PRAISE FOR

Whispers Beyond the Veil

"Exciting and engrossing, this book captures you from the first page and doesn't let go until the end. Jessica Estevao has given us a great read with a delightful heroine and a wonderful setting."

—Emily Brightwell, *New York Times* bestselling author of the
Victorian Mysteries

"You'll love the not-so-innocent heroine of this delightful new series where no one and nothing is quite what it seems. Intriguing Ruby Proulx pretends to be a medium, but is she really pretending? And whom can she trust among the many new people she meets? Jessica Estevao will keep you guessing until the very last page!"

—Victoria Thompson, national bestselling author of
Murder in Morningside Heights

WHISPERS

BEYOND

THE VEIL

JESSICA ESTEVAO

BERKLEY PRIME CRIME
NEW YORK

BERKLEY PRIME CRIME
Published by Berkley
An imprint of Penguin Random House LLC
375 Hudson Street, New York, New York 10014

Copyright © 2016 by Jessie Crockett

Library of Congress Cataloging-in-Publication Data

Names: Estevao, Jessica, author.
Title: Whispers beyond the veil / Jessica Estevao.
Description: First edition. | New York : Berkley Prime Crime, 2016. |
Series: A change of fortune mystery ; 1
Identifiers: LCCN 2016011313 (print) | LCCN 2016027976 (ebook) |
ISBN 9780425281604 (paperback) | ISBN 9780698197152 (ebook)
Subjects: LCSH: Women psychics—Fiction. | Old Orchard Beach (Me.)—Fiction.
| Maine—History—19th century—Fiction. | BISAC: FICTION / Mystery &
Detective / Historical. | FICTION / Mystery & Detective / Women Sleuths. |
GSAFD: Mystery fiction.
Classification: LCC PS3603.R63535 W48 2016 (print) | LCC PS3603.R63535 (ebook) |
DDC 813/.6—dc23
LC record available at https://lccn.loc.gov/2016011313

First Edition: September 2016

Printed in the United States of America
1 3 5 7 9 10 8 6 4 2

Cover photos: *Woman* © Lee Avison/Arcangel Images; *Old Orchard Beach Pier*
© Don Seymour/Getty Images
Cover design by Katie Anderson
Book design by Kristin del Rosario

For my sisters,
Larissa Crockett and Barb Shaffer,
who believe in listening to the voices.

ACKNOWLEDGMENTS

I owe a great deal of thanks for help with this book to a number of people. My thanks go out to my editor, Michelle Vega, who likes stories involving paranormal possibilities at least as much as I do. I'd also like to thank copyeditor Randie Lipkin for her eagle eye for detail and an extraordinary ability to keep track of loose threads.

I'd like to thank a few people from Old Orchard Beach, Maine. I truly appreciate local historian Daniel Blaney for enthusiastically sharing his time, knowledge, and resources. Jeanne Guerin, curator of the Harmon Historical Museum in Old Orchard Beach, patiently answered a barrage of my questions and pointed me toward many useful source materials. Michael Roberge graciously lent me books and unearthed photographs that fueled my understanding of life in Old Orchard during the Gilded Age.

I'd like to mention my appreciation for Noreen McDonald and the way she generously provided me with guidance concerning the world of spirit. I am grateful to Sue Yarmey for willingly sharing her knowledge of the tarot and mediumship. Mechelle Kelsey provided me with an invaluable supply of books on the subject of Spiritualism for which I am extremely grateful.

My blog mates, the Wicked Cozy Authors, have been an extraordinary source of encouragement and support. Thanks to Sherry Harris, Julie Hennrikus, Edith Maxwell, Liz Mugavero, and Barb Ross for being a part of the journey!

I also thank my children, Will, Max, Theo, and Ari for their patience. And thanks to my husband, Elias Estevao, who loves the beach as much as I do.

Chapter One

There stood my father, up on the makeshift stage. Lantern light glinted down on the brown glass bottle held outstretched in his hand. A hot wind pressed and flapped the canvas stretched above his head. Scents of sweat and hay and dusting powder melded in the unseasonably hot air. But Father appeared cool as a slice of iced melon at a picnic. He strutted and strode and worked the already-heated crowd to a fever pitch by calling out all the cures and wonderments Running Bear's Miracle Elixir would provide if only his listeners would part with a dollar.

Johnny and two other Maliseet men sat in a semicircle around the edge of the stage chanting in low tones, lending a bit of credence to the notion that the cures Father stood hawking were passed on to him by an Indian medicine man.

"Be amongst those who discover the secrets to lifelong health the red men have guarded for generations. Baldness, wasting diseases, lack of moral fiber? All these and more are banished with no more than a few doses of this potent remedy."

By the time he'd gotten a testimonial wrung out of the well-paid shills in the audience, I knew we'd sell out and I'd need to mix up another batch of what Father referred to as "Bank in a Bottle."

"I can't promise we have enough for everyone, so this is a decision you mustn't delay," Father called above the noise of the crowd. All through the tent people scrambled to their feet. Swishing skirts and stomping boots raced past me at the exit. From sleeplessness to lethargy to breathing difficulties, they chattered to each other how they hoped this nostrum would cure them all. Fortunately for Father's wallet we'd be long gone before the rubes realized the bottles' main ingredients were empty promises.

When the tent cleared, Father came up behind me and whispered in my ear, "Not a bad evening's work, wouldn't you say?" He gave me a wink, then strode toward the line to greet and encourage the customers. I watched a moment longer, then decided I wouldn't be missed if I conducted a bit of business of my own.

I HURRIED BACK TO THE TENT I SHARED WITH FATHER. AIDED BY a small bit of mirror Father used for shaving, I rubbed a burnt matchstick I saved for just such a purpose along my upper eyelashes and beneath my lower ones. I licked my lips and pressed them against a limp scrap of scarlet crepe paper and completed my costume by unpinning my dark hair and draping my lace shawl over my head.

I was always astonished at how empowering it was to transform my appearance from that of a medicine man's daughter to a fortune-telling gypsy. In my everyday attire no one would've given a second thought to a thing I said, let alone believed me to know the future. But enfold me in the guise of a foreigner and suddenly I was imbued with magical powers and otherworldly attributes.

The crowds from the show had made their purchases and were looking for other entertainments when I arrived back at the midway. I took up my usual post at a wooden folding table next to the popular magic lantern show. With a practiced hand I shuffled and cut my well-thumbed deck of divination cards and before long attracted a steady stream of customers.

I delivered rosy prognostications in a false accent for hopeful young girls and haggard old men. Years of reading the crowds had given me a feeling for what the customer really wanted to know instead of what they had asked. Subtle shifts in posture, tiny tightenings of the muscles around the mouth, widening and narrowing of the eyes all gave away what the stranger across from me held most dear.

I would have felt guilty taking their money if they went away unhappy, so I made a practice of slanting my predictions to match what they desired. People tend to get what they expect out of life. It alleviated my conscience, at least in part, to help them to expect the best.

After a couple of hours I was tired and well pleased with my earnings. Just as I had determined to pack up my cards and return to my tent, Johnny slid into the chair opposite me.

"I hoped I'd find you here." The table was a small one and I felt his leg press up against the layers of fabric covering my knee. I pulled away quickly, as any right-thinking girl would, but not before I noticed his company was not altogether unpleasant.

"You can't be here for another reading. I just did one for you yesterday." Johnny was my best customer. I had sometimes wondered if he knew how often his extra pennies were the ones that kept my belly from rumbling. Father was shockingly inept at managing money, and I had begun my card readings in the first place to stave off starvation when he had frittered away what little we had on one baseless scheme after another.

"Yesterday you didn't tell me what I wanted to hear." Johnny leaned across the table.

"Maybe you should try reading them for yourself for a change," I said, sliding the deck toward him. "You've seen it done enough times. You must know what all the cards mean by now." Johnny's eyebrows lifted as he took the deck from me. He shuffled the cards like the avid faro player he was and carefully cut the deck into three stacks. I held my breath as he turned over the top card on the first stack.

"I should have tried this myself long ago." Johnny tapped the Wheel of Fortune card. "There's hope for me yet."

"Remember it's a wheel. What comes around goes around. The wheel represents changing fortunes, not necessarily good luck or bad."

"It looks like adventure to me." He turned over a second card. "See, definitely an adventure." He placed his long finger on a card with a young man carrying a bundle on a stick.

"The Fool appears for new beginnings and youthful enthusiasm," I said. "Maybe a new life is coming your way."

"This last one is the clincher. If I'm lucky it will be a card promising a certain young lady would like to adventure with me." He turned over the last card, and I heard his quick intake of breath. His reaction was a common one, and I couldn't blame him for his apprehension.

"The Death card is not exactly what it appears," I said, hoping to ease his mind. "It doesn't usually signal the death of the body."

"What is it, then? The death of hopes and dreams?" Johnny gave me a halfhearted smile.

"It more often means a total change in your customary way of living. It gives you the opportunity to reinvent your life. For most, it's a very positive card. Taken with the other two, I'd say your life is about to undergo a radical change."

"You always manage to make everything sound like it will be just fine. I wish there was a way I could make everything turn out fine for you," Johnny said.

"Everything is fine, Johnny." I swept my hand at the shrinking crowds fading away from the ratty tents. "What more could I want than all this?"

"Ruby, don't jest. You know I'd give anything to be able to take you away from here."

"I appreciate the sentiment but you know my place is here with my father. Which reminds me, I should go. I need to replenish our supply of elixir before tomorrow's show." I gathered up the cards and slipped them back into my reticule.

I HAD HURRIED NEEDLESSLY. IT WAS LONG PAST DARK WHEN FATHER returned to our tent that night. He whistled just under his breath and there was a jauntiness to his step that filled me with dread. If it were just the jaunty step my only worry would be the whiskey I could be sure was fueling his mood. Father almost always celebrated a well-received performance with a celebratory bottle or even two. He called it his own version of a miracle in a bottle. Overindulgence generally turned him sentimental and willing to share stories about my mother, a thing he never did whilst sober.

It was the whistling that worried me. Whistling signaled an idea was foaming and churning just under the surface and he was about to burst forth with it. Whistling was the vanguard of his next grand plan, a thing I learned to fear in the course of my twenty years.

"Ruby, my love, stop bottling the hooch. We're about to move into a whole new realm of commerce." He reached for my hands and twirled me until my dress billowed and my stomach lurched. Father's good moods were not contagious.

"Father, I wish you'd stop that. You're making me dizzy."

"If wishes were horses, my dear. If only they were horses." But stop he did. "From now on we'll have no need for wishes. We'll be staying in the finest hotels instead of hunkering down in a tent hawking bottles for pennies a piece."

"What would we know about fine hotels?" I asked, hoping to delay him in sharing whatever news had brought such a glow to his cheeks.

"You'd be surprised at the things I know. I roamed the world for a good many years before you were born, you know. Fine hotels were once one of my specialties."

"You are a man of mystery, Father." It wouldn't do to tell him how often he had regaled me with stories of how he had swept my mother off her feet in the grand ballroom of a fine hotel. He had only done so when he was so far into his cups he could barely peek over the rim.

"I hope you are prepared to be rich beyond your wildest imaginings." I didn't bother to mention my wildest imaginings included a home of our own with a garden, roses scrambling along the foundation, and a wide porch overlooking the sea. I took a strengthening breath and played my expected part.

"How do you propose to make us such a fortune, Father?"

"I thought you'd never ask. Close your eyes and wait right here while I fetch it." Without another word, Father ducked back out through the tent flap. I did as I was bid, and a moment later I heard him reenter the tent. "Ta-da!" I opened my eyes and blinked.

"What is that contraption?" Father held a wooden box fitted with shiny bits of copper and black rubber tubes. Sticking out of the side was a handle that appeared to be made for cranking.

"It is nothing less than the latest in medical miracles." He dashed to the camp table and set the box upon it.

"Father, I'm not one of the rubes. There's no need to convince me it works." And he didn't. One of the things I liked best about my father was his honesty with me concerning his dishonesty with others.

"Of course, my dear. Sometimes I forget myself. This is the Invigorizer. It uses an electric current generated by cranking the handle located on the side of the box."

"But what does it purport to do?" I didn't want to encourage him, but Father exhibited a childish inclination to pout if I didn't share his unbridled enthusiasm for one of his new schemes. When I was very young I thought he truly was a miracle man and believed in him no matter how ill conceived his plans. In the past few years the realization of his fallibility had been more difficult to bear than all of the hunger, cold, or near brushes with the law added together. More and more often I was calling on my own powers of showmanship in order to keep the peace.

"It stimulates all systems of the body. It revitalizes the mind, purifies the blood, and eliminates melancholia."

"And you want to start hawking this thing along with the Running Bear's Miracle Elixir?"

"No, my dear. Instead of selling bottles of spirits flavored with turpentine for pennies apiece, we will be selling these devices for upwards of twenty dollars each. Or for the budget-minded consumer we can offer single treatments for a mere dollar. I see an entire empire building before my very eyes."

Sometimes Father forgets to turn off his showman side and he manages to con even himself into believing his pitch. It's times like these when I worry. He was going to need to be reined in quickly or we'd be without a penny to our names. It had happened more than once. Unless it was already too late.

"Is it safe?"

"Nothing could be more so. You simply place the helmet on the patient's head and then tighten the torso straps across his chest, snugging them down firmly over the heart. You then flip the toggle and a healthful current flows through the patient's body and into the ground."

"Where did you get this?"

"I purchased them from a reputable gentleman from Chicago who just happened to be in the area selling them to local doctors."

"How do you know he's reputable?"

"He had the bearing and speech of a gentleman and he produced an entire list of testimonials from satisfied patients and doctors on both sides of the border." Father's voice took on a strident note and he crossed his own arms. This would never do.

"Do you remember the Ludlow's Luxuriant Locks debacle in Toronto?"

"Please, my dear, this is nothing like that. We can't lose with this opportunity."

"By the time we were run out of town all the customers were bald."

"Never mind all that. This is our opportunity to make a mint. If all goes well, eventually I intend to settle down in one place and operate an order by mail business instead of rambling the roads.

Wouldn't you like that?" He flashed me one of the smiles that worked so well on the customers, and I felt my resistance fading. Until I remembered something.

"You said you purchased 'them.' How many of these devices did you buy?" I felt a knot in my stomach pulling firm, like it was lashing a boat to a dock. Father's business sense was appalling.

"All of them, of course. He insisted I take the lot or he was going to sell them to another qualified buyer."

"Tell me you haven't spent all the money."

"Invested, my sweet. I invested every cent."

"You promised me the last time you'd never do something like this again. There are no valuables left to sell."

"It's beneath us both for you to remind me of such a thing. Besides, I am absolutely certain the Invigorizer will completely change our lives." A deep blush crept above Father's collar. He no longer looked like the cool salesman who strode the stage only hours before.

"Every time we get the least little bit ahead you go and spend everything on something foolish. You're no better than the small boys who visit the show with their pockets ablaze with a nickel or two." Father raised a broad hand and, not for the first time, slapped me, then stomped out of the tent. He always did know how to time his exits.

I felt a hot, angry tear slide down my cheek as I sank into the wooden folding chair and stared at the Invigorizer in front of me. I couldn't begin to count how many times I had been forced to take stock of the same sort of situation, to inventory our resources. But after the last time, Father had been the one weeping when he'd been forced to sell the few small trinkets that had belonged to my mother, and I'd convinced myself he'd changed.

I had a stash of emergency money I earned from my tarot card readings and I knew enough not to give all of it to Father. The last time he had followed one of his ill-considered schemes I caught Father consulting with the man who ran a business nice people never speak of. My card money was the only thing between me and the tent—tucked out of sight and sound at the back of the show—that served lonely men and desperate women.

I carried the lantern to the back of the tent and slipped out of my gown. I lay on my cot and slid my hand under the pillow to the envelope I kept beneath it. The feel of the paper, worn smooth with so much handling, was a small comfort. As much as I told myself it did no good, I wondered, as I always did after such an altercation with Father, what life would have been like if my mother had not fled this world so soon after my birth. I told myself to be practical and to turn my thoughts to what was, not what might have been. I lay a hand against my bruised cheek and fell asleep thinking about how many readings I would need to conduct before the show pulled up stakes if I wanted to keep us fed.

B Y THE NEXT MORNING FATHER WAS STILL IN A STATE. He awoke early, thrashed and stomped about the tent loudly, and roused me without so much as a good morning.

"I shall require your assistance for a trial run of the Invigorizer. I expect you in the demonstration tent as soon as you dress." Without waiting for my reply he grabbed an Invigorizer and strode out of the tent.

I had no energy to hurry. I'd slept fitfully and dreamt of horses and wishes and streets lined with beggars who all looked just like Father. I woke often, tossing on my cot, my face still sore, wondering how Father would fare without me and how long it would take for him to return to hawking patent medicines.

Consequently, I performed my morning housekeeping duties with no degree of urgency. I smoothed the sheets atop the cots. I tidied away the bottling supplies abandoned the night before. I swept the tent and wiped down the table and chairs with a damp rag, imagining myself instead flicking a duster over a fine table in a dining room with flocked wallpaper and heavy velvet draperies.

I dressed slowly and with care, my stomach churning and a small voice whispering constantly in my ear. At its insistence I donned my best frock, my newest hat, and despite the heat, a fine wool lace shawl. Always on the alert for thieves that were more burglar than swindler, I fetched my beaded purse and added my secret savings to it. The voice told me to add my mother's tarot cards before cinching the bag tightly and hiding it away in the folds of my dress. I plucked my parasol from its customary spot near the tent flap and stepped out into the bright sunshine.

The heat of the morning promised a day as warm as the previous one and I immediately regretted the shawl. I turned back to the tent flap thinking to remove it but the voice cautioned me to hurry instead to where my father was sure to be waiting impatiently. I thought of the way he had struck me the night before, and I picked up my skirts and moved as quickly as was seemly to the far end of the show grounds.

THE DEMONSTRATION TENT WAS LARGER THAN ALL THE OTHER tents in the show and was located at the end of the midway. I dawdled past wagons belonging to magicians and sword-swallowers, jugglers and dancers. The medicine show offered much more than miracle elixirs and nostrums. First and fore-most, it sold entertainment. All the pleasures a country bumpkin could desire lay stretched out along a dusty strip of flat ground prepared to dazzle and ensnare passersby.

As I passed Johnny's tent I slowed my steps even more, trying to peek inside as the breeze lifted then dropped the tent flap. I hoped to catch a glimpse of his friendly smile before I had to face my father. Johnny was nowhere to be seen.

I lifted the flap of the demonstration tent and slipped inside. The interior was dim compared with the brightness of the day, and my eyes were slow to make the adjustment. I groped my way along to the back of the tent, following the sound of male voices.

"How good of you to grace us with your presence. You were so tardy I asked Johnny to help demonstrate the Invigorizer in your stead." Father cinched a strap across Johnny's bared chest, a heavy buckle settled right above his heart. "But now that you're here you can make yourself useful at the controls."

"Father, are you quite certain you know how to safely operate this contraption?" My stomach writhed like it was a pail full of bait worms I sometimes saw the men in the show carrying around in their off times.

"Johnny, pay her no attention. The inventor of this incredible device himself taught me to use it just yesterday. Not only that, but he kindly left me with this booklet to consult in case of any lapses in my memory." Father flapped a pamphlet in my direc-tion. "Now, Ruby, just flip that switch to check that the battery is fully charged." I held my breath as I did as he asked. I heard a quiet click and a lightbulb on the top of the Invigorizer glowed brightly.

"It looks like the card reading was right," Johnny said. "My fortune is changing. Your father's asked me to be a permanent part of the Invigorizer demonstration."

"I applaud your enthusiasm, young man. I am certain this device will be the beginning of something spectacular." Father pointed at me again. "Now switch on the toggle at the far end and watch what this can do."

And then, I heard the voice. *"Don't."* I hesitated and looked at my father once more. He flapped his hand impatiently. I reached out and gingerly flicked the switch.

Johnny stiffened. His body began to twitch, and I heard his breathing even over the rustling tent canvas. Before I could move to help him, Father shot out an arm to stop me, and Johnny toppled to the floor. Father flipped the switch back the other way, and Johnny's body lay completely still. Father and I stared at each other, standing almost as motionless as Johnny.

"What have you done?" Father took a step back from me.

"What do you mean, what have I done?" My blood pounded in my ears so loudly I could barely hear my own voice. I felt my knees giving way and I sank to the ground beside Johnny. Father knelt beside me and unfastened the Invigorizer from around Johnny's chest. Burn marks seared his tanned flesh and a bit of his skin stuck to the buckle in much the same way a scrap of ham will cling to a pan.

While I generally pride myself on my steely nerves, I felt quite faint. Father appeared to have felt the same, for he pulled his silver-plated flask from a vest pocket and consoled himself in his preferred manner by taking a good, long tug. I reached out and relieved him of it.

"Really, my dear, even under the circumstances I cannot condone you imbibing strong spirits." Ignoring him I held the flask

under Johnny's nose and prayed a discernible fog would appear
on its shiny surface. It did not.

"You killed him," Father said. The world around me seemed
to slow down and I felt my senses heighten. I was certain I heard
a noise at the side entrance to the tent but when I turned to look
I saw nothing.

"It was an accident. You told me to flip the switch. You promised it was safe."

"Irrelevant. Do you wish to be hanged?" Father stood, then
bent to grasp Johnny by the ankles. He dragged his body to the
makeshift stage and rolled him underneath, screening his body
from view with a stack of soapboxes usually used for extra seat-
ing. "The first show of the day is due to start in less than thirty
minutes. We must leave here at once."

I felt a sob working its way up into my throat, but before it
could make itself heard Father grabbed hold of my wrist and
tugged me to my feet.

"Where are we going?" Even as I asked, sounds of happy
pleasure-seekers rang through the air just outside the tent.

"Since you've gotten us into this predicament we'll have to
start over with new names in a new show as far from here as we
can get." Father's voice sounded harsh. "Come to think of it, we'd
stand a better chance of eluding detection if we separate."

"You don't want me to go with you?" I asked, hardly believing
the words slipping from my mouth.

"The authorities will be looking for a father and daughter
traveling together. It would be to our advantage to split up."

"I suppose what you are really thinking is that if you're caught
it will be easier to place the blame on me if you don't have to look
me in the face when you do it."

"I see you understand my thinking completely."

"But where will I go?"

"I suggest you head to your aunt Honoria in Old Orchard. If you're very lucky, she'll still be there."

"But that's across the border, into Maine."

"That's why I suggested it. Canadian authorities have no power in the States. Even a murderess will be safer there." Father snapped down the lid on the Invigorizer and started out through the canvas, then turned back toward me. "Have you your secret stash of money on your person? You know, the portion of your earnings you always hold back?" he asked.

I felt the weight of my coin purse tucked into the folds of my skirt. It wasn't much but it might just be enough to buy a ticket across the border. I nodded.

"Then off you go. Head out of camp before anyone misses Johnny. Flag down the first carriage you meet on the road to the train station and beg a ride." And with that, my father vanished through the flap in the canvas.

Chapter Two

I T WAS ENTIRELY MY OWN FAULT, OF COURSE. I KNOW BETTER than to ignore the voice. At least I always do in retrospect. But in the moment, in the face of difficult decisions and rational concerns, it often feels like insanity to listen to it. No matter how I tried to justify my actions, if I had listened, Johnny would still be alive. I was responsible for his death and there was no way I could forgive myself.

Now, as I felt the strong tug of the train as it hurtled south, across the border into Maine, the voice was silent. It never was one to say *"I told you so."*

I slipped my hand into the small, silken pouch containing all I could now dare claim in the world. Everything, that is, besides my parasol, wedged between the worn upholstery of my seat and the rattling window. I withdrew an envelope from my bag and gently lifted the brittle flap. From within I slid out a photograph wrapped in a letter. For the hundred thousandth time I stared at the faces of the two young women, arm in arm, wearing gowns more than twenty years out of fashion.

Curlicues, fretwork, and window boxes hung off the building

behind the smiling young women, and a sign above their heads read HOTEL BELDEN. I looked at the faded postmark on the envelope for reassurance of my decision to seek shelter with my aunt. I promised myself two things. The first was that if I made it there, and if Honoria welcomed me, I was going to go completely straight. No more cons, no more rubes. No matter what happened I was determined to live in such a way that I needn't ever look over my shoulder again. The second was that, no matter what, I would never ignore the voice again, regardless of how much it made me question my sanity.

My stomach rumbled and I was glad the sounds of the train masked the noise. One of the cars served refreshments but my funds were shockingly depleted by the purchase of my train ticket and I was unsure what lay ahead.

Across the aisle a small girl in a rose-colored dress leaned against her mother. The woman stroked her daughter's hair and bent toward her ear to whisper something that provoked a smile. I closed my eyes against the two of them, feeling like someone who stands outside in the dark peering through the glowing windows of other people's homes.

But as soon as my lids curtained the tender scene in the train, another scene unfolded before my eyes. The one that sent me fleeing. The one where I am standing over Johnny's body. The one where my father leaves me to my fate without a backward glance.

PICKPOCKETS. SO MANY DAMNED PICKPOCKETS. THE MEN WHO owned the Old Orchard Pier Company could boast all day about the good their project was doing the town but they weren't the ones out here trying to explain to yet another elderly lady why she needed

to be careful with her valuables while out in public. While pickpocketing had always been something of a concern in the popular resort
town, the coming of the pier had whipped the criminal element into
a frenzy. It seemed every petty thief on the eastern seaboard had
come to spend the summer making an indecent living.

Across the square a crowd was forming. Women in summery
dresses, their wide hats tipping precariously, stretched on tiptoe
to see into the center of the throng. More often than not, street
performers were the cause of scenes like this, but sometimes they
were more serious, even dangerous. Yancey headed for the group,
his hand on his billy club in the event he should need it. He el-
bowed his way through a ring of bystanders seven-deep. A young
woman in an emerald green dress lay on the ground. Her hat
spilled to the side of her. A handbag lay next to her hand on one
side and a battered-looking parasol on the other. At least no one
had taken advantage of her misfortune and robbed her.

"Step aside, please. Step aside." Yancey's voice rang with authority, and the inner ring of people pressed backward into the
ring behind them. Yancey knelt by the prone figure. Her chest
rose and fell slightly. At least she wasn't dead. "Did anyone see
what happened?"

"I did." Henry, one of the young boys who drove a confection-
ary cart along the beach, spoke up. He snatched his cap from his
head and leaned toward the policeman.

"Well? What did you see?" Yancey placed the back of his hand
on the woman's forehead as though he were a mother checking
for fever. Her skin seemed clammy but it might just have been
the weather rather than any sort of internal injury.

"The lady was standing just over there. She seemed like she
was looking for something or someone." The lad pointed toward

the train depot. "She took a few steps away from the station and a man came up and grabbed at her purse."

"That one there?" Yancey pointed at the handbag.

"That's the one, sir. The lady held tight to her bag and even began to bash the fellow over the head with her parasol. She got a few good licks in before she lost her balance and fell."

"Did no one help her?"

"I came a-running as soon as I knew what was happening. Things happened awful fast and it was confusing for a minute there."

"You say she slipped?"

"The man was tugging and she was just a-swinging away with her parasol and it musta tipped her right over. Her head hit the bricks when she landed on the ground. I wasn't sure if she was dead or alive."

"Didn't you try to revive her?"

"She's a lady, sir. I wasn't sure I ought to touch her." The youngster looked down at his shoes, a blush spreading up his face like a slow-moving sunburn.

"I'll need a description of the man you saw. But first, I need to attend to this young lady." Yancey slipped his hands beneath the girl's head and turned it slightly, looking for blood or a bump. Her eyes fluttered a bit but did not stay open. He scooped her up and stood. The crowd parted and watched him as he strode up Old Orchard Street toward the new police station housed in the first floor of the Odd Fellows Hall.

SOMEONE WAS DRAPING SOMETHING COOL AND MOIST ACROSS my forehead. A spot on the back of my head throbbed dully. I winced when I reached up to feel a small lump I couldn't remember acquiring. At first my thoughts were jumbled and came in images. Then, as the pictures in my mind of the train, of Johnny, of my hasty departure from my father sorted themselves into proper order I remembered my predicament. I creaked open one eye and then the other.

My worst fears appeared realized. A man wearing a police uniform sat opposite me, staring directly into my eyes. My heart beat so fast I was certain he would hear it as he leaned forward to adjust the cloth. I could not fathom how the police could possibly have caught up with me so quickly. I wouldn't put it past Father to have alerted them to the possibility of my arrival.

"You seem to have gotten yourself into some difficulty. Do you know where you are?" he asked.

"Last I knew I was in Old Orchard, Maine." I offered the gray-eyed policeman a weak smile. My instincts told me to play the part of the damsel in distress and to see where it led. There was no sense in giving up until forced to do so.

"You still are. A little while ago I brought you to the police station. I'm Officer Warren Yancey. Are you feeling well enough to tell me about the incident?"

"Other than a bit of a headache, I feel fine, thank you. However, I am not sure which incident you mean." I removed the cloth from my brow and handed it to him, hoping to gain a moment to gather my thoughts. Life in the medicine show had trained me to avoid and distrust officers of the law, as we are so often on opposite sides of it. Even without the harrowing events of the previous hours, awaking to find myself in the company of the police rattled me good and proper.

"According to witnesses, you were accosted near the train station by a man determined to relieve you of your purse." It appeared my visit to the police station was wholly unconnected to Johnny. My relief was so profound I felt myself becoming faint once more. I sagged back against the chair and shut my eyes.

"I meant to cause no distress. Please, take your time." He leaned away from me and settled back in his chair. I took the opportunity to decide on a story. I marshaled my thoughts to the pickpocket.

"I'm happy to tell you what I remember. I left the train station and had gone no further than a few steps when I felt tugging on my purse. I turned and saw a man, somewhere around thirty years old, trying his best to rob me."

"A witness stated that you gave a full measure of resistance."

"The purse happens to be my favorite." Not to mention it contained the entirety of my worldly goods. I looked down, hoping to see my purse sitting in my lap, but found it empty.

"So you raised your parasol and commenced beating him about the head with it?"

"What else could I do?"

"Did he seem surprised by your forceful reaction?"

"He did. He released his grip on my purse so abruptly I keeled right over and cracked my head against something hard. I do hope I didn't end up losing it anyway."

"After witnessing your willingness to protect it, I believe any spectators would have been too frightened to try to snatch it from you even while you were rendered senseless." Officer Yancey deposited my satiny bag into my hand. "Could you identify this man if asked at a later date to do so?" After years of reading crowds in the show, I had an eye for faces. Even without any special experience, the man would be easy enough to recognize. It's hard to forget a man sporting two gold front teeth. However, I wanted nothing to do with the police and saw no reason to continue my involvement. After all, as I had not lost my purse I needn't aid the authorities in its recovery.

"Everything happened so quickly I'm not sure I could. Although it might improve my memory if I were allowed to thrash any suspects with my parasol once more." The policeman smiled and I felt a little safer, for the moment at least.

"I would like to give such a man a good thrashing myself although I doubt my weapon of choice would be a parasol. I shall need your name and your address in order to contact you if necessary." He leaned over to a large wooden desk for a notebook and a pencil.

"My name is Ruby Proulx." The truth felt sticky on my tongue. Father and I never used our real names in the show, hardly even with each other. We had used so many false names my real one felt rusty with disuse. As a reminder to myself of my intention to go straight I had decided during my long train journey to use the name my mother had given me. If I had known the first person I would speak it to would be a policeman I might have been tempted to hold off on my rehabilitation.

"And your address?"

"I'm not certain of my address." I once again felt the gnawing concern that had accompanied me on the journey from New Brunswick to Maine. The rashness of my journey occurred to me once more. In the cold light of the police station I felt foolish for fleeing from the life I knew with nothing but a photograph tucked into a letter sent to my mother twenty years earlier.

"It needn't be the one for a hotel here in Old Orchard. I shall need a permanent address as well."

"I haven't one of those, either. I'm here in search of someone but I am uncertain as to her exact address."

"If she's a full-time resident of long standing I expect I can help you to locate her. What's her name?"

"Honoria Belden."

"Of the Hotel Belden?" Officer Yancey's eyebrows shot upward, then scrunched back down as he squinted and scrutinized my face.

"I believe so."

"How do you know Miss Belden?"

"I don't." I loosened the ties on my purse and withdrew a much-handled envelope. "This letter and accompanying photograph were amongst my late mother's things. I believe Honoria Belden is my aunt." I handed the papers to Officer Yancey and watched as he handled them carefully. He inspected the address on the envelope and then removed its contents. He read aloud from the card enclosing the photograph.

"'I am certain they have softened. Please come home. Your devoted sister, Honoria.'"

"I knew you reminded me of someone. And not just because of your unorthodox use of a parasol. The family resemblance is marked." He handed me back my things and I glanced at the photograph again. I had lain on my cot every night for years imagining what the inside of the hotel was like, what surrounded it. But most important, I wondered about the women in the photograph and whether or not I would ever meet Honoria.

"Is Miss Belden expecting you?"

"I would be very surprised if she were." I felt my stomach lurch with nervousness. If Honoria refused me I would need to call on all my skills to keep body and soul together. The purchase of the train ticket had eroded my savings. I doubted I had enough money left for more than a single night's stay in a hotel and certainly nothing left over for food.

"Then I'd say both of you are in for quite a surprise." Officer Yancey seemed amused by something, and I must confess it left me with an even greater sense of unease than before. What about a hotel was cause for such a knowing smile? "As soon as you are feeling able I will take you to her myself. It is but a short walk from here."

WITH MY HAT PRESSING UNCOMFORTABLY AGAINST THE bump on my head, we set out for the Hotel Belden and whatever might await me there. The sun blazed hot above us as we made our way downhill and toward the ocean. Seagulls circled daringly, one even snatching a bit of food right out of a small boy's hands.

"Is this your first visit to Old Orchard?" Officer Yancey asked.

"Yes, as well as my first visit to the ocean. I was determined to make straight for the beach to see it but didn't manage to get there before I met the pickpocket." Officer Yancey proffered his arm.

"If you look straight ahead you just glimpse a slice of the water." There lay a sliver of it in front of me, glittering and deeply blue. I felt a tugging in my heart as if something I hadn't realized I wanted was suddenly offered to me. Like I had been hungry but had no notion of it until I had taken a bite of food.

"Just ahead is one of our newest hotels, the Alberta House." I followed his pointing finger to an enormous four-story wooden building with a wide porch and a central tower. As accustomed as I was to large crowds and a carnival atmosphere, my experiences were limited to tents and makeshift stages. Here hotels the size of entire blocks, photographic studios, and livery stables lined the street. People swarmed in and out of carriages and restaurants. Young men swooped past on bicycles. The salt-scented breeze carried sounds of laughter up to us from the shore.

"I was imagining the view from that tower when your welcoming committee grabbed my purse."

"The view from there certainly is something worth seeing. But wait until you overlook Saco Bay from the veranda at the Belden."

"How can all this be justified?" Everywhere I looked crowds streamed and swelled. Another train pulled into the station as we approached and dozens more people alighted.

"The Old Orchard Pier Company is accountable for the current influx. This town has been a popular tourist destination for decades but with the construction of the pier, interest has reached a fever pitch."

"Is that it up ahead?" I asked. Stretching in front of us was a partially completed steel structure.

"It is. When it opens in a few weeks it will be the world's longest pleasure pier. They say it is an engineering marvel but I'm reserving judgment until it's made it through a few nor'easters."

"How long is it?"

"Approximately eighteen hundred feet, or just over a third of a mile long. The builders have even planned a miniature train to carry dancers to the ballroom at the end to spare the ladies' feet."

"How extraordinary."

"You've picked quite the time to visit. Every hotel room has had their reservations completely booked for months." I hadn't considered there might be no room for me. I only hoped there would be some way for my aunt to squeeze me in somewhere.

"You shouldn't worry though. I'm certain Miss Belden will find room for you. After all, you're family."

"You seem very sure. Are you well acquainted with my aunt?" Just saying the words "my aunt" felt strange, like I was speaking a foreign tongue. There had only ever been "my father." Anything else felt awkward on my lips.

"Everyone in Old Orchard is acquainted with Honoria Belden, or at least with her reputation."

CHAPTER THREE

OFFICER YANCEY MORE THAN MADE UP FOR THE ATTEMPTED purse snatching. His enthusiasm for Old Orchard made him seem more like a small boy than a policeman. All along our walk down Grand Avenue he pointed out the merits and histories of each hotel and eatery we passed. When I commented on the depth and breadth of his knowledge he dismissed the compliment, saying he had lived in town all his life. Then, all at once he stopped and pointed to a white clapboard–covered building.

"Here we are. This is the Hotel Belden." While it was not so large as many of the magnificent hotels we had passed, like the Sea Shore House or the imposing Old Orchard House, with its grounds running from the crest of the hill all the way down to the sea, I recognized it immediately from the photograph. Turrets, gingerbread railings, bay windows, and window boxes spilling over with pinks and forget-me-nots bedecked the outside of the building. At the top of the house ran an observation platform that must look out over the sea.

"It's even lovelier than I had imagined it," I said. Roses scrambled along the foundation, flourishing lavender sprawled along

the walkway. Officer Yancey steered me up the porch steps to the
door. He held it open for me and I felt a rush of nerves akin to
stage fright. I assured myself it was a natural response. This was
certain to be the most important performance of my twenty
years. Certainly it mattered more than convincing yokels and
rubes of the merits of Running Bear's Miracle Elixir.

Officer Yancey stepped in front of me, approached the long
oak reception desk, and tapped firmly on the bell. I could feel
myself holding my breath as I waited to see who would appear to
receive me. I forced myself to silently exhale, chiding myself for
hiding behind a policeman. I peeked around his back just as a
slim blond man emerged from a room behind the counter.

"Hello, Ben. I've brought a visitor for Miss Belden," Yancey
said. "She's a personal visitor, not a hotel guest. Is Miss Belden
in?" The man looked me up and down slowly with the palest blue
eyes I had ever seen. In the medicine show I had suffered a generous share of unwanted appraisal of my person by strange men.
It was almost always unpleasant and invariably easy to interpret.
This gaze was far more intense and I had no idea whatsoever
what to make of it. He silently nodded at Yancey and then motioned us to follow.

The man strode so smoothly and silently ahead of us it was as
though he were gliding down the long hallway rather than walking. He led us past sitting rooms and a library filled with books.
Halting, he pointed to a midnight blue portiere hanging in a
doorway at the very end of the wide corridor. He waved his hand
to show I should enter. When Yancey made to follow me, Ben laid
a restraining hand on his arm. Yancey shrugged and let loose
another smile that suggested I was in for a surprise.

I slowly slipped between the brocade folds of the portiere and found myself in a room shrouded in darkness. Heavy drapes hung at the windows and blocked out any sunlight. A solitary candle flickered on a table at the center of the room. In its wavering glow I made out four shapes seated around the table. It appeared their eyes were closed, their hands linked.

"I feel a presence. Has a spirit come to us from the other side?" A deep, rich woman's voice whispered out from the gloom. I squinted at the table, hoping to get a better look at the speaker. I stepped toward the table and as I did so the woman opened her eyes. "Someone has joined us. Come closer, if you are able." Her voice came out even more quietly. I stepped into the edge of the candle glow's reach, my heart pounding almost as hard as it had when I found myself awakening in the presence of a policeman.

Each of the people seated around the table opened their eyes and turned in my direction, their mouths circles of surprise. It was a look I'd seen almost daily at the medicine show when Father had orchestrated perfectly rehearsed miracles in front of the crowds.

"Delphinia?" The woman's voice cracked and she dropped the hands on either side of her as she rose to her feet. "I hardly dared hope you would come."

"I think there's been some sort of a mistake ma'am," I said. The woman lurched against the table, and a man jumped to his feet to offer her a steadying arm. The others leaned forward in their seats to get a better look at me. "I'm looking for my aunt, Honoria Belden." With more speed than I would have expected from a woman of her formidable size, the lady appeared at my side and wrapped her fingers firmly around my upper arms.

"George, the drapes," she said. A figure moved to the curtains and yanked them open, bathing the room in light. Standing there with a crowd of only four strangers I found myself at a loss for words. The woman grasping me did not. "Let me get a good look at you." She held me at arm's length and searched my face. I was familiar with scrutiny and skepticism during my tarot card readings and performances at the show and I expected to see it here, too. After all, what proof did I have that I was who I claimed to be? Goaded by the fear of sleeping on the beach with a rumbling belly I found my voice.

"My mother's name was Delphinia. At least that's what my father said. Mine is Ruby Proulx."

"I dreamt she'd come. Haven't I always said so, George?" The woman gripped me with even more enthusiasm.

"You did indeed." The man near the window took a step closer as if to assure himself of what he was seeing.

"My dear friends, please excuse us." She turned to the others. "This young lady and I have so much to discuss."

WITH THAT, THE WOMAN I ASSUMED MUST BE HONORIA swept me out through the portiere and down the hall. Officer Yancey was nowhere to be seen but Ben stood silently, as if awaiting a verdict, in the passageway just outside the doorway. Honoria stopped in front of him.

"Ben, I am certain you recognized Ruby on sight," she said. He nodded wordlessly. "Then you will, of course, understand that unless a mermaid appears at the front desk requesting a room you should not allow anyone to disturb us." She gave him a hurried nod, then drew me by the arm toward a wide and curving staircase. Light streamed in from a window above. When we reached the landing I could not contain a gasp. A window spanning two stories gave a view of the beach and beyond it the ocean.

"It's astonishing," I said, looking out across the flashing water.

"Have you never seen it before?" Honoria asked, pausing to allow me to admire the view.

"Only a glimpse up near the pier as I made my way here." I had longed to see it, dreamt of it, even. But every time the medicine show traveled toward the coast, Father's feet had begun to itch and he sought out a new group of performers to join, invariably farther inland.

"Then this is a day of wonders for us both." She tucked my hand under her arm and led me to a room at the far side of the second floor. She eased herself onto a violet-colored settee and patted the space beside her. "I shall, of course, wish to know how you came to be here, but what I really desire to know is what is your gift?" I felt a total fool and utterly without manners of any kind. In my haste and reduced financial circumstances I had not given the slightest thought to a present for my hostess.

"I'm very much afraid I've come completely empty-handed." My cheeks grew hot and I wished there were some way to go back and purchase a lace hankie or a fancy hair comb for her.

"I expressed myself poorly. I meant, which is your psychic gift?"

If I had not promised myself to go straight, the temptation to feign psychic ability would have been overwhelming. Between that question and the apparent séance I had interrupted, the pickings here were sure to be easy. Even with the promises I had made to myself it was going to be a test of my will not to fall back into my old ways. I conjured the image of Johnny lying motionless on the floor of the show tent and felt my resolve return.

"I'm afraid I haven't any," I said, hoping this would not influence whether or not Honoria would offer to let me stay.

"Nonsense. All the women in the family have a gift for divination and the like. Your grandmother could see ghosts, your mother was a medium, I have prophetic dreams. You must have some sort of gift."

"My mother claimed to be a medium?"

"She didn't claim to be one. She was one." Honoria's eyes widened. "Didn't your father ever mention that to you?"

"Not a word." Father had never said my mother had any extraordinary gifts. He did his best to never mention her. Even so, I was surprised that he hadn't trumpeted that story to bolster my credentials as a medical intuitive. The rubes lapped that sort of nonsense up as eagerly as our old horse did water at the end of a long day's work pulling the wagon. Honoria shook her head in disbelief.

"Preposterous. Still, there must be something. It is unthinkable that you are the first woman in the family to have no metaphysical abilities."

As kind and welcoming as she had been, I didn't know Honoria well enough to mention the voice. Hearing disembodied whispers was the sort of thing that got a person sent to an asylum. And even if she did believe me, I was not convinced myself that the voice was more than an amplified version of my intuition. However, desperate times called for desperate measures. And no one was so desperate as a girl left as much to her own devices as I had been. Clearly, I had to tell her something.

"I wouldn't claim to be gifted, but I sometimes turn to these for advice." I reached into my purse and pulled out the small deck of worn tarot cards I always carried with me. I fanned them out on the table positioned in front of the settee and held my breath, hoping they were enough to secure my position. Honoria leaned forward, knocking over a vase in the center of the table in her excitement.

"Where did you get these?" Honoria snatched them off the table and thumbed through them carefully, examining them one by one.

"I don't actually know. I've had them so long I can't remember ever receiving them." From the way tears threatened to fall from her eyes, I regretted revealing the cards. Honoria stood and crossed the room to a small mahogany desk. Unlocking the drop front with a key dangling from the chatelaine at her waist she slid open a drawer and withdrew a silken drawstring bag. Returning to the table, she handed it to me.

"Open it," she said, sitting back on the settee once more. I loosened the smooth cord and slipped my hand inside. Wrapping my fingers around the contents, I discovered a deck of cards very much like my own. The artist seemed to be the same and the amount of wear suggested they were of a similar vintage. The backs of her cards matched mine, but the images on the front were unfamiliar. "They are all from a deck your mother and I shared as children. The night she slipped out of the house and off to a new life with your father we shuffled the deck and divided it in half."

"Do you know how to correctly read these cards?"

"Your mother and I learned to read tarot before we learned to read the written word. Delphinia was always more adept at it than I. The night she left I urged her to take the entire deck as she valued it so highly but she refused, saying she would feel comforted if a part of her remained here with me." Honoria brushed a tear from her cheek. "You read them yourself?"

"I've always made up my own stories for the pictures. I would dearly love to know what they really mean." I slid the pile toward her and watched with anticipation as she scooped up the deck in its entirety and shuffled the cards with a deft hand.

"First, I'd like to watch you do a reading, to hear how the cards speak to you with no outside influence." She placed the deck in front of me and nodded encouragingly.

I had performed hundreds of readings for visitors to the show over the years, but this was different. Most of the querents' body language had been simple to read, and providing the information they wished to hear was an easy enough task.

But this time I could not help but feel I was the question. Was Honoria using the card reading to determine if I would be welcomed to stay at the Hotel Belden? And if so, was she using my ability to read the cards to decide or was she relying on the cards pulled to advise her?

"If you'd like me to, I will. I usually think of a question of my own if I am alone, or I ask the sitter to think of one if I am reading for another. Do you have a question in mind?"

"I do." Honoria leaned forward, gripping the edge of the table. A bead of sweat I attributed to nerves trickled out from under the hairline at the base of my neck and rolled down my back. "And then what do you do?"

"I shuffle the cards until one of them calls to me." As soon as the words left my lips a card jumped out of the deck and lay facedown on the table. Honoria's eyes flicked toward it but she turned her attention back to my hands.

"What do you do with a card that captures your attention?"

"I lay it facedown and repeat the process if I feel led to choose additional cards. I often pull three cards, sometimes more. Every now and again I pull only one. Especially if the picture on the card seems right to me."

I steadied my hands the best I could but was certain she could see them trembling ever so slightly as I shuffled the cards, wishing I felt more sure of what I was doing.

I concentrated on the feel of the thick deck in my hand. I sent up a silent wish that the cards would convince my aunt to offer me a place in her home. Allowing instinct to guide me I chose three cards and placed them on the table between us. I turned them over one at a time and looked closely at the images before me. Two cards were unfamiliar. The third was one from my original deck.

"What do these mean to you?" Honoria asked. I touched the first card from her deck. As I opened my mouth to answer I heard the familiar voice in my head speak more clearly than ever in my left ear.

"Homecoming. Celebration."

Bearing the warning in mind I took a deep breath and shared what it said. "Four of Wands. This card looks like good news. It tells me it concerns a homecoming and a celebration." Honoria's grip on the table loosened just enough for some pink to return to her knuckles. Watching her reaction I dared to hope I might be on the right track.

I tapped the second card. "The High Priestess," I said before repeating the next thing the voice whispered in my ear. "Trust your inner voice. Knowledge of other realms." Honoria nodded slightly.

I touched the third card and paused, waiting for guidance from the voice. It came again without delay. "The Wheel of Fortune means destiny and events set in motion. Unstoppable forces."

Honoria released her grip on the table and tapped the card I had neglected to turn upright, the one that had jumped from the deck.

"And what of this one?" she asked. I turned it over and revealed the only card from my deck I feared. I didn't need the voice to speak to me for this one. It had appeared in my readings with an accurate prediction too many times for me to be uncertain of its meaning.

"The Tower. Upheaval and catastrophe." I felt my mouth grow dry. I fought the urge to nibble on a thumbnail. If Honoria was counting on the cards to advise her, it looked like she would be unwise to extend an invitation to me to stay.

"Your mother shared one of her gifts with you. But there is room for you to develop your natural talents. Cards like the Tower have a positive side as well."

"They do?"

"Yes. The Tower also asks you to notice which parts of your life are built on falsehood. It warns you to prepare for unstable foundations to crumble."

"I am afraid I don't see how that is a positive card."

"It makes way for that which is solid and beneficial. It sweeps away complacency and demands improvements that serve the greater good."

"I see."

"Shall I tell you what I asked of the cards?"

"Only if you wish to do so." I was torn between wanting to know and being terrified to hear her thoughts.

"I asked what your arrival meant." Honoria smiled at me and I felt my worry ease a bit. "The cards told me nothing surprising. They also did not reveal how you came to be here."

I thought again of the hours on the train I had passed, carefully considering which aspects of my story I thought best to mention to my aunt. Despite my vow to go straight I'd been contemplating snipping and stitching the truth to cast Father as the victim of the accident that ended Johnny's life. It might make Honoria more inclined to welcome me if she believed I had no other family. As I opened my mouth to apply that bit of embroidery to the facts, I once more heard the voice speak with breathtaking clarity in my ear.

"Speak only truth, however conservatively."

I had always worried the voice was a sign I would end up in an asylum. It occurred to me that perhaps the events of late had driven me mad. Or maybe the blow to my head when I fell had caused some sort of damage to my brain. Only insane people heard voices so frequently and with such clarity. Then my gaze swept over the High Priestess card, the one that spoke of intuition and the inner voice. Bearing it in mind I took a deep breath and took a chance on the truth. Or at least a tidy version of it.

"My father and I argued bitterly. I decided enough was enough and that I would take the chance that you would be here and would be glad to see me."

"Just like that? Without planning of any kind?"

"I know it sounds rash and I don't wish to sound disloyal, but my father can be quite unreasonable as well as unreliable." I decided to gamble that she would be favorably swayed by a sob story. "This argument, like so many others, ended in violence. When I left, my only thought was for my safety." While strictly speaking that was the truth, I felt a twinge of guilt at the way I had presented it.

"He was heedless and impulsive when I knew him. I am sorry

to hear that with age his faults include a tendency to violence. Not that I am at all surprised." Honoria reached over and patted my hand. The sparkling stones set into the many rings decorating her thick fingers sent flashes of colored light jouncing against the creamy striped wallpaper. "I've always said your place was here with me. That's just what I wrote to Ivory when he let me know my sister had passed on."

"You offered to take me?" This was news to me.

"Certainly, I did." Honoria dabbed at her eyes with a ruffled handkerchief. "Of course I knew Delphinia was expecting your arrival. She wrote to me several times after she left home. When her letters stopped and I began to dream of her instead, I knew she was gone."

"I never knew anything about my mother other than her name and what she looked like from the photograph you sent her." I reached into my purse once more and offered her the same envelope I had shown Officer Yancey. She removed the picture and stared at it silently for some time, tears cascading down her cheeks.

"Oh, my dear girl. I knew I should have persisted unrelentingly until Ivory gave you into my care. I offered to take you as soon as he contacted me about Delphinia's passing but he refused. He said you were his daughter and he would raise you himself." Two bright spots pinked Honoria's cheeks. It appeared little love was lost between my aunt and father.

I felt a lump forming in my throat. I told myself it was just the strain of recent hours causing me to weaken. I pride myself on not falling prey to sentimental foolishness.

"That was very kind of you."

"Nonsense. I wanted you desperately. I was convinced he was holding out for a monetary consideration in exchange for you." I felt myself stiffen at the thought of my father behaving so crassly and then slumped back into the settee as I acknowledged Honoria had rightly noted Father's priorities. As long as I'd known him, easy money was his true north. One of my greatest fears was that I was cut from the same bolt of cloth.

"And he didn't take you up on your offer?"

"To my amazement, when I suggested giving him a large sum outright he said you were not to be sold like a spring lamb or a suckling pig."

"And?"

"And, I never heard from him again. I sent letters and telegrams. I placed advertisements of inquiry in papers throughout New Brunswick, Quebec, and even Ontario but no one had heard of either of you." Perhaps Father's haphazard wanderings and countless name changes were less aimless than they had seemed.

"I wish word had reached us. I would have liked to have come to you before now." I spoke those words completely without guile. Sitting there with my aunt, knowing someone had wanted to give me a stable life in a normal home felt too good to be true. Life on the road had been backbreaking and dirty. But worst of all was the loneliness. The only other child I had befriended on a show had succumbed to scarlet fever before we had known each other more than a few weeks.

"You're finally here and that's all that matters." Honoria placed a plump finger under my chin and tilted my face to meet hers. "You look remarkably like her, you know. I was certain Delphinia had finally appeared to me when you made your entrance downstairs."

"I'm sorry to have disappointed you. And for interrupting your group."

"Your appearance was in no way a disappointment. Besides, it is the business of the Divination Circle to welcome the unexpected. We must have been as much of a surprise to you as you were to us."

"I admit I was startled. Is the Divination Circle the group you were with when I burst in on you?"

"Yes. A few friends and I have been meeting together twice weekly to strengthen and develop our prognosticating abilities."

"You mean séances and such?" I felt a tingling of excitement over the surface of my skin. When I was quite young, a medium joined our show and her performances drew vast crowds. After seeing the money Madame Zeroska raked in every night, Father bemoaned the fact that we had no experience with such things. In fact, it was that very medium who gave me the idea to start reading tarot cards between shows.

"Exactly that. In truth, the Divination Circle is the inspiration for the concept of this hotel." Honoria beamed at me.

"How so?" The feverish light in Honoria's eyes suggested the hotel was her passion. If I was going to stay, I hoped it was a passion I could grow to share. Nothing is as intolerable as a zealot with whom you disagree.

"Should I assume you know nothing of the history of the hotel?"

"Until today I knew nothing more than what you can see in the photograph." We both looked at it once more.

"I would dearly love to thrash your father over the head with a parasol for keeping you in the dark concerning your heritage," Honoria said, giving me a start. Did her psychic developments extend to clairvoyance? "The property the Hotel Belden sits upon has been in the family for generations. In fact, our family has been here since the early seventeen hundreds."

"But the hotel doesn't look anywhere near as old as that." For someone as rootless as I, the idea of having family in a single spot for almost two hundred years was astonishing.

"It isn't. Early on we were farmers and merchants. It wasn't until the Staples family opened their farmhouse to boarders that the hospitality industry began to grow."

"And your family took part in it?"

"Our family, my dear." Honoria gave my hand another firm squeeze. "We started taking in summer guests in the 1850s. Over the next decade we added small cottages around the edges of the property. Your grandparents built this hotel in 1874."

"Are your parents still here?" I watched as a crinkle developed between Honoria's eyebrows. I wished I hadn't asked the question.

"They both passed suddenly the year your mother left with your father." Honoria let out a deep sigh and forced a smile back to her face. "I inherited the hotel as quite a young woman and had little in the way of guidance in its running. I muddled along year after year, despairing as I watched the competing hotels becoming larger and more elegant."

"It seems very grand here to me." What little I had seen so far had impressed me greatly. The furnishings appeared plush or gleaming. The carved woodwork was ornate and the windows and passageways generously proportioned. The unobstructed view of the beach and the bay beyond only added to its charms.

"The Old Orchard House is comprised of three hundred rooms and is planning an elevated walkway connecting it to the train station. The Fiske boasts a telegraph office and a bowling alley on site. I determined if I could not add physical amenities, I could offer a unique experience instead." Honoria rose to her feet and paced the room. "The Hotel Belden caters to Spiritualists and other seekers of enlightenment."

"You're courting psychics?" I thought of my father and how he would love just such a scheme. Something about the passion in Honoria's voice and mannerisms suggested she was more of a true believer than a cagey businesswoman.

"Exactly. The plan is to offer immersion in a multitude of spiritual subjects. I have hired experts in a number of disciplines to lead discussions, share knowledge, and to provide divination services. Table tipping, scrying, dowsing, astrological predictions all have a place here at the Hotel Belden."

"Has the idea proved popular?" Perhaps such a thing was none of my business but I spoke without thinking. If Honoria was taken aback she did not show it.

"Remarkably so. Which is a very good thing, since I've had to delay our opening for an extra two weeks in order for the staff to arrive."

"I wondered why there were so many people in town but it seemed so quiet here."

"It was a difficult decision but one that had to be made. The delay was caused by the final member of our company, a medium named Flora Roberts, who couldn't arrive until tomorrow."

"A medium must be important if her absence is enough to delay your opening."

"Offering a medium in residence is the reason we're booked solid this season for the first time in years." Honoria paused her pacing in front of one of the windows looking out over the beach.

"I hope my own appearance won't cause any disruption to your plans. You sound as though there is much to be done."

"Your timing is perfection itself. For years I've wished for someone to share the hotel with once more. Come, let me show you the rest of the property."

CHAPTER FOUR

THE WIND HAD PICKED UP AND THE TANG OF SALT FILLED THE air as Yancey hurried back to the police station. As diverting as a visit to the Hotel Belden had proven to be, his workload had become increasingly burdensome over the last few weeks. Not only had pickpockets flowed into town like a red tide, violent domestic incidents, carriage accidents, and liquor-fueled disturbances increased at a similar pace.

Frank Nichols gave Yancey a raised russet eyebrow as soon as he stepped through the door of the police station.

"Chief's been looking for you, and none too patiently, neither," Frank said through a mouthful of food. "He's in his office. Said to send you in as soon as you got back."

"Did he say what he wanted?" Yancey asked.

"Nope. But he had Jelly Roll with him so you ought to brace yourself for something rotten." Frank dabbed at his luxuriant mustache with his handkerchief.

There was nothing that took the pleasure out of a fine summer afternoon like a chat with the chief. Unless it was a talk that also included the chief's brother-in-law, Robert Jellison, known to his many detractors as Jelly Roll. Yancey took the time to place his hat on the rack near the door and to check his desk for any new messages. Deciding he could delay no longer, Yancey knocked on his superior's door and waited until he heard the growl from within.

"Very good of you to find time to make it in to work today," Charles Hurley said, his feet propped up on the corner of his wooden desk. Robert Jellison lolled in the chair opposite the desk, sunlight glinting off his bald head.

"I've been out investigating a pickpocketing case, sir. The number of sneak thefts is climbing every day."

"Petty crimes. I've got more important matters for you to turn your attention to today." Chief Hurley waved his cigar, trailing a plume of smoke.

"A young woman was knocked unconscious during the attack."

"Anyone important?" Robert Jellison asked, leaning forward with interest.

"Everyone is important," Yancey said. "But this young woman happens to be Honoria Belden's niece."

"Really?" Jellison's forehead crinkled into deep furrows. "I wasn't aware Miss Belden had any family left."

"She must be her prodigal sister's child," the chief said.

"I'd forgotten about her. Wasn't the hotel left solely to Miss Belden?" asked Jellison.

"It was. The sister, Delphinia, was disowned more than twenty years ago by her parents," Chief Hurley said. Disgust filled Yancey as he detected a note of pleasure running in the currents of his boss's voice. "She snuck off in the dead of night with a man who was in town for the summer. People said she left carrying nothing but her shoes in her hand so as not to squeak the floorboards."

"I remember now. It caused an uproar until that other

business caused even more fuss," Jellison said. Yancey had heard enough. His tolerance for family scandals and gossip was lower than most. Perhaps because his firsthand experience with them was greater than average.

"Chief, you had something you wanted me to take care of?"

"That's right." Chief Hurley stood and strode to the window. "The town fathers have made it clear that Old Orchard is on its way to being a world-class summer resort. In order to maintain that image we need to control the riffraff and undesirables."

"Are you planning to increase the size of the force, sir? We could use at least two more men to adequately patrol the increased traffic around the pier."

"No. There isn't any money for more officers. Still, the powers that be want results, not excuses." Chief Hurley shot a glance at Jellison.

"What your boss is saying is that the Indians squatting behind my latest hotel purchase need to go. And soon. We don't want them hanging around in plain sight when the pier opens."

"But they've been coming here in the summer since before there was a town. I don't see how we can ask them to leave." Yancey's collar felt as though it had shrunk by two inches.

"We're not asking for your opinion," Hurley said. "We're telling you to make them go."

"Sir, I doubt what you're asking is legal."

"You know what people said when I gave you this job. What they still say about taking a chance on you. Was I wrong to do so?" Hurley and Jellison both turned their gaze on Yancey.

"I know you took some heat, adding me to the force. I'll have a word with them."

"The Orchard Beach Pier Company expects them gone before the pier opens. One way or another," Jellison said.

"If you can't get this done, there are a lot of other men who would be happy to have your job." Hurley turned his attention to a pile of papers on his desk. "Well, what are you still doing here? Get on with it."

HONORIA MOVED LIKE A HURRICANE THROUGH THE HOTEL, blowing us from one room to the next. From the wine cellar to the rooftop balcony it was clear she loved every part of her home.

We concluded the tour in a large room at the top of the hotel. A fine lace spread covered the high bed, and a vanity table set with enameled hairbrushes, combs, and an elegant assortment of hatpins drew my attention. Nicest of all was the window seat, nestled into a turret overlooking the bay. Even with the windows tightly shut the sound of waves crashing on the beach filled my ears.

"This will be your room." Honoria said. "I do hope you like it."

"Are you sure you don't need to rent this room to a guest? You said yourself the hotel is completely booked for the season."

"Every room but this one." Smiling, Honoria looked around. "This room was your mother's and not a thing's been changed except adding electricity since she left. It's been waiting here for you all this time."

"There is no way for me to thank you enough."

"Having you here is entirely my pleasure. I expect you could use some time to rest and to change out of your travel clothes. When are your trunks being sent?"

"I'm afraid they aren't. The nature of my leave-taking was so abrupt and I boarded the train just as you see me." That was the truth, so far as it went. Returning to our tent to pack my belongings had not seemed worth the risk. I shuddered to think what might have happened if I had not listened to the voice and taken what little I had when I set out of the tent for that last time.

"Quite incredible. We shall have you fitted for some new things as soon as possible, but in the meantime there are some of Delphinia's gowns hanging in the wardrobe." Honoria waved to a massive walnut cabinet on the other side of the room. "They won't be the least bit fashionable but I expect they will fit."

"I'm sure they will be lovely."

"Have your rest, change, and come down for dinner at six. I'll introduce you to the staff then." Honoria leaned in to give me a kiss on the cheek. "I am quite certain your arrival heralds a new era here at the Belden."

As soon as Honoria pulled the door shut behind her I raced around the room, unable to contain my excitement. Everything was perfect, simply perfect. I ran my hands over the velvet upholstered wingback chair and ottoman, inspected the tiled fireplace set into the wall opposite the bed, stood at the windows, and admired the breathtaking view. I climbed up onto the high bed to test it out and did not even attempt to resist bouncing on it as vigorously as I dared.

As tired as I was, I felt certain there was no chance I could fall asleep. I awoke an hour or so later with the distinct impression someone had been calling my name and shaking my shoulder. The light in the window was slanting lower, and I hurried to the wardrobe and yanked open the door. Casting off my own rumpled clothing I felt spoilt for choice.

There were more gowns in the wardrobe than there had been women in the medicine show. I hardly knew how to choose. I felt a surge of anger as I looked around the room and considered what my life would have been like if my father had accepted Honoria's offer to take me. But then it occurred to me that dwelling on the past would not help me to enjoy my current situation. Anger had given me the push I needed to leave a life I did not wish to lead but it was not going to help me select a gown.

I wished I had thought to inquire of Honoria as to the formality of the dining room. Meals served in the medicine show's cook tent were unlikely to have prepared me for life in a hotel, especially one as fancy as the Belden. Just as I began to despair of making the right choice I heard a hesitant knock on the door. I reached for a jewel-toned crazy quilt draped over the wingback chair and wrapped it around myself. Even I knew better than to answer the door in my undergarments.

I cracked open the door and poked my head through the gap. Standing in the hall, looking down at her shoes was a girl I estimated to be a bit younger than myself.

"I hope I'm not disturbing you. I'm Millie. Miss Belden sent me to help you get ready for dinner," she said. It had not occurred to me that such assistance could be available. I had always dressed myself. Certainly there were other women in the show, but since none of them lived in the same tent as Father and me, dressing had always been something I managed on my own.

Suddenly, I felt quite shy. That was, until I noticed how

uncomfortable Millie looked. She stood shifting what little weight she had between her two feet. I was even more sorry for her than I was nervous for myself. I knew I must put her at her ease.

"Please, come in." I stepped back and gestured to the room beyond me. "I'm very glad to see you. I have absolutely no idea what to wear." Millie slowly stepped across the threshold and looked around the room.

"I've never been in this room before now." Millie lifted a finger to her mouth and nibbled at a hangnail.

I pressed the door into place and turned the solid brass lock, feeling a thrill at the luxury of doing so. Tents don't come with locks, and the rooming houses we had stayed in during the coldest months of the year were not given to such things, either. On occasion a better establishment might be fitted with a hook and eye screwed into the door and frame.

"That makes two of us. You said Honoria sent you. Do you work here at the hotel?"

"Yes, miss. In the summer, I do. Sometimes I help out in the fall or spring, too, if the need arises. I'm a maid, you see. The housecleaning kind, not the lady's maid sort. I'm not quite sure I'll know how to help you get ready." Millie's lower lip wobbled and my heart lurched. I would need an ally in the house and the odds were that Millie knew a lot more about living amongst the upper crust than I did. Sharing my own trepidation with her might put us both at ease.

"May I tell you a secret, Millie?" I asked in a whisper. She dropped her finger from her mouth and nodded.

"I've never had a lady's maid to help me dress. Why don't we figure it out together?"

Millie's face brightened into an enormous smile. "It's a deal," she said. "What a lot of gowns you have."

"That's just the trouble. There are so many of them and in truth, none of them are mine. I arrived with nothing but the clothes on my back and my trusty parasol."

"You never did." Millie's mouth hung open.

"I did indeed. So now we'll have to see what there is in here that fits me. Let's take a look."

We flicked through the choices and then decided the most sensible thing was to first settle on a pair of shoes. There were fewer of those lined up along the floor of the wardrobe, some vastly more comfortable than others.

"The red satin are certainly the best," I said, tipping my foot this way and that to admire the daintiest shoe I had ever worn.

"What about this one, miss? It goes with your name as well as the slippers." Millie held out a gown of rich red taffeta. "And will look a treat with your dark hair." I nodded, and between the two of us we managed to wriggle me into the swaths of fabric without damage to the garment or myself. It had to be rebuttoned only twice. It was a miracle.

"I hope you won't mind the lack of sleeves, miss." Millie scowled into the long mirror built into the wardrobe door. "Most of the ladies are wearing sleeves as big as hot-air balloons these days."

I stared at my reflection, hardly able to breathe both from the astonishment at what I saw and from the close fit of the bodice. "It is the very prettiest thing I have ever worn. Fashionable or not, I'm delighted with it. And do please call me Ruby." Millie smiled and moved to the dressing table. She leaned over the mirrored tray covered in brushes and combs, hatpins and boot hooks.

"Now, let's see about your hair," she said, pointing to the up-holstered seat in front of the vanity table. I eased myself onto the chair, careful not to step on the flowing hem of the dress. Millie seemed much more sure of herself with a hairbrush in her hand than she had with the layers of undergarments and the complicated mechanics of the evening gown.

I felt my shoulders pull down from around my ears as she eased the brush rhythmically through my hair until it shone in the beam of light glinting through the turret window. Deftly twisting and patting, she pinned up the heavy mass of it before adding an ornamented comb as a finishing touch.

"You've worked magic, Millie," I said as she regarded her creation. "Nothing will convince me you haven't been doing this for years." A slow blush spread over her fair cheeks as we looked at each other in the mirror.

"I've got sisters, miss, I mean Ruby. I always love helping them to do their hair for dances and such."

"I always wanted a sister," I said. "You'll have to thank yours for letting me borrow you for the evening."

"They'd be happy to share, I'm sure." Millie's hand froze in midair as a bell jangled on the wall. I hadn't noticed the contraption of buttons and a bell on the wall near the bed when I lay down earlier. "We'd best be done. The bell means five minutes until dinner."

"I shouldn't wish to be late. Especially not on my first night here."

"No, you do not. Mrs. Doyle would have come up herself to see what ailed you if you had missed her dinner. She's all het up since she heard you'd come home."

"Mrs. Doyle?"

"She's the cook and housekeeper for the hotel. Even Miss Belden's a little scared of her."

"She sounds like a force to be reckoned with."

"Oh, she is. Nothing gets past Mrs. Doyle."

"Then I guess that is all the primping we have time for to-night. I don't know how I would have managed without you, Millie. Thank you so much." I pushed back the tiny stool and stood to leave.

"You won't thank me if I let you head to the dining room without a pair of gloves. There have to be some around here somewhere." I swallowed hard. I was going to have to keep on my toes if there was any way I would fit in here at the Belden.

I tugged open a drawer of the vanity and found a pair of long black gloves. Pulling them on I rushed for the door. As I hurried down the stairs I gave myself a stern talking-to. After all, the terrors of the dining room could not be worse than those I had left behind.

CHAPTER FIVE

B EN STOOD SILENTLY AT THE BASE OF THE STAIRS AS THOUGH he had been awaiting me. He escorted me to the dining room and wordlessly opened the paneled double doors. I looked around, noticing the round tables scattered about the long room. Upon surveying the other diners I congratulated myself on selecting one of the more elaborate gowns from my mother's wardrobe.

Honoria had been right about the fit. It might have been made just for me. The satin fabric smelled a bit musty but the rich red color set off my dark hair and eyes, if I did say so myself. One by one, conversations at the occupied tables ceased as the occupants noticed me standing at the threshold. Honoria rose from her seat and met me at the door.

"Ruby, you are the vision of your mother. I should have known you'd pick her favorite dress." She smoothed her hands across my shoulders, then drew me into the room. "Friends," she said to the assembled group, "I'd like to introduce my niece, Miss Ruby Proulx." Greetings came from all around the room and I nodded to each person in turn. "This is my dear friend, George Cheswick. You may remember him from this afternoon." Honoria said.

The gentleman from the séance who had opened the drapes crossed the dining room and offered me his hand.

"Such a delight to meet you." George managed a large smile despite his mouth being weighed down by a staggering mustache.

"Likewise," I replied.

"George encourages me concerning my psychic pursuits, even going so far as to join the Divination Circle. He has become quite adept at the practice of automatic writing," Honoria said. George blushed a deep red where the swirling points of his mustache touched his round cheeks.

"And seated next to the window are Everett and Cecelia MacPherson. He's the resident radiesthesist and she's our astrologer." Honoria smiled at an older man whose most noticeable feature was his skeletal slimness and an Adam's apple larger than his nose. Seated next to him was a pale woman dressed all in black and holding a small fat dog in her lap. Cecelia flashed me a welcoming smile. Her dog gave an excited yip, then sprawled, panting, across her lap.

"I'm naught but a dowser, young lady," Everett said, his voice rolling with a heavy Scots accent. There was a cook in the medicine show from Nova Scotia with the same sort of voice. I felt a momentary tug of homesickness. "But if you need something found, I'm the man for the job. My wife, however, has much more impressive skills to demonstrate. Show her, my dear." Everett patted his wife's shoulder with a bony hand.

"When were you born, my dear?"

"February fifteenth." I wondered if she always started conversations that way.

"An Aquarius. You are experiencing important transits."

"I am?" I had no idea what she was describing. My unease

before arriving in the dining room had centered on my appearance and how to comport myself. I had not imagined I'd be conversationally disadvantaged as well.

"Yes, you are. For an Aquarius today I would predict a slight head injury, an attempted robbery, and a rescue by a handsome policeman." Cecelia gave me another sparkling smile.

"You can tell that from just hearing my birthday?" I hoped my voice did not betray my skepticism.

"Not from your birthday alone. For all that I'd need to look at a complete natal chart."

"Do stop teasing the girl," Honoria said. "Everett and Cecelia ran into Officer Yancey as he was leaving the hotel this afternoon. He told them you had a run-in with a pickpocket. Something you might have mentioned to me, I would add." Honoria shook her head at me, then led me to the last occupied table. "This young man, Ned Larkin, is our numerologist, and seated next to him is Amanda Howell, a gifted psychometrist." Ned hopped to his feet and offered a slight bow. He clasped my hand between his two damp palms and pumped it up and down with enthusiasm.

"Do let me know what I can do to make you feel welcome here at the Belden," he said.

"You already have," I said, hoping he didn't see me wincing as my shoulder made a popping noise.

"Please join us," Ned said, pulling out a chair right next to his.

"Yes, do," added Amanda from across the table. She let her gaze wander up and down the length of my gown as if trying to memorize the details in order to forbid her dressmaker from creating something remotely similar. I looked to my aunt, hoping she would require my presence at her own table but she just waved me into the offered seat and turned her attention to a woman carrying a steaming tray of food. "Honoria did not tell us your discipline. Is it by any chance the ability to time travel?" Amanda looked pointedly at my dress once more and I felt determined not to let the pleasure of wearing it dim. I called upon my years of showmanship and gave her the brightest smile I could muster as Ned pushed my chair up to the table.

"If only such a thing were possible. Have you read *The Time Machine*?" For all his faults Father believed in education. Since formal schooling did not exist on the road he made an effort to provide me with a constant supply of books in a wide range of topics. While I wished I could boast of a love of poetry and classics, the truth was my taste ran decidedly to the far more sensational works of H. G. Wells and Arthur Conan Doyle.

"As serious students of the higher realms Ned and I have no time or inclination for such frivolities." I looked over at Ned, who shifted in his chair and pleated his napkin with long fingers. He met my eyes and gave the slightest of shrugs, which I took as an apology.

"I am sure my aunt is glad to have such devoted members of her ensemble. What exactly does each of you do? I am unfamiliar with the terms *numerologist* and *psychometrist*." I directed my question to Ned, who cut Amanda off as she began to reply.

"I study the relationships between numbers and events, personalities, and life paths. It is an ancient science with predictive capabilities. Perhaps tomorrow I could conduct a reading for you?" Before I could answer I felt a sharp blow to my shin. Assuming the kick was intended for Ned, I ignored it and answered as I wished.

"How generous. Have you time right after breakfast?" I asked.

"He does not. Ned helps me in the mornings with my token reading practice," Amanda said. "Isn't that right?" She turned to Ned.

"I cannot see why you insist on me putting you through practice readings every day. You're more than prepared for the guests to arrive." From Amanda's behavior and the scorching scowl she gave me it was clear to me why she insisted on Ned's attentions. I wondered if he was being deliberately dimwitted.

"I shouldn't like to disturb a psychometry routine, whatever it may be," I said. After all, Amanda may not have seemed interested in befriending me but there was no reason to antagonize her unnecessarily. The young woman with the heavy tray arrived at our table and sat a plate in front of each of us. As I looked at the offering of tender greens, a heaping mound of mashed potatoes, and a portion of fish in a creamy sauce I realized I was famished.

"Psychometry is the challenging art of reading the energy of objects by touching them," she said.

"What sort of objects?" I asked.

"Personal possessions held close to the body like jewelry or even spectacles conduct information the most readily. But under the right circumstances I could read just about anything."

"Why do people ask for this service?" I asked.

"Because the people who appear in our lives aren't always exactly who or what they claim to be. Clients rely on me to help them to uncover harmful secrets. I'd be happy to do a reading for you if you'd like." Amanda gave me the first genuine smile I had seen from her, then snapped her large white teeth down on a forkful of beet greens. "That is, unless you have something to hide."

• • •

S HE'S THE SPITTING IMAGE OF HER MOTHER," ORAZELIA SAID.
        "People always say things like that about long-lost relatives,"
Lucinda said.

"She looks more like Delphinia than you do me," Orazelia
said.

"That's because I favor Father's side." A noticeable hush descended on the room as all three paused their clanking and scrap-
ing of cutlery on china. Yancey rushed to fill the silence and
distract his mother from painful memories and his sister from
her gaffe.

"She made an impression everywhere today. The scene at the
train station caused quite a stir."

"Is it true that she bashed a pickpocket over the head with her
parasol?" Lucinda completely abandoned any pretense of interest
in her meal and leaned so far forward the lace on her bodice
loomed perilously close to her soup plate.

"Lucinda, I'm sure that isn't true in the least. People do so
love to exaggerate." Orazelia's tone was stern but she laid her own
fork down and gave her son her full attention.

"I'm afraid the witnesses all concurred with what Lucy has
heard." Yancey paused to enjoy a sip of soup. No sense wasting a
perfectly good meal just because his family had more appetite for
gossip than for food.

"See, Mother. I told you." Lucinda stretched even farther forward, and this time managed to wet her ruffles with the tomato
bisque. She was so engrossed she didn't seem to notice. "Did you
catch the thief?"

"No, but I've given word to the men to be on the lookout for someone skulking about with a parasol-shaped dent in the side of his head. We should have him before long, I expect."

"Such high spirits. So unorthodox. It will do Honoria a world of good to have her visit. I hope she intends to stay for a while," Orazelia said.

"I wonder what people will say about her arriving so unexpectedly. There's sure to be a great deal of talk." Lucinda waved her hands about wildly. Even in the low light of the candles Yancey could see the high color on her cheeks.

"There's always talk surrounding the Belden women. At least this time Honoria will enjoy the subject," Orazelia said.

"I wonder if she's here to help Honoria with the business," Lucy said. "Perhaps she received a message from the beyond, letting her know her aunt needed her."

"I certainly hope she shows more sense than to claim a thing like that. The last thing we need is someone else bringing that séance nonsense in your lives again." Yancey felt his hand clench around his spoon. He fixed his eyes on his mother. "You've barely recovered from the last go-round with it." Something in his sister's manner gave him pause. He wasn't at all happy with the way she was chewing on her lower lip. As a child that always had meant she was hiding something. "You do remember you promised not to hire any of the practitioners at the hotel, don't you?"

"I have no plans to do so, despite my feelings on the subject." Orazelia sniffed and reached for a dinner roll.

"It's for your own good, Mother. If you'd kept on the way you were going you would have shelled out every penny you had and still not heard an answer which satisfied you."

Yancey loathed this particular conversation. When Honoria

announced her plans to renovate the Belden and create a haven for gullible souls with money to burn he worried Orazelia would not be able not resist the temptation to participate in all her friend had to offer. The dire state of his mother's finances was not his only worry on the subject. Orazelia's nerves had been shattered by the emotional highs and lows each new encounter with a self-proclaimed medium had wrought. If he'd had his way every last one of those charlatans would be rotting in a cell until they were nothing but spirits themselves.

"Well, whatever Miss Proulx's reasons are for appearing out of the blue, I'm delighted that she's here. I've always felt sorry for Honoria, rattling around in that hotel with nobody but paying guests and the Dragon."

"You know I dislike it when you call Mrs. Doyle names," Orazelia said. "She may be fiercely protective of Honoria but that doesn't make her a dragon."

"We all know how important allies are in time of trouble, Lucy," Yancey said. "If I had to guess, I'd say Miss Proulx is exactly what Honoria needs to put the past behind her."

"What makes you the authority on this particular young lady?" Lucinda asked.

"I'm no authority. I only walked her from the police station to the Hotel Belden. It was my duty to see that she was entertained on our way."

"I can't see that it was your duty to take her there at all. If she had been a grubby fifteen-year-old boy you would have left him to make his own way," Lucy said.

"But she was not grubby, nor was she a boy. Your brother has done his best to make her feel welcomed. Tomorrow, Lucinda, we must do the same."

"What a good idea. Honoria hustled her out of there so quickly I didn't even have a chance to say hello."

"We shall pay a call tomorrow afternoon. Even if she is not in we will leave our cards and an invitation to something or other. We could arrange a dinner party." Orazelia clasped her hands together excitedly and winked at Yancey in a way that left the palms of his hands clammy. If there was one thing he didn't like about his mother it was her insistent matchmaking. But at least she appeared to have forgotten to be angry at him.

"If you two will excuse me, I'm heading back out to keep my eye on the area around the station. Apparently there are pickpockets about." With that he kissed both his mother and sister on the tops of their heads and left them to their plans.

Chapter Six

Honoria caught my eye at the end of the meal and beckoned me to her with the flash of a heavily ringed finger. As the other diners filed out of the room in a buzz of conversation I made my way to her table.

"My dear, if you are not too tired there's someone who insists on meeting you this evening." A flicker of concern crossed Honoria's face and I thought of my conversation with Millie.

"Mrs. Doyle, perhaps?" I asked, hoping I wasn't going to get Millie into any trouble.

"Millie's been helping put you in the picture, I see. She is a bright girl." Honoria exhaled forcibly, her impressive bustline deflating with the effort. "Mrs. Doyle won't go to bed tonight unless she gets her own eyes on you, and I need her at her best tomorrow with so many guests set to arrive in the morning."

"I'd be delighted to meet her." I said. "Would now be a good time?" I would have expected to be overwhelmed with exhaustion after such a long journey but instead I felt alert and curious.

"Are you sure it won't be too much for you? How is your head feeling?"

"It's only a little sore." I reached up and gently pressed my fingers against the lump that had formed right below the spot where Millie had affixed the hair comb.

"Mrs. Doyle is the nurse here at the Belden along with all her other areas of expertise. If she wasn't so proud of the table she provides she would have canceled dinner and taken a tray up to your room and forced you to lie there while she spooned broth down your throat."

"But why is she so interested in me?"

"Let's just say she's devoted to the family." Honoria patted her hair and then tucked her arm in mine. "We'll find her in the kitchen."

Honoria ushered me through a long hallway leading away from the dining room and library. From the end of it came banging and clattering. Honoria paused at the doorway and drew a deep breath before giving me a wink and crossing the threshold.

"I hope you've got her with you, missy. It's bad enough I've waited twenty years too long to see Delphinia's child." The words were sharp but the voice was musical.

"She's here, Mrs. Doyle, all in one piece and ready for inspection." I squared my shoulders as Honoria stepped aside. Across the room, held at bay by a long wooden worktable covered in pie pans and carving knives, stood a tiny woman with an enormous scowl on her face. I felt my throat constrict. If Mrs. Doyle didn't like me being here would Honoria ask me to leave?

Mrs. Doyle made her way around the table and drew closer. She tipped her head back to look up at me and scowled some more.

"I'll speak to the child alone, young lady." Mrs. Doyle addressed herself to Honoria and then pointed at the door.

"I shall leave you to get acquainted," Honoria said. "Don't

keep Mrs. Doyle up too late, Ruby. I trust you can find your way back to your room when you are finished here?"

"I'm certain I can," I said, hoping I was right.

"Then I will wish you a good night. I'll see you at the breakfast table." Honoria gave a tight smile and left us alone, closing the door behind her.

"I see there's no hope you aren't who you say you are." Mrs. Doyle squinted at me as she grasped my chin with a calloused hand, turning my face this way and that. "You're the spitting image of her, especially in that gown. No wonder you gave Honoria such a turn this afternoon, thinking Delphinia had come back to us."

"Upsetting her was not my intention in coming here."

"And just what was your purpose?" Mrs. Doyle turned the full power of her blue eyes on me. Cold tugged at my stomach and I regretted eating my dinner. Honoria had said Mrs. Doyle was devoted to the family. Perhaps that was the angle to take.

"I've always wanted to be in touch with my mother's side of the family. Now seemed a perfect time to do so."

"More than likely you needed a warm bed and a free meal. You may look just like your mother but you were raised by your father. With an influence like that I'll be more surprised than not if both you and the silver are here in the morning. Running off in the night with family treasures in tow is in your blood."

"I assure you, I'm here for as long as Honoria is willing to have me. I just want to get to know about my family."

"All you need to know is that so far your father has been the worst thing to ever happen to the Beldens. I'm making it my mission to be certain you don't pick up where he left off and destroy what little remains of the family."

"Then I expect there is nothing I can say to reassure you of my intentions." I stepped out of her reach and felt the weakness in my trembling knees as I did so.

"No, there is not. You may be a sweet talker just like your father. I expect that you'll slide into Honoria's good graces just as easily as you've slipped into your mother's dress. But you shan't wriggle your way into mine." She squinted at me even harder.

"I'm sorry you feel that way." I held my breath as I stood, hoping my quaking legs would support me and that Mrs. Doyle would not see the effect she had on my nerves. "I'll take myself out of your way."

"See that you do and remember, I'm watching you." Mrs. Doyle gripped the edge of the table between her two hands.

N O ONE BUT BEN, SILENTLY MANNING THE FRONT DESK, WAS about as I hurried through the lobby and along the stairs to the refuge of my mother's third-floor bedroom. Floors creaked and voices murmured through solid doors as I passed but no one slowed my progress. I pushed open the door and was struck once more by the opulence of the room and my good fortune at arriving in such a place.

I struggled out of the unfamiliar gown and sat in front of the mirror to brush out my hair and to affix it in a braid for the night. Mrs. Doyle's words echoed in my ears with every stroke, and my hand trembled. I was convinced Mrs. Doyle would turn me over to the police if she had the least cause to do so. And what better cause could there be than murder?

My dinner stirred wretchedly in my stomach, and I cast my eyes to the wardrobe where Millie had hung my own travel-weary

gown. Surely there were other places to go. Places without someone watching my every move for signs of deception. Perhaps the
best course of action would be to slip away as quickly as I had
arrived. Usually, I would have consulted my cards when such
weighty matters pressed down my spirits but I had left mine with
the ones owned by Honoria and they rested in her room.

I pushed back the little stool and walked to the wardrobe. I
might be a lot of the things Mrs. Doyle implied. I was adept in
the art of deception. I was an excellent fraud and I was a confidence artist. I was an accomplished swindler. But I was not an
outright thief. I would not leave with anything not my own.

I unbuttoned the front of my mother's chemise and commenced to slip it off.

"Trust that your place is here." I paused as I heard the voice
distinctly through the cloth of the chemise covering my ears. Not
that the fabric mattered. Never had I so desperately wanted it to
be real, to be giving wise counsel. I tugged off the borrowed garment and reached out for the brass knob on the wardrobe door.

"Trust that your place is here." I heard the words again, even
louder now. They created a pressure in my head like that of being
underwater. I stepped back from the wardrobe and went instead to
the dresser. The drawers glided smoothly on their rails as I opened
and shut them, looking for a nightgown. I might be mad to listen
to such a voice but I remembered my promise to myself to heed its
advice no matter how strange. I tucked myself into bed, blew out
the bedside candle, and fell into a deep and dreamless sleep.

CHAPTER SEVEN

I WAS STARTLED AWAKE THE NEXT MORNING BY A KNOCK UPON the door. The comfort of the bed and the smell of the sea drifting in through the opened window left me momentarily disoriented. As I remembered where I was and why I was there I threw back the coverlet and hoped it was not Mrs. Doyle, accompanied by a policeman, at the door.

Much to my relief, it was Millie there to help me choose an appropriate costume for the day and to fix my hair into something more suitable than the braid I wore for sleeping. She told me Honoria had once again sent her and had asked me to join her in the dining room once I was dressed.

I felt my steps falter as I approached the dining room. I hoped my aunt hadn't requested my presence to tell me Mrs. Doyle insisted I should be on my way. I paused at the doorway and gave myself a stern talking-to. I told myself I was a modern woman with a decent head on her shoulders. As much as I wanted to stay I would land on my feet if forced to leave. I stepped into the dining room with my chin lifted and a smile I did not feel on my face.

Honoria sat alone at a small table near a window. Her own

smile as she glanced up at me looked welcoming and genuine. I felt my worries melt away, for the moment, at least.

"Good morning, Ruby dear. I trust you slept well?"

"I've never spent a night in greater comfort." Which was entirely true. There was no comparison to be made between the canvas and wooden folding cot I called my own at the medicine show and my mother's high bed heaped with pillows and dressed with clean, smooth sheets. I helped myself to oatmeal and a hard-boiled egg from warming dishes on the sideboard. The dining room basked in the warmth of the sun slanting through the windows, and the papered walls displayed images of colorful birds and sprigs of flowers.

During dinner the night before I had been too busy to notice the details of the room, but now I settled in to admire it at leisure. The furniture and paintings, not to mention the carpets and silk draperies, must have cost a small fortune. The renovations and upkeep on the hotel surely amounted to a great deal of money.

"I'm glad to hear it. I confess I was so excited by your arrival I couldn't settle down." Honoria slid a velvet box across the table to me. "So I used the time to locate this. I've been saving it for your return." I felt a lump form in my throat. Honoria sounded so happy and I knew I didn't deserve her kindness. I opened the box and gasped at the contents.

"This is the necklace I saw in the photo of you and my mother." I ran my finger over the sparkling red stone dangling at the end of a delicate gold chain.

"I've kept it for you all these years. It was your mother's favorite. I believe it inspired your name." Honoria lifted it from the box. "Would you like to wear it?"

"Shouldn't I save it for a special occasion?"

"Today is a special occasion. The Velmont sisters, our first guests of the season, are expected this morning." Honoria motioned for me to turn around, and I felt the weight of the pendant against my bodice.

"Is it special because they are the first or because of something special about them?"

"I understand they're very influential in Spiritualist circles and have said they will recommend the Belden to those of their acquaintance who would be interested if the experience here is all they hope it to be."

"Did they say what sort of experience they hope to have?"

"They are eager to consult with a medium. Apparently, they wish to contact their father, who has passed on to the other side." Honoria said this without any of the sneer in her voice my father's always held when discussing his marks. Nothing in her tone suggested she was attempting to deceive herself or anyone else.

"Isn't your medium arriving today as well?"

"She is expected very shortly."

"Is there anything I can do to help?" I asked.

"I would be most grateful if you would help me to greet newcomers as they arrive." Before I could respond, a carriage clattered to a stop on the street just outside the window. Honoria straightened her already impressive posture and reaching for my hand pulled me to my feet. "Shall we?"

AT FIRST GLANCE, THE VELMONT SISTERS WERE INDISTINguishable. Both were short, even given the height added by their identical hats. Both wore matte black crepe gowns even more out of fashion than the ones in my mother's wardrobe. Matching net gloves, wire-rimmed spectacles, and gray hair reinforced the impression that they were identical.

Indistinguishable, that is, until they began to speak. Unfortunately, they both stepped forward to address Honoria at the same moment.

"Miss Belden?" they said in unison.

"You must be the Misses Velmont. I am Honoria Belden and am delighted to welcome you as the first guests of the season at the Hotel Belden."

"The very first, you say? What a surprise. We're never first at anything, are we, Elva?" asked one of the other. "One doesn't like to push oneself forward unnecessarily, does one?"

"Nonsense, Dovie. We're never first because you are always late for everything." The thinner of the two sisters, and perhaps slightly older, if the lines tightening determinedly around her face were to be trusted, stepped toward me and looked me up and down. The beady look in her eye reminded me of Mrs. Doyle the previous evening. "And who is this young lady? She appears to be a relation of yours, Miss Belden. My sister and I are very keen on close family ties."

"May I present my niece, Miss Proulx?" I could feel Honoria's hand tightening around my upper arm like she was clinging to it for dear life. I wondered if the Velmont sisters were more important people than their appearance would suggest. Why else would such a self-assured woman as Honoria be so nervous in their presence?

"We only stay at family-run establishments," Dovie said. "Father only stayed at family-owned hotels and we, of course, have continued to do the same."

"You recall I mentioned Mr. Velmont has passed over to the other side?" Honoria said to me.

"How thoughtful of you to remember, Miss Belden," Dovie said, reaching out and clasping Honoria's free hand in her own small, plump one. "We are aflutter with anticipation of the arrival of your medium. She hasn't gotten here before us, has she?" Dovie swiveled her head and looked around as if hoping a medium would simply appear before her as if by magic.

"Dovie, you know we timed our visit to arrive before the medium," Elva said. "She's expected later today, is she not?"

"Everything has been arranged for weeks. She arrives on the next train from Boston and plans to begin sessions with guests this afternoon," Honoria said.

"We shall mark down an appointment as soon as we've settled in." Elva forced out an exaggerated sigh before waving a hand at the modest pile of trunks and bags behind her. "Do you have rooms for us on the first floor?"

"I'm afraid all our guest rooms are on the second floor and above," Honoria said. "I hope that won't be a problem."

"But you do have us in a shared room?" Elva asked.

"Yes, just as you requested. I'll send for a porter to carry your baggage to your room and I'll show you to it myself."

"Don't trouble yourself on our account." Dovie spoke up. "Let Miss Proulx show us the way. If she can spare the time, that is."

"It would be my pleasure. Which room are they to have, Aunt?" I asked, keeping my brightest medicine show smile affixed to my face. Considering the importance Honoria seemed to place on the Velmonts, the least I could do was to be obliging. Even if I did get lost along the way.

"I've placed them in the Beach Rose Room." Honoria cocked

an eyebrow to gesture toward the stairs nearest the front of the house. I hoped I was correct in my memory of the hotel from the whirlwind tour the day before. My best hope was that the rooms all had placards attached to their doors with nautically themed names upon them. Like my mother's room, aptly named the Crow's Nest.

"Of course, Aunt. Ladies, if you'll follow me?"

As I led the way I could hear them fussing and rustling behind me. Dovie paused to look at every picture on the walls and through every open doorway. Elva walked so swiftly I feared she would tread upon my heels. By the time I'd paused on the first landing Dovie was nowhere in sight.

"My sister goes floating off with even the most minor of distractions. She takes twice as long as I do to get anywhere at all." Elva sighed deeply and scowled. "You would not have believed all the fuss it took to get into the carriage and off to the train station this morning."

"I'm sorry to hear that. It can be a very difficult thing to be a well-organized person when accompanied by those who are not." I thought of how often I had struggled to roust Father in the morning after a night of excess. He had been a sore trial to me. Not that there was any reason to think Dovie was slow to get moving on account of a blinding headache and a roiling stomach.

"How well we understand each other, child." Elva nodded in solidarity with a single bob of her chin.

I dared to hope things had gotten off to a good start with the first guest, and I felt my spirits lift. Perhaps if the guests approved of me Mrs. Doyle could be convinced to do so, too. I forged ahead up the stairs with renewed enthusiasm. At the top of the wide staircase the hall led to the east and toward the west.

Faced with a decision, Honoria's words about the sisters' room facing the sea came back to me. The seaside was the east side, that much I was sure of. At least I thought I was.

I searched ahead at doors, looking for a sign to tell me which room was assigned to the sisters. But all the doors were the same dark walnut inlaid panels and all without a placard like my own. I took a breath and pushed open the first door I came to on the east side of the hotel. Primroses and lilacs frolicked across the wallpaper.

I pulled the door shut again and hurried to the next room, papered in seashells, and then on to the third, a room decorated with weeping willow trees and men with fishing poles. As Elva caught up with me she raised her eyebrows. Perhaps I was too hasty in assuming I had gotten on her good side.

"It seems to me you ought to know your way around your own hotel," Elva said. "Are you sure you're a member of the Belden family?" At this moment Dovie caught up with us, her hat askew on her graying head, slightly out of breath.

"What nonsense, Elva. This child is the spitting image of a very fine portrait hanging just down the hall. If you weren't always in such a hurry you would have spotted it for yourself." Dovie patted my arm with her plump fingers. "Pay no attention to my sister, child. She's always on the lookout for charlatans and confidence men. Sadly, those who seek answers to the mysteries of what lies beyond often encounter such frauds."

"I take no offense and am sorry to have been less than expert in my assistance. I am indeed Miss Belden's niece but have only arrived at the hotel for the first time myself yesterday."

"That explains things, doesn't it?" Dovie said with a voice that sounded like it was shaking a finger.

"I suppose it does. What is not explained is why you are as grown as you are and never before had visited your aunt's home. Is there something we should know about this hotel? Something that would have given you cause to stay away?" Elva asked.

"Certainly not, ma'am. My mother died when I was a baby and my father kept me with him in Canada. He had no cause to visit with my mother's people. We agreed that I was old enough to make those connections myself if I so chose. I did and here I am to do so."

"See, Elva, a nice family hotel, just like we were promised." Dovie stepped past me and opened the next door along the hallway. "Just as I thought. Here's our room." I followed the sisters inside and was relieved to notice sprigs of pink roses dotting the wallpaper. Someone had been in earlier to draw the draperies back from the windows. I wondered if it had been Millie. Once again my breath caught in my throat as my eyes took in the expanse of beach and the sparkling bay beyond.

"It's magnificent. We shall have a rest and then we will stroll along the beach and refresh ourselves with some sea air. So good for the spirit." Elva addressed her sister, then turned to me. "I trust we shall see you later, Miss Proulx?"

"I expect to see you both at luncheon. Please do let me know if you need anything at all." Elva waved me off and I hurried down the hall in the direction Dovie said she had seen a portrait of someone who looked like me.

Presently, I reached the stairs and passing them headed down a corridor I didn't remember from the tour with Honoria the day before. This side of the hotel faced the street, and without the roar of the sea the sounds of people walking by reached my ears easily. Horse hooves clopped along the street, and as I passed a window a man on a bicycle rang his bicycle bell in warning.

As I made my way down the plushly carpeted hall I happened upon a section of wall covered in paintings. I wondered if amongst them was the one Dovie mentioned. An artful arrangement of portraits painted in dark, thick oils hung in carved wooden frames. At the top of the wall hung a portrait of an old man with an extraordinary display of whiskers. His muttonchops obscured the lower half of his face but his eyes glared out at me so fiercely he made Mrs. Doyle's scrutiny seem welcoming.

Next to him, a small woman, if the birdcage behind her was to scale, sat serenely in a dark green chair, her hair pulled so severely back from her head my own scalp ached just from looking at it. A pair of pearl drops adorned her ears and a matching necklace filled the space between her neck and the low bustline on her dress. Her eyes were softer than those of the man, and a slight upturn to the corner of her mouth made me think she enjoyed having her likeness painted.

Below the older couple hung two more pictures, one of a younger, slightly slimmer Honoria. Her wavy hair fell loosely around her shoulders and her face had the roundness of youth, but it was easy to see that it was she. Unlike the older people, Honoria's face wore a bold, forceful smile, as if she would lean out of the portrait and tell the viewer an amusing story. Her zest for life was nearly as palpable in the portrait as I had found her to be in the flesh.

The final frame held a more subdued portrait. The subject sat demurely, almost shyly. Instead of Honoria's bold look, she held her head tilted, as if she were listening to something far away. Her eyes were the same dark shade as the woman in the top row and her hair curled as rambunctiously as Honoria's. She looked exactly like the woman in the photograph I had held on to for so many years. At her throat was the same necklace that now adorned mine. My mother.

I leaned forward to absorb every detail of the painting, every line, every shadow. The dress she wore for the portrait was the very same one I had chosen to wear the night before. That explained Mrs. Doyle's comment about me sneaking around and ingratiating myself. There were so many things I would likely never know about my mother. I felt a lump rising in my throat and backed away from the picture.

There was no reason to be anything but sensible. If I was going to earn my keep I couldn't spend the day standing about in hallways making myself miserable. I decided to descend via the back stairs to ask Honoria how I could further assist. After I had regained mastery of my emotions.

CHAPTER EIGHT

"Miss Flora Roberts?" Honoria asked the turbaned woman. A person looking less like a Flora Roberts I could not have imagined. This woman stood in the foyer swathed in three shawls and a bead-encrusted turban. How she had not fainted dead away from the heat was beyond me. Or from the cloud of her own perfume, wafting violently about the room.

"No. I am Madame Fidelia. You have heard of me, of course." The turbaned woman projected her voice as clearly as she projected scent. Honoria glanced in my direction as if to ask me to prompt her memory but I had nothing to offer.

"I regret to say that I have not."

"Surely the letter of introduction from my dear friend Miss Flora Roberts has reached you?" The woman squinted as if she were confused.

"I am afraid no such letter has reached me," Honoria said as the door behind her opened and Ben, assisted by a second man, rolled in a pair of brass luggage racks laden with three steamer trunks and a mound of valises. "And I regret to inform you all of our rooms have been reserved for weeks. We simply have no accommodations available."

"But surely I can have Miss Roberts's room as was mentioned in the letter?" Madame Fidelia widened her dark-rimmed eyes and looked from Honoria's face to mine. "Since she will not be requiring it."

"Not requiring it? I expect her at any moment." Honoria's face paled and she reached out a hand and gripped my arm so firmly I stifled a yelp.

"No. She no longer comes to this hotel. She sends her dear friend Madame Fidelia in her place." The bejeweled visitor unleashed a dazzling smile.

"Miss Roberts sent you to replace her as the medium at the Belden for the season." Honoria's voice cracked and her grip tightened.

"No, of course not," Madame Fidelia said. The ferocity of Honoria's sigh of relief ruffled the hair at the nape of my neck. "She sent me in her place, but everyone knows Madame Fidelia is not a medium."

Honoria gripped me even tighter and a little squeak escaped her throat, but as no words seemed inclined to follow I launched myself into the conversational breach.

"What is it that you do exactly?" I asked.

"I read the future." Madame Fidelia turned to the top valise on the mound behind her, opened it, and plunged her hand inside. "With this." She held a crystal ball cupped in her palm. I felt Honoria stiffen her spine and find her voice.

"Did Miss Roberts give a reason as to her cancellation of our agreement?" Honoria said.

"She only say to me that the spirits advised her not to come to this place and that she never ignores the counsel of her guides on the other side." Madame Fidelia glanced up and down the hall. I wondered if Miss Roberts's guides on the other side were anything like the voice I heard. Then I wondered if they had mentioned any particular reason not to come. "If you leave me standing here with all of my things I think it will look strange for your guests when they arrive, no?"

"We certainly cannot leave a friend of Miss Roberts's with nowhere to stay. I'm sure this will all be easily sorted out." Honoria turned to me. "Ruby, please show Madame Fidelia to the Piping Plover Room on the third floor." She lowered her voice into my ear. "Take her up the back stairs. I fear the force of her perfume might peel the new wallpaper in the front hall."

MADAME FIDELIA EXPRESSED DELIGHT AT THE PROVIDED ACcommodations, and I left her to rest after her journey. As I approached the back stairs Honoria's voice came toward me in a whisper. It sounded as if her voice were coming from a long way away. I crept along the hallway and followed the sound. She was nowhere to be seen but her voice seemed to be coming from a recess tucked into the corridor. It was then I realized I could hear her from the chute used for the dumbwaiter. Someone had left it open and it was possible to overhear the voices in the kitchen below.

"I cannot believe Flora Roberts canceled at the last possible minute," Honoria said. "I don't know what on earth I will do. Absolutely everything is riding on that woman," Honoria said.

"It can't be as bad as all that. You have a season's worth of bookings," Mrs. Doyle said in a louder voice than my aunt's.

"Yes, and every last one of them said in their letters that they chose to stay at the Belden because of the medium."

"Too bad the girl is proving to be about as much good as her father," Mrs. Doyle said.

"She can't help it if she doesn't share her mother's gift," Honoria said. "It seems she is only a card reader. A good one, but that shan't be enough to save the hotel."

"If only your sister hadn't run off with that good-for-nothing tramp you would have had a gifted practitioner permanently on site."

"That can hardly be helped now. I do confess I had high hopes for Ruby and the possibility that she could pick up where Delphinia left off. After all, I can read cards for the guests myself."

"You have plenty of other amusements for them, though." Mrs. Doyle must have been at her baking. Her words were punctuated by the slapping sound of yeast dough being kneaded on the wooden worktable.

"They will enjoy the other practitioners, to be sure, but you know as well as I the real reason for them coming to the Belden is the medium. If they are not provided with one they will likely leave and then we will be ruined."

"You mustn't get yourself all dithered up, child. Surely it isn't as bad as you are making it out to be." Another slap, this time even louder than the last.

"Mrs. Doyle, I tell you truly, it is. I sank every last penny I had into remodeling this place and advertising the new services we would provide. What's more, I secured a mortgage against the hotel itself to complete the project." I heard a final slap of dough, then a gasp.

"You never did such a foolish thing."

"I didn't know what else to do, Mrs. Doyle. All the other hotels around us are so much larger and more glamorous. They have ballrooms and ice cream parlors and bowling alleys right on site. We have fifteen rooms to let and a view of the sea. This was my final attempt to remain in business."

"But to mortgage the hotel. What would your parents say?"

"If the medium hadn't canceled we could have asked them. But as she did, I shall just have to figure something out on my own."

"What if you can't?"

"If I can't replace Flora Roberts with another medium I expect we'll all be out on the street. I've already received dunning letters from the bank. I thought we'd be open a month ago but was willing to wait at the medium's request, because she was so important. Every week we are falling further behind," Honoria said. Cold pulsed through my stomach and I leaned against the wall for support. The hotel looked so luxurious. It had simply not occurred to me that Honoria could be in any sort of financial trouble.

I felt irrationally tricked, as though I had fallen for a swindle that was obviously too good to be true. Hot tears filled my eyes as I considered that a new life had seemed within my grasp, but was actually out of reach.

"But what will you do if you lose the hotel?" I heard Mrs. Doyle ask. "My daughter is always pestering me to move in with her and spend my old age bouncing my grandchildren on my knees. But what about you? You've never been anywhere but here."

"As much as it distresses me to say it, I shall have to marry someone." Honoria's voice sounded as though it wavered even through the muffling of the chute.

"You never wanted to marry. You've always been so determined to chart your own course. It'll break your heart to head to the altar, especially if it isn't for love."

"If it were just on account of myself I'd take a job as a companion or even try my hand at a modern occupation like becoming a typist but now I also have Ruby to consider. I've offered her a home and I can't go back on my word."

"But you don't even know her."

"I know she is my niece and I've waited all her life to meet her. I'd rather make a practical marriage than to lose the opportunity to get to know her."

"You'll do as you're a mind to, of course. Just like you always have. I just hope it all ends up being worth it."

I took a deep breath and tried to pull myself together. I needed to think, and nothing cleared the mind like a walk. I ran up the back stairs to my room, passing Millie on the way.

"Is there anything the matter, miss?" she asked.

"I'm going out for a walk and remembered my parasol was all the way on the third floor. If anyone asks for me, please tell them I've gone to see the beach." I gathered what I needed and slipped back down the servants' stairs without being seen.

CHAPTER NINE

DESPITE THE TROUBLES OF THE DAY, IT WAS IMPOSSIBLE NOT to be distracted from them by the sights and sounds of the sea. Sunlight bounced off the waves and the gulls swooped down from above as if they wished to steal the flowers from the ladies' hats. Small boys raced up and down the boardwalk, weaving between the adults, garnering scoldings for their unruliness.

Up ahead, the pier, still under construction, stretched out like a steel leviathan whose tail had been anchored to the beach. Yesterday, I had only had a hurried glimpse of it as Officer Yancey escorted me to the Belden. I was eager to take a closer look. Indeed, all along the beach, strollers were drawn to the imposing structure. A large crowd had assembled as close as was safe, and I was as curious as the rest. Clanging and hammering echoed from where men stood atop the pier, fastening bolts and attaching beams.

I watched the work for a few moments before continuing on. I slowed as I passed a sign advertising tintypes and souvenir photographs. The scent of hot roasted peanuts and buttered popcorn wafted toward me from a cart, its metal wheels half buried in the sand near the foot of the Sea Shore House.

As I moved along the hard-packed sand my mind returned to the problem of Flora Roberts. The obvious solution was to tell my aunt I, too, was a medium. Since Honoria had hoped that I had inherited some sort of mediumistic ability from my mother she would be easy enough to convince. The real test would be with the clients. Surely most of them would have far greater experience with such matters than I.

All my life I had known people who were believers in the possibility of communication with the dead. Spiritualism was a popular movement in Canada and abroad. Even Arthur Conan Doyle, whose latest works I devoured as soon as they were released, made no secret of being an ardent believer in such things.

But even more troubling than whether or not I could pull off the deception was if I should even attempt it. Was deceiving spiritual seekers any different from deceiving people who looked for miraculous cures for their physical ailments? Was it even more reprehensible to prey on grief than on faint hopes for the future? Would it be best to ignore the voice and leave the Belden and Honoria's problems far behind? After all, it would be selfish of me to stay with Honoria if she lost the hotel. I would only be a burden to her, and over time I felt sure she would grow to resent me.

Carnival people are a superstitious lot whether they work the sideshows, the fairs, or the snake oil circuit. *Please*, I pleaded silently, *just give me a sign. A symbol, something to tell me if I should cast my fate in with Honoria and stay or if I should cut my losses and run.* And then, just as if something otherworldly had heard me, as I approached the Fiske Hotel, a bit of bright red material,

propelled by a gust of wind, careened down the beach toward
me. I bent to pick it up and realized it was a kerchief. A sturdy
woman hurried up to me, a look of relief upon her face.

"Is this yours?" I asked, extending the scarf to her.

"Yes. Thank you for stopping it." The woman's voice came in
pants. "I've chased it halfway down the beach." She paused and
dragged a deep breath into her lungs. I was intrigued by her
appearance.

Her shirtwaist was white but around her shoulders she wore
a vividly violet shawl trimmed with brass-colored disks that tin-
kled and jingled as the sea breeze tickled them. Her skin was
darker by far than mine and her hair was black with a few streaks
of silver. Fastened to a sash tied at her waist hung a pouch that
looked like the money bags most women in the medicine show
secreted into their skirts. She looked so much like an aunt of
Johnny's I thought I had been followed from the medicine show.
But then she smiled at me and revealed a full set of teeth, something not possessed by Johnny's aunt.

"It was nothing," I said. "It would have been a shame for you
to lose such a pretty thing as this." The woman took the kerchief
from my hand and tied it over her hair with a deft motion. Then
she reached for my left hand and tugged me to sit beside her on
the warm sand.

Flipping my palm up, she lowered her head over it and began
to trace the lines etched there. Then she picked up my right hand
and did the same. Holding the two side by side in front of her,
she spoke.

"You are at a crossroads. You are torn between two possibilities but you are not happy with either choice."

"You can see that in my palm?" I asked. Part of me was offended to be taken as the sort of person who would fall for such
drivel. But another part of me felt like she was just the sign I was
looking for.

"That and much more. You've suffered heartache and loss.
This is not the palm of a person accustomed to a soft life. I see a
strong fate line in both palms but they differ from each other."

"What does that mean?" I surprised myself by asking.

"It means your fate is entirely up to you. You have the ability
to stand your ground and make the life you want if you have the
courage to try."

"How can you be sure?"

"Because I have a gift. You have one, too. See this raised place
on your hand?" I nodded as she traced the outside edge of my
palm. "It indicates knowledge of the unseen, an ability to communicate with the beyond."

"You truly believe such abilities to be real?" I had no sense the
woman was working a con. She radiated a peaceful sincerity.

"Why would I not when the experiences of my lifetime prove
it to me?" She raised her hand and gestured at the beach. "Not
only are these sorts of abilities real, this place enhances their
strength."

"You think the beach makes people more able to see the future or contact the world of spirit?" Even though the thought
seemed unlikely I found it intriguing.

"I am certain of it. If you wish to build a life around your abilities, you could not have found a better place to do so."

And in a flash, I felt sure of what I had to do. I could not have
asked for a clearer omen that I should stay and take on the role of

medium. I could hardly wait to get back to the hotel. As if sensing my eagerness, the woman rose and pulled me to my feet.

As she did so she backed into a pinched-faced woman in a dusty black dress.

"Look where you are going, you filthy beggar." The woman's raised voice was loud enough to carry across the sand and draw looks from others strolling the beach. The palm reader dropped my hand and turned to the dowdy woman.

"My apologies, madam," the palm reader said. "May I make it up to you by reading your future?"

"Don't you dare touch me." The woman brandished her parasol like a weapon. Unless I was very much mistaken she was preparing to assault my new acquaintance in the very same manner I had the pickpocket the day before. "Police."

"Please accept my apology," the palm reader said.

"Police!" The woman raised her shrill voice even louder a second time.

"I only meant to help by offering to read your palm."

"More like you wanted to help yourself to my property." The gray-haired woman looked up and down the beach. "You there, police officer. Come here." Officer Yancey hurried to her side and cocked his head as she spoke rapidly.

"I assume you know how to enforce the vagrancy laws in this town, do you not?" the woman asked.

"What seems to be the trouble, Mrs. Jellison?"

"This heathen is soiling the atmosphere with her presence," the angry woman said, raising her voice even more as a fresh round of clanging and banging rang out from the pier. "She is a filthy tramp and I demand that you arrest her immediately."

There had been a wide variety of people who had visited the

shows Father and I worked. There were the poor, the ignorant, the listless, the truly ill. In every segment of society there were people who were kind and interested in others who were different from them, and then there were those who looked for ways to feel superior to their fellow man. It never seemed to be a matter of money or of background. It was more a disease of the soul. It never failed to incense me.

"How can she be a tramp if she is gainfully employed?" I asked. I found myself speaking before I gave the consequences of my words any thought whatsoever. I gave the palm reader a pointed look and hoped she could read minds as well as palms. Not that I believed either was truly possible.

"Nell works for you?" Officer Yancey asked.

"She most certainly does. We were discussing her schedule at the hotel when this woman took a notion to harangue us."

"She has no right to be accosting decent people in public spaces." The woman brandished her parasol once more.

"And you have no right to assault citizens in public spaces," I said, stepping between the angry woman and the palm reader. "Officer Yancey, you are a witness to this woman's assault upon my person."

"Ridiculous," the woman sputtered. "You placed yourself in front of me and put yourself in harm's way."

"So you admit your actions would cause harm," I said. "Officer Yancey, perhaps you should consider escorting this person to the police station and allow us to be on our way."

"How dare you suggest such a thing? Do you know who I am?" The woman drew herself up even more erectly.

"I know more about you than I wish to already. Your actions have convinced me I have no interest in furthering our acquaintance," I said. It pleased me to note the woman's face turned the color of a ripe plum.

"Who do you think you are to disrespect a woman like myself in such a way?"

"I think of myself as someone who treats everyone with the same respect they accord others," I said. My heart was hammering in my chest but it was unthinkable to back down in the face of such bigotry.

"What is your name? It is my intention to alert your family to your inexcusable behavior."

"My name is Ruby Proulx. My aunt is Honoria Belden. I am certain she would receive you with more civility than you have this lady."

"Honoria Belden? That would make you Delphinia's daughter." The woman stepped closer and pursed her thin lips as she looked me up and down. "Your pedigree explains your behavior."

"And a shocking lack of character explains yours."

"Nell, do you wish to press charges against this woman?" Officer Yancey asked.

"No, I do not," the palm reader, apparently named Nell, said. "What I wish is to continue my walk. Shall we?" She directed the question at me.

"Nothing would please me more." I tucked my arm under the crook of Nell's and turned my back on the angry woman. We walked together in silence until we were well out of earshot, and then Nell stopped.

"What is this job you have for me?"

"My aunt owns the Hotel Belden. Have you heard of it?"

"Of course. Honoria Belden is a well-known figure in this town, as is her hotel."

"Have you also heard she has transformed the hotel into a center of learning for spiritual seekers?"

"I know she has employed spiritual practitioners from many disciplines for the season," Nell said.

"Exactly. And the one type of practitioner she does not yet have is a palm reader. If you come to the hotel tomorrow I hope to have convinced her to add one to her staff."

Chapter Ten

Y THE TIME I ENTERED THE BELDEN I WAS SECOND-GUESSING
my decision to pose as a medium. Honoria stood at the reception desk greeting a new arrival. Millie pressed against a wall
biting her lip and passing a feather duster from hand to hand. I
slowed my steps in order to assess the situation. From the sound
of things an argument was well under way. A potted palm conveniently positioned halfway down the hall provided a perfect spot
to hide and observe.

"I am Mrs. Leander Stickney. This is my nephew Sanford
Dobbins. My husband, nephew, and I all have reservations for
the season." A tall, thin middle-aged lady draped entirely in dusty
black leaned heavily on the arm of a young man. "You are, of
course, expecting us?"

"We certainly are. Your rooms are prepared and I would be
happy to have the staff show you to them unless I can be of any
further assistance."

"If by *staff* you mean the imbecilic girl with the feather duster
who greeted us when we entered, I doubt we'd find our rooms
before the end of the season." The woman scowled at Honoria

and hissed a stream of air out through her teeth like she was a teakettle on the boil.

"I'm sure Millie was simply tongue-tied in your presence. Not all girls are used to interacting with a lady of refinement such as yourself." I was surprised. I had always assumed my ability to pour oil on troubled waters by knowing intuitively what people visiting the medicine show wanted to hear was gifted to me by my silver-tongued father. It had never occurred to me it could be a trait shared by my mother's family as well. Perhaps my mismatched pair of parents had more in common than I had ever considered.

"She is not the sort I would trot out to greet the guests. When I asked her to mark me down for an appointment with the medium, the foolish girl started to splutter and then told me there was no medium here at the hotel."

"Unfortunately, the medium has had to cancel and will not be joining us this season after all."

"The medium is the sole reason I booked for the season at this hotel." Even from a distance I could hear the woman exhale as though a nor'easter was brewing in her lungs. "You should have alerted me to the news before I made the journey here from Boston."

"Unfortunately, I only received word that she would not be available this morning. I would have notified you before your arrival if it had been at all possible."

"How do you propose to make this up to me?"

"I hope I may interest you in one of our other spiritual practitioners." Honoria's voice was bright but pitched an octave higher than normal. I put it down to panic. This was the time to step in if I was going to do so.

"There you are," I said, jumping into the fray. The woman

swiveled her flushed face in my direction. "I see that I was right to hurry back to the hotel."

"And who, pray tell, are you?"

"I'm Ruby Proulx, Miss Belden's niece," I placed my hand on Honoria's arm and gave it a squeeze, hard enough to make her look at me.

"I am happy to conduct a sitting with you at your convenience." I felt Honoria's muscles tense under my fingers. I turned to her and smiled my brightest showman smile.

"You are a medium?" The woman squinted at me. "But you just said a medium was not available." She swung her scowl to include us both.

"I am, but had planned to spend the summer here with my aunt in a solely recuperatory capacity." I pinched Honoria's arm to prompt her to speak. For once, she seemed to be having trouble finding her voice. "The work of a medium can be so hard on the nerves, as I'm sure a sensitive person like yourself will understand."

I was gambling on the possibility that people interested in hotels for the spiritually minded are exactly the sort of folks who like to think of themselves as sensitive. It was a statement calculated to soften her up. It worked like a charm.

"I can imagine such communications would take their toll." Her puckered mouth loosened up and smoothed out a bit, and the furrow beneath her brow that had been deep enough to plant potatoes now looked like it awaited poppy seeds instead.

"It does. In fact it can be so draining when the thread between worlds snaps, leaving the medium hollowed out and in need of utter restoration. Honoria agreed not to mention my gift in order for me to gather my strength. She is so good to me that she was willing to risk disappointing valued guests such as yourself rather than tell anyone of my abilities."

"One is always happy to do one's best for family." Honoria spoke with only the slightest hesitation in her voice. A wobble that could easily have been attributed to powerful emotion rather than uncertainty or befuddlement.

"You're too modest, Aunt." I closed my eyes and sighed deeply. "My recovery has been swift and complete. I credit the remarkable energy of this place for my speedy refreshment."

"So you are offering yourself as a replacement medium?" the woman asked.

"I consider our meeting to be fated. I don't believe I am a replacement. I believe the spirits have arranged for the cancellation in order to bring us together." I placed my free hand over my heart. "I was out walking the beach when I had my first contact from the other side in months. It said to hurry back as there was someone here who had need of my gifts most urgently. Someone who had suffered great losses and with whom those on the other side wished to make contact."

The woman's eyes widened, and I knew I had her like a fat fish on my line. I felt a familiar thrill of triumph at the success of my patter. As though this woman with her urgency and her sunken eyes were just another desperate customer at the medicine show. I felt both ashamed of myself and elated at the same time.

"And you think this person is me?" she asked.

"I am certain of it." I paused and gazed off into space, hoping I looked as though my thoughts were in angelic realms. Suddenly, I heard the voice in my head, more clearly than ever before.

"Speak of a ginger-colored dog with a missing ear sitting atop a crippled boy's lap."

I closed my eyes and began to sway slightly back and forth. In a soft voice I said, "A boy without use of his legs is making himself known to me." I paused and waited for a sign from our disgruntled guest. I heard a squeak of surprise from Mr. Dobbins and took that to be all the assurance I needed that I was on track. "A ginger dog with a damaged ear keeps watch over him in the world beyond."

"Roland is here with us?" I heard her ask, her voice climbing an octave in disbelief. "My Roland?" I fluttered my eyelids open and blinked at my surroundings.

"Please excuse me. I was just overcome by a very strong presence. It was entirely overwhelming and I am afraid it caused me to take leave of my own senses." I bit down on my lip as if concentrating feverishly on something no one else could hear. "My impression is that there was much more he wanted to say but that the atmosphere in the room was not conducive to maintaining a connection." I shrugged and focused my attention entirely on Mrs. Stickney.

"What is wrong with the atmosphere?" she asked.

"Hostility drives away all but the most unsavory of spirits." I paused for effect. "This boy had a pure quality and I am very surprised he made contact at all. He must have been strongly drawn to some energy here to cross the barrier and to contact me without me opening myself to the experience."

"It must have been Roland," Mr. Dobbins said, not keeping the enthusiasm from his voice. "This is exactly why we've come."

"I suppose in light of Roland's approval of this girl we can give the hotel a try. At least until Mr. Stickney arrives and determines whether or not he approves of the place."

"I will do everything in my power to assure your visit and that of your husband is a pleasant and instructive one," Honoria said.

"You can start to curry my favor by scheduling a sitting for me with Miss Proulx. Come, Sanford, we must rest after the difficulties of the morning." With that, she pointed at Ben, who silently fetched two room keys from the hooks on the wall behind the desk and glided up the main staircase ahead of Mrs. Stickney and her nephew.

I FELT A TUMULT OF EMOTIONS AS HONORIA HELD FAST TO MY arm and pulled me up the stairs to her private room. I gathered my courage up in both hands and commenced to embroider a pretty lie. I bit my lip for show and lowered myself gingerly onto the settee beside her.

"Please explain to me what just happened," she said.

"I have been less truthful than I ought to have been," I said.

"In which way?" Honoria's brows pulled together and I could feel that I needed to hurry this confession along. She didn't deserve any more worries in her life at the moment.

"Yesterday when you asked about my gift I told you about the tarot cards but I did not tell you that I can hear those who have passed on. They speak to me, give me messages for their loved ones." I dropped my voice to barely above a whisper and lowered my eyes to my lap as though I were afraid. "I've always kept my abilities a secret for fear of being sent to an asylum. Withholding the information from you was a reflex. I'm sorry I was less than forthcoming."

I sank back against the settee as if the confession had

physically exhausted me. Honoria pulled her hands away and clasped them to the base of her throat.

"I cannot imagine how distressing it would be to have your abilities without any guidance or reassurance that you were not suffering from an imbalance of the mind. It was very brave of you to come forward in order to help me."

"I want to help in any way that I can."

"Oh, my dear child, you have no idea how delighted I am to hear this. I knew, simply knew, you were bringing a world of good with you to the Belden and to me." Honoria's eyes filled with tears and she whisked a lace-trimmed hankie from somewhere in her sleeve. "You see, Miss Roberts canceling this morning has caused more distress than I like to admit. Most of our guests have booked their stays with us on account of the medium. Frankly, all the other disciplines are like sideshows to the main event," Honoria said. "Not that I would like them to feel that way, so I trust you will keep that in confidence."

"Of course."

"Also in confidence, I would tell you that all my capital is tied up in the renovations and staff salaries here at the Belden. Everything looks prosperous but in reality I have mortgaged the hotel to stay afloat. When Flora Roberts canceled I had no idea how I was going to survive the season. But now, you've offered the solution."

"But, Aunt, I've never really done any professional readings for anyone. Are you sure I can do it?"

"Of course you can. All you have to do is listen to your instincts and the rest will fall into place."

"I would be loath to give your clients an experience that does not meet their expectations."

"I'll tell you what. I'll **send a message** round to my dear friend Orazelia and her daughter, Lucy. You may remember them from the Divination Circle yesterday?" she asked. I shook my head. "It doesn't matter. They will come and you may practice on them. We will start at once since the majority of the guests arrive today."

"If you really think it will help, I will try." I said, letting my lower lip tremble ever so slightly.

"Ruby, I can't tell you how your honesty has saved the season."

"Does that mean I am in your good graces?"

"Even without this you would be. Why do you ask?"

"I may have behaved high-handedly, rashly even."

"How so?"

"I was out walking the beach this morning when I encountered a palm reader. She was instrumental in prompting me to tell you about my mediumistic abilities."

"But how does this end in rashness?"

"She was an Indian lady, and another woman on the beach accused her of being a filthy vagrant. She went so far as to call for the police." It was all coming back in a rush. I could feel Nell's discomfort, my indignation, and the dowdy woman's hostility all roiling in my gut. Honoria reached out and grasped my hand.

"That sounds most unpleasant."

"It was preposterous. Before I knew what I was saying I told the woman, in front of Officer Yancey, that Nell was your employee and that she had no cause to abuse her. And then as soon as we were out of earshot it occurred to me that you didn't have a palm reader here at the Belden. I thought she would make a wonderful addition to the staff. I hope I have not done wrong."

"My dear, I think it is an absolutely marvelous suggestion. I should have thought of it myself."

"So you aren't feeling cross with me that I've made this offer without consulting you?"

"I want you to feel the Hotel Belden is your home. My fondest wish is that one day it will be yours to run. Why should you not start to learn the running of the place now?"

"I'm so pleased you aren't upset."

"Ruby, my dear, I can't think of anything you could do, short of outright lying, that would make me angry with you."

CHAPTER ELEVEN

HONORIA WAS AS GOOD AS HER WORD. A FLURRY OF MESSAGES sent back and forth secured a sitting with her dear friend Orazelia and her daughter, Lucy, for that very day. As I stood pacing the room where I had met Honoria only the day before, I was glad the meeting had not been set for after lunch. My stomach tangled in knots anticipating the test before me.

I soothed myself by making preparations to the room. Setting the scene was an important part of any show. I adjusted the heavy velvet drapes to exclude all light and lit the candle on the table in the center of the room. While I had no experience personally with running a séance, I had seen it done on many occasions. Medicine shows often featured mediums as one of the acts and I had made a practice of studying their techniques. I told myself that this was simply another sort of performance like a card reading or a miracle medical diagnosis session. I looked around the room and decided there was nothing left to do but to await my clients' arrival.

I had to wait only a few moments until Honoria drew back the midnight blue portiere, and with her usual gust of energy blew into the séance room. Riding in her wake was a short, pleasantly rounded lady approximately Honoria's own age and a young, slim woman of just about mine.

"Ruby, allow me to present my very dear friend Orazelia and her daughter, Lucinda. They are eager to be your first sitters."

"We are delighted to help in any way we can. It is such a privilege to have a session with someone with a true gift," Orazelia said.

"Mother is simply smitten with the idea." Lucinda smiled at me over her mother's head as if to say she was humoring her. "I hope we aren't putting you to any trouble?"

"I should say the same to you. Thank you so much for finding the time on such short notice," I said.

"The world of spirit is where I prefer to expend most of my energy. It is a rare pleasure to be with you today." Orazelia's plump face displayed a charming pair of dimples. "Besides, we had already determined to pay you a call today to welcome you to Old Orchard."

"I wish I could stay and take part but duties call and call at this time of year," Honoria said. In the near distance the peal of the bell at the front desk rang out. With a quiet swish of the portiere, Honoria was gone and I was left to face the music alone. Both women sat in their chairs at the table and turned expectant faces to me. I drew in a deep breath and took the remaining seat.

Part of me was nervous at the thought of trying this out on strangers on my own, but the greater part of me was relieved to work through it in private. I suspected Honoria's scrutiny would have made it more difficult to focus on the subtle clues the sitters would give off as to whether or not I was on the right track concerning their loved ones.

"Shall we begin?" I reached out my upturned hands and drew in a deep breath. "An unbroken circle is important. The physical contact enhances the intention of the group to connect with those on the other side." Each of them gave me a hand and joined their other hands together.

I wasn't making up the importance of touch, but its value was not for the reasons stated. When I had worked the medicine show Father had drilled into my head from the very beginning the importance of making physical contact with a mark. If you're observant, you can learn a great deal by looking at someone's face and observing the set of their shoulders, the stiffness of their spine as they speak. But even more of their hearts and minds are revealed by the body's infinitesimal twitches and tightenings, invisible to the eye but easily sensed by touch.

I was betting the same rules would apply to those in pursuit of the spirits as it had to those in pursuit of physical cures. From the feel of their hands, Orazelia felt no fear of what she might hear. Her hand lay heavily in mine, like a sack of dried beans. Lucinda, despite her stoic appearance, displayed much more trepidation. Her hand was rigid in mine, the fingers stiff and unyielding, and she held my hand lightly, as if she feared the consequences of a stronger connection.

"Please close your eyes and think of nothing save the purpose we propose," I said, slowing my breathing and making sure it could be heard by the others in the hope they would be encouraged to match it.

Cultivating relaxation in the seeker is another trick of the trade. Calm leaves the patron more open to suggestion and more easily led into revealing their desires and concerns. I watched as they followed my suggestion and I continued to breathe deeply as

I tried to listen to their own breathing patterns. It was a technique I used many times in the medicine show.

One of Father's best moneymakers was to send men with notices ahead to towns promoting the powers of his Wonder Child. Whenever there was enough money, he had handbills printed claiming I could diagnose illnesses from liver complaints to ruptures to consumption and that with a laying on of hands I could cure most of them. What I couldn't cure for one dollar with my magnetic energy, I was to suggest bottles of his healing elixir could. For two dollars apiece. Before I was old enough for my feet to touch the decking of the wagon I could feel when I was speaking of the querent's fears and when I was addressing their hopes.

On more than one occasion I would sit in the wagon and provide consultations for hours at a time if the crowds were large enough. There was no medical value to what I did but I told myself I gave people comfort. The familiar rush of shame crept up my neck as I prepared to work the same sort of scam on my aunt's trusting friends.

As luxurious as the appointments in the room were, everything suddenly felt overlaid by a film of tawdriness that I knew emanated from me. I would never be more than a cheat and a liar, no matter how expensive my dress or opulent my surroundings. Or even how pure my motivations. As Mrs. Doyle had so eloquently pointed out, I was my father's daughter. As bad as that made me feel much of the time, it was in fact coming in handy at present. I shoved my trepidation aside and focused on the feeling in the room.

"Please concentrate on the person you would like me to contact. Bring this person clearly to mind and hold your thoughts fixed there. However, I cannot promise we will receive a visit from that loved one. The spirits have minds of their own and do not feel compelled to appear just because we wish them to do so." I creaked one eye open slightly and noticed both Orazelia and Lucinda were nodding their heads. "Once I have become aware of a presence, you are welcome to ask any questions you like. I do not promise answers but I will do my best to communicate whatever they pass on to me."

"We understand completely." Lucinda patted her mother on the back of the hand, and I wondered if perhaps Lucinda was the more capable of the two. From outward appearances she certainly seemed stronger. If her looks were any indication, Orazelia had been older than the average mother when Lucinda had been born. Age, however, was not what gave the impression of fragility. Her eyes were softly focused and her face had a look of befuddlement that Lucinda's did not share. Orazelia looked a bit like a child who had been startled out of a nap in an unaccustomed place and was searching the room for a familiar face.

Lucinda, however, seemed more like a child who would never have succumbed to a nap in the first place. Her bright, honey-colored curls bounced and jiggled with every turn of her head. Her posture, while straight, gave a sense of being poised for action rather than for showing her figure to advantage. Everything about her spoke of confidence and grace.

"We are grateful for the experience, no matter who comes to call," Lucinda said.

"Spirits, please hear our invitation to commune with us here on the earthly plane," I said, my voice pitched lower than usual and the words spoken barely above a whisper. Then stronger, as if I were desperate in my pleading. "I know there must be someone who wishes to contact these dear ladies." A subtle pull on my hands told me the sitters were willing this to be the case. I felt them both leaning toward me slightly. Time to start fishing.

"I will begin by slowly reciting the letters of the alphabet. If we are lucky, a spirit will make itself known to us when his or her initial is spoken aloud," I said. I watched them through slit eyelids as they both nodded in agreement.

"A, B, C." I spoke slowly and in a voice barely above a whisper. "D, E, F, G." On the letter G both women tightened their grip, Orazelia with a surprising degree of strength.

"G. Is there a spirit here with a connection to the letter G?" I asked, then paused as if listening. "There is a spirit here with a name starting with G. Is it your surname?" Both women sat quietly. "No, it is your Christian name, is it not?" Again, they each tensed their grip. Now I needed to know if they were expecting a man or a woman to appear, and I would need some indication of age.

"Thank you for blessing our gathering with your presence. We wish to know more about your time on our mortal plane. Am I speaking with a gentleman or a lady?" Once again I interpreted the unspoken message from my sitters.

"A female personage is with us, but I am not certain as to her age," I said. My chances of suggesting the right thing were dead even. Still, hedging my bets was even surer. "Her energy feels youthful to me, but perhaps she was simply young at heart."

"Gladys." Orazelia's voice caught in her throat.

"You can't be sure, Mum," Lucinda said.

"Was Gladys your name when you walked amongst us?" I asked, sure I had hit the mark. The fluttering in my stomach and the hammering of my heart both subsided enough for me to hear the ticking of the mantel clock. I felt a shabby sense of triumph, a familiar mingling of power, trepidation, and shame. It was a combination I had sworn to myself to leave behind with Johnny's lifeless body. Before I could chastise myself further, Orazelia leaned close and squeezed my hand harder than ever. I snapped my attention to the task at hand. "Yes, Gladys is her name. She wants you to know she is peaceful and happy on the other side."

"Gladys's happiness is the least of our concerns. As if we'd be worried about her," Lucinda said. Of all the ways in which I had anticipated the reading could have taken a wrong turn, I had not expected hostility toward a spirit visitor.

"Spirits are very sensitive to any feeling that they are unwelcome. I feel the link weakening."

"Lucinda, please, I have questions for Gladys. Do not drive her away."

"Gladys, are you still here?" I paused for effect before continuing. "She is present but I feel her reluctance to stay. Perhaps it would be best to start with something simple."

"Would you please ask her if she still seeks justice?" Orazelia wanted to know. I wondered exactly what a complicated question would involve if Orazelia felt a question concerning justice was a simple one.

"Gladys says the concept of justice is not relevant to those in spirit. She says they only feel unbounded love."

"Unbounded love was part and parcel of her way of life when she was in the flesh, too," Lucinda said. I felt her hand tugging away slightly as she leaned back in her chair. She was growing impatient with the spiritual visitor. But her mother was not. I wondered how they knew Gladys and how I should proceed.

"Lucy, my dear, please try to remember that you are a lady and that we do not say such things." Orazelia's voice sounded more sad than critical. "Ruby, ask if she needs resolution to the circumstances of her death."

"She does not," I said with conviction. The tremble in both the sitters' hands led me on. "But she realizes that the circumstances surrounding her passing are important to you. She will try to help ease your mind about it if she has the answers you seek." Perhaps I had overreached but I didn't know what else to say.

"Can she see who killed her?" Orazelia asked. I was stunned. The idea that Gladys had been murdered had not crossed my mind. Disease and even accidental death were all too common, and the loss of loved ones, even young people in the prime of life, to such events was something that touched all but the luckiest few. But something as sensational as murder was rare indeed. This was going to require careful navigation. Especially since I didn't even know how these ladies knew Gladys.

"Gladys says the details of her passing are shrouded in uncertainty. Death came upon her quickly and without ceremony." I cocked my head to the side as if to listen more carefully to the sound of Gladys's faint voice. "One moment she was here and the next she was beyond the reach of pain and suffering."

"So she doesn't know any more about who killed her than we do?" Lucinda asked.

"She says she dearly wishes she could enlighten you but that she either never knew or the information was lost in the transmutation of her soul. Gladys says that those things unneeded in the hereafter are melted away during the getting from here to there like dross from silver. The gift of death is its ability to purify the spirit and rid it of burdens. Only light and love endure the journey."

With that I felt certain it was time to bring the session to a conclusion. I sighed deeply and with a shuddering exhalation sagged back against my chair, releasing their hands. I hoped they understood the message that we were through. I fluttered my eyelids opened and through the flickering candlelight I could see the two of them looking at me.

"Ladies, I do hope you felt your time was well spent." I looked hopefully from one to the other. "I'm sorry if Gladys was not able to answer your questions."

"No one has been able to answer that particular question for nearly twenty years." Orazelia looked tired and older than she had when she entered the room less than an hour before. "It isn't your fault Gladys's murder is still a mystery."

"Most people would say it isn't a mystery at all." Lucinda pushed her chair back and slipped one slim hand into a fine lace glove. "Perhaps it would be best to try to contact Father the next time instead."

"Your father was many things, Lucy, but a truthful man he was not. Besides, after all that has happened he is the last person in this world or the next with whom I would wish to speak." With that, Orazelia pushed her chair back and gathered up her own pair of gloves. "Ruby, I'll be going now to speak with Honoria." She swished out of the room and left me alone with her daughter and an uneasy feeling as to what she would report to my aunt.

Lucinda remained seated across from me and plucked idly at her silk bag. "I must apologize for my mother. No matter how I've tried to discourage her, she has been trying to establish contact with Gladys for years. Truth to tell, I can't remember a time when she wasn't obsessed with contacting her."

"Forgive my curiosity, but why should she care so much about what happened to Gladys? I wasn't able to tell from the reading—was she a family member?" I wondered if I was breaching some sort of professional rule of ethics but my curiosity had gotten the better of me.

"You don't know who she was?" Lucinda scrunched her eyebrows together and stared at me.

"I do not," I said in complete earnestness. "How could I? I've only just arrived yesterday and I don't believe I'd ever been in contact with anyone who knew you or your family before then."

"I apologize." Lucinda's face smoothed. "I sometimes forget not everyone I meet knows everything about my family and our history."

"I'd think in a town with as many tourists as this one has, you would be meeting new people all the time."

"There are plenty of tourists, but the people of our acquaintance are few and far between. After the scandal, Mother has tended to keep to herself, making an exception for a few dear friends like Honoria."

"I did not mean to pry or to solicit a confidence. I don't wish to invade your privacy."

"There is no harm in telling you. Besides, it would be nice to tell someone myself for a change instead of having people point and whisper as I go past." Lucinda lifted her chin and looked me in the eye. "Gladys is the young woman my father is supposed to have been conducting an illicit affair with. Even more unfortunately, all evidence pointed to the notion that he was the one who strangled her."

Chapter Twelve

I found Honoria in the ladies' writing room at the back of the hotel, facing the sea. Several strands of dark hair escaped from the pile on top of her head, and even with her back to me I could read fatigue in her posture. I crossed the room, hoping her report from Orazelia was favorable.

"Am I interrupting?" I asked as she turned to the sound of my footfalls.

"No. As soon as Orazelia left I began writing up an advertisement. Now that you will be our medium, I plan to include your name in the notices I place in the papers." Honoria motioned to the seat near her. I felt my knees weaken and was grateful for an invitation to sit.

"You wish to mention my real name in the advertisements?" I was accustomed to seeing myself advertised on handbills and signs of all sorts but never using my real name. Father and I had created a long list of stage names, some of which I had grown quite fond of but never had we used our own. Doing so felt as much like breaking a taboo as would wearing trousers or lopping off my hair.

"I understand your hesitation but we are building a reputation of integrity here at the Belden. Using a name not your own only serves to create the impression you have something to hide."

"I wouldn't want to give anyone reason to suppose I was behaving fraudulently," I said, struggling to keep my voice even.

"We must be perceived to be blameless and forthcoming in every way if this venture is to succeed. Our reputation will be our greatest asset, my dear." Honoria tapped the end of her pen against the ink bottle. "I should be surprised if you have reason to fear any accusations of fraud after the report I received from Orazelia. She was positively enraptured by your abilities."

"I'm delighted to hear she felt her session a success." I paused, wondering if I should ask about Gladys. "I was unsure if the spirit that contacted us was one who would have brought distress rather than comfort."

"You've been talking to Lucy," Honoria said. I nodded. "Orazelia is distressed at not knowing for sure whether or not her husband was involved in Gladys Willard's murder."

"I understood from Lucinda that for years there has been a shadow looming over the family reputation."

"A shadow." Honoria leaned back in her chair and turned her body fully to face me. "It's more of a tornado that won't stop whipping through their lives. If you can help provide Orazelia with answers, I would be very grateful."

"I should have thought Orazelia would want to contact her husband rather than his alleged victim," I said. "Wouldn't that be the more typical path to take for such information?"

"It would if Orazelia could bring herself to speak to the man." Honoria clucked her tongue. "After all, he humiliated her and left her and her children the objects of ridicule and scorn."

"Under those circumstances, I can understand her disinclination to involve herself with him but if she truly seeks the information, I should have thought she would welcome answers from any source, no matter how undesirable."

"If you are going to continue to conduct readings for Orazelia, as she has asked that you should, I suppose it would be best to acquaint you with what is known of her sad history. You might find her behaviors easier to understand if you have a framework for them."

"I shouldn't like you to think I was asking you to betray a confidence."

Honoria snorted, most indelicately. "The only thing that could be considered still in confidence about any of this degrading matter is whether or not Orazelia's husband really did strangle the girl. Every other bit of the sordid tale is such commonly spread gossip that it has advanced into the arena of local lore. There is no reason to keep it from you and compelling reasons to share it." Honoria paused and drew in a deep breath.

"The only good thing that came of the whole incident was that it was sufficiently shocking to make your mother's elopement third-rate news. No one paid any mind to it at all once Gladys was found strangled."

"So this all happened about the same time my parents left Old Orchard?"

"The very same time. In fact, no sooner had Mrs. Doyle found the note from Delphinia explaining that she had gone than gossips arrived with the news of the murder."

"That must have been a tumultuous morning."

"It was indeed. I felt quite ashamed of myself that Gladys's murder seemed less important to me than the departure of my beloved sister."

"Did you have reason for Gladys's death to impact you personally?"

"No, not at all. She was a singer in one of the ballrooms in town. Not at all the sort of person we would have associated with."

"But Orazelia's husband was the sort to associate with girls in dance halls?" I asked.

"Unfortunately, yes. He had made quite a fool of himself over Gladys and took no trouble to hide his devotion to her. It was mortifying for poor Orazelia."

"Did Gladys return his affection?"

"She loved his generosity."

"He gave her gifts?"

"He showered her with so many presents he couldn't afford them."

"But if he loved her so much, why was he connected to the crime?"

"Because he had gone so far as to embezzle money from his employers in order to start a new life with Gladys away from the dance halls."

"How did anyone know any of this?"

"Gladys was not a discreet girl and the room in which she entertained Mr. Yancey was one she shared with another girl."

"That still doesn't explain why he would be accused of the crime."

"Gladys had no intention of settling down to be a dutiful wife to a stodgy older man. At least the girl had some sense about that." Honoria shook her head. "When he begged her to run off with him she refused. He became angry and began to shout about how much he had sacrificed to give her a life any woman in her position could only dream of."

"And someone overheard him?" I asked.

"Many people overheard him. Especially when Gladys laughed in his face and threatened to tell his employer what he had done if he bothered her again."

"How long before the murder did this take place?"

"She was discovered dead the morning after the argument."

"Did Mr. Yancey not have an alibi for the time of her death?"

"He did not. He claimed he had tried to drown his sorrows in a bottle and had succeeded in passing out on the beach sometime in the wee hours."

"No one could say otherwise?"

"He was found on the beach still in a state of inebriation, sand clinging to his trousers. No one could say how long he had been there."

"Was he convicted of the crime?"

"He died in jail awaiting trial. The court of public opinion found him guilty and has passed the sentence of murderer's children on both Warren and Lucinda. It has been very cruel."

"Lucinda seems not to have let it break her," I said.

"Lucinda is a very sensible girl in her own way." Honoria pushed back her chair and stood. "I hope the two of you will be great friends. She's come to an age where I'm afraid she will need one."

"Why do you say that?"

"Because she has always done just as she pleased, and between her unorthodox notions of the role of women and her family's unfortunate reputation she will likely be forced to compromise her principles." Honoria paused in front of the fireplace and peered into the gilded mirror hung on the wall above it. "Or learn to live on her own as I have done."

CHAPTER THIRTEEN

I AWOKE TO THE SOUND OF WAVES LAPPING AGAINST THE SHORE and a sense of unease. All night long I had tossed and turned, worrying about my first official day as the Belden's medium. According to the small clock on the bed stand I had overslept. As I hurried into a sprigged muslin gown I decided to fasten my mother's ruby necklace around my neck for luck.

I skipped breakfast and instead collected my deck of tarot cards and carried them with me to the séance room. With the Velmont sisters' habit of tardiness I was certain I would have time for a reading for myself before the pair of them arrived. Not that I necessarily believed the cards held any power to predict things but I did find using them helped me to clarify my own thoughts. And I was desperately in need of peacefulness. I hadn't the time to sit and shuffle the cards, let alone conduct a reading, when Elva's and Dovie's voices penetrated the portiere and the two ladies themselves appeared in the room.

"We're here," announced Elva.

"Right on time," said Dovie.

"It's a miracle," said Elva.

"I think there is something quite transformative about this hotel," said Dovie.

"That's what Mr. MacPherson was just telling us at breakfast. Something to do with energetic crisscrossing that all pulls together in this very spot," Elva said.

"I'm delighted to see you both no matter what the time. But you've caught me a bit unprepared," I said. "If you will bear with me I'll just put away the cards and darken the room."

"Ohhh," said Dovie. "Intriguing. Do you read cards as well as conduct séances?"

"I do," I said. Then the voice spoke to me.

"Use the cards."

Every performer needs a hook, something to set their show apart from the others, to give the audience a little something unexpected. Tarot has always been a comfort to me in times of trouble. Why not rely on them now?

"Sometimes I even use the cards as a way for the spirits to communicate," I said.

"We've never had a tarot reading or heard of them being used in a sitting, have we, sister?" said Dovie.

"How does it work?" asked Elva. She was the greater skeptic between the two of them. It was Elva I would need to convince if I were to gain their confidence and help the hotel. A practical approach would be the way to win her over.

"Spirits communicate in many ways. Sounds, actual words, images. The pictures on the cards allow the spirits to show images to the sitters as well as the medium. It can be very effective and efficient." I hoped I sounded more confident than I felt.

"Will it work for our sitting?" said Dovie. "It looks like fun."

"We certainly can try," I said. "I'll leave the curtains open in order for you to better see the cards, all right?" The ladies' thick spectacles suggested they needed any help available to see things in front of them at all. They nodded and we all sat around the small round table in the center of the room. I slid the stack of cards across the midnight blue damask tablecloth to Elva.

"Would you please shuffle the cards and then separate the deck into three stacks?" I asked.

"I am not accustomed to playing cards, Miss Proulx." Elva looked scandalized, as though I were accusing her of being a scarlet woman.

"I meant no offense. I asked you not because I assumed expertise in card handling but because it is important that the sitter has contact with the cards, that they are the ones to determine the cards selected."

"I see. In that case, I will do my best." Elva lifted the stack with her knobby fingers and dropped them easily from one hand to the other. Despite her claim of inexperience, she worked the cards as well as anyone I had ever seen. I wondered which other vices she might not want to admit to. "You're a natural, Miss Velmont," I said as she finished and split the deck neatly. "Now, I'd like you both to think of the person you wish to contact. Have you agreed ahead of time who this would be?"

"We have," the sisters said in unison.

"You needn't say who it is but I can tell you I already sense a strong male energy even before I turn over the cards." It would have been impossible to miss the reverence with which the sisters had mentioned their dearly departed father again and again since their arrival the day before.

"Remarkable," Dovie said, turning a wide-eyed glance at Elva.

"Indeed," Elva said with a great deal more reservation in her tone.

"Please concentrate on the image of this loved one as I turn over the first card. This card will signify the spirit that visits." I held my hand above the card to my right and closed my eyes. "Spirits, please grace us with your presence and deliver to us your messages of love." I opened my eyes and slowly turned over the card.

"The Emperor," I said, relieved that the voice had once again steered me along the correct path. Who better than the Emperor to stand in for a beloved father?

"That's Father, to be sure," Dovie said.

"This is a man of power and of influence. He is a respected leader and ruler of his people."

"Does he have anything to say to us?" Elva asked. I sensed that despite her skepticism, she had a strong desire to connect with the beyond. I feel a stab of guilt at what I was doing, but once again I heard the voice.

"Trust you do right."

"The next card will begin the message," I said. "The Nine of Cups, a card of wishes."

"Oh, sister." Dovie grabbed Elva by the arm and squeezed. Elva flinched and let out a faint squeak.

"And the next one?" Elva asked, tapping the third card with a gnarled finger.

"Five of Pentacles. These two elderly people show destitution and suffering. One would be right to call them beggars." My heart sank at saying this to the old ladies, finding myself fretting that they might be the ones headed for financial ruin. The Velmont sisters, however, both leaned over the card as if they could not believe their good fortune.

"What about the last one?" Dovie asked. Elva appeared to be holding her breath. Her lips were clenched and folded in on themselves as if she were trying not to let her insides escape her body.

I turned the final card and looked at the image. I waited for the voice, which had become so much stronger with each passing card. Perhaps there was something to Mr. MacPherson's assertions about the hotel. The Knight of Wands sat on his horse, brandishing a stick. I started to speak but the voice interrupted me and advised me as to the proper words.

"Generally this card signifies travel but in your case the word *ride* is being said to me instead. Does this mean anything to you?"

Elva and Dovie turned to face each other. Elva sat stiffly but a single tear rolled down her wrinkled cheek. Dovie pulled a fan from her lap and flipped it open, ruffling the cards with the vigor of her motion.

"The reading seems to have distressed you both. Would you like to stop?"

"Certainly not," Elva said. She pulled a handkerchief from somewhere in the folds of her costume and delicately blew her nose. "We are simply overcome."

"It's the message, you see," Dovie said. "Our father used to always say this to us when we were girls." Suddenly, even without a direct prompting from the voice, I knew what to say.

"If wishes were horses then beggars would ride," I said.

"Exactly. We have been searching and searching for a medium to bring us this exact message," Elva said. Dovie patted her sister on the back of her wrinkled hand and I felt the familiar pang of the outsider. I wondered if the sisters knew how lucky they were to have each other.

"Perhaps I was able to bring the message through because my own father used to say just the same to me," I said, feeling a little spooked. After all that had happened between us I was not pleased to consider he might still be influencing me.

"I just knew spending the season at this hotel was the right decision. Didn't I say that, Elva?" Dovie said.

"You did, sister, you most certainly did," Elva said. I breathed a sigh of relief and settled back into my chair. My first real séance had been an unqualified success. I was off the hook, at least for the moment.

"Ladies, I feel the spirit has left us."

"You must be exhausted. We will leave you for now." Dovie rose from her chair and touched my cheek.

"But we will stop at the reception desk and mark down another sitting for tomorrow."

"I think we should make it two. After all, it has taken us so long to be sure we are hearing from Father. He must have a great deal to say to us."

"Excellent suggestion, sister." Elva rose and took Dovie by the arm. "We will book two sessions a day for the remainder of the summer."

As I watched them go I wondered if it was possible to have been too successful. Unless I could garner new information about the dearly departed Mr. Velmont, I was going to need to rely exclusively on pluck and luck. Or on the voice in my head. As I sat slumped in the plush velvet chair mulling things over I couldn't decide which was more risky.

Chapter Fourteen

THAT GIRL WAS TROUBLE. HE SHOULD'VE SPOTTED IT FROM the moment he scooped her off the bricks in front of the train station. Even though he generally loathed gossip, this time he was grateful for the local grapevine. How could Honoria have allowed such a thing?

If Frank hadn't heard about the supposed séance from his mother-in-law, Mrs. Doyle, Yancey was sure his mother and Lucy would have kept it to themselves. Miss Proulx needed to be stopped before she did any more damage to his frail family.

YANCEY RACED PAST FLOCKS OF SIGHTSEERS IN THEIR SUMMER gowns and straw boaters. He felt his pants' garter give way and then his trouser leg tug into the safety bicycle chain. The whole machine ground to a halt with a clank and a tear in his trousers.

He dismounted, more irritated than ever. As he tugged at the shredded bits of fabric entangled in the oily chain he imagined Miss Proulx's parasol similarly shredded. There was just something about that girl that was entirely maddening. By the time he arrived at the Belden he was ready to spit nails.

Ben stood like a sentinel behind the registration desk. Yancey nodded at the man and marveled again at how he looked the same every time he laid eyes on him. Ben never looked tired, never took sick, never seemed to grow older, fatter, or less silent. Yancey couldn't remember a time when Ben didn't work in some capacity for the Belden family.

"I need to speak to Miss Proulx. Is she in?" Yancey asked. Ben reached under the desk and pulled out an oversize leather ledger. He opened it and turned it round on the countertop to face Yancey. He tapped a long, pale finger on a line with Ruby Proulx's name on it. She was busy with a client, perpetuating the same sort of fraud on another pair of ladies that she had on his mother and sister. Yancey felt his temper, usually held so firmly in check, bubble to the surface.

"Do you expect Miss Proulx to have finished with her victims before long?" he asked. Ben tapped on another line in the timetable. Ben silently shrugged. "Unfortunately, I don't have time to waste. I assume they are in the Blue Room?" Yancey barely waited for a nod from Ben before striding down the hall, the hard heels of his boots muffled by the plush carpet running the full length of the polished corridor.

Whatever qualms Yancey might have had about interrupting Miss Proulx during the course of her work were quashed as he approached the midnight blue portiere at the end of the hallway. Two almost identical elderly ladies pushed their way out through the folds in the curtains and looked up at him. Preying on the elderly was a thing Yancey simply could not stomach. The stories he heard at the police station of women such as these being targeted by pickpockets made his blood boil. Just because Miss Proulx was robbing them in an elegant parlor did not make what she was doing any less criminal.

"Good afternoon, ladies." Yancey drew off his hat, made a slight bow. "May I ask if Miss Proulx is in there?"

"Yes, she is." The tiny women spoke in unison.

"Still recovering," the slightly plumper of the two hurriedly said, as if trying to beat the other to deliver the message.

"Our father, you see," said the thinner one.

"A strong personality," they both said, again in unison.

"He can be quite tiring," said the thin one. "You may need to allow her to collect herself before she's ready for your session." The two ladies moved down the hall before he could correct their impression that he was a client. More irritated than ever he pushed through the heavy velvet draperies.

Miss Proulx stood with her back to him at the window facing the sea. Her hand smoothed the drape and light washed over her thin form. She looked like she'd benefit from a year's worth of his mother's rich dinners. She gnawed on her lower lip like she hadn't had a decent meal in months. Perhaps, from the look of her, she hadn't. The candle on the table sputtered and drew her attention. As she turned toward the noise she caught sight of him in the shadows.

"Miss Proulx, I require a word with you," he said. "I am here on behalf of my mother and sister."

"Did you wish to schedule another séance for them?" Ruby drew back the curtain and fastened it with a dark blue cord. "If so, there's no need as they've already booked another one themselves."

"I know that they have. That's the reason I'm here. I must insist that you never conduct a séance with either of them again. In fact, I forbid it."

"You forbid two grown women, neither of whom are your wife, to make an appointment with me?"

"I do. And I expect you to honor my wishes completely."

"I have no intention of doing so." Ruby stepped toward him, leaving the table with its flickering candle between them. "At least not so long as they wish to take advantage of my services."

"The only one taking advantage here is you, Miss Proulx," Yancey said, dropping his voice to almost a whisper. "If you do not leave well enough alone I will be forced to take action."

"What do you intend to do?" Ruby smiled as if the entire exchange amused her enormously. He was surprised at how attractive he found her smiling face even when she exasperated him.

"I shall mount a fraud investigation, forthwith." Attractive or not, she could not be allowed to toy with his mother's emotions. "My mother has spent countless hours and even more money on charlatans such as yourself. I will not have you playing havoc with her nerves."

"Your mother is my aunt's dearest friend. Are you telling me you would try to discredit Honoria's livelihood?" Ruby widened her eyes in amazement. "I should think concern for her friend would shatter your mother's nerves as no contact with the dead ever could."

"There is no contact with the dead to be made. You are simply giving her another reason not to put my family's sordid past behind us."

"I do not agree. Your mother found a great deal of comfort in what I had to offer. I don't see how you can desire to deny her that small joy."

"That joy comes at a very high price, Miss Proulx. I cannot believe Honoria would allow her friends to be taken in by someone exploiting common gossip. It's utterly disgraceful."

"What do you mean?"

"I mean, while I am impressed by the speed with which you researched your victims, I'm not inclined to credit you with proper morals for having done so. So tell me, how did you come to know so much about the circumstances surrounding Gladys Willard's death? Old newspaper clippings or just idle chatter with the maids in the hotel?"

"I was as surprised as your family when I was contacted by Gladys. I knew nothing whatsoever of her death or your father's alleged involvement in it before their sitting." Ruby crossed her slim arms across the sprigged bodice of her cotton gown.

"I find that impossible to believe."

"Lucinda told me about Gladys after your mother left the room. I was honored to have opened a channel to someone with whom your mother so desperately wished to communicate."

"Open a channel? Is that what you call it?" Yancey paused. "The dead are dead and they stay that way. Have you ever seen a dead body, Miss Proulx? There's nothing there to communicate with."

"I feel sorry for you, Officer. As it's clear we will not come to an understanding, I suggest you leave before my next appointment arrives." Ruby lifted her chin and nodded toward the door.

"You'd be better served saving your sympathies. I intend to run a full investigation. When I'm done with you, Miss Proulx, I'll know you better than you know yourself."

Chapter Fifteen

I stood trying not to tremble as I watched Officer Yancey's retreating back. I felt rattled by all his threats but his question "Have you ever seen a dead body?" rang loudest in my ears. I sank into the wingback chair in the corner of the room and considered my predicament.

On the one hand, the police were not to be trifled with. On the other, I had never worked a medicine show under my real name. Father and I had built long histories for ourselves under many guises but none of them had been aimed at hiding the fact that we worked in a medicine show, just in hiding which ones we had frequented. If Officer Yancey really was intent on finding things out about me he was going to run into a brick wall. I only hoped that wouldn't get me into even more trouble than I was already in.

Honoria was the one who encouraged me to conduct the séance for his family. I felt the need to speak with her to reassure myself I had not done wrong by following her suggestion. I left the séance room and hurried to the front hall, where Ben stood silently behind the heavily carved walnut reception desk. His silence pulsated, like a living thing. It was as though he were willing me to be aware of him. As I approached I could have sworn he was waiting behind the desk for me rather than waiting to attend to the guests expected to arrive throughout the day.

"Have you any idea where I might find Honoria?" I asked, stopping at the desk. Ben nodded slowly. His fair hair swished silently back and forth against his translucent forehead. He raised a long, slim finger and pointed down the hall, then with his elegant hands pantomimed opening a book. Just to be certain the message was clear, he made as if to carefully turn pages by their upper corners.

Honoria made up for any silence on Ben's part. Her voice barreled down the hall toward me in gusts and peals. I stepped into the library and found Honoria holding court with a gentleman. Their backs were to me and I had the opportunity to observe them briefly without their notice. It was a habit I had picked up whilst on the road. Strangers have much to tell us when they don't know they are saying anything at all.

The gentleman was well into his middle years and his jowls hung slackly against his collar. Unfortunately, his flourishing mustache only served to point at them like a road sign. His jacket strained against his shoulders and spoke of a recent weight gain and the reluctance to admit it. While his hair was gray it was not entirely turned and patches of dark brown hair dappled the back of his head.

He leaned closer toward Honoria and opened up a line of sight, allowing her to spot me.

"Ruby, please say hello to our latest arrival." Honoria extended a hand and drew me toward her. "Allow me to present my niece, Miss Ruby Proulx. Ruby, this is Mr. Leander Stickney. You may remember you have already met his wife and nephew." She gave me a pointed look as if to alert me to potential conversational pitfalls. I appreciated the warning. Mr. Stickney nodded slowly and deeply enough that he seemed to nearly bow. This was a first for me. In the medicine show good manners were not thick upon the ground and certainly gentlemen of this caliber were generally not frequenters of such low forms of entertainment.

"Good day, sir." I extended my hand. Mr. Stickney's jowls wobbled as he gave my hand a gentle shake and then released it.

"Just the person I was hoping most to meet," he said with more passion in his voice than seemed warranted. Warning bells clanged in my head.

"Mr. Stickney has heard reports of you from his wife," Honoria said. "In fact he's already booked a reading with you for tomorrow afternoon." Honoria looked entirely too pleased about something. Rather than reassure me, her delight turned the warning bells into gongs.

"Mrs. Stickney has nothing but the greatest enthusiasm for your abilities," he said. "She was disappointed not to find her usual medium, Flora Roberts, here as expected, but said you have done an admirable job replacing her."

"I'm only too happy to fill in."

"It was such a fortunate and extraordinary coincidence that you just happen to be a medium when the position suddenly opened." Mr. Stickney raised one eyebrow at me. My heart fluttered in my chest but my training kicked in.

"I find if one opens oneself to the extraordinary it is likely to happen," I said, offering what I hoped was an otherworldly smile. "Do you not find that to be so, too?"

"Alas, I am so insistent on proof of such things that even my friends call me Stickler Stickney. My business has taught me that the extraordinary most often has its roots in the mundane."

"May I be so bold as to ask the nature of your business?"

"I'm astonished that your aunt didn't mention it to you." He turned back to Honoria.

"I thought it possible you wished to remain anonymous." Honoria looked unruffled but I felt a wave of fear as icy as the North Atlantic cascade over me from head to toe.

"I make it a point to be forthcoming with all my investigations." He turned to me once more and his gaze felt challenging rather than friendly. It took every bit of self-control not to squirm and back away. "I am the president of the Northeastern Society for Psychical Research."

"And what is that, sir?" I asked.

"I should have thought someone in your line of work would have recognized the name of my organization immediately."

"You must forgive my niece, Mr. Stickney. She is newly arrived from Canada and has only recently come into the open about her gifts. Such a well-known organization as yours would be unfamiliar to her. I, on the other hand, am honored by your attentions."

"That explains her ignorance. Allow me to enlighten you, Miss Proulx. I am the head of a group that seeks to prove the possibility of all sorts of psychic phenomena from mediums to soothsayers to ghostly apportments," he said. "Sadly, most of what I do is to unmask frauds."

As soon as Mr. Stickney excused himself I shut the library door and leaned heavily against the frame.

"Are you feeling well, Ruby? Your cheeks are quite flushed and you're trembling." Honoria placed a plump hand on my forearm, sending sparkles of light flashing about the room from her many rings. I nodded and swallowed the lump.

"I am simply surprised to find I will be under such scrutiny."

"But as you have nothing to hide, there can be no cause for distress."

"But you said yourself that there is so much riding on the success of the medium. If I fail to impress him you could lose the hotel."

"Please don't fret. I have every confidence in you. Now, I insist we speak of pleasanter things," Honoria said, handing me a creamy envelope addressed in a firm, rounded hand. "The morning post brought this for you."

People say life is made up of the little things, and I do believe it's true. Ever since arriving at the Belden I've come to realize how many small pleasures there are in life and how much I wish to continue to enjoy them. I held the letter in my hand and felt a lump rising in my throat. This was the very first letter I had ever received. The only other one I had even touched had been from Honoria to my mother.

"I'll go open this in my mother's room, if you don't mind."

"It's your room now, Ruby. Please don't forget that I've been keeping it for you."

"Yes, ma'am," I said. As soon as I was out of sight down the hallway I began to run. I raced up the back stairs past Millie, giving her a quick smile. She raised a scrub brush in salute and I continued on my way at breakneck speed until I reached the top floor.

Settling myself in the tufted green velvet chair in the turret window I carefully slit the envelope with a hatpin. Inside was a note from Lucinda asking me to call upon her and her mother at my earliest convenience. She proposed that very afternoon if I was not already engaged. It was signed, *Your friend, Lucy.*

So there it was, my first letter and my first friend all in one delightful package. Despite my pleasure at Lucy's invitation I was uncertain of what I should do. After my disastrous conversation with Officer Yancey I could not expect him to be pleased if I were to call upon his sister. It would, however, be rude to refuse or to ignore her overtures of friendship. Besides, he had warned me to halt any efforts in the séance arena. He had not specified that I could not associate with his family in other ways.

Not to mention, if I called on Lucy it would leave less time in my schedule to conduct a sitting for Mr. Stickney. That settled it. I hurried to the wardrobe and considered which sort of gown would be appropriate for an afternoon call. Something light-weight and simple seemed best. I pulled out a white cotton gown heaving with ruffles and tucks. I held it against the length of me as I stared at my reflection in the mirrored door of the wardrobe. It was not fashionable, but it was clean and of a pleasant weight for a warm day.

On a shelf at the top of the wardrobe sat a row of hatboxes. Gathering them, a few at a time, I carried them to the bed and pried off the lids. Lifting out hat after hat it was clear to me that while they were all lovely, they were even more old-fashioned than the gowns. I tried on a straw bonnet with a bouquet of pink silk roses pinned to the side. I tied the bonnet's pink ribbons into a loopy bow beneath my chin and considered my reflection. It was the best of the lot and would simply have to do. Besides, dated or not, it was by far the prettiest hat I had ever worn.

I descended the back stairs and gathered my courage for a foray into the kitchen in hopes of asking Millie's opinion on my appearance. Mrs. Doyle stood at the sink with her back to me. Millie was nowhere in sight and I held my breath as I tried to back out of the room without being seen.

"What have you got on your head, child?" Mrs. Doyle asked, squinting at me.

"I need to pay a call on Miss Yancey and this hat was in the wardrobe." I reached up and gave it an awkward pat. "I realize it's a bit out of date but I thought it was lovely nonetheless."

"Did you, now?" Mrs. Doyle made an unladylike grunting noise exactly how I imagined a female ogre would sound just before settling in to grind a child's bones into bread.

"I'm no authority on hats but this one struck me as extremely pretty." I loosened the ribbons and lifted the bonnet from my head. "And more than that, the workmanship is lovely. The silk flowers are a bit faded but you can still see how fine the stitches are on each tiny petal." I held the hat toward her for her inspection.

"I don't need to see it up close," Mrs. Doyle said. "After all, I made the silly thing."

"I wish I had such a skill."

"You won't do your aunt much credit running around the town in something so behind the times as that is." Mrs. Doyle scowled and squinted at me again, then wiped her red hands on her long apron. "Follow me and we'll see what can be done."

I waited while she lifted a pair of shears, a roll of ribbon, and a small tin from a drawer. She motioned for me to follow her out a door at the end of the back hall. Here was a part of the grounds I had not yet visited. A high white picket fence enclosed a neat garden and contained the fragrance of vigorous plants spilling from their beds. The fence served as a windbreak and the sun beat down warmly on my bare head.

"These should do the trick." Mrs. Doyle stooped over a petite rosebush ablaze with pink roses. With a deft snip she cut three sprigs and held them out to me. "Mind the thorns."

"Which sort are these?" I asked, holding the delicate bunches to my nose and inhaling deeply.

"Cecile Brunner. They bloom from spring till hard frost and don't ask for a lot of fuss." She turned to a row of lavender and sheared off a few stems. "And this is lavender. It loves the seaside." I followed her to a stone bench in a corner of the garden tucked under an arbor mercifully shaded over with broad leaves. "Now, give me that hat." She held out her hands and I gave her the bonnet. Using only the points of the scissors, she snipped the threads that secured the silk roses to the bonnet's brim.

"Honoria tells me you are giving satisfaction to the guests with your sittings." Mrs. Doyle kept her eyes riveted on the hat in front of her as she pulled the spool of ribbon from her apron pocket and began to wind it round the floral stems to bunch them together.

"I'm glad to hear she is pleased with what I can contribute."

"I just hope you know how much is riding on you."

"She told me about how much the medium matters this season at the hotel."

"I'm not just talking about the success of the season. I'm talking about Honoria herself." Mrs. Doyle opened the tin and removed a long pin with a large green glass head. "She was devastated by the loss of her sister and then the deaths of her parents. She's managed to put on a brave face and soldier on, but your arrival means too much to her. I worry you may be a fresh source of sorrow." Mrs. Doyle jabbed the pin through the cluster of flowers and fastened it firmly to the hat.

"I know you have reason to resent my father. I am sorry for all the pain he caused the family," I said. "But I'm not my father or even my mother and do not wish to shoulder either the credit or the blame for them. I made my way here determined to make the best of things my own way. I hope you will find it in your heart to put your distaste for my father aside and to evaluate my character on its own merits."

"That is exactly what I intend to do." She handed me back the bonnet. "I was a milliner before I came to work at the Belden. I made this hat for your mother. I'm glad to see it getting some use once more." She took her leave of me without a backward glance.

I remained seated on the bench considering the formidable Mrs. Doyle. While she was clearly one to carry a grudge in both hands she was also willing to give me the benefit of her expertise when I asked for it. And she obviously was someone deeply loyal to those she loved. Maybe, just maybe if I did my best for Honoria and the Belden she would find a way to accept me. But for now, I would consider her willingness to help with the hat a sign of real progress.

CHAPTER SIXTEEN

THE DOOR OF THE SÉANCE ROOM WAS OPEN WHEN I STEPPED in to look for someone who could direct me to the address included in Lucinda's letter. Amanda Howell sat at one end of a camelback sofa while Ned Larkin perched at the other. Amanda's eyes were closed and her fist clasped tightly around a silken drawstring bag. My cards. I must have forgotten them when I left the room after the unpleasantness with Officer Yancey. Ned looked up at me, then held a finger to his lips. I stopped and silently began to watch.

I didn't like for Amanda to touch my things without asking but, despite her claims, I wasn't really afraid she would be able to learn anything about me from the cards. After all, you'd have to be a fool to imagine someone could learn about an object's owner by simply holding it. Wouldn't you?

"I have the sense this object has been in one family for many years." Amanda paused and clenched her eyes even more tightly closed. "It has traveled a long distance but is now back where it belongs."

"What else are you noticing?" Ned asked. From what she had

described at dinner the night I had arrived, this appeared to be a practice session for token reading or psychometry. I was in a hurry to get to Lucinda's but this was too fascinating to miss. I would ask for directions when they were through.

"I feel secrets and fear. Loneliness. Desperation. This object comforts the owner whose life is one of hardship." Amanda opened her eyes, then opened her hand to look at what it contained. "Where did you get this?"

"It was lying on the table when I arrived. I don't know to whom it belongs," Ned said.

"Despite the age of the item it has a youthful energy. And it definitely belongs to a woman," Amanda said. I must have made a noise, because Amanda turned her attention to the doorway and gave me an unpleasant smile. "As a matter of fact, I believe this belongs to Miss Proulx." She held out the bag to me as if challenging me to take it. Ned turned in my direction, his eyebrows pulled down together in confusion.

"I should not have thought an object like the one you described could possibly have belonged to Miss Proulx." He lifted the bag from her hand and began examining it.

"It is mine," I said, stepping into the room. "But I am afraid Miss Howell needs a great deal of practice in order to be ready to conduct sessions for guests."

"That's exactly what we were doing. Amanda has had an attack of nerves now that we know Mr. Stickney is here investigating the practitioners."

"If that reading is typical I can see why you might be concerned," I said.

"Are you saying I was not accurate in my reading?" Amanda asked.

"You guessed the owner correctly. That's at least something." I couldn't resist poking at her a bit.

"So everything else was wrong?" Ned asked. Amanda looked at me and her own expression did not require a psychic gift to interpret. We were unlikely to become friends.

"Let's just say I would continue practicing if I were her," I said.

"I am quite certain I need fear Mr. Stickney's scrutiny far less than you," Amanda said.

"Did your reading tell you that as well?" I asked.

"No, common sense did. After all, it hardly seems credible that you would announce you just happened to be a medium as soon as Flora Roberts canceled."

"What are you implying?" I said.

"I'm not implying anything. I am flat out saying that I believe you are a fraud." With that, she rose from the sofa and swept past me out the door, pressing my cards into my hand as she went. "You'll need every bit of cunning these imply you possess if you stand a chance of fooling Mr. Stickney." She scowled at me, then flounced off in her fashionable gown.

"Miss Proulx, I must apologize for Amanda," Ned said. "I have no idea what came over her. She is usually so accurate and has such a ladylike demeanor."

"Worry brings out the worst in us all. Think nothing of it."

"How understanding of you. I'm afraid Mr. Stickney's arrival has all the practitioners upset."

"Why should they be?" I was curious about the attitude of the staff.

"No one likes to be under suspicion. Besides, it fundamentally changes the atmosphere in the hotel from one of support to one of skepticism. Everett mentioned at luncheon that he feels a change in the energy here already and it has only been a few hours. Just imagine what it could do over the course of the season."

"Do you feel it yourself?"

"Numerology is more of a science. Facts, figures, and numbers are far less susceptible to that sort of thing than is dowsing, scrying, or even your own practice of mediumship. Have you done a reading since Mr. Stickney arrived?"

"I have not. I understand he arrived just after I concluded my session this morning with the Velmonts."

"So you have not yet felt any resistance in the part of the spirits or of your own guide to the change in the wind?" I could have kissed him if I were that sort of girl. Ned had given me a perfect excuse to use if I found myself in trouble with any of the clients. I could blame Mr. Stickney for silencing the spirits.

"It is likely it will be more difficult to connect with those in spirit with a doubtful energy hanging over us all. Still, we shall have to make the best of it."

"I wish there was something I could do to help," Ned said, which reminded me of my appointment with Lucinda.

"There is a way you could help me. Can you tell me how to get to this address?" I pointed to Lucinda's card.

"I know just where this is. I'd be happy to escort you." Ned crooked his arm and ushered me out the door.

ALL THE WAY TO LUCINDA'S HOUSE NED KEPT UP A STEADY stream of chatter. I was grateful for the distraction. His efforts to impress me with his knowledge of the area and his expertise in numerology drove Amanda's words from my thoughts. Mostly. But every time he paused I could hear her giving an accurate description of my emotions and my past just from touching my cards. Could it be possible for someone to possess such a talent? Or was her assessment of my character and background just wishful thinking on her part? Either way, I would do my best not to allow her to touch anything else I owned.

Ned brought me directly to Lucinda's doorstep. After assuring himself I could find my own way back to the hotel he made his good-byes and left me to my visit.

The Yancey home was small but well kept. Crisp gray paint with white trim and a profusion of flowers in the boxes at the windows proclaimed the owners of the little Cape to be house-proud. I mounted the steps to the small porch and pulled on the bell. Yapping emerged from inside before Lucinda herself flung open the door.

"Ruby, I hope you like dogs," she said, bending to scoop up a plump ball of scruffy cream-colored fur and frantic energy. "Blossom, stop barking and say hello to our friend Ruby."

"I adore them." One of the many things that played a part in my fantasy of living in a house was to have a dog. Blossom was just exactly what I had imagined, except the dog in my mind's eye had dark spots on its coat. I pulled off my glove and held my fingers out for the little dog to sniff.

"She likes you," Lucinda said when Blossom licked my fingertips.

"I like her, too," I said, feeling pleased to have passed muster. "What sort of dog is she?"

"A very naughty one." Lucinda gently patted Blossom's thick body. "I don't suppose you'd like a puppy in a few weeks, would you?"

"I would love one but I certainly can't speak for Honoria."

"I don't expect you'll have any worries there. From what my mother has to say, Honoria would give you anything you asked to keep you at the Belden. She's simply over the moon that you've come home." Lucinda stepped back into the short hallway and returned Blossom to the floor. "But let's not stand here in the doorway. The parlor's right over there."

I followed her into a small, bright room filled to bursting with bric-a-brac. Every surface simply heaved with vases, doilies, and small figurines. Needlepoint pillows clotted the chairs and the sofa. Only the floor was unblemished by decoration.

"Make yourself comfortable, if you possibly can," Lucinda said with a broad sweep of her arm. "When Mother isn't consulting with your aunt about the spiritual side of life she throws herself headlong into needlework."

"Did she create all of this?"

"Yes. She's simply a wonder with a needle and thread. Mother needs things to keep her busy and to take her mind off the past. Which is one of the reasons I invited you here today."

"I am terribly sorry if your mother was disturbed by the séance. I'd be happy to make excuses as to why I cannot hold another sitting with your mother if that's why you asked to see me." I had been hoping to make a friend of Lucinda but I understood if she was not interested.

"I wanted to see you about Mother, but I would like you to have more contact with her rather than less."

"More sittings, you mean?"

"Not so much sittings as fittings." Lucinda passed her gaze over the room and shook her head. "May I speak frankly without fear of offending you?"

"I am not easily offended. Please tell me what you had in mind."

"Your wardrobe. It simply won't do."

"My clothing was lost along the journey," I said, hoping the lie sounded convincing. "I am very grateful that Honoria kept all my mother's things and that they fit so well."

"They are very pretty but are tragically out of date. A young woman such as yourself, with looks, a social position, and a need to mingle with guests at the hotel should be dressed appropriately."

"I could not ask Honoria for money for clothing and I am afraid I have none of my own."

"I'm doing a poor job of explaining my idea. I would like you to do me the very great favor of allowing my mother to make over your gowns."

"I couldn't ask that of her. Imagine the work it would take."

"Exactly. She needs a new project. The bigger, the better. It would cost nothing to alter the existing wardrobe other than time, and she would be delighted to do it."

"It seems too much to ask."

"I am asking you to allow me to portray you as desperate and without resources to aid yourself. I'm very much afraid I'm the one asking too much."

"Will Honoria object to the gowns being altered? After all, she has kept everything in my mother's room just as it was when she left, including the clothing."

"She has been keeping everything in the room for you and she wants you to love it all and to stay with her always. She certainly isn't going to deny you this."

"I wouldn't even know how to ask. She has already been so generous, giving me a home and making me feel so welcome."

"Leave that bit to me. I shall write to her and propose that in order to best represent the Belden you need a proper wardrobe. I will suggest Honoria would be doing me a favor by allowing Mother to make the alterations."

"Are you certain she won't object?"

"Of course she won't. Even Warren couldn't complain about it. As a matter of fact, his commenting on what a shame it was that such a pretty girl as you was dressed as a middle-aged woman convinced me to formulate this plan in the first place."

Heat surged to my cheeks and down my neck. I certainly was not interested in Officer Yancey's good opinion but knowing he thought I was pretty and pitiable was strangely disturbing.

"Do you think your mother really would be willing?" I asked.

"Does it look to you as though she has space to drape another doily? Besides, we've already discussed it and she would like to do it as a way to repay you for contacting Gladys. She's looking forward to many more sessions."

"Your brother came by the hotel this morning to warn me not to conduct any more séances for your mother or you, so I doubt that will be necessary."

"He did what?" Lucinda's tone perked up Blossom's droopy ears.

"He demanded that I stop playing havoc with your mother's nerves. He was quite insistent."

"What did you tell him?"

"I told him I had no intention of stopping the sessions as long as your mother wished me to continue them."

"Good for you. I knew you were a modern sort of girl the minute I saw you no matter how old-fashioned your clothes were."

"I hope I haven't caused a rift in your home."

"Don't give it another thought. Mother will be delighted you've agreed to the project. Warren has no say in our affairs."

"If you're certain, it would be a relief to face the dining room feeling more in fashion." I thought of Amanda and her cutting remarks. It gave me a slight tremor of excitement to think of her reaction when I appeared at the table with something she could not fault.

"Then it's settled." Lucinda stood. "All this planning has made me hungry. I'll be back in a moment with some muffins and jam."

"Do you need help?"

"No. Just make yourself at home and try not to be smothered by an avalanche of needlework in my absence." Lucinda smiled and Blossom followed her out the door, her toenails clicking and scratching against the gleaming hardwood floors.

I stood and moved about the room, taking it all in. Despite the abundance of decorative items there was a complete absence of dust. The brass light fixtures and andirons shone and the windows and mirrors sparkled. I stepped to the fireplace and looked at the tintypes on the mantel. In one, a man with an elegant mustache and sad eyes peered mournfully at me. In another, a slightly younger Officer Yancey cut a fine figure in an army uniform. I was still leaning over the tintype when Lucinda returned pushing a loaded tea cart.

"I hide this in the closet under the stairs so Mother can't smother it and I can actually use it," Lucinda said, stopping the cart in front of a pair of armchairs. "You found Warren, I see."

"I thought it must be him. When was he in the service?"

"He's been back about a year. He served for eight years, more or less."

"How dashing he looks in his uniform. He looks like a man of adventure."

"If he was, I don't know about it." Lucinda sat in one of the chairs and poured the tea. I sat in the other and took the cup she offered.

"A man who doesn't boast about his daring deeds in the service of his country?" I was surprised. Not because Officer Yancey seemed like a man inclined to brag but because the men both visiting the medicine show and working it counted their time in the service as a point of honor and used it as a way to converse with other men.

"Warren won't speak of any of it at all. It is as though eight years of his life never happened. One minute he was gone with nothing more than an occasional letter and then he was back, trying to act as though he never left."

"Perhaps he did not find army life to his liking," I said. "I suppose some men don't."

"All I know is that he came back a changed man." Lucinda flicked a towel back to reveal a tempting display of baked goods. "But right now I am much more interested in discussing how we are to make a complete change to your wardrobe. After we eat, we'll write to Honoria."

CHAPTER SEVENTEEN

As much as I enjoyed my visit with Lucinda, I was ready for a little time to myself before the rigors of the dinner hour. I headed for the veranda and settled in a deep chair to read and look at the sea.

The view held me spellbound until the sounds of an argument drifted toward me from just beyond the fence enclosing the garden where I had sat with Mrs. Doyle refreshing my mother's hat. I didn't need to view the combatants. I recognized the voices of both Sanford Dobbins and Leander Stickney.

Perhaps I should have done the polite thing and cleared my throat loudly to alert them of my presence. Or even more politely, taken myself elsewhere in order to allow them their privacy. But long ago I had learned what was polite and what was useful were often very different things. I stuck my finger in my book and strained forward to listen closely. I could use all the inside information I could get for my upcoming séance session with the Stickneys.

"Sanford, I've been thinking over the incident with Flora Roberts." Leander Stickney's voice was deep and forceful. "The entire situation was very embarrassing and I've concluded I must dismiss you from my employ."

"You're firing me?"

"You've left me no choice. I only hired you in the first place because your aunt insisted."

"But you need me."

"I needed you to help keep your aunt from being taken in by every charlatan in the greater Boston area. But instead, you encouraged her in a relationship that could have done irreparable damage to our family name. After all, how would it look if a fraud investigator's wife was systematically bilked out of her fortune?"

"You never proved Miss Roberts was a fraud." Sanford's voice shot up an octave.

"I never went public with my findings but that doesn't mean I had no proof."

"You always do think of your reputation ahead of all else."

"Lucky for you someone does. If I hadn't caught on to Miss Roberts and told her I'd share my suspicions with the police if she showed her face in Old Orchard this summer she would have drained your aunt dry by the end of the season."

"You can't really mean to dismiss me. I've been an asset to the society for ages."

"No, you've repeatedly been a liability. This wasn't the first incident in which you were duped."

"If you are referring to Madame Gustav, I know what I saw. She materialized a trumpet in the middle of the séance table out of thin air."

"Madame Gustav was arrested for fraud by the Boston police the day after your session with her."

"Only because you set them onto her." Mr. Dobbins's voice was so shrill it was difficult to understand.

"Don't be so naive," Mr. Stickney said. "You know very well that the police found fishing line and pulleys and a stash of trumpets and other so-called materials of apportment in her rooms when they raided them."

"And why do you suppose that was?"

"Don't start in with that again. I've already assured you that I did not place those items in her home to incriminate her. Nor did I pay anyone else to do so." Mr. Stickney cleared his throat.

"I'll tell Permilia that you are firing me and that you're the one responsible for Flora Roberts changing her mind about spending the season at the Belden."

"No you won't. Unless you persuade my wife that leaving my employ was your idea and keep what you know about Miss Roberts to yourself, I will help myself to your trust account."

"But that was left to me by my parents. You have no right to it."

"As trustee I may disburse funds however I see fit until you turn thirty. If there's nothing left of it by then it will be your fault for displeasing me."

"It's mine upon my marriage."

"Only if I approve the match. Since I won't, I suggest you follow Miss Roberts's example and disappear."

"Permilia will be devastated. She thinks of me as a son."

"But I do not. You have until tomorrow to let your aunt know you have decided to take a job elsewhere."

A door slammed loudly, then the sound of happy whistling floated over the fence. I leaned back in the wicker chair to think. Leander Stickney was the reason Flora Roberts had canceled at the Belden—that much was clear. I wondered if my willingness to return to a life of deceit, despite my misgivings, was all for naught. If Mr. Stickney exposed me, Honoria was sure to lose the hotel anyway. But at least I wouldn't have to worry about finding a place to live. Officer Yancey was sure to provide me with accommodations in the nearest jail.

YANCEY STOOD ON THE BOARDWALK, CONTEMPLATING THE throng milling around the base of the mostly completed pier when he felt a jab between his shoulder blades. He whirled round, wearing his best policeman's scowl, only to face his sister, Lucy.

"I could arrest you for assaulting a police officer," he said. The girl had no sense at all sometimes.

"I wish I could call the authorities on you for unwarranted meddling." Lucy was angry. Yancey would have realized it even without the jabbing. Her flushed cheeks were one indication. Her arms alternating between whirling about like pinwheels and clamping across her chest were another. He wasn't going to risk enraging her further and causing a public scene by pretending he didn't know what she was talking about.

"I assume Miss Proulx has declined your overtures of friendship?"

"Of course she hasn't. But the point is that you tried to influence her to do so."

"I consider it my duty to protect both you and Mother from people like Miss Proulx."

"Being a dutiful son or devoted brother isn't a part you can pick up and put down when you feel like it, Warren. I seem to recall you had no interest in protecting us when you ran off to join the army."

"That's not fair, Lucy." Yancey felt the familiar tightening in his chest he always experienced when he remembered how eager he was to leave the scandal behind as soon as he was able. "I have apologized as best I could and have been trying to make it up to the both of you ever since."

"Well, you're going about it all wrong. If we didn't need you then, we certainly don't need you now. Besides, you aren't as much help as you think you are."

"What's that supposed to mean?"

"You work all hours, pick fights with your boss, cry out in your sleep, and then deny there's anything wrong." Lucy's face softened, just a little. "You've come back a changed man and not in ways that benefit any of us."

"You have a romantic notion of what your big brother was, and the reality doesn't match your imaginings. That's all there is to it."

"No, Warren, it isn't. You've changed and so have I." Lucy uncrossed her arms and placed a hand on his arm. "I love you but I've learned the hard way that I don't need you. And I certainly won't allow you to act as if you have a right to waltz back into my life after an absence of eight years and tell me what to do."

"So there's nothing I can do to convince you to stop Mother from consulting with Miss Proulx?"

"Not only are you not going to stop us, you should know I plan to take Miss Proulx on as my own special project." Lucy shook her head. "That girl at the hotel who reads objects has been absolutely caustic about Ruby's appearance."

"Miss Proulx told you that?" Yancey was surprised. Miss Proulx seemed too proud to share such a thing.

"Mrs. Doyle told me about it. The maids and servers have noticed. They all like Ruby and they've reported to Mrs. Doyle the jabs and snide comments they've overheard."

"Is that why you offered Mother's services at making over her wardrobe?"

"What else could I do? It would be criminal to allow such a pretty girl to feel she was unattractive. Besides, I know just how it feels to be whispered about by girls who think they're superior. I couldn't let that happen to a friend if I could possibly help it."

"I wish I'd never left you and Mother to get along on your own. I know it must have been difficult."

"You had your own grief to consider. When I was a small girl I used to envy the memories you had of Father when I had none. Now I think maybe I was better off being just a baby when he died."

"We both had our burdens to bear. I should have come home sooner."

"Mother and I are very glad to have you back. Even if you decided to become a policeman."

"You know I do this job to make sure only guilty parties are held responsible for crimes in this town."

Lucy squeezed Yancey's arm. "I know you think Chief Hurley is responsible for what happened to Father but I don't know how you think working with him will help you to prove it."

"It's the only way I know of to get to the truth."

"I can think of a better one."

"Don't say it."

"I will say it. You should ask Miss Proulx for help."

Chapter Eighteen

I SAT ON THE PORCH UNTIL THE DINNER GONG RANG ANNOUNC-
ing the meal would commence in a half hour. With so little
time, my preparations for dinner that evening were even more
hurried than the night before. Millie had no time to assist me
with my hair since the hotel had steadily filled with guests
throughout the day.

I made the best of things and managed to pin up my hair with
several tortoiseshell combs I found in a drawer of the vanity table. Despite my best efforts, by the time I reached the dining
room I felt tendrils straying from the combs and slipping down
my back.

Honoria moved from table to table, smiling at guests and faculty alike. I stood in the threshold, overlooking the chattering
crowd. I noticed that someone had thought to seat at least one
faculty member at each table to mingle with the guests. I wondered how such organization had been accomplished until I
moved farther into the room and noticed little paper cards in ornate silver holders. Upon each was written a name.

I picked my way through the room and discovered my own

name at a place near the center. Seated at the same table, I was pleased to see Elva and Dovie Velmont. Between them was a stranger. As I approached, he scraped back his chair and rose.

"Miss Proulx, I presume?" he asked, pointing at the place card.

"I am. I know the Misses Velmont"—I nodded around the table at them—"but I'm afraid I am not acquainted with you, sir."

"Dennis Ayers, at your service," he said. "The Misses Velmont have informed me you are the shining star amongst the practitioners here at the Belden." He drew back my chair and waited while I sat.

"While I am flattered that they would say so, all the practitioners here at the Hotel Belden are the best at what they do." I smiled at the Misses Velmont. "That being said, every guest has the discipline he or she favors. I suspect these two kind ladies are more partial to communication with those who have passed on than any other area of study."

"You are too modest, Miss Proulx," the plumper of the two sisters, Dovie, said.

"Father always said false modesty is as great a sin as unmerited boasting." Elva lifted her napkin from her plate and opened it with a quick snap of the wrist. Her agility surprised me and I thought I'd be lucky to be as vigorous at half her age.

"I couldn't agree with you more," Mr. Ayers said. He looked at me with a frankness that was entirely different from that of most men. For starters, he confined his gaze to my face, a notable departure from the others. "False modesty is a form of pride, even of willful deceit." Even though his voice was warm I felt a chill pass over me.

"We can assure you, while Miss Proulx may be guilty of false modesty she is certainly not guilty of deceit. Not like some others we could mention. Isn't that right?" Dovie pressed a plump hand against her fleshy bosom and looked to her sister for confirmation.

"We agreed before we came not to discuss our disappointments," Elva said, turning a stern eye on Dovie.

"Surely you are amongst friends here, Miss Velmont," Mr. Ayers said. "It sounds as though your experiences might serve as a lesson to others."

"Father always did admonish us to assist others," Dovie said, looking at Elva for approval.

"It's a rare daughter who does not profit from following her father's direction, wouldn't you agree, Miss Proulx?"

"Since you put it that way, I suppose it wouldn't hurt to discuss it," Elva said. "Sadly, there are many, many persons who have endeavored to perpetuate fraud upon us." The two sisters looked at each other and shook their heads in unison. "Especially when they realized we have the financial wherewithal to make frequent visits to their establishments."

"They think because we are spinsters we must know nothing of the world," Dovie said. "You would not believe the nonsensical mutterings we have been subjected to in our quest to make contact with Father."

"The worst was the mumbo jumbo about being drawn to the light. Father was extremely fair and suffered from terrible headaches. He'd spend hours upon hours in a darkened room avoiding light as much as possible."

"It was clear from the start none of them had a genuine gift."

"There was a phrase Father told us he would say through a medium by which we would know it was truly him speaking.

Miss Proulx is the only one to have gotten it right. She has our complete faith."

"Is that so?" Mr. Ayers turned his attention on me once more and I detected a sparkle in his eye that made me uncomfortable. There was an undercurrent to his conversation that I was unable to comprehend. Mr. Ayers seemed to be sizing me up like he was inspecting a tool in a box for its suitability for a task. As if he were hefting a hammer with a thought as to whether it was the best one for driving a nail. I would be relieved when dinner was finished and I could find an excuse to be rid of him.

"Certainly, it is so," Dovie said. "We were so pleased with our sitting this afternoon we have already set another for tomorrow morning."

"I congratulate you, Miss Proulx, on receiving such a ringing endorsement," Mr. Ayers said.

"I'm pleased the Misses Velmont are so satisfied with my help but I cannot take the credit for it. The spirits do all the work."

"Don't be so modest. I have every confidence that you are far more deserving of the credit for how effective a sitting is than you admit, Miss Proulx." He smiled again and I thought of the wolf in an illustrated storybook I had treasured as a child. All I needed were a basket and a cape to be sure he was going to swallow me in an enormous gulp.

"She's a treasure, Mr. Ayers. An absolute treasure," Dovie said.

"I can hardly wait to test out her abilities for myself," Mr. Ayers said. And then, while the Misses Velmont were turned toward serving staff bustling in with heavy trays covered with silver dishes, Mr. Ayers winked at me. It was the exact same sort of wink Father used to give me behind the backs of the bumpkins he was about to separate from their money. The only thing to do was to change the topic.

"Do you have a favorite spiritual discipline, Mr. Ayers?" I asked.

"I'm sure with your talents you must know it already," he said.

"I am a medium, Mr. Ayers, not a psychic," I said. "But if I had to guess I would venture to say you read tea leaves." I gave the Misses Velmont a wink of my own.

"What a charming notion. But my interests lie elsewhere." Mr. Ayers nodded to the waiter circling the table with a fragrant tureen of soup. The scent wafting from the serving dish momentarily distracted me and I almost missed his next comment. "My passion is art."

"You're an artist?" Dovie said.

"I flatter myself that I am."

"What brings you to the Hotel Belden?" I asked.

"I have an interest in spirit art. I wish to develop my ability to channel spirit into visual messages shown through my drawings."

"Fascinating," Dovie said. "Do you render landscapes or portraits when you commune with spirit?"

"I specialize in portraits. I pride myself, however immoderate it may seem, that I never forget a face."

"Never?" said Elva.

"Once I've seen it, no, I never do." I felt the weight of Mr. Ayers's gaze on my face. "Even if I haven't seen the face in life but rather just in a picture. On a handbill, a flyer, or even on a product label." I flushed despite my best efforts to remain calm. Something in his look made me feel afraid beyond all reason. His words meant more than they seemed on the surface, that much was certain.

Chapter Nineteen

Aɴ dinner Honoria invited the guests and Mrs.
Doyle to attend a concert at the Methodist Campground a
few blocks away. I complained of fatigue from my readings in
order to remain at the hotel but really I just wanted to spend
some more time exploring the Belden's extensive library.

To my eye, the room was the most beautiful in all the hotel.
Carved oak bookshelves lined three walls while the fourth was
made entirely of French doors leading to the veranda. Honoria
had furnished it with two deep wingback chairs and a table nestled between them. I ran my fingers over an eye-level shelf, taking pleasure in the books' crackled leather spines and embossed
letters.

One thing I could say for my father was that he was a believer
in the value of education, even for girls. It was self-serving of
him, of course. He felt an educated daughter made him look all
the wiser. We never stayed in one place long enough for me to
attend school but he always made sure I had books to read. Father had steered me toward the classics and I understood their

value, but left to my own devices I preferred more sensational stories.

Fortunately, someone else must have, too, because tucked onto a low shelf opposite the veranda were a slew of my favorite authors. I pulled out a slim volume by Laura Jean Libbey and settled into a chair for a gorge. I was pulled from my increasing interest in the plight of a naive but spirited mill girl by the sound of fierce whispering accompanying the footfalls heading along the veranda. I sank down lower in my chair, hoping if I avoided the newcomers I wouldn't have to put aside my book.

"Mr. Stickney, I'm begging you not to say anything to my husband." I recognized Cecelia MacPherson's voice.

"I told you when last we met that if I ever found you practicing any form of chicanery again I would expose you," Leander Stickney said. "Your husband has a right to know what sort of woman he married."

"I'm a legitimate astrologer."

"It would weigh on my conscience not to at least have a word with your employer. It doesn't do her credit to have a debunked practitioner on her staff."

"I assure you there's nothing deceitful in my practice. How can I convince you to keep silent?"

"There is one thing I can think of." Silk rustled and swished and the porch swing creaked as weight settled quickly against it.

"Get off of me, Leander. Your advances are still unwelcome."

"You haven't changed a bit since I knew you in Boston."

"Neither have you. You were as uncouth and unreasonable then as you are now."

"My terms are the same as well. You give me what I want and I'll keep what I know to myself. Your husband and your employer

need never know about your past." I held my breath as Leander
gave a final word. "I suggest you decide very soon." I heard hard
soles clatter away along the decking and then muffled sobs.

"Bastard," she whispered. Then she blew her nose and crept
away.

Try as I might I couldn't fall asleep. I tossed in the
high bed in my mother's room and thought about Mr. Ayers,
Mr. Stickney, and Cecelia. I wondered if I should tell Honoria
myself what I had heard. But that felt like the pot calling the
kettle black, so instead I lay fretting. I had managed to forget my
book in the library when I came up to bed.

I found a silk wrapper in the wardrobe and plucked the candle from the bed stand. As I slipped down the hallway past the
darkened guest rooms, contented snores floated out from Honoria's room at the far end. I stifled a chuckle as I thought how she
would react to hear she slept as noisily as a roustabout after a
night spent swilling hooch.

I fetched my book from the library and entered the kitchen
for a glass of milk to send me to sleep if reading didn't help. My
flickering candle threw shadows along the cupboards and crock-
ery. An uncut cake covered in icing and shaved coconut whistled
at me from beneath a glass dome. I congratulated myself for ignoring it as Mrs. Doyle would surely notice if I helped myself to
a piece. As I turned to the icebox for the milk I heard a rustling
noise in the pantry.

My first thought was mice, but the sound was too loud. I told
myself there couldn't be weasels or foxes inside the hotel and
looked around for a weapon. Mrs. Doyle was lamentably tidy.

Nowhere in reach could I see a broomstick or a rolling pin. I froze in place as shuffling footsteps approached.

My mouth dropped open in surprise as Dovie appeared before me in her nightdress. A loose gray braid draped across her shoulder and her hands were covered in white powder.

"Dovie?" I spoke to her in a low voice but she gave no indication she had heard me. She walked right past me and smack-dab into the worktable Mrs. Doyle used for breads and pies. I spoke to Dovie again, noticing she wasn't wearing her spectacles. Before I could call to her once more a light bobbed through the door and for a moment I thought I was seeing double.

"Elva, I think Dovie's sleepwalking," I said.

"I hope she didn't frighten you, Ruby."

"I was just glad she was a dove instead of a rodent."

"What are we going to do with you?" Elva took her sister gently by the arm. "And what have you gotten into now?" She dabbed at Dovie's hands with a handkerchief she pulled from her sleeve.

"I think it's flour." I nodded to the pantry. "Has she done this before?"

"Oh yes. Every time we try to contact Father she has an episode."

"I hope I didn't upset you."

"We are overjoyed that you contacted him." Elva started to lead Dovie away. "Happiness is as likely to agitate her as grief."

"It's a wonder she didn't break her neck on the stairs." Now their desire for a first-floor room when they arrived made sense. "Shall I help you get her back to bed?"

"No, dear, I've had quite a lot of practice." She pointed at the pantry. "But it would be helpful if you would repair any damage she's done to Mrs. Doyle's pristine domain."

Chapter Twenty

I SLEPT POORLY EVEN WITH ALL THE COMFORTS OF THE BED. I awakened early and, seeking breakfast, I found myself most unfortunately alone in the company of Mr. Everett MacPherson, Cecelia's husband and a man from whom secrets were being kept.

I helped myself to a boiled egg and a broiled biscuit from the sideboard and, faced with no way to politely avoid him, sat at the table with Mr. MacPherson.

"Good morning, young lady. It's nice to find that someone besides myself is an early riser."

"I can't claim always to be one but my stomach served as a wakeup call this morning and I could not refuse its urgings. Especially considering the quality of Mrs. Doyle's cooking."

"A rare one she is, that Mrs. Doyle. Cook, housekeeper, and gardener all rolled into one. If I weren't already married to my beloved Cecelia, I'd ask Mrs. Doyle for her capable hand."

"Isn't Mrs. Doyle married already?"

"Widowed, she is, for more years than you've been rattling the Earth. Her husband had taken to beating her and she left him.

She was spared the difficulty of deciding to give him another chance because he was fortunately claimed by the sea the very day she left."

"Is that how she came to be at the Belden?"

"Aye. Your grandparents heard of her troubles and offered her a position here."

"And she's been here ever since?"

"Indeed she has. Devoted to the family like they were her own." Mr. MacPherson broke off a bit of toast and popped it into his mouth. "I wouldn't want to be on Mrs. Doyle's bad side. You should have seen the rampage she was on this morning when she discovered someone had made a mess of her kitchen. A woman in rare form, I tell you." A bite of egg lodged in my throat. I had lost my ability to swallow. Just as I thought I was softening Mrs. Doyle up a bit. I took a sip of water from my cup to force the egg down before attempting to speak.

"You seem to know a great deal about Mrs. Doyle's history. How did you come to be so informed about her?"

"I'm informed, as you say, about many things, but I am especially interested in this hotel. Mrs. Doyle was happy to share some of her own part in its history with me." Mr. MacPherson scraped butter across a second biscuit, then loaded it with strawberry preserves. "This property is bewitching, don't you agree?"

"If you are speaking of its beauty, I would heartily agree," I said. The gleam in Mr. MacPherson's eyes was that of a zealot. I braced myself for whatever message he was about to extoll. At least he was too wrapped up in his own enthusiasms to leave me worrying about not spilling any secrets about his wife.

"I mean the energy here. Surely someone as sensitive to the world of spirit would sense that the atmosphere here is unusual."

"In which way?" I had noticed that the voice had become a louder, more frequent visitor since I had arrived at the Belden. But I wasn't prepared to share that even with Honoria. Still, what he had to say interested me and with a nod of my head I encouraged him to continue.

"Take my dowsing, for instance. Allow me to demonstrate." He pulled a clear crystal hanging from a chain from his vest pocket. Grasping a knob at the end of the chain firmly between two fingers he dangled the crystal above the tablecloth. I watched silently as he waited for the pendulum to stop swaying. "Ask it a question," he said.

"What sort of a question?"

"Anything you like as long as it can be answered with a yes or no. Ambiguity is for card readers and crystal ball gazers, not for dowsers. We're more the straightforward sort."

"Is today my birthday?" I asked. I watched as the crystal began to sway side to side, slowly at first and then picking up speed. I looked at Mr. MacPherson's hands in an effort to detect the source of the motion. They appeared steady as a rock.

"It says that it is not. A side-to-side motion indicates a no and a back-and-forth motion signals yes."

"Are there any other movements?" I asked.

"The pendulum can swing in a clockwise rotation for maybe and widdershins to request a different question or more likely to show that there is more information available for the asking."

"Widdershins?"

"Counterclockwise to you Americans."

"I was raised in Canada."

"That may be true but you still didn't know what it meant. Ask another question." Mr. MacPherson once again stopped the pendulum's sway and held it steady while I thought. There were many questions on my mind, the top one being how he managed to make it appear that he wasn't moving the pendulum when he so clearly was.

But other things were there, too, like what to do about Officer Yancey's determination to dig into my background? Or, more important, would I be able to convince Mr. Stickney that my abilities were real? None of these were questions I wanted to share with Mr. MacPherson.

"Are you feeling shy about the question? That's all right. You can ask anything silently and I'll dowse for it. Sometimes I prefer not to hear the question so I can't influence the reading with my own opinion."

I nodded and decided to ask if I would succeed in convincing Mr. Stickney of my abilities, as it seemed the most pressing concern. "I've thought of one." Not that I would necessarily believe the answer the pendulum offered. I wasn't saying Mr. MacPherson was trying to trick anyone. I thought it was possible he was one of those unfortunate souls who made the colossal mistake of believing his own con.

"Have you got the question firmly in mind and are certain it can be answered as yes or no?" he asked me. I nodded and he released his staying hand from the crystal. It hung motionless at first and then, with slight twitches and waggles began to stir. Then slowly but steadily it began to swing back and forth, gathering speed and increasing its arc. "That is a definite no."

"Not what I hoped. But I confess, I am not entirely convinced that dowsing works." I took a bite of my biscuit. "I hope you are not offended."

"You wouldn't be the first skeptic I've met. But I would like a chance to convince you. Will you come with me to the beach and try it for yourself?" He pushed back his chair and held out his hand.

"Now?"

"Why not? Do you have a pressing appointment so early in the morning?"

I heard Mrs. Doyle's voice bellowing down the hall about the state of her kitchen. I had no wish to encounter her in her current frame of mind. And, if the pendulum was correct about Mr. Stickney, I would do well to avoid him as long as possible. Any excuse to leave the hotel seemed appealing.

"I would love nothing more," I said as I took Mr. MacPherson's arm.

THE TIDE WAS ALMOST AT ITS HEIGHT AS WE PACED ALONG THE soft sand above the high-water mark. The morning was foggy and I was startled when a seagull dropped from the sky and landed on a large white shell. Others, drawn to its work, flocked to the same spot and drove the first gull away.

Beside me Mr. MacPherson held his arms stiffly bent at his sides. A shaft of sunlight burnt through the fog and glinted off the metal rod held in each of his clenched fists. He held out the brass rods to me. I took them in my hands and felt how warm the metal had become.

"What do I do with them?"

"You hold them firmly enough not to drop them but lightly enough so they can swing as they're a-mind to do." I adjusted my grip and he nodded with approval. "That's right. Just so."

"Now what?"

"Now you start to look for something worth finding."

"What sort of thing should I look for?"

"How about gold? That's what I look for most mornings."

"It seems an unlikely place to find nuggets," I said.

"That may well be but it is a fine place to discover lost jewelry. People are forever losing things on the beach."

"That makes sense. So how do these work?"

"You put your mind to the item you are looking for. Then hold the rods and walk slowly. When they cross you know to stop and dig."

"That's it?" I was not convinced. If it was as easy as that why wasn't everyone roaming the sand with a couple of pieces of brass wire bent into an L shape?

"Well, you do have to keep your mind fixed upon what you seek. It also helps to know what getting close feels like." He pulled a brooch from his trouser pocket and placed it on the beach a few yards away. "Hold the rods over the sand and feel the way they act." I did and they just bounced up and down slightly in the breeze.

"I feel nothing out of the ordinary."

"Now slowly walk this way." He gestured toward the brooch. "Keep the idea of gold in your mind as you walk." I felt a tingling in my hands, and as I reached the brooch the rods swung violently then crossed, one over the other.

"I did it," I said, not certain it wasn't a product of my own doing. "But what's to say I didn't cross them deliberately because I knew the gold was there?"

"I can't make you believe but maybe if you tag along you'll be convinced."

I agreed and we spent an enjoyable half hour moving slowly

back and forth over the beach, pausing now and again to check the sand for treasures. Every time the rods crossed Mr. MacPherson pulled a mesh sieve from his bag and sifted through the sand. More often than not the items he dug up were not gold but they were always made of metal. It was an engrossing activity. Almost without realizing how much ground we had covered, the pier suddenly emerged from the fog.

"I'm feeling a strong tug. This way," Mr. MacPherson said, hurrying along faster now than before. I trailed behind, struggling to keep the hem of my skirt above the incoming tide. Even from a distance I could see how excited he was becoming. It was as though he was being pulled by a magnetic force or floated along on an invisible current. Then Mr. MacPherson stopped as the rods crossed each other with a swish.

A large black mass lay spread at his feet, the waves lapping at the edge of it. Mr. MacPherson bent over. I hurried forward, abandoning the notion of keeping my hem dry, too eager to see what he had discovered. It was just like a treasure hunt in one of the dime novels Father hated for me to read. Mr. MacPherson sank to his knees on the sand. What could he have found?

"Have you found a pirate's chest?" I called out, coming alongside him.

"Oh, lassie, I wish you weren't here to see this," he said. The wind shifted and the fog streaked away from the mass in front of us. Mr. MacPherson had discovered a gold pocket watch on the beach. Unfortunately, it was still attached to the very dead Leander Stickney.

Chapter Twenty-One

"WHAT DO YOU THINK?" FRANK NICHOLS ASKED AS THEY bent over the body. "Pickpocket turned violent?"

"Perhaps. The fact that his watch is still with the body makes me wonder." Yancey pointed at the fancy and obvious chain stretched over the dead man's waistcoat. He began searching the victim's pockets. Even after hours spent wicking salty moisture up from the sand, the fabric of the victim's suit felt like money under Yancey's fingers. He pulled out a billfold and flipped it open. Several five-dollar bills and a few ones still nestled inside. Finding nothing else besides a book of matches from the Sea Spray Hotel, he turned his attention to the wound. "Nasty gash in the skull."

"It's enough to put me off my feed," Frank said. Frank's appetite was legendary. It wasn't surprising, though. His wife, Sadie, was Mrs. Doyle's daughter and every bit the cook her mother was. Yancey found himself envying Frank more often than he liked, especially when they pulled out their lunch buckets.

"Have you located the weapon yet?"

"No, but I just arrived. From the depth of the wound it had to have been something pretty heavy."

"Agreed. Have one of the other officers start scouring the area for it in case we are lucky and the murderer discarded the weapon here."

"Will do." Frank shouted to a skinny young man with a scanty mustache and sent him off with the order to search the beach for something bloody. Yancey looked down at the body stretched before him. He shook away thoughts of other times he had been in the presence of violent death and brought his attention back to the matter in front of him. The mist would make it more difficult to accurately record the position of the body, and the tide was still rising.

"Get one of the boys to fetch the photographer from up by the livery. Roust him from bed if you have to and get him down here to document this. Hurley'll have all our hides if this isn't cleared up before the pier opens."

"You can't want that guy Lydale," Frank asked.

"He's just trying to make a living like everyone else," Yancey said, then straightened and brushed the damp sand from his knees.

"Yeah, but he does it on the backs of the dead."

"Sometimes, so do we." Yancey gestured at the body in front of them. "I want any help I can get. Speaking of which, who found the body?"

"They did." Frank pointed to two figures whose details were obscured by the fog. Yancey patted his pocket for a notebook and a pencil as he started up the beach. The pair that discovered the body was sitting on the edge of the boardwalk. Before he reached them the chief loomed into view and intercepted his path.

"Yancey, have you gotten to the bottom of this mess yet?" Chief Hurley's mustache drooped in the humidity. He pulled off his spectacles and wiped the mist from the lenses on a fine white handkerchief.

"I've only just arrived, sir. I'm about to question the people who discovered the body." Yancey pointed to the pair of witnesses.

"Let's get to it, then." The chief set off before Yancey could object to his participation.

Chief Hurley reached out to shake the hand of a gaunt man unfamiliar to Yancey. Unfortunately, the young woman was not.

"Miss Proulx, it seems your real supernatural gift is an ability to attract a criminal element."

"Old Orchard does seem to be rife with violence."

"Not before you arrived, it wasn't."

"Yancey, that's no way to speak to a young lady. Are you all right, my dear?" Chief Hurley asked.

"I'll be fine once I'm allowed to return home," Miss Proulx said.

"Of course. We'll hurry things along." Chief Hurley scowled at Yancey, then smiled at Miss Proulx. "Who might you be, my dear?"

"Miss Ruby Proulx. Perhaps you know my aunt Honoria Belden?"

"Of course I'm acquainted with Miss Belden. She's a pillar of the community. Yancey, I cannot see subjecting her niece to questioning."

"I need to question her, sir. She found the body along with this fellow." Yancey tipped his head toward the gaunt man. "And you are?"

"Everett MacPherson. I'm one of the practitioners at the

Hotel Belden, and Miss Proulx and I were out using my dowsing rods when I was drawn to the body."

"Drawn to the body? How so?"

"It was the watch, you see. I had attuned my mind to seek out gold and my rods guided me straight to the watch on Mr. Stickney's waistcoat."

"So you knew the victim?" Yancey printed the victim's name in his notebook in block letters for clarity. Most of his notes were scribbles and swirls but victim's names called for more respect than that.

"He was a guest at the hotel."

"Did you see anyone else in the area?" Yancey asked.

"The only one I saw out and about was the Indian woman who reads palms on the beach. She walked quite near me not long before I came upon Mr. Stickney."

"Any idea why someone would want to kill him?" Chief Hurley said.

"I can't possibly say. I hardly knew the man." Mr. MacPherson stepped closer to Miss Proulx.

"Nor did I," said Miss Proulx.

"You don't happen to have a message about the crime from the deceased?" Yancey felt his neck grow warm under his collar as his boss arched an eyebrow at him. "Miss Proulx offers her services as a medium at the hotel."

"If only it were that simple. The world of spirit is not ours to command. If there is nothing further, I am feeling light-headed. Would it be possible for me to return to the hotel?" She batted her eyelashes at Chief Hurley and bit her lip.

"Allow me to escort you home." Chief Hurley crooked his

elbow and extended it to her. "Mr. MacPherson can surely give you any additional information you might need, Yancey."

"That'll be fine so long as I know where to find her if I need to question her further," Yancey said, tipping his hat. "You aren't thinking of leaving town unexpectedly, are you, Miss Proulx?"

"Despite Old Orchard's disturbing crime rate I do believe there are plenty of reasons for me to stay," Miss Proulx said. She and the chief slipped off through the fog, leaving Yancey unable to shake the notion he had been bested and hadn't even known he was playing a game.

"Quite a lovely lassie, that one," Mr. MacPherson said.

"She may be to some men's taste but I'd say trouble follows her like mud season follows snow melt." Before his companion could comment, Frank hailed him from across the beach. "I expect you have no plans to leave Old Orchard anytime soon, either, do you?" Yancey asked, pocketing his notebook.

"The season is already too short for my liking. I shan't make it even more so on purpose."

"You're free to head home, too. I'll call in at the hotel as soon as my business here is concluded." Yancey hurried to Frank's side.

"Lewis found this tucked into a pile of other metal bars." Frank held out a steel rod about three feet in length. Bits of sand clung to a patch of brownish-red discoloration near one end. Yancey took it and carried it to the body. He squatted next to the corpse and held the bar next to the wound.

"It's hard to tell by eyeballing it but I'd say this has a good chance of being the weapon." Yancey stood and handed the rod back to Frank. "We'll have to wait for an opinion from Dr. West, but it looks promising. Good work, Lewis." The young officer blushed and bobbed his head.

"If someone wanted to do away with this duffer they were taking a chance that there'd be something just lying around here to cosh him with."

"I don't know about that. The bar is construction material, and thousands of people have been through here ogling the pier project. Anyone could have known the pile of steel would be on site," Yancey said.

"I think we should keep an open mind about this one. It seems to me it could go either way."

"I am keeping an open mind. As a matter of fact it is so open I hate to tell you what has just occurred to me."

"What's that?"

"The bar was light enough and dense enough that I see no reason it couldn't have been swung by a woman."

"A woman? You can't mean that."

"You said to keep an open mind." Up ahead a man burdened with a load of camera equipment struggled down the boardwalk in their direction. "I'll leave you to sort out things here. I'm heading to the hotel."

CHAPTER TWENTY-TWO

Ruby, I've been looking for you. You haven't by any chance seen Mr. Stickney this morning, have you?" Honoria asked. "His wife is quite insistent that his bed has not been slept in."

"I think we should speak privately," I said, lowering my voice and glancing at Ben.

"Is there anything wrong?" Honoria reached out and grasped my hands in hers. "Are you hurt?"

"No. I'm fine, but I need to speak with you before the police arrive." Honoria nodded and led the way to the back stairs and hurried up them more quickly than I would have expected from even a woman as energetic as she. After locking the door behind us she gave me her full attention.

"I have seen Mr. Stickney. Mr. MacPherson and I came across him near the pier."

"Why the secrecy?"

"He's dead."

"Dead?"

"Quite dead. Mr. MacPherson and I are the ones who found his body and called the police."

"Did his death appear to be natural?"

"Not unless a large dent in the back of the skull can be considered natural." As much as I pride myself on a certain amount of pluck and a steel-lined stomach I really did feel light-headed as I pictured the bloody mess and clumps of sand surrounding Mr. Stickney's head.

"Oh my dear, how terrible." Honoria twisted a handkerchief around in her hands. "Orazelia told me Yancey was worried the pickpocketing in town was getting out of hand. He feared something like this might happen. That old fool Charles Hurley just pooh-poohed the notion of serious crime here in Old Orchard."

"It may not have been a pickpocket. From what Mr. MacPherson and I saw he had not been relieved of his valuables."

"Are you suggesting someone murdered him?"

"I'm afraid it is a possibility we must be prepared to consider."

"How terrible for his wife. And for his nephew."

"I'm not so sure his nephew will be sorry to hear the news. I accidentally overheard them having a very heated argument in the garden yesterday. I think we may need to tell that to Officer Yancey when he arrives."

"Ruby, we cannot discuss our guests' private affairs and conversations with anyone. It is simply not the way a hotel remains in business."

"I am not eager to discuss such a thing with the police myself, but have you considered how it may look to Officer Yancey when he discovers who Mr. Stickney was and the reason for his visit?"

"You mean Mr. Stickney's investigation into the practitioners at the hotel will cause suspicion to fall upon us?"

"That's exactly what I mean."

"That's easy enough to take care of." Honoria relaxed back

against the settee. "You shall simply have to hold a séance and ask Mr. Stickney who it is that did harm him."

"I don't think a séance will hold much sway with the police department."

"Nonsense. Yancey has known me since he was a small boy. He wouldn't think to disbelieve you."

"Honoria, he already warned me away from his family. He told me I was stirring up trouble and bad memories of the past and that if I didn't leave his mother and sister alone he would launch an investigation of me himself."

"Foolish boy." Blotches of color appeared on Honoria's throat. "This has got to be dealt with swiftly. If the hotel is embroiled in a scandal all the guests might decide to leave. Then where would we be?"

"Then we had better do a bit of poking around on our own before anyone decides to do just that."

YANCEY STOOD FOR A MOMENT ON THE PORCH OF THE HOTEL and gathered his strength. Honoria was a force of nature even when not worked up about something. The death of a guest at her hotel was bound to have riled her. It would be an Incident. Unless he was luckier than he had ever been before, she was going to try to use her "gifts" to help solve the crime. God help them all. Not that he believed in Him, either. Saying it was a reflex, like knocking on wood.

He peered through the glass in the front door. Ben was nowhere to be seen, but a very pale woman dressed entirely in black stood behind the reception desk, running her finger over a page in a large, leather-bound ledger. Her gaze shot up when the door creaked open. He heard a sharp intake of breath as she recognized his uniform.

"From your look, I take it I was not who you were expecting to see?" he asked.

"I meant no malice. It's just that I had an appointment scheduled with a guest for a sitting more than half an hour ago and he still hasn't arrived."

"You aren't waiting for Mr. Leander Stickney, by any chance?"

"I am, actually."

"I'm afraid he won't be keeping his appointment with you today." Yancey pulled out his notebook and pencil. "May I have your name please?"

"Cecelia MacPherson. What is this about?"

"Are you related to Everett MacPherson?"

"He's my husband."

"I might as well tell you since I'm sure Mr. MacPherson will tell you about it soon anyway." Yancey leaned in a little closer and lowered his voice. "Your husband found Mr. Stickney's body on the beach below the pier this morning."

"Body? Are you saying Mr. Stickney's dead?" she asked. Yancey watched as one of her slim hands began to tremble on the ledger. He was certain he had caught the barest flicker of relief just before she rearranged her face to show concern.

"Yes."

"Was it his heart?"

"I'm afraid I can't say at this time." Yancey lowered his voice as a young man with spectacles and an unruly flop of fair hair dragging over one eye approached the desk. "Could you tell me where I might find Mrs. Stickney?"

"She's a guest here at the hotel. As is her nephew, Mr. Dobbins."

Mrs. MacPherson turned and waved at the wilted-looking young man who hurried toward them. Yancey disliked him instantly. "Mr. Dobbins, this policeman wishes to speak with your aunt. Do you know where she may be found?"

"I hope more easily than my uncle. She's been asking for him all morning."

"Where is she, sir?" Yancey asked.

"I left her in the ladies' writing room just a moment ago. She sent me to ask if anyone has located my uncle yet."

"Will you go on ahead and tell Mrs. Stickney I would like a word with her. I'd appreciate it if you would remain with her during our interview." Mr. Dobbins swallowed hard, bobbing the large, knobby Adam's apple in his pale throat, and skittered off down the hall with a single worried backward glance.

Yancey turned to the desk again. "I think it is a safe bet that Mr. Stickney's is not the only appointment you should cancel for today. I'll be needing to speak with everyone in the hotel."

Chapter Twenty-three

"Mrs. Stickney, I am so sorry for your loss," Yancey said as he studied the newly minted widow as she sat opposite him in the parlor. He had been sorely tempted to send a lower-ranking officer to break the news to her. He dreaded the look he was sure he would see on Mrs. Stickney's face. The same one his mother had the night Chief Hurley delivered the news about his father's death. He was surprised to observe Mrs. Stickney looked far less stricken and bereft than his mother had. "I assure you we will do everything we can to discover who did this to your husband."

"He's in a better place, Officer." Mrs. Stickney offered a weak smile. "How I envy him. For now he is reunited with our dear little boy."

"I'm glad you're able to take comfort in that, Mrs. Stickney." Yancey didn't put any faith in such things himself but he could see how in times of distress the notion of an afterlife held appeal for others. "If you feel up to it I have some questions about your husband."

"Must you press my aunt now, Officer? Surely this could

wait?" Sanford Dobbins blinked at him through his spectacles as he leaned against the back of his aunt's chair, his slim hand drooping over her shoulder. Yancey imagined it to be unpleasantly moist.

"Of course he must ask now, Sanford," Mrs. Stickney said. "I consider it my duty to assist you with your inquiries but I cannot imagine what I could tell you about local criminals."

"I'm interested in your husband's movements over the last day or so."

"There is very little I can tell you, I'm afraid." Mrs. Stickney pursed her lips and Yancey wondered if she was considering not saying another word. "We spent little time together as a general rule and this trip was no exception."

"Let's start with something you might know. When did the three of you arrive at the Belden?"

"We didn't travel together. He arrived at the hotel yesterday. Sanford and I took a train the day before." Mr. Dobbins nodded in agreement.

"But you knew he had arrived?"

"Yes, he knocked on my door shortly before dinner to tell me he was here and that he had made appointments with several hotel practitioners. He also let me know he made other plans for dinner and would not be joining me. Is it any wonder I have come to depend so on my dear Sanford?" She reached up and squeezed his hand.

"And how about yourself, Mr. Dobbins? Did you see your uncle after he arrived?"

"I did not."

Yancey wished he could avoid the next question but there was no way in good conscience he could do so. "I don't wish to seem indelicate but I have to ask if you know how late he was out."

"I could not say." Mrs. Stickney flushed and dropped her gaze to her lap. "My husband and I have preferred separate bedrooms ever since our son died more than ten years ago."

"So you have no way to know if he returned to the hotel last night?"

"Our rooms are adjoining but I heard nothing from his. Usually, he does have the good grace to let me know he has returned at the end of the evening. Last night, he did not."

"Did you check on him this morning?"

"I did. I opened the connecting door between our rooms to remind him that he had an important appointment at ten and needed to be up and breakfasted before then."

"I assume he was not there?"

"Not only was he not, it was clear to me his bed had not been slept in. I was alarmed and went in search of Miss Belden to inquire if she had seen him that morning."

"And had she?"

"She said she had not seen him since before dinner yesterday evening. I left her making inquiries of her staff and went in search of Sanford to accompany me to breakfast." Mr. Dobbins nodded again.

"It's horrid to think we were enjoying toast and jam while Uncle Leander lay dead."

"Was Miss Belden able to ascertain the last time your husband had been seen by the staff?"

"I haven't spoken with her since."

Mrs. Stickney sagged against her chair. Despite her lack of

tears she had endured a shock. Yancey decided it best to hurry the interview along.

"I have only a couple more questions." Yancey slipped his hand into his jacket pocket and pulled out a leather drawstring pouch. He tugged it open and held the contents out for her to inspect. "Just as a matter of identification, is this your husband's watch?" Mrs. Stickney drew in her breath audibly and reached out her hand. She ran her fingers over the back of the watch and then down the chain.

"It certainly looks like his watch except for one thing." She looked into Yancey's eyes. "It's missing the fob."

"But you are sure the watch is his?"

"I am. I gave it to him myself as a gift."

"Can you describe the fob?"

"It was a miniature balance scale fashioned from gold. The pans on either side were set with a small pile of jewels. Amethysts on one and garnets on the other."

"Do you recall having seen it on his person when he left last night?"

"I did. He made a show of checking his watch quite pointedly when I mentioned how much I wanted him to accompany me to the dining room. He always fiddled with it when he found conversations to be unpleasant."

"And the fob was there then?"

"Yes, it was. His waistcoat buttons were straining against his girth and he kept plucking the fob from the gap between the top two. Most unbecoming. I told him he needed to either start a slimming regime or make an appointment with his tailor."

"So he could have been robbed?" Mr. Dobbins asked.

"It is one possibility we are investigating."

"Did you check his pockets when you found him?" Mr. Dobbins asked. "He always carried a billfold with some cash."

"His money was in his jacket pocket."

"What about his silver cigarette case?" Mrs. Stickney asked. "He never went anywhere without that in his coat pocket."

"We didn't find that amongst his possessions. Was there anything unusual about the case that might help us identify it if it turns up?"

"It was engraved 'To Stickler from Battler.' It was a gift from a school friend who was in the debate club with my husband. Those were their nicknames for each other."

"You mentioned Mr. Stickney had an appointment this morning," Yancey said. "Do you know with whom?"

"The astrologer, Mrs. MacPherson," Mrs. Stickney said. "And after lunch he was to have a sitting with Miss Proulx."

Yancey rose. "Thank you both for your time. You've been most helpful. I'll do my best to intrude on you as little as possible as the investigation proceeds."

OFFICER YANCEY, MIGHT YOU SPARE ME A MOMENT OF YOUR time?" Miss Howell stepped out from the doorway of the ladies' writing room with such exquisite timing Yancey could only assume she had lain in wait for him.

While Yancey did not consider himself the sort of man to attract enthusiastic hordes of unattached young ladies he did know when he was being pursued. Miss Howell definitely had a reason for seeking his company but he was not sure if it was for a personal matter or a professional one. He wasn't even sure which he would prefer.

After all, she was a pretty and well-spoken blonde with a pert nose and a fine figure. Although she would have to disavow the psychic nonsense to really turn his head. There were enough true believers in his family without looking to add to the problem. Miss Howell latched on to his arm and steered him down the hallway to a window seat that looked purposely built for cozy private chats. She lowered herself onto the firm cushion and pulled him down beside her with a surprisingly athletic grip.

"How can I be of assistance?" Yancey removed his notebook from his jacket pocket. Perhaps she would understand his interest was professional if he acted like one.

"Perhaps I should not speak up but my conscience and my commitment to my gifts would not allow me to remain silent concerning Mr. Stickney's death." Miss Howell looked like a cat about to lick the cream from her whiskers. "I hate to say anything disloyal about another member of staff, but keeping secrets is sure to interfere with the hotel's spiritual vibrations, which will undermine all that Honoria has worked so hard to achieve." Yancey never failed to be surprised at how quickly news spread about an investigation. By the end of the day he was willing to bet everyone in Old Orchard would have heard some version of what had happened.

"I understand you have the very best of intentions," Yancey said. "Getting to the truth about what happened to Mr. Stickney is in the interests of everyone concerned."

"If you really think I ought, I shall tell you all I know." Miss Howell leaned forward and lowered her voice. "Mr. Stickney was no ordinary guest."

"And what do you mean by that?"

"His wife had a sitting with me yesterday. She wanted me to read the energy of a toy soldier that had belonged to her son."

"How does this relate to Mr. Stickney's death?"

"I'm getting to that. I was able to tell her all about her little boy, the sorts of things he liked and how happy he was in the hereafter. She was so pleased with my help." Miss Howell cast her gaze to the floor. Yancey thought she was trying to appear modest but was unaware she was failing entirely.

"I'm sure she was extremely grateful."

"She was overjoyed to have found me and told me she was so relieved to know I was a practitioner with genuine gifts. And she would know."

"Is Mrs. Stickney an expert on such matters?"

"Her husband was. He was the president of the Northeastern Society for Psychical Research."

"Which is what, pray tell?"

"It's the foremost organization in New England for investigating the legitimacy of all manner of otherworldly phenomena and practices."

"Mrs. Stickney told you this?"

"She didn't have to tell me. Everyone in the spiritual community is familiar with the organization. Most would recognize Mr. Stickney's name. But she did tell me something else that I didn't already know."

"Which was?"

"Mr. Stickney had booked at the hotel with the sole intention of scrutinizing every practitioner in the establishment. He planned to devote his organization's entire fall quarterly magazine to his findings."

"So everyone else at the hotel was aware of the nature of Mr. Stickney's business?"

"That's my understanding. Mrs. Stickney said in case someone hadn't heard of him he made it a point of honor to alert practitioners of his aims. More often than not charlatans pulled up stakes and disappeared rather than face the scrutiny."

"And you think this has something to do with his death?"

"All I can say is that if I were in charge of this investigation I would look very carefully at Miss Proulx."

"Why would you single out Miss Proulx if he was scrutinizing all the practitioners?"

"Because fraudulent mediums were his particular specialty." Miss Howell lowered her voice even more. "I think she killed him before he had a chance to expose her. After all, who has more to lose than Miss Proulx or her aunt?"

Chapter Twenty-four

I HATED TO ADMIT IT BUT WHEN OFFICER YANCEY CAME DOWN the hall I started to perspire. And by perspire I mean I started to sweat like a roustabout hurrying to get the tents tied down before a storm. I considered trying to hide until he tired of searching for me but decided delaying the inevitable would just make things worse.

"Miss Proulx, I'd like a word with you," he said before taking me by the elbow with more gusto than I felt was strictly necessary. He steered me into the library, which he had commandeered as an outpost of the police station. "Have a seat."

"How nice of you to offer me comfort in my own home." In my experience, going on the offensive is often the best way to deal with men in general and policemen in particular.

"Your aunt, naturally, is eager to cooperate with the police in any way she can and has offered the library to me as a sort of sovereign territory. Like an embassy. I think you would be well served to consider yourself lucky that we are not having this conversation at the actual station."

"I'll keep that in mind."

"See that you do. Now, as there is much to do today, I will get straight to the point."

"Excellent. I shouldn't like you to have to spend any more time in my presence than strictly necessary." Officer Yancey had the good grace to drop his eyes to his notebook as two spots of color appeared on his clean-shaven cheeks.

"I was thinking of the need for urgency and for your inconvenience, Miss Proulx, not any personal distaste for your company."

"Whatever your motivations, you must be even busier than we are here at the hotel, so please begin."

"As you like. Can you think of any reason someone would murder Mr. Stickney?"

I knew in my heart of hearts that the truth about Mr. Stickney's occupation would come out, but I had been telling myself soothing lies ever since his bulging dead eyes had stared up at me from the beach. I'm an optimist, as are all true con artists, and a small part of me had hoped this would all stay hidden. I had been so busy trying to stay calm I hadn't even bothered to make up a story. I fought down the urge to burst out laughing. I had managed to avoid the police in connection with Johnny's death, and here I was being questioned about a murder I had not committed. It was a story so fantastical it would have been right at home as the plot of a dime novel.

I thought back to all the times I'd been in a tight spot before, and the best strategies involved either a stealthy escape or feigning ignorance and waiting to see if the fuss died down and a solution presented itself. After all she had done for me I couldn't run and leave Honoria looking as though her niece was guilty. Delay it would have to be.

"While I have been unfortunately acquainted with one of

your local pickpockets I cannot claim to be an expert on the Old Orchard criminal element. I certainly cannot speak to their motivations."

"I have good reason to believe Mr. Stickney was not killed by a robbery gone wrong."

"I have a hard time believing that. After all, everyone says pickpocketing is out of control here now that the pier is almost completed. I've heard Mrs. Doyle say that if something isn't done about them soon there will be more pickpockets on the beach than sand." I batted my eyelashes at him, but instead of flustering him he just exhaled forcibly through his nose and shook his head.

"Come now, Miss Proulx, if Mr. MacPherson really did locate him because he can find gold with his dowsing rods I'm sure you can see my point."

I was torn. I am willing to assume almost any role necessary to wriggle out of tight spots and to save my own skin. The only part I won't play is that of helpless female. Feigning ignorance of circumstances or facts was one thing. Appearing dull witted was quite another. In my experience men needed no more reason to assume women should not be allowed to vote, drive, or wear trousers.

"Of course. The gold watch was still on his person." I tipped my head to the side as if I were considering other possibilities. "But couldn't the thief have been scared off after he realized he had killed Mr. Stickney?"

"You think a brazen criminal would be so scared off he or she would leave a gold watch just lying there?"

"I can imagine circumstances where it might seem the wiser course."

"Indulge me and explain yourself."

"If he heard someone coming," I said, warming to the topic. "Or if he realized the watch were easy to identify. He might not be able to sell it without bringing suspicion of the crime down upon himself."

"You seem to have deep insight into the minds of criminals. Is there a reason for that?"

"Certainly not. It just seems to fit with human nature to run from the consequences of shameful actions. It is something any man would have been tempted to do."

"You sound well versed in shouldering guilty burdens, too, Miss Proulx." I felt my stomach grow cold and my heart thudded around in my chest. I was in over my head. And then the voice spoke in my ear.

"As do we all."

"There is no one that hasn't experience with that in some form. You, for instance, must have some sort of shadow in your past, something you wish to make right. Why else would you be a policeman?" I could tell from the flicker in his eyes my words had hit a tender spot. I just hoped it would send him packing instead of digging deeper into my history. Then, as quickly as his reaction came, it went, and he was collected and calm once more. But, more important, he redirected the questions.

"I am asking everyone connected with the hotel to share any information they might have as to Mr. Stickney's movements yesterday."

"I should have thought Mrs. Stickney would be the one to ask about that, not hotel staff."

"Mrs. Stickney reports not having seen her husband until he notified her he would not be at the hotel for dinner. So you can see we are interested in what information anyone else has to share."

Honoria had warned me about the consequences of indiscretion concerning the guests. I decided to trust her instincts and keep what I knew to myself. After all, nothing Officer Yancey had done up until this point had convinced me to abandon a lifelong habit of viewing the police as the enemy.

"Honoria introduced me to Mr. Stickney yesterday about midmorning. I didn't see him again after that."

"How convenient." Officer Yancey really was insufferable. Every moment I spent with him convinced me I was right to keep what I knew to myself.

"You make it sound as though I had arranged to avoid him. The hotel and all the obligations it entails kept me very busy throughout the day."

"You did, however, find time to pay a call on my sister, I hear." If anything, Officer Yancey's expression grew even grimmer.

"Lucinda invited me to visit her. I wasn't aware the social lives of adult women fell within the purview of the police. Or are things so very different in America than they are in Canada?" I cocked my head to the side and widened my eyes.

"Until this murderer is caught, everything is within the scope of my investigation. Every walk you take, every conversation you have, every snack you sneak from the kitchen in the night is worthy of my scrutiny."

"Does this rigorous attention apply to everyone or just to me?"

"Everyone in the hotel is being closely questioned but I think I should warn you information has come to light that could point the investigation in your direction."

"As I only met the man once, and briefly, I am surprised to hear it. What reason could I have to murder him?"

"I am well aware of the nature of Mr. Stickney's business and his real reasons for being here at the Belden. It was a remarkable stroke of luck for you that a psychical investigator should meet his death just hours before he commenced his investigation of you, don't you think?" With that, he flashed me a toothy smile and strode out of the room. I could not have stood if you had lit my chair on fire.

S EVERAL HOURS OF PLACATING THE WORRIED, CURIOUS GUESTS had taken its toll on the staff. I had just sunk into a chair in the hall to catch my breath when I heard a noise.

"Psst," said Mrs. Doyle from a doorway at the end of the corridor. "Follow me." She beckoned with a broad, red hand and scowl. I looked around, hoping she was motioning to someone else, but I found that I was alone. With all the speed of a small boy headed for a bath I made my way down the hall. She grasped me by the arm and pulled me into the small writing room reserved for the lady guests.

"I've just been speaking with my daughter, Sadie. She's married to a policeman, Frank Nichols." Mrs. Doyle sank into a chair placed beside an octagonal walnut table and drummed her fingers on its polished top. "Frank told Sadie that he thinks a pickpocket is responsible for Mr. Stickney's murder but Warren Yancey isn't convinced."

"I got that impression from the way Officer Yancey questioned me this morning," I said, sitting in the chair opposite her.

"If Yancey can be convinced a pickpocket is responsible he'll stop looking at the hotel. It's bad enough one of our guests was murdered without it looking like another guest might be responsible for doing him in."

"And?"

"And, you were the victim of a pickpocket the day you arrived." Mrs. Doyle leaned across the table and grasped my hand in both of hers. "If you were to go to Yancey and mention the murderous rage in his eyes when he grabbed your valuables it might go a long way to convincing Yancey that the thief has turned murderer."

"But I saw no such rage."

"I would not have taken you for someone to trouble herself over such small details."

"You want me to lie to Officer Yancey?" It was as if the entirety of the cosmos couldn't stand to see me go straight. No matter how I tried to pull myself away from lies and deceptions I kept finding myself pointed down the same disreputable path over and over again. "Even if I wanted to do such a thing, how could I possibly convince him to believe me?"

"The way lovely young women have always made men believe the things they say, by being charming."

"Officer Yancey does not find me charming in the least. As a matter of fact he ordered me to stay away from his mother and his sister." I paused to try to add to the indignant tone I hoped was in my voice. "He thinks I am making up my abilities as a medium and even suggested I am on his list of suspects. He wants me to have nothing further to do with his family."

"But you haven't listened, have you?" She gave me her customary scowling squint, and as always I felt exposed.

"Certainly not. It isn't for him to say with whom two grown women wish to associate."

"Excellent. Charm takes many forms, and what I've seen from Yancey is that his fancy tends to run toward independent-minded women. For all his fussing over his mother and sister he respects them. He would be less inclined to credit a thing you said if you turned tail and ran as soon as he suggested it."

"But how will I explain the fact I am coming forward with new information and changing my story at this late date? At the time of the incident I told him I had no recollection of the pick-pocket and could not describe him."

"Memory is a fickle thing. Especially if the victim has suffered a whack to the head. My great-uncle Dickson got on the wrong end of a horse's hoof and didn't know his own name for the better part of a year. We had to take turns watching him so he didn't wander off into the street and get into a tussle with four horse hooves instead of one. Then, one day, for no apparent reason, he was back to normal. Well, except for an aversion to boiled eggs. We never did figure that out."

"You really think going to the police will help?"

"I am so sure of it I've already sent a note to the police station alerting Yancey of your intention to visit this afternoon to tell him what you know."

"You did what?"

"You heard me. Now head up and change into something a bit more suited for paying calls and then stop in to the kitchen before you leave. I've a basket of gingerbread for Yancey. He can't resist it and will have much more trouble giving you a hard time once the smell of it is right in front of him."

CHAPTER TWENTY-FIVE

MISS PROULX PUSHED OPEN THE DOOR TO THE POLICE STA-
tion, bringing in the scent of the sea and something deli-
cious. It seemed to be coming from the towel-lined basket
grasped in her small hands. Yancey hadn't had time to eat since
before Leander Stickney's body was discovered. His stomach
gave a loud grumble, and Miss Proulx smiled at him and hurried
to his desk.

"It sounds as though I am right on time." She plunked the
basket right under Yancey's nose. "When Mrs. Doyle heard I was
coming here she asked me to deliver this to you. Gingerbread, I
think she said. It certainly smells like it." She peeled back the tea
towel to reveal moist, dense squares of cake with a glossy, dark
sheen to the tops.

Yancey leaned forward and breathed deeply. Mrs. Doyle knew
how much he loved gingerbread. He was quite certain there was
a reason behind her gift that he wouldn't be happy to discover.
Preserving a professional demeanor was the best way to deal with
Miss Proulx. His stomach betrayed him again with another rum-
ble. Her smile broadened and he lost his patience.

"Please convey my thanks to Mrs. Doyle. Now, if you could get on with the reason for your visit, I would appreciate it. I'm sure you haven't forgotten I'm in the middle of a murder investigation and you are a suspect."

"That's why I'm here."

"About the murder?"

"Not directly. I am here about the pickpocket who gifted me with this lump on my head the moment I stepped foot in Old Orchard." Miss Proulx winced dramatically as she reached up under her hat and appeared to touch her head.

"I thought you remembered nothing of the incident."

"Memory can be such a fickle thing."

"Unreliable, too, I often find. Especially in the case of some witnesses."

"Nonetheless, I felt it was my duty to alert you that mine has returned."

"You expect me to believe your memory has flooded back completely without explanation?"

"What reason would I have to lie about such a thing?"

"Perhaps to lead the investigation into Mr. Stickney's murder away from the Hotel Belden and down avenues which are more to your liking."

"I did not come here to be insulted. I am more than happy to take Mrs. Doyle's basket along to someone else who would appreciate it. Like that nice young man over there." She nodded toward Officer Lewis, whose uniform hung loosely on his slight frame. "He looks in need of some extra nourishment."

"Since you're already here, please share all that you have spontaneously remembered."

"It was a man who assaulted me."

"I know that, Miss Proulx, based on Henry Goodwin's testimony. He gave us a complete description of a short man with sandy hair, a pleasant expression, and bright blue eyes. You needn't have troubled yourself to come down here and tell me something I already knew." Yancey stood and reached his hand to the basket. "Now, if there is nothing else, I must return to my work."

"But that isn't at all what the man who assaulted me looked like."

"You are saying that your description does not tally with young Henry's?"

"Have you ever heard of a young woman bashing a stranger over the head with a parasol because his visage was so pleasant?" she asked. Yancey sat back down and reached for his pencil.

"I cannot say that I have," he said. "It was a unique experience."

"For myself as well, I can assure you. Now, what do you suppose could have provoked such a forceful response?"

"I could not possibly offer a scenario where a well-bred young woman would be moved to such an act." Yancey felt a twinge of something that might be guilt as Miss Proulx's face clouded over and threatened to storm.

Before she could respond, Chief Hurley and Jelly Roll emerged from the chief's office. Miss Proulx offered the chief a demure smile, then turned back to Yancey.

"Good manners have nothing to do with abject terror. The man who accosted me was a fearsome picture of wrath. His eyes were alight with a murderous rage and his grip upon my gown was so savage as to make me fear for the loss of things more valuable than a few coins and an old letter."

"So you think I should be on the lookout for a savage someone who gives the appearance of murderous rage?"

"I think you should be glad of any help the public is willing to provide since you haven't solved the murder of Mr. Stickney or the problems of pickpocketing in Old Orchard." At that, Jelly Roll whispered something to the chief, who nodded, then crossed the room to stand before Miss Proulx.

"Miss Proulx, please accept my apologies on behalf of my officer. The murder investigation has added to our burdens enormously and we are grateful for whatever help the public can provide." He turned to Officer Yancey. "Have you taken down a detailed description?"

"She hasn't given one that can be of value when out scouring the town for criminals. Unless you, sir, know what a murderous savage rage looks like."

"He was taller than I am and had dark hair. He wasn't well dressed but neither was he dirty. His clothes were just a bit shabby, really."

"Did you see his eye color?" Chief Hurley asked.

"I can't say that I remember that clearly but if I had to guess I would say brown, considering how dark his hair was."

"Did he speak to you when he accosted you?" the chief asked.

"No, he just stepped straight up to me and made a grab for my handbag. The look in his eyes was enough to start my teeth chattering." Miss Proulx looked straight at Chief Hurley and added a little lip wobble to give weight to her words. Yancey barely stifled a rude noise that could rightly be interpreted as disbelief. "I've never been so frightened in all my life." She widened her eyes so far Yancey worried they'd jump out of her head.

The chief tsk-tsked and turned to Yancey. "I've been telling you this pickpocketing situation was dangerous. I want you to make it a top priority. We can't have young ladies afraid to walk the streets of Old Orchard." Miss Proulx batted her eyelashes at the chief, and Yancey felt his jaw clenching so hard one of his teeth wiggled.

"Thank you for taking me seriously, sir. Since you seem to have the matter in hand, I'd best get back to the hotel. Things have been unsettled all day, as I'm sure you can imagine." Miss Proulx pointed at the basket. "Enjoy the treats and please give my regards to your mother and sister." With a dazzling smile for the chief and Jelly Roll, she turned to the door. Yancey's irritation grew as Officer Lewis hurried to open it for her.

The chief waved to Miss Proulx's retreating form and then turned a scowl on Yancey.

"I want you to get on this immediately. Nothing is more important."

"So you want me to set aside the murder investigation in order to look into the attack on Miss Proulx?"

"I'm not sure if you are being deliberately obtuse or if your intellect is truly unequal to the task of a police investigation. It should be clear to you that the pickpocket and the murderer are one and the same."

"Even if that were so, sir, there is very little to go on in finding the man Miss Proulx claims to have seen. Taller than herself, with dark hair and a workingman's wardrobe. How would you have me begin to find him in a town teeming with just such men?"

"You missed the crucial information, Yancey. Miss Proulx has told you exactly where to look."

"I am afraid I am at a loss, sir," Officer Yancey said, consulting his notebook.

"She said the man was a savage, filled with a murderous rage." Chief Hurley smiled at Yancey and he felt a shadow flicker across his heart. It was a smile that took pleasure in the suffering of others. "I suggest you get over to the Indian camp and make an arrest."

Chapter Twenty-six

EVEN WITH SO MUCH ON MY MIND IT WAS HARD NOT TO BE distracted by the roar of the sea and the happy clamor of the crowds as I made my way back to the hotel. All around me throngs of merrymakers and holiday visitors clogged the streets and slowed my passage. I was so taken with people watching and admiring the fashions and the frolicking I was oblivious to anyone calling my name until he was right beside me. Without warning, the sound of Mr. Ayers's voice filled my ear. Despite the warm sun on my face a shiver skittered across my scalp.

"Miss Proulx, how fortunate I feel to have come upon you so serendipitously." Mr. Ayers attempted to blind me with a radiant smile.

"We seem to encounter each other at regular intervals, do we not?" I hoped he could hear the sarcasm in my voice but if he had, he gave no indication of it.

"Since the fates conspire to bring us together, Miss Proulx, I'd like to turn this moment of privacy to our mutual benefit. If you will permit me to accompany you to your destination we might discuss a matter I have in mind along the way." Without waiting for a response, he placed his hand beneath my elbow and matched his pace to my own. Bending low, he said, "Smile, Miss Proulx. How can we speak freely if every person we pass stops to ask if you need to be rid of me?" I felt the pressure on my arm increase enough to be sure it was a threat and decided it best if I heard him out as far from the hotel as possible.

In the crowd there might be many eyes and ears but they would be far less likely to be trained on me than if we were inside the walls of the Belden. I forced a smile to my face and turned my head to look at him.

"I am not going very far, so you had best take advantage of my attention whilst it's available. What do you wish to say to me?"

"Wouldn't you like to hazard a guess?"

"I'm afraid I could not possibly do so."

"Certainly a smart girl such as yourself should have some inkling as to my intentions." When I didn't offer a guess he continued. "Very well, I'll just tell you, then, shall I?"

"I'm afraid you must. I have no appetite for guessing."

"No appetite perhaps, but certainly you have a gift for it. I wish to use your talent for persuasion to further my business interests."

"Talent for persuasion? I am still at a loss."

"Very well, allow me to be direct. I wish you to use your influence with the Velmont sisters. They are very wealthy and I want you to advise them during your séance sessions to invest in a venture in which I have a controlling interest."

"And why would I do a thing like that?"

"Come now, Miss Proulx. Or should I say Miss Prideaux or would you prefer Miss Palmer? Perhaps Miss Parker? Shall I go on?" He drew me closer and bent his mouth to my ear. "Your name may have changed but your face is the same from all the handbills and snake oil bottles that bear your image. Your father certainly was one for getting the word out about his little medical miracle worker, now, wasn't he?"

My heart clutched and thumped. My stomach thrashed. My ears buzzed and even my sense of smell felt off-kilter. As much as I did not desire Mr. Ayers to touch me, if he had chosen that moment to release my arm I believe I would have fainted dead away right there in the street. Still, there was no reason to think he knew about Johnny.

"Even if what you are saying about me is true, why would I risk the reputation of the hotel by conducting fraudulent readings?"

"Because I know why you left Canada in such a hurry."

"I can't imagine what you're talking about."

"Perhaps this will aid your memory." Mr. Ayers withdrew a small black book from his jacket pocket. "I do so like to put the time on a train to good use." He thumbed through the pages and, finding what he sought, ripped it out and handed it to me. "You can keep that as a reminder. I can always draw another from memory."

There, in smudged charcoal, were the scenes that haunted me every time I closed my eyes, every time I didn't deliberately crowd them from my thoughts. Johnny smiling, the Invigorizer strapped to his chest. My father urging me to action with an impatient wave. My own hand at the controls. My face clearly visible as I bent over Johnny's body sprawled upon the straw. Seeing the tragedy, there in black and white brought back such painful memories and made me all the more aware I hadn't been able to openly mourn Johnny's death. Still, it was a collection of drawings, not of photographs. There must still be room for doubt. I raised my eyebrows and pointed to the book.

"While I will say you are a talented artist I won't say this is proof of anything besides your unbridled imagination."

"You are a cool one, Miss Proulx, I'll give you that." Mr. Ayers smiled at me with something that looked like admiration. "If it's proof you want, it's proof you'll have." He riffled through the sketchbook and retrieved from between its pages a folded piece of paper. I was quite ashamed of myself for the way my hand trembled as I reached for it.

"More scribblings?" I asked.

"Of a sort. It's the bill of sale. I had arranged to deliver it to your father at the demonstration tent the morning of the murder." He smiled at me again, this time looking like a wolf baring its teeth. I unfolded the paper and looked it over carefully.

"This is a bill for over four hundred dollars."

"He did say he wanted them all."

"There's nothing to tie this to my father or to me."

"Your father really believed the Invigorizers were going to be the start of a whole new life for him," he said. "Take a look at whose signature is on the bottom, acknowledging receipt of the Invigorizers." He pointed to a flourishing scrawl at the bottom of the sheet. I recognized Father's style of handwriting in the signature but the name startled me. He had abandoned his self-imposed rules and truly had fallen for his own con.

"Ivory Proulx," I said.

"Yes. He signed it with his real name," Mr. Ayers said. "Did you happen to note the name of the purchaser listed at the top?" I forced myself to look where he indicated.

"Ruby Proulx." My upper lip beaded with sweat and I wasn't

sure if I felt more frightened or angry. "I never placed such an order."

"Your father felt it best to amend the original bill of sale. When I caught up with him hitching up his wagon and explained to him the price had doubled to ensure I kept what I had seen to myself, he mentioned you were the one with better prospects."

"He told you to come after me?"

"It was the only sensible thing to do. He convinced me that your wealthy aunt would be in a position to help you repay me." Mr. Ayers plucked the paper from my quaking hand and tucked it back into his pocket. "He said if I hurried I could catch the same train you would take to Old Orchard. That's exactly what I did."

"You make it all sound so easy."

"It was. Almost as easy as it would be to convince the police that someone like yourself, who has already killed once, is responsible for the death of Mr. Stickney. I think this paper and a telegram to New Brunswick would be all it would take to slip a noose over your lovely neck."

"So if I convince the Velmont sisters to invest in your sham company, the debt will be paid and you'll give me the invoice?"

"Precisely. You'll have ownership of the evidence tying you to Johnny's death and I'll have my money."

"Why do you think they'd listen to me about matters of finance?"

"I don't. But they will listen to advice from their dearly departed father flowing through you. If he were to tell them to invest in my company, they would certainly do so."

"And you think I would save my own skin by swindling two little old ladies?"

"I am certain of it. It is not as though you are a woman of scruples. After all, how many little old ladies did you sell your father's miracle cures to? How many did you encourage to seek relief in a bottle of empty promises rather than the advice of a doctor?" He released my arm and I stumbled backward and sagged against a tree trunk. "I see you need time to think. I'll say my good-byes and will await your decision." He tipped his hat in my direction and strode away.

CHAPTER TWENTY-SEVEN

OF ALL THE INFURIATING WOMEN HE HAD EVER MET, MISS
Proulx took the cake. Yancey was disgusted with Miss
Proulx for pointing her finger at the Indians. He would have expected more from Honoria's niece. After all, Honoria was so
broad-minded it made most people uncomfortable. Between her
talk of women's rights, equal opportunities for Negroes, and her
fascination with people from other cultures it seemed incredible
she could be nurturing a bigot to her outsize breast.

It just went to show how deeply such things ran. And that
people are more than their biology, their lineage. Which was the
only cheering thought wending its way through Yancey's mind as
he landed at the bottom of Old Orchard Street and turned left
onto East Grand Avenue.

Just ahead was a flat piece of ground used for time beyond
memory by the Indians who traveled down from Maritime Canada and points north in Maine to spend the summer, as had their
families for generations. According to the Indians Yancey knew,
their people had gathered on this stretch of sand ever since there
was a beach to gather upon.

Elders in the community credited the waters at Old Orchard with healing properties and made a point to bathe when it was warm enough to do so. Younger people seemed less inclined to believe in the power of the water but they did take benefit from the tourist trade. Some, like Nell, interacted with the vacationers by telling fortunes or selling medicines and cure-alls. Others put on shows of strength or shared stories, songs, and dancing. Not that all the stories, costumes, or dances were native to eastern Indian tribes.

Wild Bill's show had created assumptions amongst whites about what Indians were like, and the white people had no interest in the differences between Indian groups. Most of what was being demonstrated and displayed belonged west of the Mississippi, but that fact was of no concern to the audience and simply a matter of good business for the performers. Yancey wondered what the Indians he had known in the South Dakota Territory would have made of the mixed-up display spread out on this eastern shore.

Yancey turned left and entered the campground proper. Tents flapped in the steady breeze and a small girl barreled into him as he passed. He watched as the girl dashed away, chased by a boy just a bit smaller than she. They disappeared behind a line of tents, and Yancey stood alone with his memories of another little girl with dark glossy braids and a fleeting smile. Nothing he did seemed to ease that memory. Yancey steeled himself for the flood of emotion he knew would accompany his trip into the camp.

People all along the rows of tents looked up as he passed. Some waved out of recognition, some from a friendly nature, some not at all. But everyone saw him and noted his presence. His instincts told him this was a group braced for trouble. And why wouldn't it be? A white man had been found dead not a quarter of a mile from where they lived. Yancey would be hard pressed to think of anyone the rest of the town would rather be found guilty of the murder than the Indians.

Yancey stopped and asked a young man where he could find Nell. The man shook his head and hurried away. Yancey asked again, this time an older man with whom Yancey had once shared a walk along the beach at sunrise. The man smiled at him and escorted him to the front of Nell's tent. Without a door to knock upon Yancey decided the thing to do was to call out a greeting. Before he could raise his voice the tent flap lifted and Nell appeared in the gap.

"You're late."

"How did you know I was coming?" Yancey asked.

"You would not believe me if I told you. So we shall not waste our time. Are you coming in?" Nell held the flap open wider and beckoned with her free hand. Yancey hesitated and looked around. "Are you worried for your reputation, being seen with me?" she asked.

"No, I am concerned for yours."

"I've already invited you in—that should be enough to assure you I am unconcerned. Besides, I am certain you do not want all eyes and ears on what you wish to say." Yancey nodded and stepped into the tent. He looked at the small space and the simplicity of the interior and was struck by the contrast to the way his mother filled their home.

The tent was comfortable, cozy even, with a lightness that came from the spareness of the decor. Yancey felt he could breathe and breathe deeply, that there was no chance he would ensnare a lacy doily with the power of his lungs or knock over a china statuette if he moved too quickly. Nell gestured to a neatly folded stack of blankets and, after seeing Nell settle herself on another, Yancey sat.

"You are here about the dead white man."

"I'm here to ask about that and also about a pickpocketing incident that occurred recently. My chief thinks the two may be connected."

"What do you think I can tell you?"

"There's a witness who saw you passing close to the body at the time it was discovered."

"And so you come to ask if I am involved in what happened to this man?"

"No. I came to ask you if you saw anything or anyone strange as you passed by."

"You are not here to arrest me?"

"I am only here to ask you questions. With all the time you spend there, I consider you to be an expert on the beach. If anything were amiss you would have noticed it."

"Everything on the beach is now unusual."

"Unusual how?" Yancey leaned forward, hoping for some scrap of information that would turn the investigation away from the Indian camp and back toward Jelly Roll and the chief.

"Everything is disturbed by the building. Even the seagulls are skittish. The fog has been especially heavy and my eyes seem to play tricks on me at night when I am out walking."

"If you know something that could help catch who killed that man you should tell me."

"As I said, it was foggy. If I had seen a body anywhere I would have stopped. I can't say I would have run to tell the police. You know how they are." Nell smiled at him and let loose a deep laugh. "Most of them would have arrested me on the spot and then come for the men in my family, too."

"I wish I could contradict you, Nell, but you're probably right." Yancey paused and considered how to proceed with the next question. The real reason he had come to the camp.

"Why are you really here?"

"There are troubles brewing with the police. A young woman has made an accusation against a man who tried to grab her valuables a few days ago." Yancey pulled his notebook from his pocket and pretended to consult the words written upon it. He wanted to look official in some capacity and his emotions were threatening to overwhelm his good sense. "Her description of the man could easily be interpreted as an Indian man by someone eager to do so."

"This woman who accuses us, is she friend or family to Mr. Jellison?" Nell asked, her arms folded across her chest.

"Why do you ask that?" Yancey was curious as to what Nell heard that he had not. Jelly Roll had a finger in a great number of pies.

"Because he keeps walking through this camp like he owns it. He was here last week with another white man and they were discussing bathhouses and where they will put them once they finally get rid of us."

"Are you sure that is what they said?"

"Of course I am sure."

"Why were they not more secretive about their plans?"

"I believe they think we can't speak English so it didn't matter if they were overheard. Yes. They want us gone before the end of the season. Mr. Jellison doesn't think it is a good image for the town for us to live so close to the pier. He said we'd scare away the tourists," Nell said.

Yancey knew about Jelly Roll's plans but he was disgusted to learn that the man had been so bold about it. He also knew the answer to his next question but, still, he had to ask it.

"Do you know who the man was who was with him?"

"Everyone knows him. It was your boss, Chief Hurley," Nell said. "Now, I have told you things of value and you have not revealed the name of our accuser. Do you think she was sent by Mr. Jellison?"

"There's one way to find out. I'll go to the Sea Spray Hotel this evening and poke around, asking some questions about Mr. Jellison and whether or not he has a connection to the pickpocketing victim."

"Will you tell me who she is?"

"I'm not sure that is fair to the young woman."

"Is it fair that Indians are accused without reason or that we are considered to be of less worth than all the white newcomers to this beach?"

"No, Nell, it's not." Yancey looked at the woman sitting across from him. He thought once again of a little girl with a shy smile and thin brown arms. "The young woman is Honoria Belden's niece, Ruby Proulx. You met her on the beach a few days back."

"I remember this girl. She offered me a job."

"I'd think twice before accepting it."

"You think she means us harm?" Nell asked.

"I would not presume to have any idea what goes on in that girl's mind." Once again Yancey noticed a crescendo of frustration building in his chest at the thought of Miss Proulx and her outrageous disregard for his wishes or for convention. "But I am certain what my boss is thinking. He just wants someone to be arrested for the murder, the sooner, the better."

"And you think we will be blamed?"

"I think it likely unless I can discover that someone else is responsible for both crimes. But, you're the one who tells the future, not me."

"Give me your hand." Nell reached out her own.

"You know I have no use for such things," Yancey said. "Telling the future is impossible."

"What you believe is possible and what I know to be so is as wide a distance as the expanse of the sea. Give me your hand."

"Will it be faster to let you read my palm than to argue?"

"Undoubtedly." Yancey slid off the pile of blankets and moved within easy reach of Nell's grasp. She turned his palm upright with a practiced motion and began to trace the lines with a gentle finger.

"You have a strong lifeline and a deeply etched line of fate. And here, on the heart line, I see something most surprising." Despite himself, Yancey leaned in closer. "Do you see this star formation right here?" Nell touched a burst of lines placed part-way along a deep groove running up the center of Yancey's right hand.

"Yes."

"This star is seated at the intersection of your fate line and your heart line. It is a very uncommon mark." Nell picked up Yancey's left hand. "You have it here, too, which makes it all the more unusual."

"And you wish me to believe there is something significant about the strangeness of these grooves?"

"What I wish is not the point. And what is most strange is not the grooves but what else I saw."

"And what was that?"

"I just saw the same stars, in the same places, on another pair of hands very recently."

"I don't suppose you know the name of the person whose unusual lines match my own?"

"It would do you very little good if I didn't." Nell gave his hand a firm squeeze then released it. "I saw the very same thing in the hands of Honoria Belden's niece."

CHAPTER TWENTY-EIGHT

IT HAD TAKEN ME HOURS TO FALL ASLEEP. BETWEEN THOUGHTS of Johnny and worry over Mr. Ayers's threats I had tossed and turned all night. Worst of all was the cold realization that my father held me in even less regard than I had believed. By the time my eyes were growing heavy, the early morning sun slanted through the windows of my room. When I awoke hours later than usual I decided the best course of action was to do a little investigating on my own. After all, if Mr. Stickney's murderer was discovered Mr. Ayers would have less to hold over me. I dressed quickly and hurried downstairs.

SANFORD DOBBINS WAS ONE OF THOSE YOUNG MEN WHO NEVER seemed to arise before noon. It was easy to guess I could find him in the breakfast room cleaning up what little remained in the silver chafing dishes. I felt just a bit sorry for him as I surveyed his plate filled with dried-out clumps of scrambled egg and limply congealing bacon.

"Good day, Mr. Dobbins," I said, settling in a chair next to him. "I've been remiss in not yet offering my condolences on the passing of your uncle."

"How kind of you," Mr. Dobbins said.

"You and your aunt must be absolutely devastated by this sudden and tragic loss." In truth, Mr. Dobbins and Permilia Stickney had both appeared discontented and sullen before Mr. Stickney's death. If anything, they had both seemed a bit more animated since his demise.

"I don't know how we will go on without him," Mr. Dobbins said. "The loss to us personally and to the psychical society is incalculable." Mr. Dobbins was quite a showman. If I hadn't overheard his argument with his uncle I would have thought they were very close. "No one else has done as much to protect the public from fraudulent spiritual practitioners as he."

"From the brief conversation I had with your uncle I understood him to be a skeptic."

"My uncle joined the psychical research society not out of an interest in proving such things to be possible but to prove they most certainly were not."

"It sounds as though he was a man who might have had any number of mediums who would be happy to hear he had passed on."

"Not just mediums. He had it in for any psychic practitioners." Mr. Dobbins scowled as he bit into a piece of flaccid toast. "He never met a single one he didn't actively seek to discredit."

"It's a wonder no one did away with him before now."

"Old Mr. Velmont warned him a thing like this was likely to happen if he didn't develop a more open mind."

"Mr. Velmont? Was he related to the Misses Velmont who are staying here?"

"Certainly. He was their father. My uncle served under him as vice president of the society for about a year before he started haranguing and harassing him for being gullible and incompetent. He called him addled in one of the last society meetings Mr. Velmont attended."

"That seems quite cruel."

"He felt it was in the best interest of the society. He made a point to expose those practitioners Mr. Velmont had given the stamp of approval just to create doubt in the minds of the other society members. In the end Mr. Velmont was forced out and my uncle took over the presidency in his place."

"I should think discovering that the Velmont sisters were booked at the same hotel must have been awkward."

"Not for me or for Permilia. We both count the Velmonts as friends. If it bothered my uncle he never let on."

"How long ago did all of this take place?"

"About a year and a half ago. Uncle Leander joked about starting the New Year off on the right foot with a new president for the society. As matter of fact, during the society's annual New Year's Eve celebration he promised business would not be as usual in 1897. And it wasn't."

"How so?" If Mr. Dobbins felt I was being too inquisitive he gave no indication of it. But then, men are so often eager to do the talking with the slightest persuasion by a seemingly interested young lady.

"Mr. Velmont died within six months and it was openly mentioned by many people, his daughters included, that my uncle's actions had led to his broken spirit and ultimately his death. Those members of the society who were genuinely interested in proving psychic phenomena exist complained they felt unwelcome and

ridiculed. By the end of 1897 the society, myself being the exception, was made up solely of critics and debunkers."

"So there no longer existed a spirit of open-minded inquiry?"

"I was the only one left and I assure you, since I needed the
job as my uncle's secretary, I kept my opinions to myself when I
was with him."

"Did your aunt know you felt different?"

"My aunt and I are very close. She understood and respected
my reserve. As I'm sure you'll agree, life does require one to have
a few secrets." Mr. Dobbins dabbed at his sparse mustache and
dropped his napkin into his plate. As I watched him leave I
couldn't help but wonder if the secret of the killer's identity was
one of the things he and his aunt shared.

I THOUGHT LONG AND HARD ABOUT APPROACHING CECELIA. SHE
had been kind to me and I hated to repay that with suspicion.
But with the cloud hanging over the hotel and myself in particular, I felt I had no choice. Perhaps I could find a way to broach the
subject without seeming too accusatory.

Cecelia stood on the beach a ways down from the hotel, looking out over the ocean, while her fluffy little dog, Bisbee, occupied
himself by digging a hole at her side. Cecelia was so engrossed in
her thoughts that when I called her name she jumped.

"I'm sorry to have disturbed you. Would you prefer that I leave
you with your thoughts?" I asked.

"You are welcome to stay. I could use the company." She
turned to me and gave a halfhearted smile. I crouched down next
to Bisbee and looked into the hole. What could be so interesting
down there? "Besides Bisbee, I mean."

"I thought that dogs were supposed to be good company," I said. "Not that I've ever had one."

"Never?"

"No, never. My father thought they carried disease and wouldn't allow it." And he was never sure if there would be food enough for us, let alone a dog.

"Bisbee is often good company. One of the best things about him is that he never has any opinions about what I have to say. I can tell him anything and he loves me just the same."

"Unconditional love. That sounds nice."

"It is. I highly recommend getting a dog of your own," Cecelia said. I stood and opened my parasol over my head.

"Perhaps I will be so fortunate one day," I said. "This seems to be a good place to think."

"The hotel feels a bit small at present."

"Mr. Stickney's death has cast a pall over the hotel. I hope it doesn't ruin the season for Honoria. And for the rest of you," I said. Cecelia let out a burst of laughter and shook her head. "Or would it be safe to say that your summer will improve now that he's no longer a part of it?"

"Why would you say that?" She turned to me, this time without the smile or the laugh.

"I heard you arguing with Mr. Stickney on the veranda the evening before he died."

"What are you talking about?" She squinted at me but I think she did so in order to scrutinize my face rather than because of the sun.

"I was hiding in the library reading and your voices came in through the French doors." I felt my face flush, and not because of the heat reflecting from the sand. "I didn't mean to eavesdrop.

I was just really enjoying my book and I didn't want to be disturbed. By the time it was clear you had settled in for a private conversation it had become too awkward to make myself known."

"I'm sorry we put you in that position. I suppose I should explain."

"I'd feel a lot better if you did," I said. "I like both you and Mr. MacPherson and I'd hate to have a shadow on our friendship."

"Walk with me, then, and I'll tell you all about it." Cecelia linked her arm in mine and set off in the opposite direction of the pier, toward Camp Ellis. Bisbee ceased his excavations and trotted alongside as soon as his mistress moved. "The things I am going to tell you, I hope you will keep in confidence."

"I cannot promise to do anything that will compromise the hotel or my aunt."

"I think you can be sure what I will reveal will in no way enhance the hotel's reputation should it become common knowledge." Cecelia looked around and, seeing no other strollers near enough to overhear, continued. "Mr. Stickney and I were acquainted five years ago, before my association with the Belden."

"I understood as much from what I overheard. He seemed to have had a hand in some misfortune that had come your way."

"At the time it felt like everyone and everything was wrapped up in misfortunes and misadventures."

"You said five years ago. Does this have anything to do with the Panic?"

"It had everything to do with the Panic. My family lost everything when the economy collapsed. My father's family had been in banking for several generations but his was one of the hundreds of banks that closed. His heart had been bad for years and it couldn't take the shock. When my late husband realized the situation we were in he stepped in front of a train and left me to find my own way in the world."

"How terrible."

"Even though I knew from the start he'd married me for my money and family connections it was still a shock."

"But how does this relate to Mr. Stickney?"

"As I said, I was desperate. People were out on the street, standing in bread lines. I had to find a way to support myself and I had no intention of doing so by marrying again if I could think of any other way." Cecelia grimaced. "Then I thought of the medium my mother used to consult."

"You decided to set yourself up as one, too?"

"I did. It was remarkably easy to say the right things, especially to society ladies."

"You researched them?"

"I had been amongst their type all my life and found it quite simple to dole out the sort of information they really wanted to hear."

"And Mr. Stickney investigated you?"

"He did. I made the mistake of adding props to my sittings and he exposed me as a fraud."

"What sort of props?"

"I added the usual knockings and rappings on the table but I specialized in apportments."

"Apportments?"

"With your own abilities I would have thought you would be an expert."

"I hear voices and sometimes I use tarot cards to help me translate the messages. That's the extent of what I do."

"Materialized objects, that's what apportments are. They appear out of nowhere and have the greatest impact if they have some sort of association with the deceased the sitter is trying to contact."

"But they weren't real?"

"They were real objects but they didn't appear from the other side." Cecelia stopped walking and turned to face me. "They dangled from fine threads in the gloom above the table."

"How did you manage such a thing?"

"I had a partner in crime. My personal maid was as much a victim of the situation as I was so I suggested we stick together."

"So you were the face on the scam and she worked behind the scenes running the threads and following the cues?"

"Exactly. You sound like you know more about how such things work than I would have imagined." Cecelia stopped and gave me her full attention.

"I must have read something similar in a dime novel."

"I see." Cecelia kept her eyes fixed on my face. I turned the subject back to her and reminded myself not to open my mouth so wide in future.

"But Mr. Stickney was not so easily convinced as other sitters?"

"No, he wasn't. He told me he was eager to contact his dearly beloved mother. Our appointments ran along the usual lines and I suspected nothing."

"So he met with you on several occasions?"

"That is the best way to make money in this game. You start out with enough proof that contact has been made but never give out all the information at once. Then they have to come back."

"And you get an idea by spending time with them of what the deceased was like?"

"Clever girl." She gave me another curious glance. "Yes, but after some time the client gets restless and you need to provide them with an increasingly dramatic show."

"And that's where the apportments come in?"

"My assistant, Emily, would lower the items on cue. A single daisy led to our undoing." Cecelia shook her head. "It was the color blindness that did it."

"Color blindness?"

"It had been something of a joke for the two of us when she was my maid. Emily couldn't tell red from green. She was forever laying out the wrong hat to go with a gown or a mismatched pair of gloves."

"And this impediment led to a crisis with a daisy?"

"Since the room would be dark except for the glow from the candle at the center of the table it was easy enough to fasten items to the end of a length of thread and to direct it over the table using a fishing pole. Emily manned the pole, and after the apportment made the rounds in front of the astonished sitters I would pluck it from the air and place it on the table for inspection. It worked like a charm."

"Until the daisy?"

"Yes. Emily grabbed a spool of red thread from the sewing basket instead of a green one to attach the flower stem to the fishing rod. When I reached up to remove it a bit of a red thread tail remained on the stem. I didn't notice it but even in the low light Mr. Stickney did."

"Did he threaten to turn you in to the authorities?"

"He told me to immediately cease my mediumistic pursuits." Cecelia surprised me by rooting around in her sleeve and fishing out a lace-trimmed hankie. She dabbed at her eyes before continuing, and I had no trouble believing her show of emotion was not a performance. "He remarked that my circumstances must indeed be desperate if I was willing to debase myself in such a way for so little sure reward. He offered to not expose me and to allow me to continue my business if I agreed to take him on as my client for far more debasing activities to be performed in darkened rooms."

I felt my stomach churn. There had been many times when Father had spent all our earnings on strong spirits or poorly considered schemes. I was always very uneasy in my mind at those times when I had spotted my father whispering with the man who ran the grubby tent at the far edges of the show. I hardly dared let myself consider what sort of bargain Father might have been trying to strike.

"From the conversation I overheard I can only assume you decided to no longer ply your trade as a channel?"

"I gave it up immediately and left Boston. I've never been back. Fortunately, I met my dear Everett not long after. He encouraged my interest in astrology and I have made a decent living from it ever since."

"Does he know about your encounter with Mr. Stickney?"

"He knows nothing of my troubles or of my time as a medium. It only lasted a few short months and I thought it best forgotten. I have the feeling you might understand the desire for a fresh start."

"Perhaps. What happened to Emily?"

"Emily and I parted ways. I could not convince her to accompany me and we completely lost track of each other after that."

"You do know it looks suspicious that Mr. Stickney died after threatening to expose you to your husband?"

"I understand but I didn't kill him."

"Do you have an alibi?"

"I do but I would rather not say."

"And I would rather that it can be proved that no one from the hotel was involved in the murder of a guest. You can see how that is likely to damage the business."

"I am thinking of the hotel's reputation. I'd still rather not say."

"Then I am afraid I will have to mention what I overheard to Officer Yancey."

"Wouldn't that hurt the hotel and your aunt?"

"It would, but if it would end the speculation as quickly as possible then I think it's the lesser of two evils." Cecelia bent over to pat Bisbee. I think it was to stall and consider her options.

"That man has brought me nothing but bad options and grief."

"If you tell me where you were last night perhaps this will be the last time he troubles you."

"I was at the Sea Spray Hotel next door. I didn't want Honoria to feel I was being disloyal."

"What were you doing there that you couldn't do at the Belden?"

"Despite his public reputation as a temperance man, Mr. Jellison's hotel is one of the few places in town where you can go dancing and order a drink, too."

"How do you think Mr. Jellison is getting his supplies?"

"I can't say that is something I know about but I've heard rumors about stills in the area and also liquor being brought down from Canada. I expect he doesn't have much trouble."

"Isn't anyone worried about being caught?"

"Not really, from a legal standpoint. Most people simply end up paying a fine. Jellison has his reputation to lose so he's more cautious than most."

"Facing the wrath of Honoria and a fine at the courthouse is a lot less worrisome than staring at a murder charge," I said.

"I think I might rather take my chances with the police than with Honoria."

"Is there anyone who can vouch for you being there?"

"Mr. MacPherson was with me."

"As much as I think he's an honest man, I think he's likely an even more loyal husband. Is there anyone else who might remember you being there?"

"Mr. Jellison would remember."

"Why would he remember you?"

"Everett made a bit of a fuss. He was asked to leave and to not return. It was all very embarrassing." I was shocked to hear it. Mr. MacPherson was such a mild-mannered man.

"What could he have done to provoke such a request?" I asked.

"He felt Mr. Jellison was speaking to me in an overly familiar manner. I'm afraid Everett's only real fault is his jealousy."

"He caused enough of a scene to be thrown out?"

"I am sorry to say it was very embarrassing and I felt utterly humiliated. He actually started shouting and if I hadn't stepped in and calmed him down I believe he would have struck Mr. Jellison." Bisbee strained at his leash and stopped just short of a rivulet of water running to meet the sea. "Goosefare Brook. This is as far as Bisbee and I go unless the tide is at its lowest point."

I made my excuses and watched as they walked back toward the hotel. Only the sound of the train drew my attention as I stood wondering if Cecelia's **secret** past was really a secret or if her jealous husband had felt the need to turn his rage on Mr. Stickney. After all, if he was angered when a man simply complimented his wife, how would he behave if he knew someone had made such outrageous overtures to her? As much as I didn't want it to be him, there seemed good reason to worry that pleasant Mr. MacPherson might be more complicated than he seemed.

Chapter Twenty-nine

I HAD PLENTY TO THINK ABOUT AS I WALKED BACK ALONG THE beach. In addition to the murder investigation and Mr. Ayers's threats, there were still the practicalities of running a hotel to consider. Up ahead a familiar figure squatted on the sand next to a young woman dressed in a bathing costume. I waited until Nell released the girl's hand and collected her fee before approaching her.

"Hello, Nell. I was surprised not to see you at the hotel this morning. Was there some confusion about the date you would start?"

Nell stared at me, then turned her back and started to walk away. I hurried to catch up and tried again.

"Have I done something to offend you?"

"Yes." Nell turned to face me and stuck her fists on her hips. I searched my memory for where I had gone wrong. My first foray into employee management was not likely to impress Honoria. If she meant what she had said about me learning the ropes in order to take over myself one day, clearly I had a long way to go.

"I'm happy to apologize if you tell me what I've done."

"You think an apology will make up for telling the police you were assaulted by an Indian?"

"I did no such thing."

"I've been told different."

"The only thing I've said about you to the police was the day we met on the beach when I told Officer Yancey that horrible woman with the parasol was completely unprovoked. I never said I was attacked by an Indian." I was flummoxed. My statement at the station the day before had not indicated any such thing.

"Officer Yancey said you accused an Indian man of trying to rob you."

"Officer Yancey told you that?"

"He did."

"Nell, I don't know how to convince you, but my words were misinterpreted." I held her gaze with mine. "Officer Yancey and I are not on good terms. He may have told you those things to turn you against me."

"Yancey would not lie to me. He believed what he said was true."

"Is there nothing I can do to make you believe me?"

"If Yancey comes to me to say you have told him it was not an Indian man who attacked you then I will accept the position at the Belden. But until then, I do not wish to associate with you."

As soon as I returned from my walk with Cecelia, I searched the hotel for Honoria, in order to share what I had learned. I found her in the parlor rearranging needlepoint pillows on the tufted settee.

"Why didn't you tell me about the conversation between Mr. Stickney and Cecelia right away?" Honoria asked.

"You had enough worries without wondering, with cause, if one of the staff in your employ was involved. I decided to look into it further before adding to your burdens."

"You are such a treasure, my dear. How do you propose to verify Cecelia's alibi for the time of the murder?"

"I'll go to the Sea Spray Hotel tonight and ask the staff and if need be, Mr. Jellison himself," I said with a lot more confidence than I felt.

"I cannot possibly accompany you," Honoria said. "We shall have to find someone else."

"I should have thought you would be the ideal person to chaperone me to a neighboring hotel."

"I'm afraid Mr. Jellison and I have quite a history of antagonism. I vowed long ago I would never set foot in his establishment and I intend to keep my word." Honoria was visibly quaking with indignation. "Are you quite certain there is no other way to pursue your investigations?"

"None that I can think of. Is there anything I should know about the feud between yourself and Mr. Jellison before I enter the lion's den?"

"Only that he has coveted my property for all the years I've owned it. He offered to buy me out as soon as your grandparents died and it was left to me. He was more than insulting when I refused."

"Why would he insult you?"

"He believes women to be incapable of running a business and even went so far as to say he felt we should not be allowed to own property. He said that to me in front of my own guests and then had the audacity to propose marriage as a remedy for my incompetence." Honoria flicked a fan back and forth in front of her face but even her vigorous movements of the thin silk didn't seem equal to the task of cooling her temper. Her cheeks displayed a bright spot high on each, and a crimson stain spread down her throat and across her wide expanse of bosom. If she were older I would have worried for her heart.

"I can see why you wish to avoid him."

"I had no inclination to marry before his proposal, not after seeing what happened to my sister." Honoria paused and clucked her tongue. "No offense, my dear."

"None taken."

"But Mr. Jellison cemented my resolve never to do so. I determined to make my own way in business and in life. But even after all these years I feel him circling and scheming. He still wants the Belden and is just waiting for me to lose it to the bank so he can buy it on the cheap, knock it down, and add more rooms to his existing hotel."

"Where did you hear a thing like that?" I asked.

"Mrs. Doyle's son-in-law overheard Mr. Jellison and Chief Hurley discussing his plans. Jellison said he didn't believe I'll last the season."

"Did the chief agree with him?"

"Apparently so." Honoria exhaled forcibly.

"Are Mr. Jellison and the chief close associates?"

"They're family. After I refused his proposal Mr. Jellison soon after made an offer of marriage to Chief Hurley's sister. She accepted, making them brothers-in-law."

Suddenly, an idea occurred to me. "Did this conversation take place before or after Mr. Stickney's murder?" I asked.

"A few days before. Why would that be important?"

"What better way to ensure your hotel failed than to arrange for a guest to be murdered?" Honoria looked at me with widened eyes.

"Do you think he would go that far to acquire the Belden?"

"You know him far better than I. What's your feeling?"

"I wouldn't put anything past him."

"Then it's more important than ever that I go to the Sea Spray and verify Cecelia's alibi."

"You cannot possibly go there alone. Perhaps I should ask Lucy and Yancey to accompany you."

"I hardly think staff at a hotel serving illegal spirits are likely to be forthcoming in front of a police officer."

"You're right, my dear. But we can still ask Lucy. Now all you need is a gentleman to accompany you both." At the doorway I heard a discreet throat clearing.

"Perhaps I could be of assistance?" said Mr. Ayers. "It would be my distinct pleasure to escort Miss Proulx anywhere she would wish to go."

"How kind of you to offer, Mr. Ayers. We would be delighted to accept your offer, wouldn't we, Ruby?"

"Find an excuse." The voice practically shouted in my left ear. But nothing whatsoever came to mind. With a heavy feeling I could only force an insincere smile to my face and mutely nod.

"That's settled, then. I'll just ring the Yanceys and invite Lucy."

NOT ONLY WAS LUCY EAGER TO ACCEPT HONORIA'S INVITA-tion, she arrived only a short time later carrying a large white carton tied up with string. Ben relieved her of it as soon as she stumbled through the door.

"Would you make sure this ends up in Miss Proulx's room?" she asked, holding out the box. He nodded and slipped silently up the stairs, carrying the parcel himself.

"What is it?" I asked.

"Come and see," she said, tugging me by the hand as we followed in Ben's wake.

We mounted the stairs, tripping and giggling. Mrs. Doyle appeared at the bottom and scowled up at us, I assumed on account of all the noise. But she didn't scold us, so we grew even sillier and noisier as we rounded the bend in the staircase at the first landing. By the time we arrived at my door we were both breathless and I had almost forgotten to dread the evening ahead with Mr. Ayers.

The box sat on the bed, and Lucy flung herself down beside it.

"What a wonderful room. It's like a tree house."

"I've been trying to think just what this reminded me of. Like being in the book *The Swiss Family Robinson*."

"Only far more luxurious." Lucy ran her hand over the coverlet. "I've been in and out of this hotel all my life but I've never been in here before."

"How did you know where it was?"

"Because I'm nosy, silly. Whenever we visited as children, Yancey and I would sneak all over the hotel, opening doors and looking inside the rooms. This one was always locked. When I asked Mother about it she said we mustn't ever try to sneak in here because it was being saved for Delphinia's return."

"Honoria told me it had been kept just as my mother left it."

"I'm glad it was. The only thing I would possibly consider changing is the clothing in the wardrobe. Do you have any scissors?" Lucy plucked at the string on the box. I went to the vanity and opened the top drawer. As I looked in I heard the voice whispering in my ear.

"Is all as it should be?"

I couldn't say why exactly, but I had the sense that the gloves and hair ribbons were not exactly as I had left them. Try as I might I couldn't be sure. I retrieved the scissors before Lucy could ask if something were amiss. I had no desire to change the tenor of our visit.

With a deft snip she sliced through the string, then lifted the lid. The sea breeze ruffled folds of tissue paper and I caught a glimpse of deep amethyst silk. Lucy held back the rustling sheets.

"Go on. Lift it out," she said. My hands trembled at the smooth, cool feel of it as I raised one of my mother's gowns and held it against my body.

"I don't know what to say."

"Say you'll try it on this instant," Lucy said. She jumped up and began to undo the hooks at the back of the gown I was wearing. "I'll play lady's maid, shall I?" Before I could say anything at all she had the old gown off me and the newly made-over one spread out for me to step into. As I slid the smooth drape of it up over my arms I felt like bursting into tears. It was too much.

"I cannot believe your mother could make such a drastic change in so little time." I twirled to and fro in front of the long mirror set into the wardrobe. "She's a miracle worker."

"She'll be delighted to hear you are so pleased with it. It looks as though it was made just for you."

"It makes me almost look forward to this evening." I spoke without thinking, and realizing how rude that must sound I clapped a hand over my mouth.

"Is it my company?" Lucy's tone was light but her eyes looked sad. It occurred to me she had perhaps wanted a friend as much as I.

"I assure you, it is not." I sat on the bed, hoping I wasn't crushing the gown, and motioned for her to join me. "May I confide in you?"

"That sounds serious," Lucy said. The twinkle was back in her eyes and I knew I had done right to risk sharing a bit of my worry with her, even though I wasn't being entirely truthful about my relationship with Mr. Ayers.

"Honoria accepted Mr. Ayers's offer to accompany us without asking if I wished to encourage his attentions."

"And you do not."

"There is no one I would rather encourage less."

"Is he making determined forays in your direction?" Lucy's voice dropped to a conspiratorial whisper.

"Unceasingly. But I feel I mustn't offend a guest in my aunt's hotel." I sighed. "I am in quite a predicament and I fear something as social as dancing might serve to fan the flames of his intentions."

"Leave him to me. I will make it my mission to keep him so occupied all evening he hasn't the time to disturb you."

"You would do that for me?"

"Of course I would, silly. What are friends for?"

Chapter Thirty

The moment we entered the Sea Spray I tucked my hand in the crook of Lucinda's arm and hinted to Mr. Ayers that we needed to withdraw to the ladies' washroom. As soon as we were out of earshot I explained myself.

"Lucy, could I trouble you to distract Mr. Ayers now?" I asked. "I don't want to spend any more time with him than absolutely necessary."

"Leave it to me." I watched with admiration as Lucy flicked open her fan, then swayed off toward the ballroom. With no idea how long I had to get on with my investigation I flagged down a passing waiter and asked where I might find Mr. Jellison. He pointed me toward the far end of the ballroom.

"He's always somewhere on the dance floor. Mr. Jellison has an eye for the ladies and he never misses an opportunity to take a twirl with a pretty one." I thanked him and made my way to the ballroom, glancing over my shoulder now and again for Mr. Ayers.

As much as it felt disloyal to admit it, even in the privacy of my own mind, I could understand why Honoria was worried about competing with the larger hotels. The Sea Spray was simply magnificent. From the sparkling crystal chandeliers bejeweling the ballroom ceiling to the gilded moldings and the ornately carved columns, the effect was opulent and enchanting. The sound of the orchestra filled my ears and the swirling skirts of the dancers took my breath away.

Ever since arriving at the Belden I had counted myself lucky to have skimmed and slid past any social ineptitudes. I had survived the terrors of the dining room and had conducted myself admirably despite a perplexing array of cutlery and stemware. I had navigated the culture of séances and had even made inroads into the world of fashion with Lucinda's help.

Still, I was not prepared for dancing. There had simply been no opportunities to learn on the road with the medicine shows. Well, at least not the sorts of ballroom dances everyone in the Sea Spray seemed to have mastered. I doubted a jig to a rousing fiddle tune would be on the slate that evening. My confidence fled and my steps faltered. I knew I had to locate Mr. Jellison if I wanted to ask him about Cecelia's alibi but the desire to hide and to search for him from the shadows was overwhelming.

I hugged the wall of the ballroom and to my relief noticed a potted palm that promised to provide the perfect cover. I stepped behind it and settled in to search for Mr. Jellison in safety. Between the flash of the dancers, I thought I spotted my quarry. A bald man in a violently plaid jacket stood with his back to me in the center of the room. But before I decided how best to approach him, Mr. Ayers and Lucinda twirled past only inches from the palm. I ducked back, sure I had not been discovered until I heard an unwelcome voice calling my name.

• • •

The band broke into another tune, and as partners switched and spun Yancey caught sight of Miss Proulx. She stood in the corner by a potted palm, more of her hidden behind it than not. If he weren't so sure she was up to no good, Yancey would have been convinced she felt shy and overwhelmed by the crowd.

But that couldn't possibly be the case. A more forthright and obstinately independent young woman he had never met. Even his sister, Lucy, paled in comparison with Miss Proulx and her self-sufficient nature. Surely, a social gathering like a dance held no terrors for her.

Certainly, she couldn't be worried about her appearance. Yancey knew his mother and Lucy had taken great pleasure in beginning to make over Delphinia's wardrobe, bringing it up to date. He wished they hadn't done such a good job with the gown she was wearing. She looked even more infuriatingly lovely than ever. Before he could talk himself out of it, Yancey picked his way through the crowd.

"Good evening, Miss Proulx. Are the gentlemen here so little to your liking that you prefer the company of the botanical specimens?" Yancey asked. Miss Proulx's already-impeccable posture grew even more rigid at the sound of his voice. If he didn't know better Yancey would have said she was frightened.

"I find the company of this palm particularly soothing." Despite their earlier unpleasantness Yancey felt an uncomfortable thump in his chest as he realized she looked unhappy to see him. Why should he care about the opinion of a strange girl with a dubious past?

"But a plant hasn't the ability to ask you to dance, Miss Proulx."

"Precisely." Yancey couldn't be sure, on account of all the noise, but he thought he detected a quaver in Miss Proulx's voice.

"Is your dance card so full you seek respite by hiding?"

"I'm afraid that is not it. If you must know, this is my very first dance and I simply don't know how it's done." A faint blush touched Miss Proulx's cheeks, giving an even more appealing glow to her face. If Yancey didn't know better he would think she was telling the truth and was in fact sharing an embarrassing piece of information with him.

"Then I would be honored to teach you. May I have this dance?" Yancey held out his hand and gave a slight bow. With no thought to the answer he stepped forward and pulled Miss Proulx from her hiding place. With a deft hand he drew her to the edge of the dance floor and proceeded to step backward with a surety he did not know he possessed.

"I don't recall accepting your offer," Miss Proulx said, appearing flustered. Yancey thought it suited her far better than her usual competent control. He adjusted his hold on Miss Proulx's back and steered her farther into the center of the room. For reasons he didn't wish to consider he felt eager to be seen guiding her about the floor.

"I'm not surprised, considering the problems you have with your memory. Maybe it will come back to you, like the description of the pickpocket." He felt her hand tense in his own and a flicker of worry flitted across her face. He had spent enough time with people with a guilty conscience to know she was hiding something. "Now, let's speak of more congenial things."

"Such as?"

"Your lovely gown and the handsome pendant you are wearing. Both seem familiar somehow." Yancey assumed he was on safe ground. His mother and Lucy seemed to chatter endlessly on the subject of fashion.

"That's because this gown has been hanging in your dining room for the last several days as your mother altered it for me. The necklace is one I expect you have seen in a portrait of my mother." A hint of what looked like a genuine smile touched Miss Proulx's lips. "Honoria said it has been passed down through the women in my family for generations."

"It must mean a great deal to you, then." Yancey nodded toward his waist. "I have my father's pocket watch and there's nothing I would trade for it."

"I see we understand each other. At least concerning heirlooms, if nothing else." Miss Proulx's hostile gaze returned and Yancey felt his breath catch. "Your behavior following my visit to the station yesterday is the reason that even if I did know how to dance I would not wish to dance with you."

"I am sorry if you felt I did not take you seriously, but the murder of Mr. Stickney was and is my top priority."

"If it's such a priority I wonder that you have time to spare for dancing."

"My investigation brings me to the Sea Spray. When I saw you cowering behind the shrubbery I felt it my civic duty to ask you to dance."

"Do your civic duties also include spreading lies to my acquaintances?"

"I haven't the foggiest notion what you mean."

"You know what you said to Nell."

"Nell, the palm reader?"

"Yes. She said you told her I accused an Indian man of being the one who attempted to rob me. However did she get that idea?"

"You said the man was in the grip of a savage, murderous rage, did you not?"

"I believe I said something to that effect."

"You pointed your finger right at the Indian camp."

"I did not."

"You described a dark-haired man, probably brown eyed, behaving like a savage."

"And you naturally concluded the word *savage* was one I would use interchangeably with *Indian*?" Miss Proulx had stopped dead in her tracks. All around them the other dancers continued to move to the music.

"Chief Hurley made that assumption, not me."

"But you were the one who went to the Indian camp and told Nell I had accused one of her friends or relations."

"I went at the chief's insistence. However, I will admit I thought he had correctly interpreted your meaning."

"I meant no such thing." Miss Proulx shook her head with sufficient gusto to send tendrils of hair spilling from their pins. "I was shamefully embarrassed when Nell told me she no longer wants to work at the Belden. I've never been so humiliated in all my life."

"I apologize, and if it will help I'll tell Nell myself that your words were misconstrued." Yancey stepped toward his partner and drew her nearer to him, pulling her out of the way of a passing couple.

"That's a start," she said. Yancey winced as Miss Proulx stomped on his foot. "Oh dear, I'm afraid I am not getting the hang of this at all."

"You're doing fine. Just keep your eyes up and allow me to lead."

"I have not found it in my best interest to allow gentlemen to direct me."

"In the ballroom it is customary for the man to lead, no matter how modern his partner believes herself to be."

"You seem to know everything. How to dance, how ladies should behave. Is there anything you don't know?"

"I don't know why you would attend a dance when you don't know how to waltz? Especially a dance at the Sea Spray? You must be aware that Jelly Roll is not one of your aunt's bosom friends."

"Jelly Roll?"

"My apologies. I refer to Mr. Jellison, the proprietor."

"It sounds like Honoria is not the only one who dislikes him."

"He has his supporters but I'm not one of them. You haven't answered my question."

"Is this part of the murder inquiry?"

"I am attempting to make polite and charming conversation with my dance partner. It's also customary." Yancey watched the way Miss Proulx's mouth opened and then snapped shut again without a word. Really, she was very pretty when she wasn't saying something provoking. It was too good to last.

"I'm here precisely because my aunt is not on friendly terms with her neighbor. Mr. Jellison was overheard telling your boss how he planned to acquire the Belden at a drastically reduced price from the bank when our season proved disastrous financially."

"And you came here to see for yourself the sort of man he is?"

"Amongst other things." Miss Proulx looked around the room as if searching for someone.

"Are you holding back information that concerns the investigation?"

"I am not sure I can trust the police. I don't mean you particularly but . . ."

"You've heard the chief is related to Jelly Roll."

"I have. Unfortunately, it makes me suspect the entire department may not act in Honoria's best interests."

"Honoria is my mother's oldest and dearest friend. Chief Hurley does not garner more of my loyalty than my mother. Or your aunt."

"I remain unconvinced."

"What if I told you my visit with Nell is the reason I am here? Something she said set me to wondering the same things about Mr. Jellison you have mentioned."

"Truly?"

"I give you my word."

"I appreciate the confidence you shared but I believe I will keep my thoughts to myself."

"I see. In that case I am left to guess at your purpose here. Since I am loath to believe you are the sort to frequent an establishment in search of illegal substances, I can only conclude you are here to conduct your own investigation on behalf of Honoria."

"And what if I am?"

"I sincerely hope you will be persuaded to stop immediately. Not only would I consider you to be obstructing a police matter, I would be worried for your safety. After all, someone has murdered a man of far greater size and strength than your own."

"How flattering of you to concern yourself with my safety. Does that mean I am no longer a suspect?"

"It is too early to tell. It isn't just your safety that worries me. It's my own." Yancey flashed a smile down at Miss Proulx. "If you should come to harm I shall have to answer to both my mother and my sister. It doesn't bear thinking about."

Yancey felt a tap on his shoulder and turned to see one of the guests from the Hotel Belden standing behind him.

"I hope you don't mind but Ruby promised me a dance, and with such a crowd I consider myself lucky to have found her. I'd hate to lose her again," Mr. Ayers said.

Yancey remembered him from the round of questioning he had conducted at the hotel after the murder. He hadn't much liked his easy smile and unflappable attitude at the time. He liked him even less now that he was calling Miss Proulx by her given name. The only consolation he had was that Miss Proulx looked even less eager to dance with Mr. Ayers than she had to dance with him. It looked more like she had been asked to take a turn about the room with a wheelbarrow full of fresh manure.

"Although Miss Proulx and I are not on a first-name basis I know her well enough to be certain how little she would think of me if I didn't ask her permission before handing her off. Miss Proulx, what do you say?" Yancey's breath quickened when he felt a tightening on his palm and he was preparing for the pleasure of sending Mr. Ayers away with a flea in his ear when she answered.

"I do seem to remember promising Mr. Ayers a dance. Now would be most agreeable." She slipped her small, warm hand, encased in its mesh glove, from his.

"I should check back in with my partner anyway."

"Still haven't caught the murderer yet, Officer?" Mr. Ayers said, taking Miss Proulx by the hand and stepping toward her.

"Sadly, no. But as Miss Proulx and I were discussing earlier, my business here has more to do with pickpockets anyway."

Chapter Thirty-One

As inexperienced a dancer as I was, the difference in my two partners was obvious even to me. Officer Yancey had held my hand gently and steered me round the floor like he was a champion at the egg-and-spoon race. Mr. Ayers stepped closer to me than seemed strictly necessary and contrived little slips and collisions of our bodies that felt as intentional as they did unwelcome.

"Miss Proulx, have you thought about my offer?" Mr. Ayers asked.

"Is that what you are calling it? An offer?"

"Why not? If we are going to be working together so closely, should we not make the experience as agreeable as possible?"

"I prefer to hold my nose and make it quick when I have to force down something vile."

"Quick is not what I have planned for our partnership." Mr. Ayers pulled me even closer. "I envision a long and lucrative endeavor."

"After thinking it over, I don't see as I have any choice."

"I knew from the moment I laid eyes on you that you were a sensible girl."

"I suppose that is meant as a compliment but you'll understand if I'm not flattered. I'll do as you ask but there will have to be some rules to the arrangement."

"Do you really think you're in a position to make demands?"

"Perhaps not, but consider that I can apply myself with more or less enthusiasm to the task you have demanded of me."

"What is it that you want?"

"I want your assurance that you have no intention of draining the Velmont sisters dry." My morals had often been as flexible as a sideshow contortionist but even I had some scruples.

"Certainly not. For one thing, that would attract suspicion that we are both eager to avoid." Mr. Ayers tried to look scandalized by the suggestion but ended up looking more like his lunch had not agreed with him. "For another, I find it's far easier to run one game over the long term than it is to set up many short ones."

"How do you propose to run this particular con?" I asked.

"I want the sisters to receive directives from their father. All you have to do is to pass along the information I feed you during their sittings. I leave the details of convincing them entirely in your capable hands."

"How long do you plan to force me into helping you?"

"You make it sound so ugly. What sort of term do you propose?"

"We're done as soon as I've repaid you the amount you and Father agreed upon for the Invigorizers."

"Come now, I thought you were sensible. Is this the sort of businessman you think I am?"

"What, then?"

"If your father had paid as he agreed I would have had a lump sum to invest. Instead, I have to wait while the funds trickle in.

I require compensation for the delay. You will put yourself at my disposal until the end of the season."

"And what happens then?"

"If I feel my account has been cleared we will go our separate ways."

"That's your final say on the matter?"

"I suppose I could shorten the term to a fixed amount of money if you found a different way to compensate me. I could do with the attentions of a lovely young lady such as yourself." My stomach squeezed and I felt unladylike sweat flash into my palms.

"I'll take my chances with the entire season."

"As you wish," he said, maneuvering me with vigor to the far side of the ballroom. As the dance mercifully came to an end Mr. Ayers released my hands, bowed, and backed away, leaving me to look once more for Mr. Jellison. Only a few feet away I noticed Officer Yancey speaking to the man himself. Officer Yancey had his notebook open in his hand. I hesitated. Even if I had enjoyed dancing with him more than I wished to admit, I hadn't changed my mind about keeping my inquiries to myself.

Before I could decide what to do, Mr. Jellison called out to me.

"Miss Proulx, isn't it?" he said. "Please join us." I took it as a sign I should proceed. Officer Yancey scowled at me and I thought it likely Mr. Jellison was hoping my appearance would make it less likely that Yancey would pursue his questioning. I nodded to both gentlemen and tried to use my eyebrows to tell Officer Yancey he should not feel hobbled by my presence. He seemed to understand me.

"Mr. Jellison was just telling me he was surprised to hear

there are rumors afloat that he has plans to expand his holdings to include the Belden and the Indian campground near the pier."

"The idea never crossed my mind. But now that you mention it I shall have to give it some consideration," Mr. Jellison said. "After all, it's the only neighborly thing to do."

"Coveting your neighbor's property is not most people's definition of neighborly," Officer Yancey said. I nodded in agreement.

"The time for small hotels and bands of roving Indians is past. By the new century Old Orchard will be the premier summer destination in the Northeast. Offering to purchase the Belden before Honoria's financial troubles get the better of her is the merciful thing to do."

"I wasn't aware you had access to Honoria's financial information," I said.

"It's still a small town, Miss Proulx, despite the number of visitors we host here," Mr. Jellison said. "And I would have to be a fool to not understand how the murder of one of Honoria's guests is likely to impact reservations and staff morale." Mr. Jellison beamed down at me and I felt I needed a good long soak in a hot, soapy bath.

"I think you underestimate the loyalty of our guests and staff."

"I think you overestimate them. Why, just this week we've hosted several of your guests and most of the staff." Mr. Jellison smiled again.

"Like who?" I asked.

"You, for starters, Miss Proulx, and the gentleman who accompanied you here this evening. The astrologer and her husband and the unfortunate Mr. Stickney have all been here within the past few days," Mr. Jellison said. "Not that we've entertained them without incident."

"What sort of incident?" Officer Yancey asked. He had put his notebook back in his pocket and sounded conversational instead of official.

"There was a misunderstanding with the astrologer's husband. A very jealous sort of man. He was vehemently opposed to me speaking to his wife. He made such a scene I had to ask him to leave."

"You said Mr. Stickney was here. Do you remember when?"

"It must have been the night before last because he was here at about the same time as the astrologer. He left not long after they did."

"How can you be so sure of that?" Officer Yancey asked.

"Because after the argument with the astrologer's husband, Mr. Stickney came up to me and asked if we had any vacancies. He said he had concerns about the Belden already and witnessing the unprofessional behavior of the staff convinced him he should move himself and his wife."

"And did you have vacancies?"

"I assured him we would be happy to accommodate them both, and he left shortly thereafter. Sadly, he had no need for the room by the next day."

"And you can prove this?" I asked.

"Officer Yancey is welcome to speak with the front desk. There will be a reservation marked down in the book." His attention was pulled elsewhere and he raised his hand to someone. "Business calls, Yancey. If you have more questions they'll have to wait until tomorrow." He gave us each a brief nod, crossed the ballroom, and tapped a dark-haired man on the shoulder.

Something about the man struck me as familiar, but from across the room I couldn't quite put my finger on it. Then Mr.

Jellison said something that made the man throw back his head and roar with laughter. And that's when I saw them. The light from the chandelier glinted down on his face, and I grabbed Officer Yancey by the arm.

"If you believe the murder and the pickpocketing are connected, you might want to question the man speaking with Mr. Jellison."

"Albert Fitch?"

"I don't know what his name is but I am acquainted with him."

"You know Albert Fitch?"

"There was one more thing I suppose I should have mentioned about the pickpocket."

"You mean besides the fact he was not an Indian?" His tone did not do him credit. It was hard to believe someone as pleasant as Lucinda shared a bloodline with Officer Yancey.

"He had two gold front teeth." I admit to having taken no small satisfaction in the look of astonishment that flooded his face. He recovered himself with haste and waved his hand above his head. Out of nowhere another officer appeared.

"Frank, looks like we might finally have a chance to get somewhere with our old friend Albert Fitch."

"Have you been sampling the hooch?" Frank said.

"Miss Proulx here says he's the man who snatched her bag." An enormous grin spread over Frank's face.

"You don't say?"

"I do say," I said. "Do you need me to fill out a report or something to make it official?"

"Your word is good enough for me to keep an eye on him, miss." Frank tipped his hat, nodded at Officer Yancey, and slipped off into the crowd.

"That's it?" I asked. "You plan to simply keep an eye on him?"

"That's exactly what I intend to do." Officer Yancey took my arm and steered me away from the noise of the band to a secluded table at the edge of the dining room. "Albert Fitch has been in my sights for a long while. I've heard rumors of his involvement in everything from illegal stills to horse thefts from the livery but I've never been able to get the chief to authorize me to bring charges against him and have never caught him in the act."

"Why won't your chief bring charges?"

"He's a favorite of Mr. Jellison's, which makes him someone protected by the chief." Officer Yancey sighed deeply. "But if I have an upstanding citizen swearing he is involved in pickpocketing it is worth further investigation."

"Do you think he could have killed Mr. Stickney?"

"Let's just say I am hoping that by keeping an eye on him we'll catch him with Mr. Stickney's missing watch fob."

CHAPTER THIRTY-TWO

ALBERT FITCH HAD BEEN A BUSY BOY FOR MUCH OF THE NIGHT. He stayed at the Sea Spray, making eyes at the ladies and selling illegal hooch on the sly until after two in the morning. He stopped off at a rooming house for another several hours of card playing. Dawn had long since lightened the sky as he staggered toward a ramshackle cottage a few blocks from the shore and let himself in. Before the door closed behind him, young Henry Goodwin slipped out through it and set off toward town. Even without his Peanutine cart he was easy to recognize. Despite his energetic bearing, Henry walked with a pronounced limp. Rumor had it the boy's father had caused his injury but no one was entirely certain.

With the promise to send Lewis to relieve him, Yancey left Frank watching the house, then followed Henry as far as the livery stable on Old Orchard Street. He was sure Henry would be there at least long enough to hitch a donkey to one of the many Peanutine wagons that dotted the beach throughout the summer.

Yancey hurried across the street to the station, where through the plate glass window he saw Lewis seated at Frank's desk scattering powdered sugar from a half-eaten fritter all down the front of his uniform jacket. He jumped to his feet when Yancey pushed open the door.

"Is the chief in yet?" Yancey stuck his hand into the grease-stained paper bag on Frank's desk.

"No, sir." Lewis wiped his fingers on his uniform. "Do you want me to call him, sir?"

"Absolutely not," Yancey said. "Frank and I have had Albert Fitch under surveillance all night long and I want you to go over to the Goodwin place and relieve him." Yancey stifled a grin. If Officer Lewis had had a tail he would have wagged it clean off.

"I'll get right over there, sir." Lewis jumped to his feet, abandoning the half-eaten fritter on the desk. "Just as soon as you tell me where the Goodwin place is located." Yancey gave him the address and told him to ask the patrolman stationed down on Grand Avenue to accompany him.

"Don't approach Fitch and don't let him know you're there." Yancey waited until Lewis dashed out the door to help himself to the fritter left on the desk. He picked up the greasy bag left there, too, and found two more. Time to tackle Henry.

YANCEY PACED ON THE STREET NEAR THE ALBERTA HOUSE, waiting for Henry to clatter past with his peanut-shaped cart. Henry was one of several cart drivers who sold the popular peanut and molasses confection, Peanutine, up and down the beach all summer. Yancey waited until Henry was at the end of Old Orchard Street and almost on the sand before he followed him.

It was still early, with only a few people looking for shells or walking with friends. Thomas Lydale, the photographer, called out to him as he was setting up for a day taking souvenir photos in his booth at the edge of the boardwalk. Yancey kept Henry in his sights as he stopped to greet Thomas.

"I've got those photos of the murder scene ready up at the shop whenever you want to see them," Thomas said.

"I'll try to come by this evening if nothing holds me up," Yancey said. The photographer nodded and Yancey hurried after Henry, whose donkey was starting to put more distance between them than Yancey liked.

No one wanted candy yet, so Henry looked up eagerly when Yancey approached.

"I don't suppose I could interest you in an apple fritter, could I, Henry?" Yancey asked, extending the bag. Henry tensed his grip on the donkey's reins and peered down from his perch.

"What's it going to cost me?" he asked.

"I'll give you these in exchange for a description of the pickpocket you saw assault the lady near the train station."

"I already told you what he looked like."

"But this time I'd like you to tell me the truth." Yancey rattled the bag. "I already know it's Albert Fitch, I'd just like to know why you wouldn't identify him." Henry looked up and down the beach. The nearest person was the photographer, who was well out of earshot.

"Who's Albert Fitch?"

"He's the guy you passed in the doorway to your own house this morning."

"Oh, that guy." Henry bit his lower lip. "Sometimes he asks people to do odd jobs for him."

"Did you ever do any odd jobs for Albert, Henry?" The older Goodwin boys had been mixed up with Albert Fitch since their parents had both died of scarlet fever several years earlier, leaving a very young Henry in the care of his teenage brothers. They'd done whatever they could to keep a roof over their heads and food in their bellies. Rumor had it that a fast buck could be earned helping Albert Fitch.

"Albert offered me a way to make more money in an afternoon than I do all day driving this cart."

"What did Albert have you do?"

"All I had to do was go swimming."

"That's it? Just swimming?"

"Well, no. He told me he wanted me to drop something off at the bathhouse at the Sea Spray first but he'd pay me to do it and then I could swim all afternoon."

The Sea Spray again. Yancey felt the tingling along his scalp he always did when he was sure he was onto something. He held out the fritter bag.

"What did he want you to drop off?"

"I don't know. He told me not to look. He gave me a drawstring pouch and told me to put it in cubby number seventeen at the bathhouse."

"Just put the bag in the valuables storage at the bathhouse and then go swimming?"

"That's it. He said to tell the lady at the entrance that Albert sent me with something for cubby seventeen."

"What did she say?"

"She let me in without paying, gave me a key, and pointed to the room just past her. I went in, unlocked door seventeen, and stuck the bag in the cubby."

"Was there anything else in there?" Yancey asked.

"Another bag."

"If I were you I would have peeked into that one."

"You wouldn't if you really knew Albert." Henry gulped down a second fritter in three big bites.

"Did he ever have you go swimming again?"

"A few times, but when my brother Tippy found out, he gave me a hiding."

"Did Albert get someone else to do it?"

"I don't want to get anyone in trouble."

"I'll find out one way or another. If you're worried about someone it'll go easier on him if I'm not annoyed when I track him down."

"Tippy took over. He didn't want me to work for Albert."

"Does Tippy still make deliveries to the bathhouse?"

"Yeah. Albert shows up at our house. He leaves a bag with Tippy for him to take to the bathhouse that day."

"Henry, best mind your brothers and stay away from Albert." Henry shrugged and turned his best smile on a lady approaching the cart.

Yancey hummed a little tune to himself as he set off to invite Lewis to go for a swim.

CHAPTER THIRTY-THREE

ISCOVERING THE IDENTITY OF THE PICKPOCKET THE NIGHT
before and mulling over the possibility that I might have
ended up like Mr. Stickney had weighed heavily on my mind.
Adding to my unsettled feeling was the task I had agreed to per-
form for Mr. Ayers. Since there seemed to be little to do about
Mr. Stickney, I decided to set things in motion with the Velmont
sisters as soon as possible.

It took a little searching but I found them in the side garden
sheltered by the high wooden fence from the sea breeze and the pry-
ing eyes of passersby. The sisters stood facing each other, Elva holding what looked like a bowling pin in each hand. They both looked
over as I stepped through the gate. From the tension in the air and
the grim looks on their faces I had the sense they'd been arguing.

"Hello, ladies. Have I interrupted something?"

"Ruby, my dear, you are just the person to help us with an important decision," Elva said. "I am trying to convince my sister that
our interest in physical fitness is best expressed through the private
use of Indian clubs rather than by some less seemly means."

"I wouldn't call it unseemly," Dovie said.

"My sister has gotten quite a wild notion in her head."

"Ruby, would you be willing to consult Father for us? Elva refuses to consider joining me until she has his approval."

"Perhaps if you tell me what is on your mind, Dovie, he will be moved to whisper his thoughts in my ear." I smiled and nodded.

"I wish to bathe in the sea. My sister feels Father would not approve," Dovie said. "She knows she wants to go at least as much as I but she doesn't want to disappoint Father by acting in a way that attracts the wrong sort of notice." Dovie leaned forward with shining eyes and for just a flickering moment I could clearly see the young girl she had once been.

"I always wanted to test the waters when I was younger but Father never would give his consent," Elva said. "He felt the bathing costumes were much too immodest."

"*Scandalous* was the word he used," Dovie said. "But recently the messages you've been relaying from Father indicate a mellowing of his forceful opinions. Perhaps he will think differently of such things from the other side?"

I could see no harm in turning Father Velmont into the sort of man who helped his daughters to enjoy themselves for once. Especially the serious Elva. If I could lie to them to save my own skin with Mr. Ayers I could certainly lie to them for their own pleasure.

"Please give me your hands and we will see what can be discovered," I said, extending my arms to each of them. I drew in a deep, salt-laden breath and allowed my head to loll forward. "Father Velmont, can you hear me?" At the base of the veranda a seagull cried out and I felt the sisters' hands squeeze my own in surprise.

"That wasn't him, Elva," Dovie said.

"It sounded just like him whenever his dinner was late," Elva said.

"He's just arriving. I hear him coming closer and closer. He says he knows your question and he has an opinion."

"What is it, Father?"

"The other side provides a higher and purer perspective. He sees time in a long and expanding way and feels there is no need to cut yourself off from wholesome enjoyments because of the small minds of others."

"Oh, Father, are you certain?" Dovie asked.

"Quite. But he has something else he is showing to me. He's saying you should take stock. Does that make any sense to you?" I decided to slip in the bitter with the sweet. I knew Mr. Ayers would be hounding me at every opportunity and things would be easier if I had some progress to mention the next time he cornered me.

"We inventoried the china and the linens before we closed up the house for the season. Could that be what he means?" Dovie asked.

"Perhaps, but he is repeating himself, only louder this time, and I doubt he would do so if that were the correct interpretation."

"Father did tend to shout when he felt he was not being understood. Didn't he, sister?" Elva said.

"In addition to his voice I hear a crinkling, rustling noise like leaves of paper," I said, hoping to lead them toward stock certificates.

"I've never felt the need to inventory the library, have you?" Dovie turned to Elva.

"No. I have not. We will be sure to do so as soon as we return home at the end of the season. I expect Father had some valuable volumes."

"He did prize his library," Dovie said. I searched my mind for any subtle way to introduce the topic of Mr. Ayers's company but felt the task was beyond me at the moment. Anything that came to mind seemed too obvious. I told myself I would revisit the subject at our next sitting. I decided to move the topic to the sisters' possible involvement with Mr. Stickney's death.

"Take spiritual stock. Do you have something on your conscience, something that would be best confessed to someone in authority?" I peeked at them through slightly parted eyelids. Dovie's face flushed a deep red and Elva's eyes flew open and she looked at her sister. Then each of them took a deep breath and seemed to come to a decision. Elva spoke up first.

"I am certain that if either of us is keeping any secrets it is motivated by the best of intentions and that neither of us has done anything we should regret. Father would be most pleased with us both."

"Father always said family is more important than anything else," Dovie said. From the determined looks on their faces I doubted there was anything they would be willing to tell me now.

"He has left us, ladies," I said. "I believe you should feel emboldened to go for a bathe. The weather looks fine for it this very afternoon." I was pleased to see broad smiles pass between the two of them.

"We can only consider going ahead with it if you consent to accompanying us as our guest," Elva said.

"I haven't a bathing costume," I said.

"Neither have we but I understand they rent them next door at the Sea Spray bathhouse. We can all go right now."

"Don't worry about any sittings you may have had scheduled

this morning. We had already requested until after lunch for ourselves."

"But since you've already spoken with Father we can take the morning off."

THE VELMONT SISTERS MET ME ON THE VERANDA, AS AGREED, fifteen minutes later. It was early, yet the sun beat down on us as we walked along the sand and I was grateful for the comforting shade of my parasol. The tide was at its midpoint and crowds tramped along the hard-packed sand in clusters of three and four. Small children with shovels and tin pails squatted at the water's edge, constructing castles and sea creatures from the damp sand.

"With this heat I am glad we are going no further than next door," Elva said. "It is most convenient to have something so nearby." I thought fleetingly of Mr. Jellison's expansion plans and how the boardwalk stretching from his hotel to his bathhouse might extend to the Belden the following summer if things didn't turn around soon for Honoria.

As we stepped up onto the grayed wooden planks of the boardwalk I caught sight of a scrawny young man who seemed vaguely familiar walking to the bathhouse ahead of us. As we drew closer I remembered where I had seen him. It was Officer Lewis from the police station. I wondered if he were part of the effort to follow Albert Fitch.

I increased my pace and the Velmont sisters kept up. We reached the end of the boardwalk, which terminated in a long wooden building. At the entrance sat a red-cheeked, middle-aged woman.

"Good morning, ladies. Are you here to enjoy a dip in the sea?"

"We are," Dovie said. "It's our first time giving it a try."

"Father has finally approved," Elva said as she drew out a coin purse from the folds of her gown. "How much for three of us?"

"That depends on whether you've brought your own bathing costumes or if you prefer to rent them?"

"We shall need to rent them." The attendant quoted a fee and Elva drew the coins from her heavily beaded purse.

"This is all very convenient," Dovie said, peering along the airy corridor.

"Would you like a key to a locker where you can secure your valuables?" the attendant asked. Elva nodded. "If you'll head down the hall you'll find everything you need."

We stopped at a small room filled with swimming costumes, and the attendant helped us each find our size. Mine was easy enough to discover and I left the two older ladies in the attendant's capable hands as I went to change. I found it more difficult than I would have anticipated to struggle into the unfamiliar garments. I placed my own clothing into a basket dangling from a wire attached to a pulley system running along the ceiling. As soon as the garments were loaded into the basket, as the attendant had instructed, I pressed a bell button fitted into the back wall of the booth and the wire on the pulley whisked the basket away for storage.

As I wrestled with the stockings that accompanied the bathing costume, I heard Elva greet someone. I recognized Madame Fidelia's heavily accented voice answer her as she let herself into the booth to the right of mine.

Even though I had emboldened the Velmonts to attempt sea bathing I found myself delaying my exit from the booth. I felt foolish and utterly exposed. While it was true that my calves were encased in heavy stockings, the shape of them was clearly on display for all to see. I hadn't found a bathing costume amongst my mother's things and I wondered if she would approve of my behavior. I found myself wishing, not for the first time, mediums were real and that I could ask my mother for the sort of counsel the Velmonts believed they received.

But I didn't have any such comfort. I was, as always, responsible for deciding for myself how to behave. I chided myself that I was a modern woman; it was nearly the twentieth century, after all. I hauled back the curtain and bolted through before I could lose my nerve, and collided with a young woman departing the booth next to me.

"Pardon me," I said. "Are you injured?"

"Not in the least," said the woman, who looked at first glance remarkably like Amanda. As I looked her over more carefully, I realized she was a similar type. Blond, slim, and taller than me, with flawless posture. "Are you?"

"No. But I seem to have lost my bearings. I was certain I heard an acquaintance of mine enter your booth."

"It's easy to mistake sounds at the beach. Something about the breeze and the background noise of the waves distorts things. On a foggy day it is almost impossible to tell which direction sounds come from." She lifted her hand in a farewell gesture and walked off through the exit. I waited until she left and then gently pulled back the curtain of the booth next to mine. It was empty, but I still couldn't shake the feeling something strange had just happened.

CHAPTER THIRTY-FOUR

THE TIDE WAS STARTING TO COME IN, AND ROILING WAVES slapped at the back of Yancey's knees, threatening to knock him off-balance. As unreasonable as he knew it was, Yancey blamed Albert Fitch for the sea being rough. Yancey leaned against a barnacle-encrusted outcropping of boulders that thrust up from the beach. Locals and tourists alike clambered over Googins Rock, named after a settler, Patrick Googins, who sheltered there from a hostile group of Indians with a prior claim to the beach.

Despite the fact he was on duty Yancey felt distracted by a young woman wearing a bathing costume. She'd hurried toward him and was perched disconcertingly near on the rocks. She, too, faced the bathhouse and didn't seem to notice as his glance kept drifting over. He forced his attention back on the bathhouse exit, watching for Lewis to appear.

Instead, Miss Proulx, also clad in a swimming costume, moved into view, a Miss Velmont clinging to each of her arms. They moved unsteadily across the sand into the surf. To Yancey's complete amazement all three of them hopped and jumped over the low waves like small girls. After a few moments of vigorous splashing the plumper of the sisters pointed toward Googins Rock. Miss Proulx steered them in Yancey's direction. As they approached, the woman next to Yancey gave a gasp loud enough for him to hear over the crash of the waves. She scrambled off the rock and hurried toward Camp Ellis, the sun glinting off her bright blond hair.

Miss Proulx gave Yancey a smile as they reached the outcropping, but the Velmonts took no notice of him until he greeted them.

"Ladies, you seem to be enjoying yourselves," Yancey said.

"We are indeed," Dovie said. "We've never had such fun. Even though the water is very cold."

"Have we been introduced, sir?" the slimmer of the Velmonts asked. Miss Velmont had been very cooperative when he'd interviewed her after Mr. Stickney's murder. Yancey wondered if she was getting a bit soft in the head.

"Officer Yancey, at your service, ma'am."

"Oh, young man, you must think I'm losing my mind." A charming blush colored the elder Miss Velmont's crepey cheek. "There's something very wrong with my head, but it's my eyesight, not my memory."

"The ladies didn't want to risk losing their spectacles in the surf so they left them in a locker in the bathhouse." Miss Proulx tucked tendrils of dark wet hair back into her ribbon-trimmed bathing cap. "They are finding it difficult to make out much of their surroundings."

"We're quite blind without them."

"How adventurous you were to head into the ocean without them," Yancey said. "I doubt I would be so bold." The Velmonts both giggled like schoolgirls and Yancey felt his own spirits rise as Miss Proulx beamed at him.

"That's just what I told them," Miss Proulx said. "Are you here for a bit of swimming yourself, Officer Yancey, or is your purpose a professional one?"

"I am here in the same official capacity as last evening." Yancey suddenly had an idea. "You ladies left belongings in the lockers at the Sea Spray bathhouse?"

"That's right," the slim one said. "Should we be worried about their security?"

"Not at all," Yancey said. "If anything, the locker room is a bit too well guarded for my liking."

"Too secure for a policeman?" Miss Proulx said.

"It's too safe because I'm a policeman. But you aren't."

"What an idea." The slimmer Miss Velmont flushed again.

"I don't see why there shouldn't be lady police officers, do you, Miss Proulx?" the plumper one said.

"I am quite certain the world would be far better off if women were involved in every profession."

"Does that mean you're up for one more adventure this morning?" Yancey asked. "It would be a sort of temporary police assignment."

"I am, but I cannot speak for my friends." Miss Proulx turned to the older women.

"Father always encouraged us to cooperate with the authorities, didn't he, Elva?" The plump one squinted at her sister.

"I suppose he did admonish us to respect the police," the elder one said. "What do you need us to do?"

THE ATTENDANT ON DUTY LIFTED THE KEY TO THE VELMONTS' locker and handed it to Elva.

"Ruby, would you be a dear and fetch our things from the

locker?" Elva placed the key in my hand and then turned and let out a piercing shriek. She raised her knobby hand and pointed down the hallway.

"What is a man doing in here?" Even with all my years reading people, if I hadn't been in on it I wouldn't have had the foggiest notion Elva hadn't actually seen a man enter the ladies' section of the changing rooms. Righteous indignation rolled off her like steam from a tugboat.

Dovie was no less impressive with her bout of the vapors. Somewhere between Googins Rock and the bathhouse entrance she had perfected the art of the swoon. The poor attendant at the bathhouse entrance hadn't known where to look first. And the chaos spread from one dressing booth to the next as word of a man in the bathhouse ripped shrill screams from patron after patron.

In the midst of the turmoil I slipped behind the attendant's desk and plucked a brass key from the hook labeled SEVENTEEN. Ducking into the room on the left I found the correct locker and turned the key. I bent down and peeked into the small wooden cupboard. I reached in and grabbed hold of a grubby cloth bag.

I tucked it into the waistband of my bathing bloomers and returned the key to its board. Elva stood outside a booth at the center of the hallway. When she saw me she arched an eyebrow. I nodded and she spoke up.

"My sister and I will catch our deaths standing around in these wet bathing costumes. It's bad enough there are unauthorized persons roaming about without fearing for our health as well."

"I'll send for your things right away, ma'am."

"Thank you. For my young friend as well, please." Elva helped

Dovie into the nearest booth and snapped the curtain shut. I felt a bit sorry for the attendant as I watched her hurry toward the clothing storage room at the back.

I felt sorry for her, that is, until I loosened the drawstring at the top of the bag in the privacy of the changing booth. I sat on the stool in the corner of the stall and shook the contents of the bag into my lap. Locker seventeen was a place to secure valuables, all right. But I doubted anyone headed for a day at the beach would need to store two ivory cameos, four silver cigarette cases, and a half-dozen gold pocket watches. From the inscription on the inside of one of them I felt certain the murder of Mr. Stickney had been solved.

CHAPTER THIRTY-FIVE

WORKING WITH THE POLICE HAD BEEN MORE EXCITING AND more satisfying than I would have imagined. I felt curiously elated, having been on the side of the angels for a change. In fact, I was in such high spirits Mrs. Doyle found my presence grating and shooed me out the door and down to the general store for some nutmeg and an ounce of tea.

The day was so lovely I decided to forgo the dummy train and instead headed back to the hotel on foot. As I passed the train station someone stepped close and clamped down on my arm.

"I think you've been avoiding me," he said. "If I had to guess, I'd say you're having second thoughts about getting the Velmont sisters to invest." Mr. Ayers didn't even bother with an insincere smile and his usual pretense of good manners. His shift in demeanor signaled a worrying change in his attitude and I fought the urge to twist from his grasp. Calling attention to his behavior would only make things worse.

"It's not as easy as you might imagine to convince the sisters to part with their money. Elva is quite savvy about such things," I said, hoping I sounded more at ease than I felt.

"I should think convincing them that their father wants them to invest with me should be a great deal easier than getting them to believe he would encourage them to go sea bathing. But you managed that now didn't you?"

"You've been keeping an eye on me?"

"Both eyes and both ears." Mr. Ayers took a step closer. "And what I've observed has left me convinced that you aren't sufficiently concerned about my financial situation."

"It is far easier to convince people to do things they already wish to do," I said. "I am building a rapport with the Velmonts and that takes time."

"I see. If you need more time I shall have to allow it." Mr. Ayers nodded to the necklace nestled against my throat. "I will take that while I await the rest of what you owe me."

"The necklace isn't mine to give. It belongs to my aunt." I felt a rush of anger as I thought of what Honoria had said about keeping the necklace safe for me all these years. I considered that if he took it I would not have it to pass along to my own children one day as so many women in my family had done before me.

"Then you won't miss it. I'm sure it is worth enough to buy my silence for another few days."

"I couldn't possibly give it to you." Mr. Ayers pressed even closer and towered above me. I'd seen men give the look he was giving me right before they dragged their wives into their tents and took a belt to them. I tried to step back but Mr. Ayers intensified his grip on the underside of my upper arm. With the speed of a cat his other hand shot out and gripped my own and, despite my best efforts, a squeak of pain escaped my mouth. Tears sprang to my eyes and it seemed to spur him on. He increased the pressure on my right hand and I felt my ring finger wrench out of place.

"You will give me that necklace or I will drag you into the alley behind the livery and enjoy hurting you in unmentionable ways before I remove it from you." Mr. Ayers's eyes were shining with excitement, like the happy children I had watched running up and down the sand with their kites. I could only nod. I was afraid if I spoke he would hear how frightened I truly was and that was no way to bargain. He released his hold on me and nodded to the necklace.

I looked around, hoping someone would notice me and interrupt us, but despite the crush of people swirling round the station, no one did. Before I could signal to a passing stranger, he shifted his stance to shield me from view. I squinted through the crowds and even tried to spot a police officer.

My legs threatened to give out from under me both from fear and from the pain in my hand. But no rescue appeared from any quarter, and sensing Mr. Ayers's increasing impatience I decided to give in. I reached up to undo the clasp, but between the gloves covering my hands and the pain in my finger I couldn't manage it.

"You'll have to do it," I said, hearing the tremble in my voice as I lowered my hands. I flinched as his fingers lingered on the sides of my neck, pressing firmly before moving to the clasp. I didn't even feel the chain snap or the weight of the pendant lift before it was gone. Mr. Ayers flashed me a terrifying smile, then turned and disappeared into the crowd.

THERE WAS JUST SOMETHING SO SATISFYING ABOUT THE LOOK on Albert Fitch's face. After leaving the Sea Spray bathhouse Yancey had tracked him to a boarding house on Atlantic Avenue. Fitch had looked more amused than worried when

Yancey cuffed him and shoved him into the back of a waiting wagon.

Even sitting chained to a table in the police station with the bag of loot from the bathhouse in front of him he slumped back in his chair as if he had nowhere better to be. It wasn't until Yancey mentioned murder that Fitch even seemed to be paying attention.

"Considering your connections, Albert, you might have gotten away with it if you had coshed some poor mill girl over the head or, better yet, one of the Indians. But you made the mistake of killing a wealthy guest from one of the fancy hotels. You know as well as I this town is built on tourist money. No one is going to let you go around murdering the moneyed visitors."

"I don't know what you're talking about." Albert Fitch shifted in his seat. A little bead of sweat ran down the side of his face and got lost in the dark stubble on his cheek. Yancey had waited for months to see Fitch squirm. It did the heart good.

"Maybe this will clear things up for you." Yancey opened the bag and began to spread the contents on the table. "You don't seem like the cameo-wearing type to me."

"You can't tie any of these things to me. And you can't pin a murder on me, neither."

"But I can. We have a couple of people who are more afraid of the noose than they are of you. It is astonishing how quickly some people will cooperate once they hear the word *murder*." Yancey lined up the six pocket watches in a neat row. "Your mistake was being greedy and cocky. If only you had left just one thing alone you could have probably continued operating as you have for the foreseeable future." Yancey pulled silver cigarette cases out of the bag one at a time. He opened them each and laid them in front of Albert.

"I didn't kill anyone."

"See this case here?" Yancey tapped on the final one he pulled from the bag. "See the engraving? Very distinctive, wouldn't you say?"

"I wouldn't know." Albert's eyes shifted to the floor. "I can't read."

"Well, that's a shame. I'll read it for you then, shall I?" Yancey cleared his throat. "'To Stickler from Battler.'"

"So?"

"So, the man found dead under the pier with a big old dent in the back of his head just happened to have owned a cigarette case with exactly that inscription. And the funny thing was, it wasn't in his possession when we found his body."

"I didn't kill nobody."

"So you keep saying. But I'm a practical man and I just don't think any other explanation makes sense." Yancey leaned forward. "I know you gave this bag containing a dead man's case to Tippy Goodwin to drop off at the bathhouse. I know it was secure in the locker at the bathhouse until someone working for me removed it. I know the dead man didn't have his case or his watch fob when his body was found. Which makes me pretty sure you did it."

"Maybe I did take it but I didn't kill him." Albert chewed on his lip like it was a cheap steak. "I'm not a violent man."

"How did the young lady at the train station get a lump the size of a clamshell on her head if you are not a violent man?"

"She gave as good as she got." Albert's cheeks reddened a bit. "I should have been the one pressing an assault charge."

"I think that situation serves as an example of the lengths you're willing to go to, to get what you want. Unless you have more luck with a judge than you do with young ladies, you're going to swing."

"I took it off of him. I did. But I did it at the Sea Spray. Mr. Jellison and I have an arrangement."

"I'm not surprised."

"I make the rounds in his ballroom, cloakroom, and especially in the back room where the hooch is flowing." Albert leaned forward. "He gives me free rein to take whatever I can from anyone I please. He lets me use the lockers to make deliveries to my fence, and I give him a cut of the profits."

"What does that have to do with murder?"

"I took the cigarette case off the guy at the Sea Spray. He was in the hallway heading out and I lifted it from him. I didn't look it over at all and even if I had, so many of those things are engraved, and like I said, all the words look the same to me. I tossed it in with the stash of others I had once I got home and didn't give it another thought."

"So you want me to believe you took it off him before the murder and you didn't even know you had it?"

"That's the God's honest truth."

"Unfortunately for you, I'm not much of a one for God." Yancey scraped back his chair and stood. "Frank, I'm heading over to Lydale's studio for some more evidence so we can finish off this investigation, and then, since it looks like this case is well in hand, I'm going home for some dinner and a couple hours' sleep. You'd be happy to keep him company, wouldn't you?"

"I can't think of anything I'd like more." Frank pulled open his desk drawer and brought out a truncheon and a pair of brass knuckles. "Don't hurry back."

CHAPTER THIRTY-SIX

YANCEY HUMMED TO HIMSELF AS HE CROSSED THE WIDTH OF Old Orchard Street to the photographer's studio tucked in next to the livery. Not a bad day's work. One murder solved, a pickpocketing ring broken, and Jelly Roll exposed as the criminal Yancey had always suspected him to be. He couldn't wait to see the look on the chief's face when he told him it wasn't the Indians, but instead his brother-in-law who was behind all the pickpocketing. Unless he already knew.

The bell jangled as Yancey pushed open the door, and Thomas Lydale emerged from the back room.

"I'll be right back with the photographs." He held up a finger and stepped back through the door. Yancey doffed his hat and occupied himself by looking at the souvenir picture cards pinned up along the shop. There were dozens of them tacked to the walls, none of which looked posed. Women in summer gowns strolling the beach with men in straw boaters, workmen setting the pilings for the pier, even one of Henry Goodwin sitting high on his Peanutine cart.

Most interesting, at least in Yancey's eyes, were the photos taken at the Indian camp. He had captured people moving along the paths between tents, people carrying wares to sell on the beach, mothers lifting children. Nell appeared in more than one of the pictures, often bent over a palm, giving a reading.

In one photo, a small girl smiled at the camera, and Yancey's heart turned over. If Jellison and the chief had their way, the Indians wouldn't be in Old Orchard next year to be photographed. But with Jellison finally shown for what he was, maybe there was some hope his expansion plans would be quashed.

"Here they are," Thomas announced, returning to the shop. He set a cardboard carton on the counter positioned at the far end of the room. Yancey joined him and watched as Thomas pulled out a meticulous record of the crime scene. Judging by the number of photos he had taken, the photographer had patience and an eye for detail.

"How did you manage with the fog so thick?"

"Luck and lanterns." Thomas tapped a photograph with a long finger. "The wind shifted almost as soon as I arrived. I lit a pair of lanterns to help with shots of the victim."

"It must have worked. The images of the victim are very clear," Yancey said.

"Photographs of the dead always are," Thomas said.

"They must make some of the most satisfactory subjects. Perhaps we could call on you in future if we are faced with the unfortunate need of your services."

"I don't think some of the other policemen would be happy for me to be a regular part of investigations."

"It isn't personal. Frank just hasn't gotten over the photo his mother had you take of his family."

"I thought his father looked very lifelike in that portrait,"

Thomas said. "The widow was very pleased with the way I posed him sitting in his favorite chair."

"That was part of the problem. Frank's mother gave him the chair after the photo was taken and every time he walks through his own living room he remembers how alive his father looked and it gives him the willies."

Thomas shook his head. "People can be so hard to please."

"Is that why you started taking those sorts of shots?" Yancey gestured to the wall of candid photographs.

"I take those photos because they show subjects I find interesting." Thomas strode across the room and pulled several of the images from the wall. "Do you know how many rich, sour-faced women and their spoilt daughters I photograph on any given day?"

"I'm guessing too many."

"Any is too many. But their fees allow for me to take photographs of ordinary people doing ordinary things." Thomas spread an array in front of Yancey. "Like these folks right here."

"Like the ones you took at the Indian camp?"

"I believe in documenting life as it occurs, because it's always changing. In the same way you wanted a record of the crime scene, someday someone will want to know exactly what life was like as we lived it, and that includes boot boys and mill girls and secret meetings and arguments. Not just posed pictures of pampered socialites." Thomas's face lit up as he spoke and he waved his hands over the images. "Do you only investigate murders of the wealthy?"

"Of course not. All lives have value."

"I couldn't agree more. And those lives are all made up of moments like the ones I capture. Look at this one of the train station I took this very afternoon," Thomas said. "There's so much bustling, so much energy and excitement there. It's a wonderful place to head with my detective camera," Thomas said.

"A detective camera?" Yancey's attention snapped away from the photos and focused on Thomas.

"That's what they're called but they aren't only for those in your profession." Thomas pushed another photo toward Yancey. "People tend to behave differently when they know they are being observed. I use a variety of hidden cameras to capture truly candid images. For example, I took this one with a camera disguised as a parcel."

"A parcel?"

"Yes. It's a camera wrapped with brown paper and tied with string. I hold it under my arm and no one is ever the wiser."

Yancey bent over the photo, incredulous that something snapped from inside a paper wrapper could be worth viewing. But, he had to admit, it had worked. The photo was remarkably clear and filled with detail. In fact, in the foreground he recognized Mr. Ayers from the Belden. He was wearing the same sort of smile Yancey had wanted to wipe off his face when he swooped in and danced off with Miss Proulx at the Sea Spray. One of his hands was gripping the arm of a young woman and the other seemed to be resting on the bodice of her dress.

"Do you have a lens?" Yancey asked, the blood beginning to pound in his ears.

"Of course." Thomas removed a small one from his vest pocket and handed it to him. "Does that clear things up?"

Yancey bent over the image and held his breath. Ayers's hand was wrapped around a pendant dangling from the woman's neck. Thomas had perfectly captured the terror on Miss Proulx's face.

"No, Thomas, it just makes me ask more questions." Yancey

felt worry bear down upon him. "Do you mind if I borrow this one?"

Yancey's good mood had fogged over as he walked home. He was still pleased with the conclusion of the investigation but he couldn't get the photograph of Miss Proulx out of his thoughts. Hoping Lucy could set his mind at ease, Yancey went looking for his sister as soon as he opened the door.

Lucy stood at the kitchen sideboard shelling a batch of early peas into a tin bowl. Each pea hit the metal dish like hail on a barn roof. Poor Blossom sat at her mistress's feet, ears flattened against her head to block the sound. Yancey wished he could do the same.

"Are those for supper?" he asked. Lucy turned at the sound of his voice and nodded.

"Mother and I have been so busy all day we just got around to starting supper. Why are you so late?"

"I've solved the Stickney murder and got to the bottom of the pickpocketing ring all in one fell swoop."

"So why don't you look more triumphant? Are you sure you've blamed the right person?"

"It's going to be a rip-snorting shocker if the murderer it isn't the man I arrested."

"Who was it?"

"Albert Fitch."

"That's convenient."

"What's that supposed to mean?"

"You've had your eye on Albert Fitch ever since you joined the force. And now you've got him for the two worst crimes to hit town in twenty years." The oblique reference to Gladys Willards's murder hung for a moment in the air between them. "So why aren't you capering around like a spring lamb?"

"I'm concerned about some information that has come my way about Miss Proulx."

"As a policeman or as a gentleman?"

"I'd like to think a policeman can be a gentleman." Yancey felt unreasonably cross even as the words slipped past his lips.

"I mean, are you worried about her as a man interested in an eligible young lady? Or are you still convinced she's committed a crime?" Lucy rolled her eyes at him. "Ruby is very dear to me and I won't help you to pester her with your ridiculous accusations."

"The police do not pester. We investigate, we interrogate."

"Call it whatever you like." She winked at him. "But if you're interested in Ruby, you ought not let it wait. She has at least two admirers already."

"What a popular girl." Yancey felt a tickle of annoyance. "Mr. Ayers isn't one of them though, is he?"

"In fact he is. But I don't think you have to worry about the competition from that quarter. When he accompanied us to the Sea Spray, Ruby asked me to distract him."

"She did, did she?"

"She was quite desperate about it. He was determined in his attentions and she didn't want to seem to encourage him. As the hotel owner's niece, she was in a difficult position. Of course she didn't want to offend him. That wouldn't be good business."

"Did she seem frightened of him at all?"

"Ruby, frightened?" Lucy laughed. "You're teasing me. Ruby wouldn't be frightened of a lion in her linen cupboard. I've never met a more spirited girl."

But Yancey did remember Miss Proulx appearing frightened for just a moment when Mr. Ayers cut in on their dance at the Sea Spray. She had hidden her feelings quickly but he had definitely seen the look on her face, felt the tightening of her small hand in his own, like she just needed a safe place to cling to when Ayers had appeared.

"Has she confided any concerns to you about him? Have his advances become aggressive?"

"Not that I know of. Besides, I'm sure Ruby can take care of herself. As a matter of fact I understand she's been helping take care of your problems as well as her own."

"Did Miss Proulx come round crowing about that?" He thought he had made it clear she was to be discreet about her role in the bathhouse break-in. What's more, he thought she had actually agreed.

"Certainly not. Honoria told Mother, who, of course, told me."

"Miss Proulx's help today with the pickpocketing problem was invaluable but I can't see working with her again," Yancey said. "Fitch's arrest is the first real break I've had in linking the chief to corruption and the first step in clearing Father's name. I won't risk being laughed out of court because I involved a phony soothsayer."

"Never say never, Yancey." Lucy turned back to her peas. "Dinner will be ready in an hour. Go sit in the parlor and I'll bring you a tray when it is ready. You look done in."

CHAPTER THIRTY-SEVEN

A S MUCH AS I GENERALLY ENVIED MEN THE ABILITY TO WEAR trousers I was grateful for the way my long gown hid my trembling legs. I found an unoccupied bench beside the board-walk and gratefully sank down onto it. As I watched the gulls circle overhead and the waves inch farther and farther out to sea I felt my pulse slow. Fatigue overwhelmed my body and my spirit as the tension from my encounter with Mr. Ayers faded away.

It was clear I had to convince the Velmonts sooner, rather than later, to invest in Mr. Ayers's scheme. The necklace was the only valuable thing in my possession. The look in his eyes had convinced me he would be all too pleased to take payment out of my hide while he waited for cold, hard currency.

As much as I wanted to put off seeing Mr. Ayers ever again I was going to have to chance meeting him at the Belden. After all, I could hardly hope to convince the Velmonts their father pre-ferred to converse with them about financial investments on a boardwalk bench. I gathered my wits and what was left of my courage and slowly made my way home.

Mrs. Doyle spotted me as I made my way to the back stairs.

"You've taken your sweet time getting back. Honoria's been looking everywhere for you and so have I. Have you got that nutmeg I sent you after?" In all the upset I had completely forgotten she had sent me on the errand that put me in Mr. Ayers's path.

"Yes. It's in my bag." My wrenched finger throbbed as I reached into the folds of my skirt for my drawstring purse. I couldn't disguise a sharp intake of breath as I tried to loosen the strings.

"What's the matter with you, girl?" Mrs. Doyle stepped forward and seized my wrists. I flinched and she gave me one of her familiar scowls.

"I'm fine. You just startled me, is all."

"I hardly think so. Your hands are shaking." She pointed at my purse, whose jouncing and swaying mirrored the movement of my trembling hands. She plucked the bag from my fingers and without hesitation but with more gentleness than I would have expected, tugged off my gloves, one at a time. "What's this then?" She pointed to my ring finger, now swollen and flushed almost purple.

"I caught it in the door of the store on my way out."

"You expect me to believe you caught just the ring finger in the door? No other fingers were injured?"

"I admit, it was very peculiar." The way Mrs. Doyle was scowling at me left me feeling as transparent as her tomato aspic salad. "I was a bit clumsy, I suppose."

"I've met a lot of women who are this sort of clumsy." Her voice dropped so low I almost didn't hear what she said next. "I used to be one of them until I snuck out of my marriage bed in the night with my baby in my arms and found a place here working for your grandparents."

"That was very brave of you." I felt my heart soften toward this woman Lucy called the Dragon. It sounded like Mrs. Doyle had good reason to be such a fire-breather.

"Sometimes so is telling the truth."

"I never claimed to be brave, just that I am inclined to be clumsy."

"You didn't happen to be clumsy in the company of Mr. Ayers, did you?"

"What makes you suggest that?" Mrs. Doyle was hitting too close to the truth for my liking. It was enough to make even a hardened skeptic like Officer Yancey believe in psychic phenomena.

"He asked if I had seen you. When I told him I sent you to the general store he rushed straight out the door. I wondered if he had found you." I opened my mouth to lie and say I hadn't seen him when I heard the voice in my ear.

"Falsehoods do not deceive her."

"We spoke briefly near the train station." I fought to steady my voice. "Has he not returned?"

"No, he hasn't."

Relieved, I gritted my teeth and pulled on the drawstring of my bag once more, then removed the brown paper–wrapped nutmeg from it. "I'm sorry for keeping you." With that, I hurried up the stairs and into my room. I closed the door behind me and locked it, more grateful than ever for the ability to secure myself against the outside world.

ELVA AND DOVIE WERE THRILLED WHEN I MENTIONED AT DINner that their father had an urgent desire to communicate with them at their earliest convenience. I invited them to join me in the séance room after the meal was over. I hurried ahead of them, wondering how I was going to manage to conduct the reading. I wished I could rely on my cards to help guide me through the session, but my hand hurt far too much to shuffle them.

Nor could I stand to join hands in a circle with the sisters, which left me completely cut off from my usual ways of evaluating my impact on my sitters. One of the things I had learned about running the most convincing show was to stick as close to the truth as possible and to let the person opposite you feel they were allowed to see the real you.

I decided it would be best to place my cards on the table, so to speak, and to let the ladies know about my injury while avoiding naming Mr. Ayers as the culprit. After all, in my experience, ladies of a certain age and a sheltered sort of existence secretly hanker for word of the sensational.

I removed my gloves and turned on the lights to best allow them to see my swollen finger and the purple bruises blooming on the back of my hand. I placed my pouch of tarot cards in the center of the round table and awaited their arrival. Before long the sisters took their seats.

"Ladies, sometimes the universe conspires to offer us opportunities through adversity." I lifted my bare hand from my lap and stretched it toward them. "As you can see, I am in no fit shape to shuffle the cards for our session or even to turn them myself."

"What have you done to yourself?" Dovie leaned over my injuries with her hand held to her throat.

"I think it's unlikely Ruby would have done such a thing to herself, sister." Elva gave my face a sharp glance. "Who did this to you?"

"I was accosted at the train station and foolishly tried to

prevent another pickpocket from helping himself to my valuables. This is the unfortunate result."

"But I thought our help at the bathhouse earlier today would have put a stop to the pickpocketing here in town," Dovie said.

"I very much doubt such a group could be quashed so easily or quickly as that," Elva said. "But you ought to report it to Officer Yancey. He should be aware the investigation is by no means over."

"I was so rattled by the whole thing I just headed for home. It never even occurred to me to go to the police."

"Did the thief manage to take anything in the end?"

"Unfortunately, he took the necklace given to me by my aunt. It was a family heirloom which had belonged to my mother." I felt the loss of it afresh and a lump formed in my throat. I willed the tears threatening to spill over to recede and leave me in command of my emotions. They refused to be coerced and I was touched when Dovie pulled a handkerchief from her sleeve and handed it to me.

"Have you told your aunt about the robbery?" Dovie asked.

"I haven't wanted to trouble her. The hotel is a great responsibility and I hesitate to burden her further."

"I'm sure she would want to know. I'm quite certain she would want you to have your injuries looked after." Dovie and Elva exchanged a look, then Elva continued. "Are you quite sure you are up to a session this evening? I'm sure whatever Father has to say can wait." As much as I appreciated their kindness I couldn't imagine sleeping a wink if I hadn't moved toward solving my problem with Mr. Ayers. I dreaded the thought that the injuries to my hand might be the least of my concerns.

"Spending time in the realm of spirit is the best tonic for anything that ails me. I would prefer to go ahead with our session but

I will require some assistance from the two of you." I nodded to the cards. "I find I am unable to loosen the ties on the bag, let alone shuffle the cards. If you could do so, it would be a great help." Elva nodded and removed the cards from their pouch. I held my breath as I waited. Instead of the voice, my left ear filled with a rustling, crackling sound like a radio dial tuned to where there was no station.

She shuffled them as deftly as the first time we had used them and then placed the stack in front of me.

"Thank you, Elva. Now, Dovie, since this is a message for the both of you, I think it would be best for you to handle the cards as well. Would you cut them into three stacks and then turn over the first card on each pile?" Dovie did as she was told, and I pondered the images before me, hoping the voice would chime in with some words of wisdom. I couldn't help but notice that although the voice was silent the message from the cards was loud and clear.

The reading may have been about the Velmont sisters but it was warning them to beware of treachery and deceit. The cards were warning them about me. Never before had I had this happen. I felt sick to my stomach. I silently called to the voice to advise me, to tell me I was not so very wrong to try to save my own skin, but it refused to answer.

I remembered what Honoria had said about the fact that the cards have multiple meanings, often more complex ones than are apparent at first glance. I felt the ladies' eyes on me; they were clearly uncertain that I was fit to conduct the reading. Another flicker of guilty unease fluttered across my heart before the image of Mr. Ayers's smiling face as he crushed my hand filled my memory. Time to put their minds, and mine, at ease.

"The Magician is a card of skills and talents. Your father would like you to know he thinks it's time for you to learn something new. To turn your hand to something that might seem almost magical in its rewards."

"We are here at the Belden to develop such skills," Elva said. "Does he speak of that?"

I bent closer to the card, appearing to consider Mr. Velmont's words. I shook my head.

"No. He approves of your purpose here and believes you to be destined for success with your metaphysical inquiries but he urges me to turn my attention to the second card." I reached out my good hand and tapped the Three of Wands. "This speaks of investments. In creating new wealth. It involves risk but it's a calculated one."

"Father was never in favor of such things in his lifetime, was he, sister?" Dovie asked. "Remember the way he went on and on about how relieved he was not to have speculated wildly like so many others during the Panic five years ago?"

"I do. It seems most unlike him," Elva said. "Are you quite sure the cards are speaking to you as clearly as usual, Ruby? You have been through quite a trauma and someone as sensitive as you might be particularly affected by such a thing." I might have imagined it but I could have sworn I heard the voice chuckling at me.

"I am certain. Remember how much your father has changed his stance on sea bathing since he passed to the other side? He is altering his opinion on the subject of investing as well."

"What is the rest of the message?" Dovie asked. I focused on the final card in the reading.

"The Seven of Swords is a warning to beware of deception

and theft. Your father would like you to develop your skills in the area of finance so you can invest without too much risk."

"That sounds more like Father, doesn't it?" Dovie said. Elva nodded slowly.

"Does Father have any recommendations as to where to invest?" she asked. I closed my eyes and leaned back. After a dramatic pause I answered.

"He says to be open to possibilities that are right at hand. An opportunity will be in front of you shortly and he would like you to consider it carefully and not simply dismiss it, as you have no experience in such matters."

"How exciting. Perhaps we will become tycoons, sister." Dovie's face pinked becomingly. Elva pushed back her chair and stood.

"Come along, then. We have work to do." Elva paused and turned to me. "If Father has anything else to say we will be in the library reading the financial section of the latest newspapers." With that, the ladies left me alone to wallow in relief and guilt. I had taken the first step toward digging myself out of a mess. I just wished I hadn't also taken the first step toward getting such trusting ladies into one.

CHAPTER THIRTY-EIGHT

THE MOON FLOATED HIGH AND BRIGHT. YANCEY HAD SLEPT far longer than he had intended. He had been nodding off when Lucy brought him a supper tray. He couldn't even remember her coming in to clear it away. It was only the sound of the mantel clock striking midnight that had jolted him awake and alerted him to his responsibilities. He should have relieved Frank from duty hours before.

The station was the only building on Old Orchard Street where a light glowed within. Frank looked up as Yancey pushed open the door, a look of total wretchedness playing over his face.

"I'm sorry I'm so late, Frank. It was unforgivable of me. You've been out as late as I have and I don't even have a baby at home to interrupt what little sleep I've managed to snatch." Yancey stopped at his friend's desk and sat on the scarred wooden edge.

"In truth, I've been dreading you showing up." Something in his tone made Yancey's blood ice over. Frank's appearance wasn't one of exhaustion, it was one of misery. "I've got some bad news."

"What is it?"

"Albert Fitch."

"What about him?" Yancey felt his neck and shoulders tense as though he were anticipating a physical blow.

"You know how you asked me to keep him company while you were gone?" Yancey nodded; felt his throat dry up. "I did. And I admit, I worked him over pretty good. But I swear, he was still breathing when I left him." Yancey craned his neck to look to the back room where they held those under arrest. It was no more than a windowless room closed off by a metal door fitted with a sturdy lock.

"I don't want to hear this, do I?"

"I didn't go at him very long. About six whacks into it he was wailing for his mother. I gave off and went back to my desk. I must have nodded off because the next thing I knew the chief was hollering at me from the lockup to explain myself."

"I'd appreciate that myself. What is the problem, besides the chief dropping in when he was off duty?"

"When I stepped into the lockup Fitch was dead. His face was all bruised and his mouth and nose were all busted up. But I swear, he wasn't like that when I left him."

"You think the chief had something to do with it?"

"I don't think nothing. I just know he said that this sort of thing happens from time to time and we'd all be best off if there wasn't any fuss. He wouldn't say any more about it if I didn't."

Yancey walked to the lockup and threw open the door. It was empty, leaving no trace of Albert Fitch or what had happened in the small room.

"Where's the body?" Yancey asked, hearing Frank's footsteps behind him.

"Gone. The chief and I loaded it into the back of the police wagon and covered it with some feed sacks. Hurley drove it off himself and said I should tell you that the pickpocketing investigation should head in a new direction."

"And you're sure Fitch was dead when you loaded him into the wagon?"

"I know a dead body when I see one. We both do."

"So either you or Hurley killed our prime suspect in the murder of Leander Stickney and the person we know was the face of the pickpocketing ring. Is that what you're telling me?" Yancey could feel a burning in his gut, a familiar sense of frustration that stemmed from tangling with authority figures who abused their positions.

"That about sums it up." Frank looked stricken. "But, the pickpocketing in town should stop being such a problem now no matter what. And the state is spared the expense of a trial."

"What matters is that the testimony Fitch could have given against Jellison, and maybe even Hurley, died with him." Yancey pounded the wall with a clenched fist. "We've got no more to go on than we did before we uncovered the loot in the bathhouse."

"I'm sorry, Yancey. I wish I'd never started in on Fitch."

"If wishes were horses, Frank. Go on home and get some sleep."

"Are you sure you don't want to go instead?" Frank's glance drifted toward the door.

"If there's one thing I'm sure of, there's no way I'll catch a wink tonight no matter what. You go."

"My mother said things always look better after a good night's sleep."

"Considering the state of the case right now, let's hope she's right."

• • •

THERE WAS NO DOUBT ABOUT IT. THE BODY SPRAWLED ON THE sand in front of the seawall was that of Dennis Ayers. The incoming tide had soaked his lower legs, leaving a salty rime on his light trousers, but it hadn't carried him out to sea. Instead, it had left him lying within a few feet of Googins Rock and just out of sight of both the Sea Spray and the Belden.

"I must not have had a good night's sleep, because this is hardly what I would call *better*," Frank said, pitching his voice as low as he could while still being heard over the pounding surf. He glanced over his shoulder to where Jelly Roll stood observing it all.

"I'm sure if he could voice an opinion, Mr. Ayers would agree with you," Yancey said.

"You worked with Miss Proulx on the case yesterday. Maybe you could ask her what Mr. Ayers had to say about it."

"No thanks. Have you forgotten the way that case turned out?" Yancey asked. Frank had the good grace to blush as Yancey crouched over the body and gave it the once-over. He gently turned the victim's head and gingerly touched the skull, carefully feeling through the hair. "No injuries to the head. This victim wasn't killed in the same manner as Mr. Stickney," he said.

"Think this was a pickpocketing, too?" Frank didn't even try to suppress a tonsil-rattling yawn as he bent over the body.

Yancey hadn't liked the dead man's familiar attitude with Miss Proulx or his slick prattle, but he wouldn't have wished this death on anyone. He pried open Ayers's mouth, revealing a swollen tongue. He lifted one eyelid, noting burst blood vessels marring the whites of the eyes.

"If it was, at least we know Albert Fitch couldn't have done it. I am wondering if Jelly Roll knows more about this than he's letting on." Yancey loosened the tie around Mr. Ayers's neck and unfastened his collar. There, beneath his clothing, lay a linear bruise. Barely wider than a clothesline, it encircled the victim's throat. "Strangulation with a rope or something similar." He pointed to the marks, and Frank nodded as he wrote something in his notebook before straightening.

"I'm not sure I want to know about it if he does. I'm up to my eyeballs in hot water already." Frank shot another glance over his shoulder. "Here he comes."

"Any leads, Officers?" Jellison asked. "Besides the unfortunate Mr. Fitch?"

"I'm sure when there's something to report you'll hear all about it." Yancey slipped his hands into the pockets of the victim's striped cotton summer jacket and turned up a cigarette case, a crumpled calling card, and a handkerchief. Inspection of his left trouser pocket yielded nothing but lint and the wrapper from a peppermint candy. He slid his hand into Ayers's right pocket and felt something hard and cool.

Even in the low light of the early morning the ruby pendant in his hand sparkled and winked at him. His stomach sank. He would have recognized Miss Proulx's necklace anywhere.

"You got something there, Yancey?" Jelly Roll asked, coming closer.

"Nothing that concerns you." Yancey slipped the evidence into his own jacket pocket and walked away. There was no way he wanted gossip spreading about Miss Proulx's possible guilt unless it was absolutely necessary.

Yancey looked back and watched as Jelly Roll tried to strike

up a conversation with Frank instead. Yancey retrieved the necklace from his pocket and inspected it more closely. The slender
gold chain was broken as if it had been wrenched from the wearer
rather than unclasped carefully. With growing concern, he set
about scouring the shore for anything, besides his nagging suspicions, that could flesh out the story of what had occurred.

The beach was filled with the usual detritus. Shells and drift-
wood lay scattered around the body. Yancey toed piles of seaweed
to the side to inspect below them. Tucked beneath a pile of drying seaweed buzzing with sandflies he glimpsed something midnight blue. A length of cord. He teased it out, then rolled the
width of it between his finger and thumb.

"What've you got there, boss?" Frank had managed to shake
Jelly Roll and, still yawning, fetched up beside him.

"Looks like it might be the murder weapon. A length of cord
is a very handy thing to strangle someone with if you haven't a
great deal of strength." Yancey tucked the cord into his jacket
pocket and leaned back against the seawall to think.

"Finding the murder weapon is a good start, isn't it?" Frank's
sleepiness fled from his face, replaced by widened eyes and an
eager tone to his voice.

"It depends on whether or not you want to see the Hotel
Belden go out of business."

"What does that cord have to do with the Belden?"

"I seem to remember some just like it used as a holdback for
the drapes in the séance room at Honoria's hotel."

"You don't suspect Miss Belden of killing one of her guests,
do you?"

"No. I don't suspect Miss Belden." Yancey caught sight of
Lewis striding along the sand. Thomas Lydale, laden once more

with photographic paraphernalia, lagged behind. "But I'm afraid there is another lady at the hotel I will need to question."

"Please tell me it isn't my mother-in-law."

"Afraid of Mrs. Doyle, are you?" Yancey couldn't blame him. Frank's wife was a gem of a woman, but marriage to her came at the high price of family ties to Mrs. Doyle.

"I'm quaking in my boots. There's been no end to the misery in my house since the last time you went to the Belden and questioned everyone."

"Rest easy. I have another lady in mind. Can you take over here with documenting the crime scene?"

"If it means I don't have to go into the Belden with you, I'll even deal with Lydale without complaint."

"I have a lead I need to follow before I make inquiries at the Belden. I'll come back for Lewis in a bit." Yancey set off across the beach. Of all the reasons he could be headed for the hotel, the least appealing he could imagine was to collect evidence to arrest Miss Proulx.

Chapter Thirty-Nine

YANCEY LET HIMSELF INTO THE SÉANCE ROOM AND CAREFULLY inspected each window. Lewis stood and watched as Yancey confirmed the drapery tiebacks were a perfect match for the cord from the murder scene. The third window he checked was partially hidden from view by a silk folding screen. He felt his heart strain against the lining of his jacket when he noticed the far drape was held back by a length of packing twine rather than blue cording. He retraced his steps to the foyer.

Elva and Dovie Velmont stood near the registration desk, watching him approach. They bent their heads toward each other and whispered animatedly back and forth. With a simultaneous nod of their fluffy white heads they turned toward him once more.

"Officer Yancey, you are just the man we wanted to see," one of them said. He wasn't quite sure which sister was which. He motioned for Lewis to stay put and moved down the hall to greet the elderly pair.

"It's a sign, isn't it, sister?" said the other one.

"I am at your service, ladies." He knew he ought to tell them he was at the Belden on urgent business but he was relieved to find an excuse to delay confronting Miss Proulx. Yancey gave a bit of a bow, unleashing a twitter from the plumper of the two sisters. "How may I assist you?"

"We wish to report a crime," the thin one said. "On behalf of a friend."

"A friend of yours, too, we suspect." The plump one twittered again.

"What sort of a crime?" Yancey asked. The desk's gleaming walnut and polished brass fittings shone so brightly they made his eyes hurt. Lack of sleep was taking its toll. If he didn't make a special effort he would mishandle the upcoming interview.

"I'm not sure how you would classify it. It was either a robbery or an assault."

"Who was the victim?" Yancey asked, quite certain of the answer.

"Ruby," they answered in unison.

"Was she severely injured?"

"She didn't feel the need to seek the ministrations of a doctor but she was not able to use her hand for the card reading she conducted for us yesterday evening." The sisters nodded at each other in agreement.

"Which hand was injured?"

"Her right one."

"Do you know what was stolen?" Yancey asked.

"That was the worst part. The thief absconded with her mother's heirloom necklace. Such a heartbreak."

"We couldn't convince her to tell you or even Honoria what had happened."

"Ruby is always such a thoughtful girl, never wanting to trouble others."

"We worried that she might feel we had betrayed a confidence by gossiping to the police but when we saw you standing right in front of us we felt it was a sign."

"Did she give a description of her attacker?" Yancey asked.

"Oh dear, we never thought to ask for one."

"Ladies, you did right to bring this to my attention. Criminal behavior cannot be allowed to run unchecked. Do you know where I can find Miss Proulx?"

"I believe I saw her enter Miss Belden's office before we arrived here in the foyer."

"You've both been a great help." He motioned for Lewis to follow him, then walked slowly down the hall, not wishing to think about why it was that he didn't want to question Miss Proulx.

Just outside the door to the office he paused and listened. Honoria's booming voice and Ruby's higher-pitched one came through the thick wood. He chided himself for cowardice, then knocked with more force than necessary on the door. Millie, the maid, opened it and a look of fear passed over her face.

"Yancey, how lovely to see you." Honoria waved him into the room, a beaming smile spread across her face. There were days when Yancey loathed his job. This whole week had been full of them.

"As much as I wish it were, this isn't a social call." He motioned for Lewis to follow him into the room. "I'm here to ask you some questions about your guest, Mr. Ayers."

"He isn't here. He never came back to the hotel last night. Very poor manners not to let us know ahead he planned to stay out all night," Honoria said. "Ben waited up to let him in, as he hadn't asked for a latchkey." Yancey heard Lewis's pencil scratching across his notebook.

"Do you know when he was last seen?" Yancey asked.

"He left the hotel in the afternoon with the intention of attending a concert at the amphitheater," Honoria said. "What's all this about, Yancey?"

"There's been another tragedy."

"Has something happened to him?" Honoria asked. Despite his question being directed at Honoria, Yancey kept his eyes firmly planted on Ruby. A flicker of apprehension flitted across her face, but almost as soon as it appeared it vanished. If he hadn't known to watch her he would have missed it entirely.

"His body was found near Googins Rock this morning," Yancey said. "This was in his pocket." Yancey held out the necklace. Honoria stood and leaned toward him, bracing herself against the desk with her plump hands. Her face drained of its usual high color and the contrast between her skin and dark hair made her look frail. Yancey hated to contemplate what his mother would say when he returned home.

"That looks just like Ruby's necklace."

"I thought so, too." Yancey returned the necklace to his pocket.

"You said he's dead? Is some sort of lunatic targeting my guests?"

"He's been murdered, and while I believe there's a connection to your hotel, I don't think it's an anonymous lunatic."

"Since he had Ruby's necklace do you think Mr. Ayers was part of the pickpocketing ring?"

"I don't believe so. I believe she knew when it left her neck," Yancey said. "Miss Proulx, will you permit me?" Yancey crossed to where she stood and reached out to take her right hand. He felt like a brute when she let out a squeak of pain as he tugged off the glove and inspected her injuries. Her ring finger was purple and swollen to twice the size of her other digits.

Yancey knew well enough where his responsibilities lay but he couldn't help but feel the world was better off without the sort of man who would do that to someone so much smaller than he. Just as Yancey was about to release her hand he recalled Nell's words. He turned Ruby's hand over instead and bent close. There in the middle of the intersection of two lines on her palm was etched a distinct star. It was all he could do to keep himself from tracing it with his own finger. Annoyed with himself for his lack of professionalism, he resumed his line of questioning.

"I understand you were the victim of another aggressive thief yesterday." Yancey raised Miss Proulx's injured hand for Honoria and Lewis to see. "Are you more able to identify this attacker than you were the last one?"

Yancey felt Miss Proulx's body grow rigid as he kept a lingering grasp on her hand. She tugged her hand away and he reluctantly released his grip.

"It all happened so quickly. And besides, the last time I gave a description to the police my words were twisted and used against innocent people. It hadn't occurred to me to attempt to do so again."

"I wish you felt you could be honest with me. A man might not be dead if you had." Yancey placed the photograph he had gotten at Thomas Lydale's studio on the desk. "It looks to me like you did know your attacker." Yancey placed his finger just above the image of Miss Proulx.

Honoria leaned over the photograph and Yancey thought he detected a flicker of surprise as she recognized what was taking place in the scene set before her. Yancey found himself admiring her quick recovery as she raised her gaze to his own.

"This proves nothing. All I see is a man behaving in much too forward a manner to an innocent girl." Yancey heard the dismissal in Honoria's tone. "There is nothing to connect this photograph and the murder." Honoria crossed her arms over her daunting bosom and pelted him with a look that would have sent him packing if it weren't for the other evidence in his possession.

Yancey withdrew the drapery cord from his pocket. "This was found near the body. We believe he was strangled with it."

"What does that have to do with the hotel?" Honoria asked.

"It's a drapery tieback from your séance room. I've already checked and one is missing from a window there."

"Anyone could have taken it."

"The photograph shows Miss Proulx in a heated exchange with Mr. Ayers. You said yourself he never returned home, so she is the last person we can say for sure saw him." Yancey held up a hand to stop Honoria from sputtering an interruption. "No one had better access to the murder weapon than she or, as far as we can tell, a reason to kill him. Miss Proulx, it is my duty to take you to the station for questioning."

Ruby started to sway slightly, and Honoria moved quickly to her side and wrapped a steadying arm round her.

"It wasn't Ruby," Honoria said. "I did it."

"Honoria, that isn't true." Ruby's voice was shrill, and Yancey was certain she believed what she said. All at once she looked far younger than her years and utterly lost.

"It is. And I can prove it." Honoria released Ruby and returned to her desk. She yanked on a drawer and rummaged inside. She opened her hand to reveal Mr. Stickney's missing watch fob. "I meant to take the whole watch so you would think a pickpocket had killed him but I heard someone coming and this was all I managed to grab in my hurry to not be discovered."

"But why would you kill either of them?" Ruby asked, her voice quavering and small.

"Mr. Ayers told me he knew I had killed Mr. Stickney to keep him from reporting in his publication that my hotel employed frauds. He wanted money to keep quiet. I arranged to meet him out on the beach to make the first payment."

"And you strangled him with the cord?"

"I did. There's nothing I wouldn't do for my hotel. Or for you." Honoria gave Ruby a long look. Yancey wasn't sure what it meant but he felt he was missing a silent message passing between them. Yancey held out a hand and Honoria dropped the watch fob into it.

"Honoria Belden, I am placing you under arrest for the murders of Leander Stickney and Dennis Ayers."

"Of course. Ruby, I'm trusting the hotel to you." Honoria slipped her hand into her pocket and pulled out her jangling set of keys, which she thrust toward Ruby. "Mrs. Doyle and Ben will help you with anything you need. Please break the news to Mrs. Doyle yourself. I'd rather she not hear it from someone else."

CHAPTER FORTY

ONORIA STRODE OFF WITHOUT A BACKWARD GLANCE. I watched, feeling completely unmoored. As I sagged against the doorframe I heard a sob. Millie sank into the desk chair, tears running down her face.

"This is all my fault." She stared at the desk and let out another shuddering sob.

"I think you'd better tell me what this is about." I shut the door firmly and turned the key in the lock.

"It's about Miss Howell."

"Amanda?" I asked. "What about her?"

"While you were out with the Velmonts she was in your room."

"What makes you say that?"

"I was coming along the hallway with a tray for Mrs. Stickney when something caught my eye."

"Yes?"

"Your room is the only one at the end of that passage and as I stopped to shift the weight of the tray I saw Miss Howell letting herself into your room."

"Did you call out to her?"

"No. I had to make haste. Mrs. Stickney is impatient and I didn't want her to complain to Mrs. Doyle."

"Did you see her face?"

"No. Just the back of her head and her dark dress. She was behind the closed door as quick as a wink."

"And you didn't see her coming out?"

"Mrs. Stickney kept me for some time. By the time I got back and worked up the courage to let myself into your room there was no one in there."

"Then what happened?" I was curious but I still didn't understand why Millie was so upset. Maybe Amanda was just borrowing a hatpin or snooping through my newly refurbished wardrobe. She had already performed a reading on my tarot cards, and my parasol had been in my possession, so there was no way she could have gotten any information about me from the contents of the room. Prowling around wasn't nice but it did not a crisis make.

"I decided to check if anything had been disturbed or taken."

"And?"

"Nothing had been taken but I found something that didn't belong to you."

"I haven't noticed anything in there that wasn't present when Honoria first showed me the room."

"That's because I took it out and gave it to Honoria." Millie hung her head. "I never meant her to come to harm from it."

"What did you find, Millie?"

"I checked the jewelry box to be sure nothing was missing and right there in the bottom, sitting amongst the brooches and earrings, was a watch fob made of gold in the shape of a tiny set of scales." Millie drew in a ragged breath. "It was just like the one Honoria gave to the police."

As soon as Millie managed to stop crying, I sent her off to pack a bag for Honoria. Remembering my promise to my aunt, I decided next to speak to Mrs. Doyle. I headed for the kitchen and found her pulling gleaming glass jars of pickles from a shelf in the pantry.

"Do you have a moment?"

"No, I don't. I'm up to my eyeballs rearranging dinner plans." Mrs. Doyle's face was as flushed as a pint of strawberry jam and her hair curled damply around her face. She squinted at me in her usual alarming way. "You don't know how the turkey I'd planned for dinner ended up all dried out, do you?"

"No. I have no idea. I need to talk to you about something more important than turkeys."

"That just goes to show what you know. That turkey is the most important thing in my day. Someone peeled back the paper wrapper and now a whole side of it is dried out to a fare-thee-well. Just like the beef roast the day Mr. Stickney was killed. There must be some sort of a lunatic at the hotel with a grudge against my supper plans."

"I'm sorry to hear it. Would you like a glass of water?"

"Of course I wouldn't. If you have something to say you'd best get on with it. I haven't got all day." Mrs. Doyle blew out a loud breath. I was surprised it wasn't made of fire. Her impatience burnt up whatever reservoir of tact I might have had.

"Mr. Ayers has been murdered. Honoria's confessed to killing both him and Mr. Stickney. Officer Yancey just took her to the police station." Before that moment I wouldn't have believed so few words could change someone's world. But watching Mrs. Doyle collapse into a heap in the nearest chair, the life drained out of her face, I discovered that they could.

"She never did any such thing."

"I can't understand it. Officer Yancey arrested Albert Fitch for Mr. Stickney's murder yesterday. Why would she confess to both crimes? Millie found Mr. Stickney's watch fob hidden in the jewelry box in my room and gave it to Honoria."

"She was trying to protect you," Mrs. Doyle said. "According to my daughter, Albert Fitch is no longer in custody."

"The police let him go?"

"Frank told my daughter Albert died while in custody. If Honoria confessed to both murders I'm sure the department is relieved to have a new suspect before the pier opens."

A hot tear slid down my cheek and a choking feeling filled my throat. I put my head down on the table and began to sob. I felt Mrs. Doyle's strong hand stroking my hair. "It's all my fault. If only I'd told Honoria the truth in the first place, none of this would have happened."

"You'll feel better if you get whatever it is off your chest." Mrs. Doyle lifted my head with her firm hands and held my face between her work-roughened palms, squinting at me like she always did. "No matter how terrible you think it is."

"I had no intention of putting the hotel in jeopardy." I tried to steady my voice. "It all started with Mr. Ayers."

"What about him?"

"Honoria confessed because Officer Yancey had a photograph of Mr. Ayers ripping my mother's pendant from my neck."

"Why didn't you report him?"

"I was buying his silence."

"What the devil were you paying him for? Did he have some sort of hold over you?"

"He knew things about my past that I didn't want Honoria or anyone else to discover."

"Everyone needs someone they can trust." Mrs. Doyle lowered her hands to my own and squeezed them encouragingly. "Even if you don't trust me, you can trust that we both want what is best for Honoria and for the hotel." I wondered what it would be like to take the chance, to be myself without guise, without guile. I drew in a deep breath and made a decision.

"Mr. Ayers knew my father in Canada. At his place of employment."

"Did he also work for the medicine show?"

"No, he was just passing through," I said. And then the realization washed over me. "You knew Father and I worked a medicine show?"

"Yes."

"Does Honoria know?"

"Of course she does. She thought if you wanted to talk about it you would bring it up yourself. That's why she never mentioned it."

"But how did you know?" It never occurred to me there could be people from my mother's past who were in on the secret.

"Where did you think your parents met?"

"Father said he swept my mother off her feet in the ballroom of a fine hotel."

"He danced with Delphinia at the Old Orchard House and made quite an impression. I remember she came home that evening floating on air." Mrs. Doyle clucked her tongue at the memory. "But they met the day before at your father's show when he asked for volunteers and picked Delphinia out from the crowd. The show was in town for less than a week before they snuck off together in the night."

"What did her parents say when they discovered she was gone?"

"They disowned her. She wasn't married when she left, and it cast a taint on the family name. Publicly decrying one daughter was the best way to salvage the prospects for the other."

"But Honoria wrote to say she thought they would be willing to reconcile."

"She did. The coldness between them was ruining your grandmother's health and even your grandfather could see something needed to be done. He said if Delphinia was willing to come home all would be forgiven."

"But she never made it back, did she?"

"No. Honoria never received a response to her letter, and then began to dream of Delphinia soon after she posted the message. The next word we received was from Ivory, informing us of your birth and your mother's passing."

"Did my grandparents take it hard?"

"Your grandmother lasted long enough for us to receive the letter announcing your father would not relinquish custody of you to them. As soon as we heard that, her heart just gave out. Before she died she made Honoria promise to get you back here." My throat constricted and more tears splashed down over the folds of my gown. Not only had my aunt wanted me, my grandmother had, too. "None of us thought you should be raised in such an awful situation and by such a scoundrel."

"Now that I'm finally here, I think it would be better if I never had come."

"Well, you certainly have made a mess of things. Anything else you want to confess?"

"Mr. Ayers wanted me to use my connection with their father to influence the Velmont sisters to invest in his dummy corporation."

"Did you do so?" Mrs. Doyle kept her hands on mine.

"I couldn't bring myself to do it properly. I made some vague hints but then just last night, after he injured me, I tried to get them to draw the conclusion Mr. Ayers wanted. I never wanted to do something like that to those two sweet old ladies."

"So he stole Delphinia's necklace?"

"He took it as payment until the Velmonts bought shares of his fake stock. I didn't want Honoria to know the necklace had gone missing or why. But I didn't kill him."

"I know you didn't." Mrs. Doyle narrowed her eyes. "I can see it."

"You see lies?" That explained all the scowling and squinting. Maybe she hadn't disliked me so very much after all.

"I see auras. They hover around everyone like a colored mist."

"Some mists look like lies?"

"The colors surrounding people change to match their thoughts and feelings. Auras are clear, like a shaft of sunshine through a clean window, when the person speaks the truth and is filled with good intentions. It grows muddy when the person intends to damage another."

"Is my aura muddy?"

She shook her head. "You tell white lies. Even when you're conducting a reading your aura just becomes pale, faded. Which is why it's a white lie. It's like someone mixed a quantity of white paint into your aura."

"What does that tell you?"

"It means, like all white lies, yours are intended to make things easier or to shield others from pain."

"So you knew I wasn't a medium?"

"Of course. I've known several mediums and your aura isn't like theirs." Mrs. Doyle sat back and looked at me appraisingly. "I expected you to be clairaudient."

"Clairaudient?"

"Do you hear a voice that isn't there? Telling you to do or not to do things?"

"How did you know about that?"

"Your mother and grandmother and great-grandmother before her were all clairaudient. Every generation has at least one woman who can hear voices. Since you're the only Belden in your generation, I assumed you were the one."

"I am. It's how I've been able to conduct the readings for the clients. There's a voice that advises me."

"I'm delighted you've inherited your mother's gift. I thought perhaps because you weren't born here in Old Orchard you were not blessed with it. Can you summon it at will?"

"I often hear it when I use the cards," I said. "But sometimes it just appears in my ear unbidden."

"Delphinia used to have excellent luck simply asking for guidance and then listening for an answer."

"I've tried in the past but it never worked."

"I think you may find it works here. As Mr. MacPherson keeps mentioning, Old Orchard is a special place." Mrs. Doyle tucked a strand of my hair behind my ear. "Don't look so discouraged. You've done well for someone completely without guidance."

"Even though it's often been useful, I've worried that I was insane."

"Well, you aren't. But you do need Honoria to make the most of your gifts." Mrs. Doyle shoved back her chair and stood. "So go sit somewhere quiet and ask the voice how best to go about getting her home."

CHAPTER FORTY-ONE

HEEDING MRS. DOYLE'S ADVICE TO SEEK SOMEWHERE QUIET I headed to the séance room. No sooner had I pulled my card pouch from the recesses of my skirt and settled myself at the table than the Velmont sisters slipped through the velvet portiere and sat down next to me. Both of them looked concerned and pulled their chairs close. I must have appeared as overwhelmed as I felt.

"Ruby, did Officer Yancey find you?" Dovie asked.

"As much as I wish he hadn't, he did indeed."

"We never should have meddled." Elva drummed her knobby fingers on the tablecloth.

"When we saw him coming out of this room earlier we both felt it was a sign that we should tell him about the attack you suffered yesterday," Dovie said.

"But from the looks of you, we have done wrong," Elva said. "We didn't mean to betray your confidence. You have every right to be angry with us."

"Ladies, it isn't that. I might as well tell you, since the news will be everywhere before long. Officer Yancey has just arrested Honoria for the murders of Mr. Stickney and Mr. Ayers."

A surprised silence hung in the air and I sensed something pass between the sisters.

"Then it's settled, don't you think?" Dovie turned to Elva, who nodded, then cleared her throat.

"We would appreciate it if you would accompany us to the police station. We intend to turn ourselves in for the murder of Mr. Stickney."

"Ladies, Honoria has already confessed."

"I'm afraid she's a liar," Elva said. "She must be because I am the guilty party."

"It wasn't your fault," Dovie said.

"Sister, we agreed on a course of action," Elva said. "I'll take the blame."

"The actions were mine."

"You know I assured Father I'd keep an eye on you. I have failed, so the blame is mine." Elva's voice grew shrill.

"Ladies, perhaps you could be more specific," I said.

"It was the bloody handkerchief, you see," Dovie said.

"My handkerchief," Elva said.

"I think it would be best if one of you explains," I said. The sisters looked at each other, then nodded. Dovie picked up the tale.

"The morning the police arrived to announce Mr. Stickney's murder I awoke in the wee hours to the sound of Elva bent over the washbasin scrubbing at something. When I asked her about it she told me to go back to sleep. I pretended to do so. She finished up with the washing and hid a square of fabric below a towel on the drying rack."

"I didn't know you were watching, sister," Elva said.

"I always was a good actress. When Elva left the room a moment later I slipped from bed to inspect what she had hung to dry. It was one of her handkerchiefs, and despite her vigorous efforts there were bloodstains on the white fabric."

"How does this make you a murderess?" I asked.

"As I was inspecting the handkerchief I noticed discoloration below my fingernails. It was dried blood."

"You've seen with your own eyes that my sister is not always herself." Elva leaned forward. "You recall when we first arrived that she sometimes wanders in her sleep."

"The night I found her in the pantry?" I asked. Elva nodded.

"Poor Elva can't always catch me before I slip out. She must have been too tired to hear me go."

"I try to keep an ear open even while I sleep but I think the sea air must have been too much for me. I woke to a knock on the door. Mr. Dobbins had kindly brought Dovie back to our room. He said he couldn't sleep so he took a walk and found her on the beach near the pier."

"When I asked Elva about it she said it was nothing." Dovie reached out and placed a plump hand on Elva's arm. "After we heard Mr. Stickney was dead I asked her again. She said I returned with blood on my hands and that since she had cleaned me up so well no one would need to know what had happened."

"No one but Mr. Dobbins, that is."

"Are you sure it was blood?"

"I haven't achieved the age I have without some passing familiarity with such things. It was blood."

"When we heard about Mr. Stickney being killed, naturally we assumed the worst."

"Even if you did find blood on your hands, why would you assume you were guilty of his murder? Couldn't you have simply cut yourself?"

"I was in no way injured. And there is something else. Elva and I had good reason to wish Mr. Stickney dead."

"Because of what he did to your father?" I asked.

"How did you know about that?" Dovie asked.

"Father must have told her," Elva said. Even though I felt a twinge of guilt, I thought it wouldn't assist matters to admit I had been gossiping about the two of them with Mr. Dobbins.

"We knew the Stickneys planned to spend the season here and we came, too, with the notion that we could in some way exact revenge," Elva said. "When Mr. Stickney died I was certain our evil intentions had come to pass even if Dovie took action whilst asleep."

"It is the desire of the heart, you see. We wanted him to die and he did." Dovie nodded as if it all made complete sense.

"Mr. Dobbins made everything very clear to me when he suggested there was no need to tell the police about Dovie's nighttime wanderings." Elva bunched and unbunched the folds of her skirt between her knobby fists.

"Mr. Dobbins suggested to you that Dovie might have been involved?"

"He did."

"When was this?"

"Shortly after the police arrived to notify Mrs. Stickney of her husband's death," Elva said.

"He assured us that after all we'd done for him, we could count on him not to divulge what he knew about me and my murderous heart." Dovie's voice cracked and tears shone in her eyes. It was impossible to imagine either of the Velmont sisters as murderers, but Dovie the less likely of the two.

"What sort of favor had you done for him?" I asked.

"He credited us with introducing him to his true love," Elva said.

"We should have known what would happen," Dovie said "Men are so susceptible to blondes, don't you think?"

"It was all so romantic and we were delighted to be able to encourage young love to bloom." Dovie's cheeks pinked becomingly and the years melted away from her face.

"Secret trysts, furtive notes, messages sent through bouquets, it was all very exciting. Until the end." Elva shook her head.

"Without a word she simply disappeared from the Boston Spiritualist community."

"Who was she?" I asked.

"Flora Roberts," Elva and Dovie said in unison.

"The Flora Roberts whom I am replacing?"

"The very one," Elva said. "The Spiritualist community is not very large, after all."

"When did all this happen?" I asked.

"Just last week."

"Why didn't you mention to Honoria or me that you already knew Flora? Or that you were so well acquainted with Mr. Dobbins?"

"We didn't wish to embarrass poor Mr. Dobbins. After all, he was so distressed by the whole affair that we thought it best to let the entire matter drop," Elva said.

"We were a little ashamed of ourselves for having helped foster the relationship, considering how it all turned out," Dovie said.

"We allowed them to meet at our home, you see, before or after our sessions with Flora." Elva cleared a lump in her throat. "Sanford knew his uncle was very critical of any young ladies he wanted to court and was eager to press his suit without Stickney's watchful eye on them."

"We did wonder if now that Mr. Stickney is dead whether Mr. Dobbins will marry his true love after all," Elva said. "I do love a happy ending."

I felt a buzzing along my skin, an aliveness that always accompanied the sense I was on the right track when I performed readings.

"Not that there will be one for us, I'm afraid. Ruby, would you accompany us to the police station? We would appreciate a friendly face when the long arm of the law clamps its steel bracelets around our wrists," Dovie said.

"I think it would be best to investigate this matter a bit further before turning yourselves in to the police. I am still not convinced either of you had anything to do with the murders."

"Why do you say that?"

"A ruined roast."

"I'm afraid that hardly clarifies things for us."

"Elva, was there sand on the floor of your room the morning after Mr. Dobbins returned Dovie to you?"

"I don't remember any."

"Did you say 'a ruined roast'?" Dovie said.

"I did. Ladies, I'm receiving a message from your father." I still felt a little guilty but Mrs. Doyle would have said the lie was white. "He wants you to know the blood on Dovie's hands came from her nighttime wanderings. He's showing me an image of her peeling back the paper wrapper on a roast of beef in the pantry."

"Do you hear that, Sister?" Dovie turned to Elva, a look of hope on her face.

"He wants you to keep your confession to yourselves until I can look into this more thoroughly."

"If Father thinks it best then we must content ourselves with waiting." Elva took Dovie by the arm. "Come, sister. Let's leave Ruby to her work."

As soon as their voices faded down the corridor I closed my eyes and thought about the voice. I slowed my breathing and decided to leave my cards on the table untouched. I wanted desperately to share my mother's ability to consult the voice at will. I couldn't help but feel that wish had more of a chance than ever at being fulfilled, since my intention was to help my aunt and to save my mother's childhood home.

I focused my thoughts on proof to convince the police that Honoria wasn't guilty. I asked silently how such a thing could possibly be managed. I felt a sort of tingling along the top of my head and along the back of my neck as though a strong shaft of sunlight was bathing me in its glow. And then more loudly and distinctly than ever before I heard it.

"Consult the crystal."

CHAPTER FORTY-TWO

THE OBVIOUS THING TO DO WAS TO APPROACH THE CRYSTAL reader but the voice had mentioned the crystal, not its reader. Ben was conveniently missing from his post at the reception desk so I had a bit of privacy in which I could check on Madame Fidelia's schedule. No one had arranged for sittings with her for the next two hours. If I were lucky she would be out enjoying the day instead of holed up in her room. If I were even luckier she would have left her crystal ball behind.

I ascended the stairs and made my way along the back hall past the family portrait gallery. Perhaps if I ever got to the bottom of this problem, I might have my picture added to the collection. But first, I needed to get Honoria back to her proper place in the hotel.

I raced to Madame Fidelia's room and after receiving no answer to my knock, fitted the correct key into the lock. I glanced around, then stepped inside, closing the door behind me. I moved to the gleaming wooden vanity whose drawers seemed a perfect place to store something as delicate as a crystal ball. Apparently

Madame Fidelia did not agree. All the drawers yielded were lacy, monogrammed handkerchiefs and a collection of gloves and a sewing kit complete with a thimble and a tiny pair of scissors. Vexed, I opened a trinket box. Inside were three burnt match ends.

I hurried to the wardrobe, daunted by the memory of the enormous pile of trunks accompanying her arrival. I flung open the doors and to my surprise found few gowns adorning the bar. They were, however, unusually bulky for summer use. I ran my hands over one garment, giving it a closer inspection. I lifted the hem of a drab black affair and below it spotted a rose silk gown. Checking each costume I discovered at least one and sometimes two other gowns secreted beneath.

Hatboxes perched on the shelf above the clothes pole. I slid them out one after the next and found nothing of interest inside the first two. As I pulled out the third I heard a clunking sound as something heavy landed with a thud against the shelf. I reached up on my tiptoes and saw a black bound book that must have been wedged in behind the box.

It looked familiar, and when I opened it I realized why. It was the pocket sketchbook Mr. Ayers had at the ready at all times. I snapped it open, searching for any pages covered with the scene of Johnny's death. I felt weak with relief as I realized there were none. As I leafed through the book looking for any other damaging drawings, I recognized guests and staff from the hotel, the Sea Spray ballroom, the unfinished pier. Mr. Ayers indeed had a good eye.

I turned the page and slowly moved my eyes over it. At first glance I noticed only a sea of strangers. As I looked more closely I recognized two familiar faces. Sanford Dobbins stood near the edge of the sketch. But he was not alone. Right next to him, with her arm linked in his, was the woman I had encountered at the bathhouse.

I RACED AROUND THE HOTEL LOOKING FOR CECELIA. WHEN I found her in the ladies' writing room she was less enthusiastic about my idea than I would have hoped.

"I thought you'd be happy to help Honoria," I said. "If she doesn't return the hotel will close."

"And I thought I had your assurance my past would stay in the past," Cecelia said. "This would bring it all to light."

"Not necessarily. Everett and the other staff members needn't know. If you are discovered, it won't work anyway."

"But what about the policeman?" Cecelia asked. "Can he be relied on to keep quiet?"

"I'm convinced he's a man who knows how to keep secrets. Besides, he needn't know that you are the expert. He already thinks very little of me. It won't be a stretch to allow him to believe you are simply helping me and that I am the one who's the expert on fraud."

"If you believe he thinks very little of you, you aren't the psychic you're reputed to be," Cecelia said. "If you promise to allow everyone to believe I am simply helping I'll do it. But we will need a few supplies."

"May I leave that in your capable hands while I take care of one other detail?"

"What would that be?"

"Inviting the guests."

• • •

Yancey looked up as the door flung open and Miss Proulx, with flushed cheeks and a spring in her step, launched into the station. Something about her arrival made him check his tie for spots and tuck in his shirt.

"I have proof of who killed Stickney and Ayers," she said. "Here." Miss Proulx held out a black book. Yancey took it from her hand and opened it. Inside were pencil drawings of faces, none of which he recognized. "I marked the relevant pages." She pointed to a scrap of paper serving as a bookmark. Yancey turned to it and saw exactly what she meant.

"This is interesting but it raises more questions than answers. How do you expect these drawings to help Honoria?"

"I don't. I had hoped they would pique your curiosity sufficiently to convince you to help me to gain the rest of the proof." Miss Proulx smiled at him and he felt himself working to keep from smiling back. "If we combine our areas of expertise I've no doubt the truth of this matter will out."

"I'm not sure your area of expertise is something a court would be inclined to accept. Are you planning to go on the witness stand and channel the spirits of the victims? I doubt very much a judge will go for that sort of thing."

"I don't need to gain the confidence of a court," Miss Proulx said. "I think it would be much more effective to preach to the choir. And to answer your question, channeling the victims was exactly what I had in mind."

"Of course, I should have thought of that before." Yancey knew he sounded snide but it beggared belief to think she could actually be making such a ridiculous suggestion. "Why spend all this time running around questioning suspects and collecting evidence when all you had to do was ask who murdered them?"

"I can't just ask who murdered them. It doesn't work that way." Miss Proulx patted his hand like he was an old man in need of soothing. She really was the most difficult woman he had ever met. Besides Honoria. "But the sitters don't need to know that."

"You want to run a fake séance?"

"Why not? According to you I have plenty of experience with such things. It's the perfect way to get the information from true believers. I just need you to listen in the wings."

"That's it?"

"Well, there is one more thing." She smiled sweetly and batted her long eyelashes. "Do you think you can persuade a couple of your officers to dress up like ghosts?"

Chapter Forty-three

WHEN I TOLD HER I HAD BEEN ADVISED BY MY GUIDES THAT an urgent message from her husband was forthcoming, Permilia readily agreed to a sitting. At my urging she convinced Sanford, the Velmonts, and Madame Fidelia to join her. In fact, she was so eager I worried we would not have time to prepare.

Fortunately, Millie was joining the séance, too, and had arrived early to help me set up. The darkened séance room was lit only by a single, flickering candle in the center of the table. I cast a final glance around the room as the sitters pushed through the portiere.

"Please take your seats and join hands," I said. "The room clamors with restless spirits." Permilia seated herself at my right and Dovie took the left. The others filled in the remaining seats.

A feeling of expectation permeated the room. All around me the sitters fidgeted in their seats. Their obvious agitation increased my own nervousness. This was no ordinary con. There was so much at stake. And much of the success would depend on Officer Yancey and the part he needed to play. He was hardly the sort of partner I would have chosen for such an endeavor under normal circumstances.

Prepared or not, it was time to give it my best try. I lowered my eyelids until they appeared closed and began to sway slightly back and forth. Permilia gripped my hand as a shroud-wrapped figure approached from the shadows. It raised one hand toward the sitters and the other to the back of its head. Mrs. Stickney gave a squeak and Mr. Dobbins gasped.

From the other side of the room a second, slimmer figure drifted toward the table. It staggered and lurched before raising both hands to its throat.

"I feel the unquiet spirits of Mr. Stickney and Mr. Ayers at hand." I paused and my face slowly moved from one figure to the other. "Have you come to expose those responsible for your deaths?" Mrs. Stickney squeezed my hand even tighter as the specters slowly nodded.

"Was it a pickpocket, Leander?" Permilia asked.

"He says the guilty parties are known to us all," I said.

"Who was it who left me a widow?" But as soon as she asked the figure directly, it faded back out of sight.

Dovie sniffed deeply. "I smell flowers," she said. An overpowering scent of roses and lavender filled the air as a shower of petals cascaded onto the table from above. "An apportment. What does it mean?"

"The spirits are trying to speak but I sense conflict in the room," I said. "Someone here does not want the truth known." The figures came back into view and both pointed at Mr. Dobbins.

"They can't mean me. Why would I harm either of them?" With that, a handkerchief monogrammed and trimmed with delicate lace landed in the middle of the table atop the flower petals and scattered blooms. Elva tugged a hand free and picked it up.

"Who is *FLR*?" Permilia asked.

"Flora Louise Roberts," Elva said. She waved the handkerchief at Dovie. "We helped Mr. Dobbins choose this for her before their engagement was broken."

"Surely, it is not the same one," Mr. Dobbins said.

"What engagement?" Permilia asked. "Sanford, were you engaged to Miss Roberts?" She looked at her nephew, who simply swallowed hard and said nothing.

"Mr. Stickney says he knew of their secret engagement. He also says the handkerchief belongs to Miss Roberts and it points to her guilt," I said.

"But Flora isn't here. How could she have harmed Leander?" Permilia asked.

I withdrew my hands and raised them swiftly toward the ceiling. I heard a sharp intake of breath and then a dark wig drifted in from the shadows and hovered right in front of Permilia. I reached for it and dangled it in front of Mr. Dobbins's face. "She's been here all along." I pointed across the table to the empty seat Madame Fidelia had just vacated.

The portiere parted and Officer Yancey loomed into view, stopping her in her tracks.

"Have the spirits left us, Miss Proulx?" Officer Yancey asked. I nodded. "Then if you would be so good as to let in some light I think we have some questions in this world for Madame Fidelia."

"I'll just open the curtains then, shall I?" I asked in a loud voice but I made no effort to hurry. I waited until the drapes had stopped flapping and I was sure my ghostly helpers had made it through the French doors and offstage.

"That's Flora Roberts," Elva said, pointing to a young, blond woman whom Officer Yancey held firmly by the arm.

"It certainly is," Dovie said. "What are you doing here, my dear?"

"None of this would have happened if your husband wasn't such a disgusting old man," Flora said to Permilia.

"What is she talking about?" Permilia turned to Sanford and all the starch went right out of his spine.

"Your husband had a habit of pressuring mediums who wanted to avoid exposure to provide him with their favors," I said. "Instead of giving in to his demands, Flora disappeared from Boston."

"Mr. Dobbins said she left because he broke off their engagement after his uncle accused her of fraud," Dovie said.

"He thought that was what happened but Flora wasn't going to give up a wealthy husband so easily. She posed as Madame Fidelia in order to keep an eye on Mr. Dobbins."

"But why did she kill Mr. Stickney?" Elva asked.

"Mr. Dobbins went to Madame Fidelia for a reading after his uncle told him he had decided to dismiss him from his employ. After hearing his financial prospects were endangered Flora determined to fix the problem. She contacted Mr. Stickney and said she'd reconsidered his proposition. She arranged a meeting at the pier, where she struck him with an iron bar, then tried to make it look like a pickpocketing gone wrong," I said.

"Sanford wouldn't kill his uncle over a job. He has a trust fund," Permilia said.

"Mr. Stickney threatened to raid the trust if Sanford didn't go away quietly," I said.

"You have no proof that Sanford's uncle threatened to dismiss him. The word of a newly minted medium is hardly about to stand up in court." Flora's eyes blazed as she spoke.

"I don't believe any of this," Permilia said. "Sanford would never kill my husband."

"He didn't kill him. He didn't even know Madame Fidelia was actually Flora until after the murder. Perhaps she panicked or just wanted to confide in someone but she let him in on her secret. They were certain the police could make no connection between Madame Fidelia and Mr. Stickney so they kept up the charade, at least for the time being."

"But what about Mr. Ayers?"

"I was led by the spirit of Mr. Ayers to his sketchbook hidden in Madame Fidelia's room and containing drawings of her as both women." I pulled the sketchbook from my lap and held it open to the relevant page. "As an artist, he had a trained eye. He noticed the similarities between Madame Fidelia and the young woman he saw in Mr. Dobbins's company on a few occasions." I pointed to sketch after sketch showing the same woman dressed in two very different sorts of clothing.

"He may have had artistic talent but being a successful blackmailer was his true calling. At least if the price written at the bottom of his sketches of you was any indication." Officer Yancey took up the story. "So how did he approach you? Was it during one of the sessions with Madame Fidelia?"

Flora and Sanford exchanged a look. She held herself erect, her lips pursed and her shoulders back. She gave her fiancé a slight warning shake of the head. It was time to make sure Sanford was more afraid of the dead than he was of the living.

"Your uncle is with us once more. He says to tell you he regrets the example he set for you and hopes you will show yourself to be a better man than he," I said. "That unlike him you would do the right thing when it is hard instead of the wrong thing whenever it was easy."

Mr. Dobbins started to shake. He turned to Flora. "I told you my uncle would come through from the other side. That we would never be rid of his presence."

"Keep quiet, Sanford." If Officer Yancey hadn't been holding on to Flora's arm I think she would have lunged at me in an entirely unladylike fashion. "She's just trying to trick you into confessing."

"Your uncle says he regrets his remarks about your gullibility and that you were right about Madame Gustav. He did plant evidence in her apartments and then point the police in her direction."

"I knew it." Sanford's eyes glowed with triumph. "I told him my belief in her abilities was not fair grounds for his insistence on dismissing me. I'm not so easy to fool as he thought."

"I'm sorry to say it, young man, but I'm afraid you just foolishly admitted you had reason for your fiancée to kill Mr. Stickney and for you to then kill Mr. Ayers in her defense," Elva said. Sanford's Adam's apple bobbed and a deep flush suffused his face.

"Sanford's job loss and an anonymous sketchbook are hardly enough to prove either of us killed anyone," Flora said.

"There is a bit more we can rely on in court," Yancey said. "An employee at the Sea Spray bathhouse testified that she regularly removed a dark wig from one of the changing room baskets. She also mentioned there were never any wet bathing costumes from that same booth. When we showed her the sketchbook the locker room attendant confirmed seeing you enter and exit a booth dressed as two different women."

"There's nothing to say Sanford knew Flora was here," Permilia said.

"Actually, there is. We also have proof that after Madame Fidelia used the bathhouse to change into Flora she met you in town." Yancey held up the photograph taken near the train station, showing the two of them together. "Frank, Lewis, we're ready for you."

The two officers appeared at the door and took charge of Flora and Mr. Dobbins. The Velmonts each took one of her arms and helped the weeping Mrs. Stickney out of the room.

Chapter Forty-four

A
ND THEN I FOUND MYSELF ALONE WITH OFFICER YANCEY.
"That was quite a performance. I think you would have
stood a good chance of pulling one over on Mr. Stickney if he had
lived to book an appointment."

"Is that supposed to be a compliment?"

"It is. I've met a lot of criminals but I've never used one to
catch another."

"One incident of embellishment hardly makes me a criminal."

"Embellishment? Is that what you'd call it?"

"Considering I'm in the presence of a policeman, you can
hardly blame me for putting a bit of a shine on an ugly truth."

"There was nothing ugly about the way you set out to help
Honoria and the hotel."

"What else could I do?" I felt my chest constrict. "She put her
reputation and even her life in danger to try to protect me."

Officer Yancey reached out and gently touched the back of my
hand. "For a young lady like you, Miss Proulx," he said, leaning
daringly close, "I can see how someone could be quite tempted to
take such a chance."

I admit I have found myself in many an awkward position with the police in the course of my travels with the medicine show. I had even been on the receiving end of overtly flirtatious, even bawdy, remarks from them from time to time. But I had never before found myself on the receiving end of a policeman's sincere regard.

As a matter of fact, excepting Johnny, I had never attracted the wholesome notice of any eligible young man. Both patrons and fellow show workers alike saw girls who worked the medicine show as sport. Long ago I had learned to ignore the leering, to dodge most of the groping. What I hadn't mastered was the art of accepting honorable intentions. I felt flushed, flustered, and completely out of my depth. Making light of the situation was the only way to keep myself from stammering.

"Does this mean you believe in my abilities?"

"I didn't say that."

"Just because this case is solved does not mean the world is not still filled with mysteries."

"I agree. One that still isn't cleared up to my satisfaction is how your necklace came to be in Mr. Ayers's pocket."

"Would it put your mind at ease if I explained what you saw in the photograph?" I asked.

"It might." I had seen the look on his face countless times. It was the expression of a man who desperately wanted to believe the promises of Father's concoctions or the guidance provided by my cards. I was surprised to wish the best course was to be honest with him. I sent out a silent call to the voice for advice.

"The truth will not serve your purpose." I should have known the ease between us could not be expected to continue. I made up my mind and started to weave a story he would be happy to hear.

"For some time Mr. Ayers had been making unwelcome advances toward me. I couldn't seem to be rid of him and as Honoria's niece I couldn't very well rebuff one of her guests."

"Lucy mentioned you were in an awkward position with him."

"*Awkward* doesn't begin to describe it. He chased me through the hotel, along the beach, and on more than one occasion into town."

"Including the afternoon of the photograph?"

"Yes. When he accosted me at the station he told me he wasn't happy that I was cultivating friendships with other male guests. He implied I had behaved inappropriately and that he would be expecting me to confine my attentions to him once our engagement was announced."

"You had accepted an offer of marriage from Mr. Ayers?" Officer Yancey's tone was tinged with disbelief.

"Of course not. What's more, he had not made one. I feared his mind was unbalanced."

"You looked frightened in the photograph."

"I feared for my life. Especially when I made the mistake of telling him I had not agreed to be his wife."

"Is that when he turned violent?"

"It was. He crushed my hand with tremendous force and as he did so he threatened to take me behind the livery and take unmentionable liberties with me if I did not agree to marry him."

"That explains your expression in the photograph and your injuries, but not the theft of your necklace."

"Fearing for my virtue and possibly my life I assured him I would be delighted to accept his proposal." I paused, gratified by the look of disappointment on Officer Yancey's face. "Of course I had no intention of going through with a wedding. If he was willing to chance such violent behavior with an acquaintance in a public place, what might he do to his wife behind closed doors?"

"It doesn't bear thinking about." Yancey's forehead furrowed. "But how did your necklace come to be in his pocket?"

"All at once his attention turned to the necklace. He moved his hands around my throat and said he was quite certain I cared more for it than I did for him. He tore it from my throat and stuffed it into his pocket. He said I could have it back on our wedding night."

I felt a hot blush steam its way up my cheeks. Officer Yancey, I'm sure, assumed it was caused by my mention of the wedding night. In fact, I was heartily ashamed of how such a convincing string of lies simply and easily rolled off my tongue.

"Why didn't you go to Honoria and tell her what had happened?"

"Because she was busy all evening with her duties at the hotel and I didn't manage to find her alone for a private chat. You appeared with news of his death before I managed to do so."

"So that's why she confessed? She thought you might actually be involved?"

"I'm afraid so. I still haven't been able to reassure her that I did nothing wrong."

Yancey stepped to the French doors and opened one. "You aren't the only one who can make loved ones appear," he said to me. He made a waving motion and Honoria swept into the room, her head high and her arms thrown wide. I rushed to her and felt the crush of her embrace as I heard the voice once more thrum in my ear.

"Trust that your place is here."

CHAPTER FORTY-FIVE

RUBY, IT'S HERE." I RACED DOWN THE STAIRS TWO AT A TIME, following the sound of Honoria's voice to the reception desk. She held out a large envelope. "Mr. Lydale just brought it by."

"Have you seen it yet?"

"I wanted to wait for you." I lifted the thick flap and slipped out the photograph. I was struck at once by how well Mr. Lydale had reproduced the original image. Honoria and I stood arm in arm in white summer gowns. Curlicues and fretwork and flower-filled window boxes hung off the building behind us. He had even managed to position us in the same spot in front of the Hotel Belden sign.

"It's perfect," I said, feeling a lump gathering in my throat. "But are you sure you could spare the expense?"

"I shouldn't worry about that anymore. I've paid off the mortgage."

"How?"

"All thanks to you," Honoria said. "The Velmonts took me aside and told me their father had advised them to take charge of their own investments."

"They did?" I felt guilty all over again. Even with Mr. Ayers dead and gone he was still making trouble.

"Don't worry. Mrs. Doyle told me all about Mr. Ayers's part in that." Honoria smiled at me. "The ladies were so impressed with the way your channeling exposed Flora and Mr. Dobbins that they asked to invest in the hotel. They've taken over the note in exchange for a percentage of the profits and a lifetime tenancy at the hotel. Oh, and they insisted on daily sessions with you."

"But I thought we agreed that séance was to be my last," I said. With Mrs. Doyle's help I had confessed to Honoria that I was not a medium. "I don't want to go on deceiving them."

"Your mother always said the voice she heard only advised her for the good. For herself and for others," Honoria said. "Has that not been your experience?" I thought about my own experiences with the voice and the sorts of things it had whispered to me over the years.

"That's exactly what I've experienced. The only problems have come of not listening to it." My heart squeezed as the image of Johnny smiling at me over my deck of tarot cards filled my mind.

"Delphina couldn't identify the source of the voice she heard. She never believed she heard directly from those who passed over."

"Why not?"

"She said the voice she heard was always the same rather than a multitude of different voices."

"I only hear one voice too and it has become louder and more helpful since I arrived in Old Orchard."

"It seems to me that it would be a shameful waste of your gift to refuse to use it because you are concerned about the way it's labeled." Honoria smiled at me. "But, the decision is yours. I would never ask you to do something against your conscience."

I couldn't deny that the voice had provided comfort to the Velmonts, and had assisted with solving the murders. It had helped me to finally find a place to belong. This time I didn't need to run my cards or ask the opinion of a voice from beyond the veil. My own voice was all I needed.

"Let's ask the Velmonts if they prefer their sittings in the morning or afternoon."

HISTORICAL NOTE

While *Whispers Beyond the Veil* is a work of fiction, the seaside town of Old Orchard Beach, Maine, is entirely real. Most of the events, people, and places mentioned in this book are entirely from my imagination, but a few are a matter of record.

People have been visiting the shores of Saco Bay since the end of the last ice age, more than ten thousand years ago. Groups of native peoples from what is now known as New England and the Canadian Maritimes gathered to enjoy the pleasures of the comparatively warm ocean waters and the unusual sugar-fine sandy beach. These rare qualities may have led to the reputation Old Orchard developed amongst the earliest visitors as a place of healing waters.

As early as 1657, European descendants began to see the appeal of Saco Bay as well. Interactions between new arrivals and existing residents were frequently tense. By the time this story takes place, native peoples were treated as the interlopers.

The Hotel Belden is just a fond imagining on my part. However, the hospitality industry in Old Orchard dates to 1837 when guests began staying at the E.C. Staples farm for $1.50 a week. Rail service with connections from Montreal arrived only two miles from the beach in 1853 and by 1873 the Boston and Maine Railroad stopped in the center of town.

By 1898, the town was a premiere tourist destination, equally popular with wealthy families who came for the season and mill workers who stopped by for the day from neighboring Biddeford and Saco. Luxury hotels, boarding houses, ballrooms, bathhouses, and, of course, the famous pier, were all a real part of the bustling scene at the time this book takes place.

Also popular at the time was an interest in Spiritualism. Americans from coast to coast attended public meetings where those serving as mediums channeled messages from the dead for members of the audience. Private gatherings to conduct séances and to develop paranormal abilities with other believers were very popular.

Not everyone was convinced that Spiritualism was anything more than an intersection of grieving dupes and skillful con artists. The Northeastern Society for Psychical Research only exists in the pages of this book. An actual organization, the Society for Psychical Research, was founded in 1882 for the purpose of investigating claims of paranormal abilities. Debunking fraudulent mediums comprised much of the society's early work.

Pickpocketing truly was a serious problem in Old Orchard at the time Ruby would have been in residence. Maine was the first state in the nation to enact laws that prohibited the manufacture and sale of alcoholic beverages except for those for medicinal or industrial purposes. The exact regulations varied in stringency over the years but laws restricting sales continued until 1934, a year later than the national prohibition.

Today, the town of Old Orchard Beach continues to enchant tens of thousands of visitors each summer with its beautiful beaches, nostalgic amusements, and welcoming locals.

Jessica Estevao is the author of the debut novel in the Change of Fortune Mysteries, *Whispers Beyond the Veil*. She loves the beach, mysterious happenings, and all things good-naturedly paranormal. While she lives for most of the year in New Hampshire, with her dark and mysterious husband and exuberant children, she delights in spending her summers on the coast of Maine where she keeps an eye out for sea monsters and mermaids. As Jessie Crockett, she writes the Sugar Grove Mysteries for Berkley Prime Crime. Visit her online at jessicaestevao.com.